About the author

Simon Conway is a former soldier. He is a director of a
not-for-profit organisation dedicated to the eradication of
landmines and other explosive remnants of war. *Rage* is
his second novel.

Also by Simon Conway

Damaged

SIMON CONWAY

Rage

HODDER

A CIP catalogue record for this title is available from the British Library

ISBN 978-0-340-83965-2

Typeset in Plantin by Hewer Text UK Ltd, Edinburgh
Printed and bound by Clays Ltd, St Ives plc

Hodder Headline's policy is to use papers that are natural, renewable
and recyclable products and made from wood grown in sustainable forests.
The logging and manufacturing processes are expected to conform
to the environmental regulations of the country of origin.

Hodder & Stoughton Ltd
A division of Hodder Headline
338 Euston Road
London NW1 3BH

Maisy and Nelly

Thanks: Phil Robertson, Jules Welstead, Nick Sayers, Kate Robinson, Paddy Nicoll, Tom Dibb, Olivia MacDonald, David Smith, Jo Bloom, Ran Van Der Wal, Zoe & Kate Conway, Therese Lyras, Sue Mitchell, Marshall Robinson, Martin Buckley, Richard Moyes, Robert Cooper, Banksy, Audrey Gillan, Cameron Milne, Hedvig Boserup, James Rawlings, Richard Elsen, Steve Russ, Katy Grant, Tim Waller, Miranda Murphy, Gordon & Sue Conway, Alison Locke, John Gray, Aslan Mintaev, Sam McCleod, Guy Willoughby, Fergus Nicoll, Fay Mackenzie and Mary Jane Nicoll.

Author's Note:

There's no truth in it

'We may not be interested in chaos but chaos is interested in us.'

Robert Cooper, *The Breaking of Nations*

'There are four basic human needs: food, sleep, sex and revenge.'

Banksy, *Existencilism*

Jonah Said

The vehicle crackles and burns, somebody's meat.

In my mind's eye the last moments spool frame to frame as if by strobe light: the final striptease as the remaining sections of the car's bodywork and chassis are ripped apart and spin away. Then I am in freefall, hurtling through the air on the blast wave.

Strange to say, I've done this before, the same damn thing. Twice now a tank mine has whipped me raw and catapulted me into the sky. It's an odd sensation, a sort of grotesque and turbulent rebirth. The first time I was lucky and another man died. It was my last days in the Balkans and they had sent a genuine Englishman to replace me. Born in the United States, with a Palestinian father and a Guyanan mother, I've never really counted as a true Englishman.

The true Englishman was younger and eager to sing the praises of one side over another. Bosnians, Serbs or Croats – I don't remember which. I wasn't listening. I was already full to the brim with the feuds of the world. Out of courtesy, I gave him my seat beside the driver and the front offside wheel hit the mine. He died in my seat – they never found his legs – and I crawled away minus an eye, using the vehicle's broken antenna to probe the ground for further mines.

I used to think I was invincible. I believed it wholeheartedly. I can also tell you with some conviction that I have used up more than my fair share of luck. The well is dry. This time I do not expect to survive.

I land flat on my back, in a rain of debris. I try to scream but I have no voice or breath. I am spread-eagled like a sacramental offering and there is a roar like the buzzing of a thousand flies in my ears.

I must keep my nerve. There is not much time.

THE ZONE

Bled al-Siba: Lands of Insolence

March 2003

'And the Lord said unto Satan, "Whence comest thou?" Then Satan answered the Lord, and said, "From going to and fro in the earth, and from walking up and down in it."'

The Book of Job

Selling used cars in Umm Qasr

The first I heard of the cars was up in the Zone, at the Desert Palm bar on the Iraqi side of Umm Qasr. The Palm was a hole. A portable stereo was knocking out mangled balalaika music. Three Russian paratroopers swayed like charmed snakes in the middle of the floor and there was nothing to drink but house-distilled cha-cha that tasted like bleach.

Back then, I had a rant loose inside me. There were times when it felt as if I was about to burst into flames.

I'd flown into Kuwait International that afternoon on a commercial flight from Heathrow. I'd missed the RAF flight. They must have decided that it was worth the expense of a ticket just to be rid of me. I wasn't interested in Kuwait. I wanted them to pack me off to Mount Alice in the Falklands. I wanted to have nothing to do but throw stones at penguins and wait for the occasional has-been rock band choppered in for entertainment. I wanted the Stranglers minus Hugh Cornwell in some windswept Nissen hut with only thirty-four people for an audience.

The last thing that the general, a squat terrier of a man named Monteith, told me before packing me off to exile in Kuwait was that I was basically a good man but that I was riding astride some dark and occasionally explosive forces. Monteith was well known for his formidable religious conviction. I expected him to invoke the name of Satan.

In fact, I'd been counting on it. I remembered that
Monteith had talked a lot about Satan in the last hours
before the first Gulf war. He was a colonel then, commanding a mixed battle group of rough Highland jocks and
effete Geordie tankies. I was his Arabic-speaking inter-
preter. Monteith believed that God and the Devil were
engaged in a wager and the outcome was by no means
certain. He made us kneel in the sand beside his armoured
vehicle and, as a white dust as fine as flour settled on
exposed flesh and oiled gun parts, he prayed out loud:

*'Even that it would please God to destroy me; that he would
let loose his hand, and cut me off! Then should I yet have
comfort . . .'*

I would have touched wood if there had been any. In
those days, like so many of the mad and mediocre, I loved
all things fateful. Instead, I crossed my fingers, while those
around me groped for lucky charms, family photos and
such, any kind of protective shit. It didn't make a blind bit
of difference; after that a clock was inexorably ticking.
Someone was bound to die. In the event, three soldiers
were brewed up in an armoured personnel carrier mis-
takenly hit by an American missile.

I've had a bad time these last four years, at times very
bad. I've dug about in the rubble of my own ground zero
and I've learned that you can turn a life on its head in just a
few short moments. A single phone call or a wrong turning
down a shaded track can twist it into a new and ugly shape.
I've seen things. I've seen the tangled limbs of murdered
children in a grave and I've had my own marriage snatched
from me.

I folded and unfolded the complimentary newspapers. I
drank whisky miniatures back to back. I slept for a while

and when I awoke the late afternoon sun was hot in my eye and my head was throbbing. As I looked down through the window I watched the plane's shadow running over the pale green water of the Gulf.

I could see the submerged hulks of Iranian tankers sunk during the Iran–Iraq war. The plane was about two hundred metres offshore. There was a white sand beach and beyond it the rebuilt city, with its blinding ziggurats of steel and glass and the twin pot-bellied needles of the Kuwait Towers.

More than a decade before, I had gone to war to secure the flow of gas guzzled by American cars. Since then I had gone to and fro and up and down, and I had certainly gone down. The world, by contrast, had come around full circle and was on the brink of war again. This time, though, it seemed that I would be a spectator and not a participant. I had not flown out to join the ranks of the coalition armies that were poised to invade in a few days' time. No. A different fate awaited me. I was being sent to the strange purgatory that is the United Nations.

My job was as a military observer, tasked with patrolling the Demilitarized Zone – the Zone – the nine-mile-wide strip of sand-and-gravel desert, extending six miles into Iraq and three miles into Kuwait, that started from Ar Ruqi on the Saudi border and curved in a crescent shape northeastwards to Umm Qasr, the Zone's only town and Iraq's only port. The narrow strip of land sandwiched between the US 3rd Infantry Division and 1st Marine Expeditionary Force on one side and the Iraqi Republican Guard on the other.

I stepped out of the plane's cabin into a hot wind filled with stinging sand.

There was a Norwegian waiting for me on the tarmac, a clutch of baby-blue laminated passes dangling on his pigeon chest. He was tall and thin-necked with a mouth crowded with bad teeth. He blinked constantly.

'Jonah Said?'

'That's me.'

'Nobody warned us that you were coming,' he said.

He took off in the direction of baggage reclaim. When I caught up with him he was standing by the carousel, glaring impatiently at the sparse gathering of other passengers: Kuwaitis mostly, dressed in white dishdasha robes.

'Listen,' the Norwegian said, 'I have an important meeting in the Zone.'

I'm pretty sure that was the first time I heard the word *Zone*. I'm sure that there was something about the way he said it, a marked significance that to my febrile imagination suggested a sulphurous whiff of far-off treasure, of fresh blood and plain piss-yourself fear. Or maybe that's hindsight talking.

'OK,' I said. 'I'm in.'

'You must wait in the car,' he insisted.

'No problem.'

'As long as I have made myself clear,' he snapped.

'Crystal.'

'Where are your bags?' he demanded.

'I don't have any other luggage.'

'What?' He took a look at my one small canvas bag and my *Buddhist Punk* T-shirt and his face was rent with sudden fury. 'What are you talking about?'

'This is it,' I said.

'What? This is it? This is it!'

People turned and stared. He was clearly in something

of a state. So I removed my sunglasses. I fixed the Norwegian with my one good eye and stretched my mouth out into its most ferocious grin. He recoiled under the force of it. I can have that effect.

'Screw you,' I said.

Really it's the eye that does it: a raw welt of muscle and tissue peeping out from between my eyelids. Usually it's well hidden but I lost my glass eye, along with the contents of my stomach, in the back of a black cab on Constitution Street in Edinburgh a few hours before my flight.

'I'm sorry,' the Norwegian stammered.

'This is it,' I told him, getting into the swing of it. 'Me. Here. One bare, forked and fucked-up fellow.'

The Norwegian's hand pawed at his chest.

'Who are you?' I demanded.

'Odd. Odd Nordland,' the Norwegian told me, and then plaintively, 'I do logistics.'

From the terminal to his Land Cruiser, I was subject to an account of Odd's lousy childhood and his disintegrating home life. On the King Faisal Highway, I learned that Odd was recently divorced. She ran off with her dentist. Odd let out a strangled laugh, a moist and unpleasant noise.

He said, 'She takes all my money and then she tells me that I'm childish and selfish and uninteresting.'

I let him talk and watched him smoke a packet of cigarettes. I had it in me to stop him dead, to smash through his self-pity. Did he think that he was unique? I had my own list of carefully hoarded words: morose, self-absorbed, egocentric, ill disciplined, lazy and violent; the kind of words that lie about in language like unexploded mines in a field. I could have traded a few. We could have played scrabble.

And then night fell and we were in the potholed forecourt of the Desert Palm and from the expression on Odd's face it was clear to me that, whatever it was that he had got himself involved in, he lacked the necessary qualities to see it through.

'You don't want to go in there alone,' I told him.

Adjusting our eyes to the almost total absence of light in the bar, we negotiated our way around the paratroopers and asked the Iraqi barman for a beer.

He shook his head. '*Nyet Peevo. Vodka.*'

I admire that in barmen, their adaptability. They pick up the necessary language. He produced two dirty tumblers from behind the bar and sloshed liquid into them. We retreated to a dark corner table that was sticky with grime. The three swaying paratroopers followed our movements closely. The stereo blared on abrasively.

'Who are you meeting?' I asked him.

He knocked back the vodka and immediately broke into a fit of coughing.

'Go easy,' I told him.

'A woman,' he explained, 'the wife of a businessman.'

I laughed out loud. 'You're expecting to meet a woman, here?'

'Yes,' he insisted.

'In case you hadn't noticed, this isn't the Rotary Club. What's her name?'

Odd wagged his finger at me.

I should have got up and walked out right then. The guy was an idiot. I could have walked away unscathed.

Then one of the paratroopers sat down opposite us and stared at me for a long time. He didn't speak. From time to time he swigged at a bottle of Cossack and his small black eyes seemed to get smaller and shinier. Odd offered him a cigarette and he took it without letting his eyes off me, crushed it and sprinkled the strings of tobacco on the floor. Odd flushed from his neckline to his forehead. His hands started to shake. I let a smirk play at the corners of my mouth. The Russian was puzzled.

'Why,' he said in Arabic, 'are you so relaxed?'

I answered him in Arabic. I explained that since I was British and sitting opposite a Russian I knew that I was amongst friends.

The Russian wasn't impressed. 'You're a foreigner,' he said, spitting on the floor. 'All foreigners are filth. All this is your fault.'

He gestured angrily around the room but I could see that he meant more than just the dinginess of the bar. I didn't point out to him that he too was a foreigner on foreign soil. I wasn't necessarily looking for trouble; I wasn't averse to it, that's all. The Russian's companions came to join him. They slumped heavily into the seats and we were boxed in.

'We were allies fifty years ago,' I said. 'Your country and my country stood alone against Hitler, we defeated him together.'

He brought his pitted face to within a few inches of mine. 'You have no idea how we suffered. No idea at all.'

'That's bullshit,' I told him. 'Everyone in my country knows what happened at Stalingrad. Resistance there turned the war around. The whole world owes you.'

At this the Russian's companions roared with approval. The first Russian looked put out, muttering that he still reckoned that all foreigners were filth. Then I understood: he was from Volgograd, the city that used to be Stalingrad. It seemed to me that I had said the right thing. The Russian's friends dragged him away.

I looked across at Odd. He was clutching his chest again. No. My attention fixed on the front pocket of Odd's crumpled blue shirt. I slapped the hand aside and removed a sheet of paper from it before Odd could intercept my move.

'Bastard,' Odd said, falling back into his chair.

I unfolded the sheet and laid it out on the table.

'What is it?'

Odd massaged his arm and assumed a pained expression. 'You know you won't find them without me.'

'Just tell me what it is.'

'A bill of lading.'

'Explain.'

Odd volunteered the information in the same confessional spirit as he offered every other scrap of his life. I watched him smoke another packet of cigarettes.

The cars were in a forty-foot container: two metallic-black 4.6-litre armoured Range Rovers with smoked-glass windows.

'They were stopped in transit and forgotten about for thirteen years,' Odd explained. 'I'm asked to do an inventory by Department of Peacekeeping in New York as part of an audit. Sure, it's not the first time they have asked, but I do it properly, you understand. There are thousands of containers left lying around after the war that were owned by companies that were put out of business by the invading armies. I have logged two thousand four hundred and twenty-two containers in the last three months and opened six hundred and thirty-nine in the last three weeks: all over the Zone and in the military bases. Look, I have calluses on my hands.'

In the noise and dislocation of a place that was unfamiliar I tried to understand what he was saying.

'First I make a database because every container has a

unique reference number, then I cross-reference against any existing paperwork, invoices, consignees' addresses, packing lists and bills of lading. I have stacks of paper. I realize that everybody keeps records of everything but they don't know where. You understand, it's a complicated business. The UN is not an organization with motivated people. I don't get help from anybody. So I start to open the containers by myself.

'They were lost in transit,' he explained and gave another blast of that desperate laugh. 'You understand? Nobody cares. So nobody knows.'

I didn't need to ask him what he was going to do. He was going to try and sell the cars; after all, no one was going to miss them, or so he thought.

'I need the money,' Odd explained. His ex-wife had wiped him out. I could sympathize with that. Certainly, in the wake of my separation, I had come to understand the belief that the only route to existential improvement lay in the acquisition of money.

Odd had made contact with the widow of the original consignee and offered to sell the cars to her.

'We set up the deal,' he explained, 'and then all we have to do is recover the containers and fix the paperwork.'

'We . . . ?'

'Yes,' said Odd, a desperate streak in his voice. 'You and me. Partners. Fifty-fifty. Agreed?'

'Why don't you just sell them in Kuwait City?'

Odd said, 'There's no market for used cars in Kuwait City.'

I refolded the sheet of paper.

The Russians were back, with a full bottle this time. Now we were old friends. There was much slapping of shoulders and many toasts. To Stalingrad, the Murmansk Convoy, Alamein.

I had the folded sheet under the span of my hand and as we shifted in the booth to make room I slid it across the table and into my pocket. Odd regarded me with a kind of dreary resignation. I could see what he was thinking; Odd was ripe for ripping off and he knew it.

The Russians wanted to know how it was that I could speak Arabic. I explained that my father is a Lebanese Palestinian and that gained me a further chorus of approval and more vodka. Another bottle was produced. I didn't tell them that I was born in the United States or that my mother is a Guyanan Catholic or how I ended up attached to a succession of Scottish highland regiments. I've had character poured into me through a strange filter. I'm a mongrel. There was a time when my wife called it hybrid vigour.

I hardly registered it when Odd staggered off towards the toilets. Soon afterwards the Russians insisted that I join them in a mad spinning dance amongst the tables and chairs. The barman looked on, bored and oblivious. At some point I lost my bearings, fell over and slid under a table. I lay there for quite a while, maybe hours.

When I climbed out from beneath the table, neither the Russians nor the barman were anywhere to be seen.

I went into the toilet. It was even darker in there, the only light source a single red bulb hanging from some antique-looking flex. Odd was slumped in one of the stalls with his eyes raised to the ceiling and the pupils coagulated into milky jelly. He'd had his throat cut. The blood was black in the light from the bulb. I had never seen so much blood come from one person. It was everywhere, splashed all over the walls and a great inky pool of it on the floor as if some part of him had liquefied. There was no way that he had done it to himself.

I stood still, helplessly gazing at the body for a few moments. Then I went back to the bar and found a light switch. The bar looked even dingier bathed in fluorescent white light. I couldn't see a phone and I had no number to ring. I badly wanted a cigarette. I contemplated an open packet on the bar counter, but I had made a vow.

Fossils, ghosts, hostages

The Mutla Ridge is one of the few places with any visible elevation in Kuwait. In daylight, from the top of the ridge you can see right across the bay and if the city is not smogged up, you can just about make out the silhouette of the Kuwait Towers.

That night the moon was full, lending everything the silvery-white patina of bone. From where I was standing I could see the oblong shape of the Kuwaiti police post and the gleaming new Japanese-built satellite earth station and, directly beneath me, piled beside the highway, the bleached hulks of hundreds of burnt-out cars, trucks, buses and tanks. A wayside shrine to the last days of the first Gulf war: the vast, ridiculous turmoil of an army in rout that the combined aerial might of the US Air Force, Navy and Marine Corps had swept through like a hot and scouring wind.

I understand that this is what it is to be handcuffed to some solemn scrap of history. I remember driving the 'Highway of Death' in the early hours of 26 February 1991. It had been raining. Oily black rain. We drove slowly through the wreckage, the kill zones; the armoured personnel carrier's tracks splashing through pools of dark and bloody water.

I'm not sure why I chose to drive down to Mutla after the Desert Palm. Maybe it was for the simplest of reasons: I knew where it was. Where the hell else was I going to go? What I knew for sure was that I had to get out of the bar in case whoever it was that killed Odd decided to return.

I staggered out of the door into the parking lot. The moon was out and the lot was filled with stark shadows and harsh silvery light reflected on a spill of broken glass that crunched underfoot. The Land Cruiser had been ransacked. The remote head and the transceiver for the HF radio had been ripped out of their mountings and smashed. The seats had been slashed and the padding was coming out in fistfuls. My bag was gone and with it my passport and army ID card.

I felt it more keenly than before, the need to be far away immediately. I was sure that I had escaped a similar death only because, in my drunkenness, I had found a dark corner in which to pass out. Passed out and passed over. Perhaps there was some scrap of luck left in me. Certainly, I could not be sure that I would be so lucky again. There were no keys, so I hot-wired the car. Another skill mastered in my teenage years.

I took the expressway back out of the Zone to Mutla. There was plenty of traffic, convoys of tank transporters thundering out of the darkness and heading for the border, but no one was using lights and no one noticed the lack of mine.

It was cold without any windows. A sobering and penetrative cold that made me wonder at my own emotions. The stark truth was that an insinuating thread of pleasure was woven into my response to the death. It wasn't that I had any particular reason to dislike Odd. I didn't feel strongly about him. The furtive spark of satisfaction had nothing to do with hostility or a sense of justice about what the Norwegian had been trying to do in selling the cars; it was something larger – it was the thrill of survival. The beast got him and missed me. I had been spared.

At Mutla, I abandoned the car by the side of the road and set off on foot through the wreckage. I took out the bill of lading and unfolded it for the last time. After quickly scanning the information that it contained, I tore it into small pieces that I scattered amongst the wreckage as I walked.

A lot can change in twelve years.

Back in 1991 the western nations were riding a tide of interventionism. I was giddy with battle, embarked on an adventure in putting the world to rights. I'd seen the pictures of Halabja. I knew that Saddam had used poison gas on his own people. I believed that there were just and unjust wars: forms of killing that were necessary and forms that dishonoured us all.

A month after the end of the conflict and I was on a plane home, a spark of conquest that leapt across the world. I was newly married and ecstatic to be alive.

At the airport arrivals gate we grinned from ear to ear. My wife and I kissed for the longest time.

'Skinny malink', I called her.

'Come,' she said, leading me by the hand.

She drove back from the airport with her dress around her waist. She was naked under it and my hand slipped in and out of her. We hardly got in the door. We made hungry love on the hallway carpet with my knuckles pressed into the jute weave and her legs scissored across my back. She had her eyes wide open and her lips curled back, revealing her chipped front tooth. I plunged into her with the same exultant passion that had carried us across the desert into Iraq. I'd never felt more alive. Abruptly she was brought to that last point of pleasure and let forth an exultant wail. And I was tempted. But I kept on going and as I continued, the noises that emerged from our opened mouths expanded in breadth and range until finally the tumult rose from deep within me and was spent inside her.

On the Mutla Ridge, I found myself gasping for a cigarette, fumbling in my pockets for a nonexistent lighter. For over ten years I had tried to give up cigarettes. Over and over again I gave up. And then I lost my family.

Before the split I hadn't had a cigarette for a year. Twenty minutes after that phone call and I was bumming cigarettes off a Serb militiaman at a checkpoint in Bosnia and was, after a week of battling myself, hooked again. Every cigarette after that smelled like a brimming ashtray discovered on the morning after, but it was not tar that made me gag.

What went wrong? With my marriage? She found someone else. With the world? Srebrenica, Bali, the bodies in the church at Nyarubuye in Rwanda, Mogadishu, the twin towers, the sack of Mazar al-Sharif, anywhere in Congo. The recognition that people don't want peace – men and women, old and young – they want victory. The admission that, in the worst depravities of war, there is no fundamental minimum of humanity, there is no distinction between man and beast.

So why did I give up smoking again? Why do I fight each day? Because I am determined to retain some sense of self-control.

In June '99, a few short months after my marriage collapsed, I stood at the lip of a trench overgrown with scrub oak in a tiny hamlet called Cikatovo near Glogovac in Kosovo and, drawn by the smell – the kind of smell that only cigarettes can hide – I squatted down on my heels and stared along the line of the trench. The Serbs had made a half-hearted attempt to collapse the walls of the trench before fleeing, so that it was difficult to know for sure how many were buried; just a few probably – perhaps not enough to fit the definition of a mass grave – but body parts were visible in the dappled light, a torso here, a hand there, a child's foot in a shoe.

A warrior does not kill prisoners. A warrior does not kill children. A warrior does not rape women. You cannot treat war as a personal vendetta. I gave up cigarettes. I know it's not much. In fact it's ridiculously little. What could I do?

The Russians arrived soon afterwards in a couple of resprayed UN Cherokees, the paint job on the cars so bad that even by moonlight the black lettering showed through. Somewhere in the darkness around me were more than 100,000 combat-ready coalition troops, but I might as well have been on the moon.

There were seven Russians carrying metre-long black batons. I recognized the three paratroopers from the Desert Palm amongst them. It took a while for one to look up. He pointed. I contemplated running but there was nowhere to run to. Instead I raised my hand and waved. They fanned out into an arrowhead and climbed the ridge towards me.

'Hi,' I said, to the Russian from Volgograd, as they encircled me. They glanced at each other meaningfully. What else was I going to do? Say, 'I'm British, take me to my embassy,' in my clipped and ridiculously plummy voice? Received Pronunciation – more like rammed down my throat, by the numerous schools that I drifted through but never belonged to and the military academy that tried and mostly failed to make a soldier of me. What alternatives did I have? Try and explain? That made me laugh, a nasty and cynical laugh, which, as it turned out, was all the provocation they need.

I'm not sure which one of them hit me first or where. I didn't even brace myself. There was no tension in me: I gave myself up to their blows like a man falling off a tall building.

Korobko was a small man who was once powerfully built. Some evidence of this was still visible but he had gone to fat. He was wearing a crumpled grey-green uniform and his trousers were held up by a thick leather belt slung beneath the broad expanse of his belly.

He was almost completely bald. His face was puffy and sallow, as if he was struggling with an illness. He had heavy bags below his eyes and his upper lids were plump wattles, so that there were only small slits for him to peer through. To me, he looked like a small and angry box.

I was in a freight container. My arms were pinned against the wall by a couple of Russian paratroopers, who were bent almost double. Korobko had the end of a baton, its paint worn with usage, wedged under my chin. Sweat spilled from his damp forehead.

'What do you think you're doing,' Korobko said, 'in my town?'

Korobko had two front-row gold teeth and the glint of others further back in his mouth and his breath stank of vodka. He seemed determined to share his hangover.

'I told you, I'm a soldier,' I replied.

'Your papers?'

I rolled my only eye.

Korobko shook his head. 'Your mother.'

He turned his back on me and stamped back over to the table, sending the single caged bulb dancing on its cord with a flick of the wrist. Shadows pitched and yawed, making hunchbacks of us. He considered my remaining possessions: G-Shock watch, Nokia mobile phone, Oakley sunglasses, leather wallet and my old, cracked leather belt from MacKenzie of Arran. He picked up the wallet and emptied the contents onto the table: some dollars and sterling, my solicitor's business card, a Bank of Scotland Visa card way over its limit and, tucked away in a sleeve, two folded pieces of paper. One was a piece of self-reflective humour, a photograph cut from a Sunday magazine of a polar bear slouching in a state of angry shambles on an ice floe. The other piece of paper was the map of my heart. Ignoring the bear, Korobko reached out for it and I drew up the slack in my captors' grip.

There are some protective totems for which I would gladly exchange teeth. My daughter drew the house when she was small, laid thick the layers of wax crayon so that no white would show. The drawing was scored like some ancient map with crease marks from being folded and stored. You could scrape the colour with your nail.

He gave me a studied glare. 'You're like all of them. You cause the death of that guy and yet you seek to accuse the Russians.'

Her name was written in the bottom right-hand corner, partially obscuring what may have been a rabbit or a horse, in that looping, childish style of nursery school teachers everywhere. He held up the picture, gripping it between the thumb and forefingers of both hands and made a sudden motion as if to tear it. I bounced the Russians off each other and was almost on him before they had me down again.

'Don't,' I hissed.

Korobko tossed the drawing onto the table and wiped my spittle off his shirt with the back of one grubby hand. I let gravity and my captors' grip drop me down into a slouch.

'My name is Said,' I told him, through gritted teeth. 'Jonah Said, I'm a British Army officer.'

'You're an Englishman. Frankly speaking, you think the world is not good enough for you. You must idealize everything; turn it into some kind of stupid fairytale. You think this is a fucking movie? Name-rank-number?'

'My name is Said. I'm a British soldier, posted here on a UN mission. Like you.'

'Not like me. You are a spoiled westerner. You have no idea.'

'That's right. I don't have the first clue. So, why don't you tell me what this is about?'

'I will tell you. This man comes to my office. He says he wants to open containers. He says he has come to count UN property. I say what UN property? I tell him to go away and come back with the correct requisition papers. Two nights later you go with this same man to a bar on the Iraqi side that is a regular place of my soldiers. You drink strong vodka. You insult my soldiers. You argue with this man. You follow him to the toilet and you just kill him. You are trying to make it look like robbery. You try to frame my soldiers.'

'That's not what happened.'

'Why did you kill this man?' Korobko demanded.

'I didn't kill him.'

'What was it he was seeking?'

'I don't know.'

Korobko's baton slammed into my stomach and I slumped further down on the steel floor with the wind knocked out of me.

'Why did you go to the Desert Palm with this man?'

'I don't know,' I gasped. The existence of the Range Rovers and the bill of lading I had destroyed were details that I had decided not to share with him. A wave of nausea rose and subsided within me.

Taking a fistful of hair, Korobko lifted my head and started gently tapping the end of the baton against the side of my jaw. Clearly he wished me to believe that he intended to remove some teeth. I wasn't fooled. He had not used my daughter's drawing against me and it was the only weakness that I had chosen to show him.

'I was just along for the ride,' I told him.

Korobko frowned. 'Ride?'

'You've got the wrong guy. I'm just an impartial observer.'

The light bulb died with a cheery little pop.

Korobko swore softly in the darkness. I felt the soft whisper of air as the baton passed just millimetres from my face. Then I listened to the sound of Korobko's boots retreating across the container floor and his knuckles tapping on the door to be let out. For a few moments I caught a glimpse of moonlit asphalt and the dapple of camouflage netting and the silhouette of Korobko in the doorway. Then my captors threw me down and strode after him. The door slammed shut and I was plunged into total darkness.

I crawled over to the mattress in the corner of the container. I stretched out and listened to the whisper of voices and footsteps that filtered through the steel walls. An insect I couldn't see crawled over my hand and I brushed it away.

'*Fuck you*,' I whispered, and then again for good measure, '*Fuck you.*'

Beams of light shone out of nothingness and were fractured by a whirl of black cloth. There was a figure approaching, hands pulling at the hood of a robe. I cowered in the corner. Then there was a torch in my face and my eye was filled with dazzling prisms.

I was surprised to hear a woman's voice speaking in English. 'It's a clear violation of his rights and of your mandate. You can't hold him like this.'

A second, unfamiliar voice, with a Russian accent, replied, 'The matter is he's a suspect.'

'Christ, Nikitin. There's such a thing as due process. Even here.'

The man identified as Nikitin protested, 'He stole a UN vehicle.'

'He's a UN observer. He's entitled to drive UN vehicles.'

'You say that.'

'He's UN, I'm telling you. He's just been posted in.'

'And the dead Norway?'

'Turn the body over to the embassy.'

'The incident is being investigated by the police.'

'The Iraqi police? The Mook? Don't make me laugh.'

A hand took my upper arm and the woman's voice said, not unkindly, 'On your feet.'

Within seconds we were out of the container and into a grotto of camouflage netting. There was a blaze of light and then cool shadow and the sensation of entering a biblical city or a walled medieval town. Rising above us was a warren of routes and dwellings, a jumble of wooden and

steel stairways, exposed balconies, passageways and alleyways. Everywhere there were washing lines and TV and
radio aerials.

I was following a very tall, dark-haired woman in a black
robe as she strode across the stage created by the pool of
light from a skylight far above. Russian soldiers struggled
to keep up with us. I could hear distant noises – an
argument, chickens, pop music – and smell cooking,
garbage, sweat and urine.

I called out, 'Where am I?'

'Not Kansas,' the woman replied briskly.

'And you're not Judy Garland,' I retorted.

She spun around to face in my direction, with her
hands on her hips and her elbows out at angles, and
anything else that I might have said became an irrele-
vance, because I was thinking that she was by some
distance the most beautiful woman I had ever seen.
To my eye she was five-foot ten-inches with a mane
of hair as black as cane molasses and her teeth were
bright white, her provocative grin a slash of light in the
encircling gloom. I felt a heady rush of excitement. I
wanted my closed, tightly furled heart to open.

'We're in the Russian compound,' she said, looking me
in the eyes, clearly aware of the effect she was having.
'We're in one of the old British warehouses in Umm Qasr
port. There's about six or seven hundred Russians in here
without a fan between them. They have no showers, no hot
meals and no place to take a shit. It tends to make them
irritable. So, if it's OK with you, I'd like to leave.'

I wanted to reach out with one hand and touch her, to
place my fingers against the slender curve of her neck. I
wanted to fix her unreal beauty in the here and now.

I saw the hot blood rise in her cheeks. She threw up her

arms in exasperation, turned on her bare heels and strode away.

'Sure, let's go,' I said, grinning. I hurried after her.

We emerged from the building on the far side into daylight. We were walking across a large courtyard formed by a wall of double-stacked freight containers, whilst beneath our feet was a carpet of fish bones that glittered like salt. The sun had not yet cleared the container wall and it was still cold.

There was a battered Nissan Patrol parked by the entrance to the compound. I noticed that the woman's ankles and the skin of her bare brown feet were covered in floral hennaed patterns.

'My name's Jonah,' I called out.

'I know,' she said.

There was a sudden commotion off to our flank and the woman cursed. Korobko had reappeared and he was shouting and gesticulating at the guards on the gate. Abruptly a hand gripped my shoulder and a thick knot of soldiers placed themselves between the woman and me. My good humour was abruptly doused, leaving me with my usual dark comedy.

'*Ribbet*,' I called out. I was being dragged back to the building, my heels raising clouds of bone dust.

'I'll get you out,' she shouted.

'*Ribbet!*'

She yelled, 'Why do you keeping saying that?'

'If you'd kissed me I'd have turned into a prince,' I shouted.

Back in the container, Nikitin supervised the replacement of the light bulb. It was difficult to tell because none of them wore any visible rank, but my guess was that Nikitin was Korobko's deputy. I was tempted to ask him how many Russians it takes to change a light bulb but he was downcast and would not look at me, concentrating instead on the foul-smelling cigarette he was smoking. Clearly Korobko had humiliated him. Unsurprisingly, I was not filled with compassion. I asked him for some shoe polish. He let out a plume of smoke as blue as a car exhaust and shrugged noncommittally.

When they were gone I began to pace the length and breadth of the container, striding back and forth in zigzags and figure of eights, slapping the walls as I passed.

In the weeks after the collapse of my marriage I strode the length of bedrooms and hotel rooms. I walked up and down the aisles of darkened aeroplanes. I walked the thirteen miles of Manhattan from the Broadway Bridge at 225th street to South Ferry. I know what I am. I have seen a maddened polar bear pacing its zoo enclosure, lumbering back and forth in the prison space, back and forth, with its head bobbing and the groaning whistle of its breath a strange mad ululation.

At some point, from speakers lashed to bullet-pocked minarets, came the tinny and echoing sound of the muezzin calling the faithful to prayer.

Spicy

Spicy's voice preceded him. 'Cheers,' he said as the bolts were thrown on the container door. 'Thanks very much.'

He cut an unlikely figure in a Ralph Lauren shirt that was caked in dust but might once have been fire-extinguisher red and a pair of baggy khaki shorts that only accentuated the thinness of his legs. He wasn't wearing any socks, just a pair of down-at-heel deck shoes. He had an untidy mop of hair that he kept out of his pale, almost colourless eyes with a frequent flick of the head.

'Eat my chuddies,' he said, without movement of his upper lip. 'You're an ugly fucker.'

'So I've been told,' I replied from the floor where I'd been lost in the comforting rhythm of working polish into the leather of my boots with my fingers. Nikitin had come up with the goods; it wasn't Kiwi but it would do.

Polishing her shoes was something that I had always done for my daughter: rising early and working the blue into her sandals and then taking a brush to them until the flowers shone through the polish and gleamed. I held those shoes as if they were something unbearably precious.

'I've been sent to rescue you,' Spicy told me as he consulted his plastic Saddam Hussein wristwatch. 'Running a bit late. Sorry about that.'

'I liked the other one better,' I replied, meaning the woman.

Spicy wasn't about to give up. 'Jonah, isn't it?'

'Uh-huh.'

'Lieutenant Titus Rhodes-Spicer of the Grenadier Guards,' he said, 'Spicy to you. I'm the UN Military Information Officer, though what that means is as much of a mystery to me as it is to everyone else in this god-forsaken hole. The good news is the Russians have agreed to let you go.'

I ignored him and considered my hands. They were covered in black polish. My hands are coarse and my fingers are calloused. The nails are chewed and ragged. They are weapons, really, not instruments. By contrast my father has fine fingers. Before Alzheimer's, my father was an accomplished geneticist. As a child, I remember being conscious of my father's fingers pressing the flesh on my back as if trying to summon forth the discrete physical, mental and emotional potentialities that he knew I contained. I remember on a different occasion brandishing yet another sheet of D-minus homework in his face and taunting him, 'Nature or nurture, Dad?'

I was always a smartarse. Somewhere in the birth canal or the back garden, in the playground or on the football pitch, I took my father's wisdom and smashed it up. Ironically, Alzheimer's is making the same short work of him.

The last time I saw him my father said to me, 'What are those things moving around by themselves?'

'People,' I replied.

He said, 'Who are you?'

'I'm your son.'

Every surface of the interior of Spicy's Land Cruiser was smeared with a powdery covering of sand. The seats were ripped. It looked like a wreck but appearances can be deceptive. As well as the Codan HF and Motorola VHF radio sets, he had a satellite phone, a dash-mounted GPS and a customized in-car CD system with massive speakers, so that it was all sound. Beside me was a plastic cool box packed with cans of soda and behind me, in the storage space, a Tirfor winch and ground anchor, a first-aid kit, a couple of spades and some sand tracks.

'Fasten seat belts,' said Spicy. 'The Rocky Mountain roller-coaster to Saddam's Magic Kingdom is about to depart.'

At the entrance to the camp, freight containers were arranged in a herringbone pattern, so that Spicy had to slalom back and forth half a dozen times, passing though the narrow channel between steel walls. Russian soldiers were perched on top, looking down on us as we steered through.

'And outside,' Spicy announced, kicking off his deck shoes, 'the hollering gobs of humanity.'

As we approached the narrow exit, sweating Russian guards in flak jackets dragged barbed-wire entanglements aside and there was a sudden rush of beggars towards the car. Spicy pressed his fist down on the horn and we swept through the crush, scattering people in our wake. Then we were rattling over railway tracks, blasting a wall of Prodigy out across the port, the sound echoing amongst the derelict cranes and bomb-damaged warehouses.

'*Smack my bitch up*,' Spicy sang over and over again.

I turned in my seat to watch the road behind. Seconds later an old black Mercedes accelerated out of a narrow lane between warehouses and fell in behind us.

'We've got company,' I shouted above the music.

'Your first recognition lesson,' Spicy yelled, watching

the rear-view mirror. 'Mukhabarat. We call them the Mook. Saddam's bogeymen. Brutalized orphans, mostly. They wear sunglasses and as a rule they call on their victims after dark.'

Revealed in daylight, Umm Qasr was a sprawling and shabby town of mud-brick hovels with corrugated iron roofs. The main street was marked by piles of slashed tyres, mounds of rubbish and shell craters left over from Desert Storm and the Iran–Iraq war. Wide strips of dirt with truncated stumps were visible where tree-lined avenues might once have been. On every wall there were flaking murals of Saddam Hussein. The entrances to narrow alleyways suggested labyrinths beyond.

'Lots of e-traffic back and forth to Blighty about you,' Spicy said.

We rattled up and down through the potholes with the Mercedes following close behind. In the centre of town, clusters of women in black robes with red-hennaed hands squatted on each street corner, waving away flies from plastic buckets of fish. They stared at the vehicle as it passed.

'The boss has got you down as a troublemaker, especially after last night. It seems the Mook feel the same.'

'Who's the boss?' I asked.

'What?'

I raised my voice. 'Who's in charge?'

Spicy turned down the volume. 'The lines of command are ferociously complicated. Nobody is ever really in charge at the UN. Everything is disavowed.'

'You said "boss". You used the word.'

'So I did.' He rolled his eyes. 'Lieutenant Colonel Hanbury. He's the senior British officer attached to the

UN here in Kuwait and therefore nominally in charge of the British contingent to the UN. That's you and me. He wants to meet you. I'll take you to see him tomorrow.'

'What does it mean to be a UN observer here?' I asked.

Spicy shrugged. 'It means you get to stare wistfully into the desert and when the time comes you get to watch the Americans come crashing through the fence. You want the tourist spiel?'

'Yes.'

'OK. The official mandate of the United Nations Iraq/ Kuwait Observer Mission is to monitor the Zone and the Khawr 'Abd Allah waterway; to deter violations of the boundary and to observe any hostile action mounted from the territory of one state against the other. In real terms that means you get to sit in a barely defended patrol base in the middle of the desert with the Americans on one side and the Iraqis on the other.'

I considered this information. 'And when the Americans invade?'

'I should get out of the way. They have great big tanks.'

We watched a Russian patrol coming down off the roof of a graceless concrete blockhouse that might once have been an administrative building, darting across the open spaces created by shell holes and retracting their pickets.

'When did the Russians arrive?'

'A few months back. They are the resident infantry battalion, here to support the UN mandate. In theory they're here to protect you, though somebody should explain that to them. There used to be a Bangladeshi mechanized battalion but they got posted to some other zone. Eritrea, I think. Apparently the Russians leapt at the chance.'

'So what's so special about the Zone?'

Spicy grinned lewdly. 'The Zone is a spit of land bereft of all social order. Anything is possible in the Zone.'

'And that makes it worth it?'

'Oh yes.'

'It wasn't like this before.'

'Of course it wasn't. Things have changed. In fact, nothing is the same. The Gulf Arabs are a disillusioned and resentful bunch. The ruling families may be great allies but they're lousy rulers. One day soon the whole region is going to explode and when the jihad comes it doesn't matter how much of our expensive weaponry the Emir and his no-hoper family have got stockpiled, they'll go down like chaff and we'll be hightailing it with them. That just about covers the residents.'

On the subject of UN personnel he was even more forthright.

'Don't mess with the Africans, especially not the Nigerians; they'll beat you to death. The Chileans will knife you in the back, ditto the Romanians. The Argentinians will hate you; that should be self-evident. The Turks don't see a joke and neither do the Greeks, so no Cyprus gags. The Bangladeshis and the Pakistanis will detect "the foreign hand" in your every word and gesture. Don't worry about the French: they'll ignore you. The Thais are the nicest people that money can buy and the Chinese are the nastiest. As for the Americans, I've never met such a bunch of self-righteous, ill-informed morons. Though, as in all situations, there are exceptions.'

'And the Russians?'

'For a start, don't drink with the Russians. I thought that you might have learned that lesson.'

In a sudden spirit of confession, I said, 'I'm not sure that it was the Russians who killed Odd.'

'As I understand it, you were comatose under a table. It follows that no one is going to consider you a reliable witness.'

Spicy had a point. I had no more idea of who killed the Norwegian than anyone else.

Around the next corner, a shabby concrete mosque thrust its angular minaret from amongst the shapeless buildings around it. An amplified voice, transcendent with anger, was coming from the tower, echoing all around. Then we heard shouts, shattering glass and the rattle of stones against walls.

'That's the thing about peacekeeping,' Spicy said, in a resigned tone. 'It's not about keeping peace; it's about struggling against anarchy.'

At an intersection a crowd of barefoot women in black robes were wailing with their henna-stained fists raised to the air. They ran towards us.

Looking left and right, Spicy slowed to a roll.

'Hold on,' he shouted, glancing anxiously in the rear-view mirror. He attempted to back up but the Mercedes deliberately blocked our way.

'Fuckers,' Spicy said.

We were engulfed. Shrieking women pounded on the roof, the bonnet and the windows. I lowered the window to shout at the driver of the Mercedes and soon realized that I had made a mistake. A woman came around to the passenger's side with her eyes fixed on mine. She was screaming, her mouth opening and closing. The air reeked of burning rubber. The woman parted her robe with one hand to reveal a long curling violet scar that snaked across her naked chest. She'd had a breast removed.

I was stunned by her anger. There was no doubt that I was being held responsible for her injury.

I felt a sudden coldness in my upper arm, followed by a rush of liquid. My shirtsleeve was soaked in blood. The woman had reached in with her other hand and stuck a curved, elaborately carved knife in my arm.

'Fuck!' said Spicy.

I reached across and without thinking pulled the knife out. Blood flowed down both sides of my arm. I dropped the knife out of the window and rolled it up. There was a hiatus while the women stopped pounding the car and contemplated this apparently unexpected turn of events.

I thought I could feel my blood pressure dropping.

'Drive the fucking car,' I said.

'Righto,' said Spicy, nodding gravely. He put his foot down and accelerated away, scattering women left and right.

I looped my belt around my arm and pulled it tight with my teeth in an attempt to stem the flow of blood. Already my trousers and the car seat were sticky with blood.

'What the fuck is going on?' I said.

'It's the Zone,' said Spicy as if no further explanation was needed.

A rain of stones met us halfway along the next block. We drove down a narrow alley and plunged into smoke. Out of the smoke came a chanting gang of teenagers, boys with scarves tied across their faces. They hurled themselves against the walls as we passed. At the far end of the alley was a square strewn with stones. There was a skirmish line of Russian troops advancing, while behind them soldiers, posed like medieval archers, fired gas canisters that came spinning against the sky.

Across the square was a crumbling stucco wall topped with sheets of corrugated iron and razor wire. A drooping UN flag hung over a sandbagged gate. Signs in Arabic and English were pasted around the entrance.

Spicy pumped the horn and sped across the square. Huge figures in flak jackets and blue berets burst from the steel doors and fanned out, dropping into a watchful crouch as we approached.

Inside, for a few seconds, it was like stepping into another world. A world of burnished bronze windscreens and blue and white flags; rows of white Land Cruisers, Discoveries and Grand Cherokees parked against the dusty stucco walls. Then the first tear-gas grenade landed in the courtyard and bounced away under a Discovery. Clouds of smoke and bitter gas drifted towards us.

'That was . . .' Spicy paused, 'interesting.'

He grinned, revealing his strangely pointed canines, and arched his eyebrows in an expression clearly intended to be comical.

I stumbled out of the Land Cruiser and fell into the arms of a Danish soldier.

'The hospitals here have no facilities. No incubators. No drugs. No electricity. Today another kid died of leukaemia. Cancer is through the roof here, a twelve times increase in cancer mortality. It's like Hiroshima: an increased percentage of congenital malformation and an increase of malignancy. The local imams blame it on the dust from depleted uranium shells fired by American tanks in the battles here during the war. They whip up the local people. And the local people are Shias, a disenfranchised group like the Kurds; they are the lowest of the low. The bottom of the pile. We bear the brunt of their frustration.'

UN Observer Mission Headquarters was located in what had been a British army hospital during the Second World War. We were in the medical centre, the site of a former dispensary. I was sitting in a plastic chair in a pair of shorts while a German army nurse named Dieter was stitching my arm. He was crying, the tears rolling down his cheeks as he pushed the needle in and out of the meaty flaps of skin.

'Of course, although they are supposed to be here to protect us, the Russians don't like us much,' he said. His eyes were bloodshot and appeared almost closed. 'Which explains why they are so indiscriminate with the tear gas.'

It transpired that the knife had passed through my arm without damaging anything vital.

'You will have another scar to add to your collection.'

'I'm thrilled.'

Finishing, Dieter slid away on the castors of his chair and wiped away the tears with the back of his hand. He scratched at his neatly trimmed goatee beard.

'You know they say that scars are the way we know that our past is real.'

'I've had a busy time,' I replied.

Dieter stared. 'You look tired,' he said.

'I tell you it's exhausting,' I added.

'I guess it is,' he replied carefully.

He reached for a pill bottle on the shelf behind him and shook out a couple of capsules into his palm. He held them out at arm's length.

'You want something to help you sleep?'

'No,' I told him regretfully. 'Off limits. Cheating.'

'Please yourself,' said Dieter and, making a funnel of his hand, returned the capsules to the bottle. 'More for everyone else,' he added wryly.

He showed me to a small, whitewashed room with a camp bed and a sleeping bag.

'I have left you a uniform. It's German, I'm afraid.'

I climbed into the sleeping bag and rested my bandaged arm on my chest. 'German is fine,' I said.

'We're not so keen on a war,' he said.

'I can safely say the war is going to pass me by.'

'Maybe that's a good thing,' he said. He paused in the doorway. 'Welcome to the Zone, Jonah. Sleep tight.'

Wormwood

Driving south out of the Zone on the expressway the following morning we passed columns of tank transporters and oil tankers, then the theme park Entertainment World, before seeing the first signs of Camp Doha. I lifted myself far enough off the back seat to stare at mile after mile of chain-link fence, topped with helixes of razor wire. The fence was broken only by the barriers and dragon's-teeth chicanes of the American complex and after it the British gate. There were acres of containers stacked four high beyond the fence.

Odd had told me that he'd opened six hundred containers in three weeks, in Camp Doha, Umm Qasr port and the sectors of the Zone. I pressed my fingers against the tender, swollen skin at the back of my head and asked, 'Is it as big as they say it is?'

Spicy lifted his eyebrows at me in the rear-view mirror. 'Camp Doha? Bigger. Someone told me that, amongst everything else, they've got forty-eight million Meals Ready to Eat stockpiled in there. You could hide the Ark of the Covenant and nobody would ever find it.'

'Am I supposed to take that as a hint?' I asked.

'Take it how you like,' he retorted.

We drove on down the expressway into Kuwait City. The streets were filled with Filipinos in the orange coats of 'Tanzifco' workers, one every fifteen feet or so, silently sweeping the streets.

'What do you think of Kuwait?'

'I hope that's a joke,' Spicy replied good-humouredly. 'They can't even clean up their own shit. They have to get someone else to do it.'

A couple of nights later I heard a joke, not a particularly funny one but illuminating. A Kuwaiti is asked if sex is work or fun. He thinks about it for a while. 'Fun,' he says. 'If it was work I would get a foreigner to do it.'

'Kuwaiti society is a club sandwich,' Spicy explained, 'arranged strictly by caste. The Kuwaitis are the bread: the oil barons and the royal family, assorted family members and clingers-on sitting at the top; and the Bedouin, the caretakers and tea makers, at the bottom. In between are the meats and the cheeses, arranged in strict hierarchical order; at the top, just underneath the most privileged Kuwaiti families, come the Americans and beneath them the Europeans. Beneath the Europeans you have the Egyptians and the Palestinians, who are, in turn, superior to the Pakistanis and Bangladeshis. Then you have the rest of the hired help: the Filipinos, the Indonesians and the South Koreans, and finally at the bottom of the heap the blacks, Africans mainly from Ethiopia, Somalia and Sudan. Does that illuminate things for you?'

'I suppose.'

'So what else do you want to know?'

'What did you do to end up here?' I asked.

'D'you want to answer that question first?'

I returned my attention to the cars behind. In each car, I observed that the driver seemed to be engaged in a con-versation on a mobile phone.

'I'm accused of kidnapping someone,' I said, finally.

'Far out,' said Spicy. 'Tell me more.'

'I don't think that would be a prudent idea,' I said.

'Fully understand, old chap,' he said. 'Careless talk and all . . .'

We drove down through al-Wafra, Kuwait's garden; its dusty main street lined with Indian restaurants and small shops with gaudy plastic kitchenware and cheap cotton dishdashas hanging from the awnings. Then we were amongst irrigated fields of strawberries and tomatoes that stretched southwards to the border with Saudi.

My wife Sarah phoned me in Bosnia on St Valentine's Day 1999, nearly six years into our marriage. She said, 'There's no easy way to say this. You don't make me happy. I love Douglas. I want to spend the rest of my life with him. Don't come back.'

There wasn't any easy way to hear it, either. Certainly there is no easy way to describe the emotions that followed on the heel of that particular phone call. My world was torn apart.

I knew one thing only: I had to get back. My memory of what followed is fractured and disordered: the cramped interior of armoured personnel carriers and Land Rovers, freezing hangars and cell-like transit accommodation, helicopter landing sites and airport departure lounges. It's all run together in a goulash. I was sleepless and delirious. I strode back and forth like that maddened polar bear at Edinburgh zoo. I smoked cigarettes tip to tail.

I got as far as Glasgow airport in thirty-three hours and then the weather defeated me. There was a squall out over the Western Isles and they cancelled the plane that was due to take me across to the island that Sarah and I had made our home.

I finally arrived twenty-four hours later, an already advanced and intractable insomniac. My head felt like a burnt-out husk. I'd lost the fight before I'd begun. When I confronted my wife, I could only summon the energy for a simple question. 'Why?'

She replied, 'There's no point in character assassination now.'

I cannot describe the trajectory of their relationship, how it started or in what manner it developed. I wasn't there.

I had not realized the extent to which my wife's world had contracted. This was the woman who hitch-hiked solo across Africa, who caught malaria in Sudan, climbed volcanoes in Indonesia and survived shipwrecks in Central America. She had been worldly and valiant, terrifying and wonderful, truly a world-swallower.

And then she changed. She withdrew into family and family-like ties, into the 'white bread' agrarian community of a tiny island. To her I suppose I became some big-talking Cyclops who couldn't tell slurry from silage. She turned her back on me in bed and although night after night I pressed myself against the base of her spine, the answer was always no. No. Until my head was boiling and I signed up for the army again and shipped out to Bosnia.

I wonder if she thought that I was going to keep going off to the terrible corners of the earth and that one day I wasn't going to come back. I wonder if she left me because she thought that I was going to leave her.

Revenge

We were in the Tower Restaurant on the roof of the National Museum of Scotland on the night of the Cowgate fire. Alex was drinking an espresso. He had a Range Rover full of broad-shouldered, ex-Hereford types waiting down on Chambers Street. I was drinking a glass of Veuve Clicquot – the widow – Alex had demanded it. The old town of Edinburgh was in flames behind his head.

'You went out there that night. She knows your face. You know what that means.'

Alex lifted his Oakleys for the first time in twenty-four hours, rubbed his eyes and adjusted them to the muted lighting. He surveyed the abandoned tables and empty bar, the wash of spinning blue light against the far wall. He did a sudden double take and spun around in his chair.

'What the fuck is going on out there?' he demanded loudly.

People looked back from the glass wall.

'The Cowgate's on fire,' I explained.

He seemed insulted. 'Does *anything* mundane ever happen to you?'

'What is that supposed to mean?' I protested.

'Did you really want this to happen? Did you want to get caught?'

'Fuck off,' I told him.

Our waiter returned. He said, 'Is everything OK?'

'No, Kevin,' said Alex. 'Things are not fucking OK. We need another bottle, two bottles in fact.'

The waiter retreated.

'You'll probably never eat here again,' said Alex. 'Do you realize that?'

I couldn't tell whether he was being melodramatic. I was remembering another night, at another restaurant, back in the summer of '99; the night that Alex suggested revenge.

We were in Quo Vadis. Alex was drinking an iced latte. He had a different Range Rover full of goons on a double yellow line outside. I was drinking a raspberry martini; as usual, Alex had insisted. One of Damien Hirst's cow's heads was floating in formaldehyde behind his head.

'You're losing weight and you're looking pale. Your hairline is receding,' Alex had said.

'I've been through a rough patch,' I replied, resolving to shave my head immediately.

'So what is this disaster that I must be apprised of?'

It was unsettling and humiliating. There were times back then when I felt like the Ancient Mariner, compelled by fate to recount my sorry tale over and over again.

'The straight face is impressive,' Alex told me when I was done.

'I didn't mean this to happen,' I said.

'Are you sure?'

'Wait a minute.' I held my hands up in front of me. 'It's not what I expected to happen. You think that my wife leaving me for someone else was part of my cunning master plan?'

'The world is full of surprises, Jonah, and most of them are fucking unpleasant.'

'But I don't understand,' I said.

'You'll never understand.'

'That's comforting.'

Alex stretched then slouched back in the chair. 'Clearly, what you require is a seriously cathartic experience.'

'Please.'

'I'm serious.'

'Like what?' I asked.

'Revenge. What else is there in this world?'

'It's a couple of months too late for a crime of passion,' I said.

'There are some people who owe me a favour,' he said vacantly, 'people from former days, unattributable people.'

I assumed he meant some acquaintances from Belfast. I said, 'What are you thinking?'

'We'll lift him. Strip him and throw him in a cellar. Let him lie in his own filth for a few days.'

'You mean lift Douglas?'

Alex waved his hand. 'Don't tell me his name.' He leant forward. 'He'll be getting off lightly. The Taliban would have chopped his hands off, or worse. The Chechens would have thrown him down a gravel chute.'

'This isn't Chechnya or Afghanistan, Alex. We have laws here.'

'The people I'm talking about are professional,' he said, 'very professional.'

'What will it achieve?'

Alex stared at me and, after a brief incredulous pause, he said: 'It'll make you feel so much better.'

I must have looked doubtful.

'We're going to hell, Jonah. Why not take a few with you?'

They lifted him from the agricultural show at Lochgilphead. In the car park after the show, he was approached by a tall woman with long brown hair poking out from under a white crocheted hat and striking blue eyes. She spoke with an English accent and bore a deliberate resemblance to my wife. They knew what Douglas's taste ran to. The woman explained that her car wouldn't start and asked him to give her a push. She smiled winsomely.

I imagine him hunkering down behind the boot of the car, a nondescript blue Ford Sierra, his jeans riding low on his hips, revealing the pale flesh at the top of his buttocks. The needle went straight in, the unidentified man coming up behind him, hooking his arm around Douglas's neck to brace him and sticking the needle into the muscle. Douglas was swiftly bundled into the back of the car and driven ten miles. Then he was bound with plastic cable ties, gagged and blindfolded and transferred to the boot.

I followed a very public routine. I booked in and out of Dreghorn barracks on the southern outskirts of Edinburgh. I set memorable patterns of behaviour and in doing so I acquired an unassailable alibi.

On the second night after Douglas was lifted I lounged in the television room in the officers' mess. I exchanged pleasantries with the padre and ruffled the jowls on his overweight black Labrador. I went to bed early. Some hours later, dressed in black, I went out through my window and up the bank that led to the playing fields. I followed the line of Scots pine that fringed the rugby pitch and squatted in the shadow of a tree close to the path that the Ministry of Defence Police patrol never deviated from. Unknown to them, there was a hole in the security fence concealed behind a clump of brambles. My soldiers used it and I had been aware of its existence for some time.

I eased myself through the rent in the steel links and I

was in thick woodland overgrown with rhododendrons. I could hear the whoosh of the occasional car on the bypass. I followed the line of a stream and then I was adjacent to the road and Alex was waiting for me in a car that I had never seen before.

'Anybody see you?' Alex demanded.

I shook my head and he started the car. We drove north into Perthshire and beyond. Alex was uncharacteristically quiet. We left the main road and soon we were in a landscape of darkness unmarred by sodium light.

Eventually, Alex stopped the car. He took a 1:50,000-scale map from the glove compartment, a Silva compass and a small pen torch with a red filter. He stared at the map for a few seconds and rotated it slightly in his hand to orientate himself.

'We're here. You're going there. It's about a kilometre and a half. Avoid the farmhouse.' He consulted his watch. 'You have exactly one hour.'

'Thanks,' I said, my hand poised on the door lever.

'Wear the balaclava.'

Traditionally it is the adulterer who disguises his face. 'No eye shall see me,' I told him.

'Don't do anything stupid.'

A woman was standing in the steading doorway, cast in shadow, so that I was reaching for the door handle before I saw her. We did not speak. She offered me a cigarette and I refused. She lit one, leaning against my chest to shield the lighter, and as the flame illuminated her elfin face I realized that she was deliberately revealing herself to me. It was not lost on her, this resemblance to my wife, and I was half out of my mind. I couldn't help myself. I reached out – like a child reaches for a flame – and rested my hand against her cheek. She turned her head slightly and ran her tongue along the inside of my fingers.

'Sarah,' I said.

She grinned and raised her jaw, a thread of spittle bridging the gap between my fingers and her mouth. I did not know who she was, this woman. I had never seen her before and I did not expect to see her again. But I wanted to fuck her, immediately, there against the steading wall. I wanted to mark her as mine. I sometimes think that that is all I need to heal me, palliative sex. Enough sex will make the pain go away.

'Go on,' she said.

She dropped the cigarette and ground it out with her heel. She then reached down, picked up the butt and stuck it in her pocket. She raised her eyebrows at me and turned and walked back across the yard to the cottage.

A single candle burned in the steading. It stank of piss, faeces and fear. Terror imparts to shit a smell that is all its own – thin and shaming. It reminds us of the helplessness and fear that is our common heritage, our common origin in shit and screams.

Douglas was lying face down on a bed of straw, naked but for a pair of underpants. His flesh was a blotch of red and white. His blindfold had been removed for my arrival and his eyes rolled in my direction as I entered.

I did not speak. I took no action to reveal my identity. I didn't need to. I simply squatted down about five feet from him with my big bony knees beside my ears and my large ungainly hands dangling forward of them. How long did it take for the realization to come? Four minutes? Five? I'm not really sure. Suddenly his eyes widened dramatically and he started to thrash spastically on the straw.

When he had stopped, something like a soft mewling sound came from behind his gag. I understood then why Alex told me not to do anything stupid. I could so easily have killed Douglas. I did not need a weapon. I had my hands and my feet and my teeth. I did not need to use my imagination: I had seen dismembered bodies, arms detached from torsos. I felt the hunger for it rushing through me like wind. One second I was freezing and the next I was sweating sulphur.

And just as suddenly, I'd had enough – the fury abated as fast as it had arisen. I stood up and staggered out. I leant against the steading wall in the starlight. I pulled the balaclava off my head and let the sweat turn cold on my face. I shook my head. I felt mightily sick at myself.

The woman approached from the cottage. She closed the door to the steading which I had carelessly left open and offered me another cigarette.

'I don't want a cigarette,' I told her, too vehemently.

She shrugged and lit herself another. Again the flame of her lighter illuminated her face but the illusion was shattered. Her hair was dyed, her accent was false and I imagined that sometime the following day, somewhere on the road to Stranraer or the ferry back to Ireland, she would remove her coloured contact lenses and throw them to the wind. She was not my wife.

'You'd best leave,' she said.

As for the rest, I can only go by what Alex told me. Douglas was hosed down, given a boiler suit to wear and abandoned on a lonely stretch of road somewhere up in Sutherland. The Ford Sierra was found thirty miles away in a lay-by on a minor road. It had been torched; there were the charred remains of clothing, though nothing was clearly identifiable. There were no usable prints.

I got away with it. Everybody was convinced that I'd done it – of course they were – but I was in no mood for confession and they had no evidence.

A few weeks after Douglas was released, I found myself back in Bosnia.

For over three years, I got away with it. Then, in an unrelated investigation, a military policewoman who had been a member of 14 Intelligence, the undercover unit working in Northern Ireland, was arrested and offered immunity from prosecution in return for testimony.

Alex leant across the table at the Tower Restaurant while our fellow diners watched the flames leaping from the roofs of the old town.

'You could leave,' he said, 'go somewhere without an extradition treaty.'

'Fuck you,' I told him.

The following morning I was in General Monteith's office and soon after that I was on the road to London and a flight to Kuwait. No one could say that Monteith didn't take care of his own.

Golf

When I eventually found him, Colonel Nigel Hanbury, Deputy Chief Military Observer to the United Nations Mission in Kuwait and head of the British contingent to the UN, was standing at the base of an African palm with a pile of golf balls at his feet. An old leather golfing bag, threadbare at the seams, leant against the bole. His golfing shoes had lost their colour, as had his hat, which, it seemed to me, might once have been blue. When he took it off to wipe his brow, Hanbury revealed a bald leathery pate. Everything about him was faded, leached of colour by the relentless Kuwaiti sun. He was clearly an old-timer, a loan-service Gulf man who had long ago slipped off the career ladder – his blood too thin to contemplate return.

'Looks like it's going to be hot, young man.'

Hanbury was staring out across the broad, flat expanse of neatly clipped grass. Everywhere there was the gentle chugging sound of sprinklers.

'Do you play?'

'No, Colonel.'

'I had a feeling you didn't.'

I found myself considering how much it must be costing to water an entire golf course, the sort of calculation that devastates the mind. I don't like golf. There is something unnatural about the manicured and obedient landscape, its artfully created obstacles and rigid hierarchies; the implication of social and economic distances between those who belong and those who don't.

'There's a flask of coffee in the car, John.'

'Right.'

I staggered back in the direction I had come from. There was a single, immaculately polished white UN Discovery in the car park and beyond it the desert and the occasional outline of an oil derrick. On the horizon CH-53 Sea Stallion helicopters with under-slung loads were ferrying equipment across the desert.

Spicy had gone. I felt as if I was on the farthest edge of something. I certainly didn't feel I was part of any impending war. I wondered how I was going to get back to the Zone.

I tapped on the mirrored window of the Discovery and listened to the electric whirr of the window being lowered. Without giving me a glance or waiting for me to ask, the driver passed me a flask. I understood that I was being put in my place.

As I was turning to leave, the driver said, 'I'd call him "sir" if I were you.'

I considered this information. 'How do you manage?'

'Grit my teeth,' he replied.

By the time I got back to the tree Hanbury was preparing to take a shot. He had his feet planted firmly apart and with his hat tilted low on his forehead he seemed oblivious to my presence. I watched him take the shot, the club rising and falling.

Hanbury called out, 'Fore!'

As far as I could tell, we were the only people there. 'Actually, sir, my name is Jonah.'

Hanbury glanced in my direction without comment and

then returned to squinting after his ball. I drank some coffee.

If he was looking for a way into the subject he settled on what I considered to be an obscure approach. 'You get any sleep last night?'

'I'm fine, thanks,' I replied and gave him my best smile. I needn't have bothered; he didn't even look at me. However, I was encouraged by the pained expression on his face: 'And yourself?'

Hanbury shook his head. 'Damn funny business. Bring my clubs, will you.'

He strode off down the fairway in search of the ball. Dutifully, I followed. At least my muscles were getting a stretch after the beating I'd taken.

Hanbury asked, 'Did you know him well?'

'You mean Odd? No. Not at all. I met him at the airport.'

'I don't know about you, but he always struck me as being something of a loner. Not one of the team. Now where's that damn ball?'

He stared about him in exasperation. Then he reached across and gripped my sleeve. It was the first time that he had really got a look at me and I felt the jolt travel down his arm. I'm no freak but up close the absence of an eye can be disconcerting. I suppose the bruises didn't help. My face was mostly chartreuse with livid streaks of indigo. The skin around my blind eye was bruised and there was a zigzag-shaped graze across my forehead.

'I know he stumbled across something,' Hanbury said when he had recovered sufficiently.

'If he did, he didn't share it with me,' I told him.

After a pause, Hanbury said, 'What were you doing up there?'

'I don't know,' I said. I wasn't going to tell him about the cars. 'Odd said he had a meeting with someone.'

'Someone?'

'A woman.'

His lip curled. 'A woman?'

'Yes.'

'Did you meet this . . . person?'

I shook my head. 'Didn't show.' Then I added, 'There were some Russians.'

'These days, there always are,' Hanbury sighed.

'Maybe they killed him.'

'Maybe they didn't.' Hanbury let go of my sleeve. 'Odd was poking around, opening up containers and looking for things. Imported goods. Forgotten things.'

'Perhaps he found something,' I said.

Hanbury returned to contemplating the fairway. 'Personally, I blame the Americans; their bloody container-security initiative.'

'I'm sorry, I don't follow.'

'Suddenly they want us to open all the boxes with no thought for the consequences, typical bloody Americans. You know that back in August 1990 the Iraqis destroyed every single computer in Shuaiba port? They thought they were televisions, got the hump when they didn't work and smashed them. Can you imagine the chaos that caused? Thousands of containers strewn across the country and no records: twelve years later and we still don't know what was lost or misplaced. Now the Americans are demanding of the Department of Peacekeeping Operations that we open and catalogue everything in the Zone. It's a bloody feeding frenzy out there.'

'I'm sorry, I still don't follow.'

Hanbury regarded me with a kind of schoolmasterly impatience. 'You're not very sharp, are you?'

'Not really,' I conceded.

'At least you're honest. I'll be straight down the line with you, John. It was a nice little earner for a select few personnel, the odd container here and there – sugar, flour, cooking oil – non-perishable items. It is difficult enough to make a living in this world and nobody missed what was found.'

'I think I'm beginning to understand now, sir.'

'One learns to live with these things, John. It is regrettable but there's no point rocking the boat, especially if it's going to make the situation worse.'

'Sir.'

'And then New York is broadcasting the fact that there are all these uncatalogued containers littered around the Zone and in the various military bases. The timing couldn't have been worse; the Russians have only just settled in and are already providing cause for alarm. On top of that we're about to go to war. I shouldn't need to tell you, war makes people greedy.'

'You think that Odd may have found something valuable?' I asked, in my most innocent voice.

Hanbury stroked his moustache with his thumb and forefinger. 'I want you to retrace Odd's steps. Start where he did. I need to know what he found.'

'That doesn't seem very sensible.'

'Why?' he demanded.

'I thought I was under suspicion.'

'Don't be ridiculous,' Hanbury said. 'I don't pretend to understand the motivation of my fellow human beings, John. I just want to be sure that Odd didn't find something sensitive.'

'Sensitive?'

'Something that might fall into the wrong hands,' he explained. 'You're in a unique position: people are going to think that you know more than you actually do. They may confide in you.'

'And if they do?'

Hanbury studied me carefully before replying. 'You'll make money here,' he said. 'If you're not greedy you'll find that there's plenty for everyone. The Kuwaitis are accommodating hosts. They'll turn a blind eye to most things.'

I had to stop myself from laughing. 'Sir.'

Hanbury grimaced. 'You know you won't get anything out of Kuwait without my signature.'

'I'll bear that in mind.'

'I suggest you do. I suggest that you consider the implications very carefully.'

I kept quiet for a moment and then said, 'Is there anything else?'

'Yes, as a matter of fact there is,' Hanbury replied. 'One Mary Moriarty, the proprietor of the Port of Leith bar in Edinburgh, called the Ministry claiming to have your glass eye in her possession. Apparently a taxi driver handed it in. They gave her the address of the Outward Bound room at the Foreign Office, so I expect that it will drop on your doormat imminently. Apparently the taxi driver expects you to reimburse him for soiling the inside of his taxi. I'd send a cheque if I were you.'

'Yes, sir.'

'And, John.'

'It's Jonah.'

'Try and stay away from the Sheep Market.'

'I'm afraid I don't know what you're talking about.'

'Good,' said Hanbury sceptically. 'Keep it that way.'

'Message received.'

'Sir,' Hanbury added.

'Message received, *sir*.'

'Good man.' He made as if to turn away but changed his mind abruptly and stared at me as if a thought had just struck him. 'You're not a policeman, are you? No. Customs? Jesus, you're not MI6, are you?'

'No, sir.'

'They let your sort in now, don't they?'

'Actually, sir, my mother's a peer.'

'Not inherited, surely?'

'No,' I conceded. My mother is a formidable woman: a former chair of the Human Genetics Commission, sometime barrister, now elevated to the Lords, where she is one of only twelve black peers.

'Rather proves my point,' he said triumphantly and then, 'My driver will run you back up to Umm Qasr and, for God's sake, when you get there find yourself a British uniform.'

Back in the car, it soon became clear that that Hanbury's driver wasn't going to take me back to the Zone. Instead he dropped me by the side of the road opposite the Mutla police post.

'Someone will come for you,' he told me, but I wasn't sure whether to believe him or not.

I asked, 'Do you have any water?'

'No,' he said. The Land Cruiser drove off.

I looked around. Of course I wanted a cigarette. I walked back through the wreckage and climbed the nearest dune. The coarse-grained sand was slate-grey. Beyond it older dunes – a deeper oxidized yellow – stretched away to the horizon.

'Come and talk to me,' I yelled after a while. 'Somebody! Anybody!'

I watched a lizard – *tubayhi* the Bedouin call them – scurry across the sand, its tail coiled like a watch spring. Above me a hawk traced figure of eights in the sky. It seemed that every place in the world, no matter how harsh, had made a home for some creature.

For the second time Spicy rescued me. I was beginning to feel like the package in a game of pass-the-parcel at a children's birthday party; stripped of skin, fought over and surrounded by an air of heightened, and mostly un-deserved, expectation.

'Fancy meeting you again,' said Spicy.

On the way down the hill Spicy produced a rolled baby-blue beret from his pocket and handed it to me.

'Welcome to Smurf-land. You are here as a United Nations observer. You last more than thirty days, or thirty days pass without the war kicking off, and they'll give you a medal out of a cornflake packet, hold a parade and chopper in the general to pin it on your chest.'

'I can't wait,' I said and put on the beret.

'If you belonged to any other nation they'd have given you a medal already, just because some titless letterbox knifed you at a set of traffic lights.' He winced, theatrically. 'How's your arm?'

'It's OK.'

Spicy was clearly relieved; he ran his hand through his hair and grinned. 'How was your meeting with Hanbury?'

'He asked me if I was MI6.'

'There's not much to do here,' Spicy explained. 'Idle minds generate spectacular rumours.'

'I didn't come here to draw attention to myself.'

'Too late,' Spicy replied. 'You were the last person to speak to Odd and Hanbury clearly believes that he stumbled on something valuable.'

'Odd was jumpy, that's all I know,' I said. 'I got off a plane and he was there and not very pleased to see me. I was an inconvenience.'

Spicy grinned. 'Come on, Jonah. No one's going to believe that. People think you know something that they want to know.'

'Hanbury told me I wouldn't get anything out of Kuwait without his signature.'

'He has a nose for these things.'

In the vehicle Spicy produced a can of 7UP from the cold box and pressed it into my hands.

'Drink that, matey. You look dehydrated.'

A few minutes later we slowed as we passed a UN Land Cruiser parked on the far side of the road with a Kuwaiti police cruiser parked behind it, its bank of lights flashing. The driver was squatting disconsolately by the side of the road, his head in his hands. A couple of Kuwaiti policemen were standing at the back of the Land Cruiser. They were methodically throwing vodka bottles onto the asphalt, each impact a sudden spray of reflected blue light.

Spicy lit a cigarette. 'God, how I loathe this place.'

'What do you know about the Sheep Market?' I asked.

Spicy gave me a sideways look. 'How long have you been here?'

'Not long.'

'You pack a lot in, don't you . . . ?'

'Mostly, I get taken places by you,' I retorted.

'There's that,' Spicy conceded.

'So? What do you know about the Sheep Market?'

'In good time,' Spicy said, returning his attention to the road ahead.

I stared out at the passing desert. 'Where are we going?'

Spicy glanced at me. 'Home.'

'Home?'

'Your home for the foreseeable future: Patrol Base Three, Southern Sector; one of the most benighted spots on earth.'

'Great,' I said.

'We're all just waiting for a war,' said Spicy. Then he stifled a laugh. 'Except you, Jonah; you look as if you've already started.'

I drank my 7UP.

The Gujaratis

At first I thought it was a pillar of dust, a twister sweeping towards us, then a vial of coloured glass – blue and a myriad of other colours – shimmering in the jellied heat. It was the strangest convoy, three massive eight-wheeled trucks roaring across the desert, their engines spitting and popping, their chassis and bodywork a patchwork of steel plates streaked by the nozzles of acetylene gas axes. The sides and welded doors plastered with looted armour plates.

Spicy grinned from ear to ear. 'The Gujaratis!'

He braked and pulled over to let them pass.

The first two vehicles were South African, the third Slovak: the first a second-hand recovery vehicle built on a Skimmel chassis with an armoured cab; the second a Casspir troop carrier with an armoured v-shaped hull to deflect and channel the blast of anti-tank mines; the third a Tatra crane, with a traversing jib and a raised front-mounted dozer blade.

'Who are they?' I asked.

'The lost of the earth,' said Spicy, 'freelance salvage merchants waiting to go in behind the invading Americans.'

I watched as the Skimmel rolled to a halt beside us and the air brakes let out a long, drawn-out hiss.

'They're from somewhere in Gujarat.'

'Alang,' I guessed.

'Yes, that's it,' said Spicy. 'How did you know that?'

'I've been there.'

'You do get around.'

The escape hatch on the roof of the cab clanked open and two skinny brown arms appeared, followed by a man's matted head and his bare shoulders tattooed with dark blue starbursts.

'*Namaste,*' Spicy cried out of the open window. 'Aziz, how the devil are you?'

'Not bad, Spicy mate,' the man replied in a Brummy accent. 'How ya doin'?'

'Tip-top,' said Spicy. 'Pukka.'

Aziz shook his head. 'You crack me up, you do.'

The man levered himself out of the hatch and dropped to the sand below. A crowd of grinning Gujaratis followed, clambering out of the doors and hatches. Within seconds they had surrounded the Land Cruiser. To look at them you'd think they'd been out in the desert for months. They were caked in sand and their hair hung in ropes down their backs. Only their teeth shone from their blackened, un-washed faces. They wore copper wire in their beards and coins, electronic circuitry and the small bolts and springs from the firing mechanisms of weapons as jewellery.

The man with the tattooed shoulders rested his forearms in the car window frame.

Spicy introduced us. 'Jonah, this is Aziz.'

Aziz reached across Spicy and we shook hands.

'Your men want some water?' Spicy said.

'That's very good of you, Spicy,' replied Aziz, stepping back from the car. 'Out you come, then.'

Spicy went around to the boot and started distributing bottled water. The Gujaratis snatched off the bottle tops and drank greedily, the water leaving dark streaks down their chins and running down their chests.

I got out of the car. Aziz nodded to me and scratched at his matted beard.

'You're from Alang?' I asked.

'Me? Walsall, mate. You don't come from Alang, you end up there. You know it?'

'Yes,' I said.

'How come?'

'I heard about it, in a bhang shop in Diu. It was years ago.'

'You went as a tourist?'

'You know how it is; I was looking for a beach.'

The beach at Alang in Gujarat: the largest ship-breaking site in the world. Driving there, you saw the smallest items first, brass fitments, life jackets, doors, wooden panelling and porcelain, in stacks or hanging from awnings on the roadside. The chandlers' shops were crammed together one after the other on the roads that led like spokes towards the beach. There were plates of reinforced glass, portholes, lifeboats and a thousand miles of pipe work in stacks, steel plate, pistons and boilers. Finally you reached the sea and the beached hulks of supertankers and container ships covered with a multitude of people as small as ants. Everywhere there was the crackle of gas axes and the clang of hammers and chisels on steel and the thud and crash of falling bulkheads.

Aziz shook his head. 'It's not a beach for building sandcastles.'

'You're right there,' I said.

He held up his hand to shield his eyes from the sun and squinted at me. 'You're the new guy, aren't you? The one that was knifed in the riot up in Umm Qasr?'

'That's right,' I said.

'I thought there couldn't be too many one-eyed observers.'

'I only get half the pay.'

'That's funny,' he said drily. He gazed at me for a while in silence. Then he said, 'There's a lot of traffic about containers on the scanners. People know the dead man was opening sea cans. People think he found something to sell, otherwise why else go up to the Desert Palm? No one goes in there except lowlife, middlemen and Russians.'

'I only saw Russians.'

'The Mook are doing a spaz up in Umm Qasr, running around asking questions. I expect that's why you've been sent down here out of harm's way.'

I shrugged. 'I just go where I'm told.'

'If you know something, my advice to you is to spit it out. There's too much at stake.'

'I'll bear that in mind,' I said.

'I'm serious,' he said. 'War's coming. The Americans are in their tanks revving the engines. It's no more than a few days away. I'd say ten days tops. So nobody here is interested in polite negotiation, Jonah. There isn't enough time. The wrong people get hold of you and you'll wish you'd never been born.'

Spicy joined us, running his hands through his dripping hair. 'So what's up, Aziz?'

'Waiting, mate,' Aziz replied before walking down the side of the Skimmel towards the Casspir. He ducked under the overhang of the capstan winch. 'Waiting for the war. India has a huge appetite for scrap metal and we mean to feed it.'

We followed. Spicy asked, 'Have you got a contract?'

'Government work? Don't make me laugh,' Aziz said.

'The Yanks have sewn the whole thing up. Bechtel and
Fluor have people in Kuwait on the starting blocks.
Halliburton already has the oil fires. There's no look-in
for anyone else. Our window of opportunity is going to be
very narrow indeed. A few days rushing in on the back of
the invasion.' He climbed on the tow hitch and stared in the
back of the Casspir. We joined him, our feet on the
tailgates. The bed of the truck was filled with huge spools
of copper. 'There are still a few pylon lines for stripping on
the Iraqi side, though I don't know why we bother. There's
people made a lot of money from copper in the early
nineties but it's getting so you've got to drive further and
further to find it. There's not the same margin.'

'So where are the margins?' Spicy asked.

Aziz jumped down from the tow hitch and we jumped
down after him. 'Right now? It's all speculative.'

'Sure,' Spicy prompted him, 'speculate.'

'At a guess and given the traffic on the scanners, I'd say
lifting and transporting sea cans.' He leant back against the
armoured body of the Casspir and looked straight at me. 'If
you've got a crane.'

'That figures,' Spicy said.

'I understand that there are a lot of containers?' I said.

Aziz nodded. 'Yeah, you could say that. You'd need to
know what you are looking for – but if you've got the
location and the plate number, it'd be easy. You could have
a deal worked out in no time.'

Spicy and Aziz glanced at each other and then back at
me.

Aziz gave me a lazy smile. 'If you've got the plate
number . . . ?'

'Not me,' I said.

Spicy lit a cigarette.

'Where are you taking him?' Aziz asked.

'Down to Patrol Base Three. The Bangladeshis are pulling their observers out and Jonah's been sent to replace one.'

'Gotta get on,' said Aziz suddenly. 'Thanks for the water.'

'Don't mention it.'

Aziz gazed at me. 'Take my advice, Jonah.'

We watched in silence as they clambered back into the vehicles and roared away.

When the dust had cleared Spicy asked, 'What advice was that?'

'To reveal my secrets.'

Not something I was planning to do in a hurry.

King of a sad castle

Patrol Base Three was a sad castle, makeshift and neglected. Its buckled watchtower was, to use one of my
daughter's expressions, extremely 'rickety-clackety'. It
looked like something out of Dr Seuss. A hundred feet
high and coated in a thick layer of rust, it featured a
distinctive dogleg earned in one of the tank battles that
ended the first Gulf war. I quickly discovered that I was the
only one prepared to climb to the top of its precarious
ladders. Immediately, I liked it up there, away from the
chaos and trouble of other people. It promised to hinder
my relentless pacing and perhaps lend a kind of clarity to
the events of the previous days.

From the battered steel crow's-nest the desert stretched
in every direction, dirty brown like an old chamois leather
and scored with tracks, mostly Bedouin trails that never
seemed to lead anywhere. Away to the west you could see
the ancient gash in the desert caused by long-forgotten
water that was the Wadi al-Batin and away to the east on
the edge of the Zone sleek black Apache helicopter gun-
ships prowled like hunting wasps.

Below me and arranged in a horseshoe was the patrol
base: seven Portakabins raised on breeze blocks, with flat
aluminium roofs and windows; a shed containing food and
drinking water; another shed for the generator, a container
for storage and a water bowser for washing. There was a

three-metre-high chain-link fence surrounding the base to keep out the Bedouin who would otherwise have stripped it bare long ago. There was just one entrance. The paint on the Portakabins had blistered in the heat and you could brush it off with your palms. There was air conditioning but it was mostly defective. There were two battered white Land Cruisers parked outside the sandbagged Portakabin that served as an operations room and a third with its front end stoved in and its chassis bent, resting against one of the watchtower's legs.

There was nothing to suggest why the base was situated where it was, other than the ancient and unused watch-tower. About five hundred metres beyond the fence was the shadowy entrance to an underground bunker, a for-ward observation post once used by the Iraqis.

I shared the patrol base with seven others, fellow passen-gers temporarily stranded on what was effectively a desert island.

The first I met was an Armenian major named Hadzhik Matirossian. He was big, with dark eyebrows and a thatch of black hair flecked with silver. There was something sad and perhaps kind about his face, but his eyes were guarded as if protecting something inside himself.

I was standing on uneven linoleum inside the Portakabin that served as kitchen and recreational room. Hadzhik was defrosting two cans of beer in a saucepan of boiling water on a primus stove. He'd put them in the freezer to cool quickly the night before and then forgotten about them.

He grimaced. 'No vodka.'

'On the contrary,' Spicy told him, hefting a cardboard box full of Absolut bottles through the doorway and setting it on the table. 'We have a surfeit of the stuff.'

He started unpacking the box. Hadzhik nodded solemnly and as Spicy introduced us he said, 'I am very pleased to meet you.'

Beyond him a small figure in bright green was bobbing up and down on a sofa, attempting to meet my eye. When I looked in his direction he sprang to his feet and shook my hand vigorously. 'Ishfaq. From Bangladesh. We are all looking forward to meeting you, John,' he said.

'Jonah.'

'Of course. We hear you are a Scotsman.' He continued to pump my hand. I decided that my provenance was too complicated to attempt to correct him. 'It is never difficult to distinguish between a Scotsman with a grievance and a ray of sunshine. P.G. Wodehouse. Ha! Very good. Of course, I'm a colonel.'

'Good for you,' I said.

'You are my replacement. I am leaving. My country needs me.' He indicated the two suitcases by the sofa. 'Lieutenant Rhodes-Spicer is taking me to the airport, isn't that right?'

On the far side of the room on another sofa an elongated figure in the blocky, geometric camouflage of Sweden lay sprawled with his eyes closed and earphones in his ears.

'Per,' said Hadzhik, his hand gripping the Swede's shin.

Per opened his eyes, yawned and removed the earphones, releasing a pulse of dance mix. He swung his legs off the sofa and sat ruffling the blond shambles of his hair with his hands. When he looked up, I reached forward and shook his hand.

'The last of the observers,' he said, contemplating me. He half-heartedly waved a hand at Spicy and then swung himself back onto the sofa. He reinserted the earphones and closed his eyes.

Hadzhik raised his eyebrows and passed me a beer. He said, 'We have always been an unlikely combination. Come, we shall take the tour.'

We walked over to the operations room, across the courtyard formed by the horseshoe of raised Portakabins, past plastic tables sheltering under tatty camouflage netting that was strung with Christmas lights and a cabinet with a television hooked up to a satellite dish. There were a number of bottles, mostly beer and vodka, strewn across the compacted sand. Ishfaq struggled after us with his suitcases.

'For a long time we didn't get many visitors,' Hadzhik explained. He noticed me looking at the wreck of the Land Cruiser resting against the watchtower and said, 'Your predecessor was not a good driver.'

'The brakes failed,' protested Ishfaq, hurrying to catch up with us.

'The brakes were undamaged,' Hadzhik told him.

'Go and get in the car, Ishfaq,' Spicy said drily, 'or I'll leave you here for the Americans.'

'That is no way to speak to me, Lieutenant Rhodes-Spicer,' said Ishfaq.

'I'm not joking,' said Spicy.

'The operations room,' said Hadzhik, pausing at the entrance to a Portakabin, with more than a hint of irony in his voice. 'Apparently we have a new operations officer.'

Just inside the door there was a large black man wearing a dirty khaki T-shirt sprawled on a plastic chair. He had his hands resting on the shelf of his barrel-like paunch and his feet squeezed into a pair of bright yellow flip-flops decorated with artificial daisies. He was snoring loudly.

There was an army kit bag propped against the wall beside him.

'Who's the snoring fellow?' called out a second man from a swivel chair as he accelerated towards us down a narrow space between banks of dusty monitors on one side and a Perspex-covered map on the other. 'He's been asleep since I arrived.'

He rolled to a stop. 'I'm Sal. Major Sal Kapoor. Pakistani army. I've just been transferred down from the Intelligence cell in Umm Qasr.'

He was wearing camouflage pants and a black polo neck and black-rimmed glasses that made him look self-consciously urbane. The map behind him was marked with coloured pens detailing sectors, units, boundaries and borders.

'The snoring guy is Colonel Charles, the base commander,' Hadzhik informed him.

'That figures. You must be the Armenian, right?'

'Hadzhik.'

'Pleased to meet you.' They shook hands. 'Hey, Spicy.'

Spicy nodded. 'Sal.'

Sal transferred his attention to me. 'You must be Jonah, right?' He shook my hand. 'So tell us, Jonah, what did Odd find in his searching? The emir's gold? Pearls? Heroin? Sarin? A dirty nuke – I'm sorry, a radiological dispersion device?'

'I don't know,' I said. 'He didn't tell me.'

'Shame. A great shame,' he said. 'You have arrived in the Zone at an exciting time, a time of celebrities.' He patted the knee of the sleeping man. 'I'm sure that even the colonel here will be very excited when he wakes.'

'You know how to work this stuff?' Hadzhik asked, waving at the stacks of hardware, the array of computer screens and snaking cables behind him.

Sal feigned an expression of outrage. 'Stuff?'

Hadzhik shrugged.

'No one's touched any of the surveillance equipment for years,' Sal explained, 'but the microwave link is still up and the browser history is illustrative: Teen sluts, Asian sluts, all kinds of sluts. It seems that you guys have been taking the opportunity to improve yourselves.'

Spicy said, 'Sal's got a brain the size of the Mekon's. Even his shit has brains.'

'And you have shit for brains,' Sal retorted.

'He finds things,' Spicy explained, unperturbed, 'plucks them out of the air.'

'What sort of things?' I asked.

'Things about people,' said Spicy, 'you, for instance. Come on, Sal, don't tell me you haven't been bitraking.'

'I've been following some lines of enquiry,' Sal conceded.

'Well what have you got?' Spicy asked.

'The biographical basics and a few other choice morsels.'

'Spit it out, man,' Spicy demanded. 'I'm intrigued.'

'May I?' he asked me.

I shrugged, unaware of what I was letting myself in for. 'Fire away,' I told him.

'All right. Jonah Angus Said, born April 1, 1970, in Sacramento Mercy hospital, California. You hold dual citizenship. Your British Army ID number is 527189 and you hold the military rank of major. Your mobile phone number is 07939 999359. You smoked Marlboro cigarettes from 1986 to some time in June 1999. At some point you switched from Reds to Lights. You have one daughter and she has blue eyes and dark hair. You've been questioned but never formally charged by the military police in two separate investigations since 1991. You're right-handed. You have one eye, you lost the other in an anti-tank mine incident in Gornji Vakuf in April 1994. The mine was a TMRP6 – you turned right on the top of Raitci hill and you should have turned left. Your blood type is O negative. You're heterosexual. You visited a brothel in Cologne in 1992 and paid for it on Amex. Your wife left you on Valentine's Day in 1999 and, choicest of all, a couple of months later your friend Alex Ross employed two former members of 14 Intelligence, the British Army's covert surveillance unit, to arrange the kidnap of your wife's lover. One of them, a military policewoman, is currently under investigation on unrelated charges but has been offered a deal by the Crown Prosecution Service in return for information. You'd better pray she doesn't take the deal.'

I stared at him, struck dumb.

'Good, huh?' Spicy leered.

'There's more,' said Sal. He rolled away to a computer terminal past a blocky HF transceiver and data modem and beside it a black moulded plastic VHF transceiver. 'Lots more. You're a fat data file, Jonah. You lost your glass eye three days ago in the back of an Edinburgh black cab, No 4389. You were baptized a Catholic. You speak Arabic. Your mother's a baroness. You arrived in Kuwait with only hand luggage. You used to be a regular visitor to a webcam site called Jenny Cam.' He paused and smiled. 'She was a pioneer.'

'Enough already,' I said.

'It's all out there.' Sal waved his arm diffidently. 'It's all just floating about amongst the conspiracy theories and chitchat, raw data; you have to know how to snatch it and map it. Make connections.'

Hadzhik smiled and rested his hand on my shoulder. 'Come on, let's go and wave off the Bangladeshi.'

We walked out to Spicy's Land Cruiser. Ishfaq was in the passenger seat, with his seat belt on. 'Come on,' he called out impatiently. 'I have to go home.'

'Everyone is desperate to get out of here,' said Spicy.

'I'm happy here,' said Hadzhik.

'I'll stop by in a couple of days,' Spicy told me, 'to check you haven't gone doolally.'

'Thanks,' I said. 'And thanks for getting me out of the Russian base.'

'Don't mention it,' said Spicy, winking. 'The pleasure was mine.'

Before he left, Spicy rolled down the window and said, 'Jonah.'

'Yes?'

'Try and stay away from the Iraqis.'

We stood and watched the dust trail as the Land Cruiser headed towards the horizon. Eventually I looked across at Hadzhik. 'So?'

Hadzhik raised a speculative eyebrow.

'I've been told to stay away from the Sheep Market and the Iraqis,' I told him.

Hadzhik stuck out his lower lip. 'Which one do you want to do first?'

'I'm easy.'

'You want to see the Iraqis?'

'Yep,' I nodded. 'I want to see the whites of their eyes.'

'Let's get some water,' he said. 'It guarantees a warm reception.'

We filled the back seat of the Land Cruiser with six-packs of purified water and drove out into the desert, following the incoming tyre tracks. After a few minutes we joined Crown Route, the main north–south feeder route.

Crown was a two-lane highway of compacted gravel that ran between barely discernible sand dykes. It was marked at irregular intervals by steel pickets with military signs; plywood squares with the silhouette of a crown spray-painted on them.

The air-con was broke so we drove with the windows rolled down. I could feel the grains of sand in the air scouring my forearm on the sill. Everywhere were the signs of relentless sandblasting. The windscreen was almost opaque.

'Not like home, yes?' Hadzhik said, lighting a Marlboro with the flick of a gold-plated Zippo. There was something unnerving about his grin.

'Not like home,' I agreed.

'Cigarette?'

'No thanks.'

'Not since June '99?'

'That's right.'

We turned off Crown Route and headed west through a minefield on one of the little-used east–west roads. The cleared lane through the minefield was marked by rows of iron stakes driven into the ground.

'I'd have killed him,' Hadzhik said. It was obvious that he meant my wife's lover.

'I was the lucky one,' I told him. 'I don't have to live with her.'

'That's true,' he conceded, 'sometimes the worst is for the best. When a man steals your wife, there is no better revenge than to let him keep her.'

'Amara al-Hijara'

The first thing we saw was the radio mast and then the red and black of the Iraqi tricolour and beneath it a cluster of drab-looking tents and tarpaulins weighed down with stones that was the Iraqi police post. We stopped about fifty metres short of the encampment. Nothing stirred. The land baked. Our presence felt wrong somehow, like an intrusion.

A sharp-nosed and skeletal dog emerged from behind some rolls of wire and watched us approach.

'*Salaam aleikum*,' Hadzhik called out.

There was a short delay and then a reply came from someone crouching behind a barricade of corrugated iron sheets. '*Salaam.*'

'Get the water, Jonah,' Hadzhik instructed. 'Move very slowly.'

And then as one they rose from behind the barricade and stood posed like villains in a spaghetti western. There were seven of them, their faces the outline of bone. No better than the malnourished and humiliated POWs I remember from the first Gulf war. They seemed as stripped of expectation as the dogs that hung around the margins of the camp.

Their leader was a Kurd named Sadeq. He was lean and unshaven, with a couple of days of greyish stubble surrounding his moustache. He welcomed us in with a proud and solemn demeanour. Hadzhik had explained to me that there would be a Ba'ath party member amongst their number and that any overt sign of friendliness might be dangerous. We handed the six-packs of water across to them and at their invitation climbed over the barricade.

It was cool in the tent and after the glare outside it was dark and restful. Clothes and plastic bags hung on nails on the pillars holding up the canvas. The Iraqis laid their Kalashnikovs to one side and we sat in a circle.

We nodded and smiled but said little at first. They offered dates from a bowl and one of them came with a tray of bitter coffee in plastic mugs.

The coffee loosened tongues. I discovered that Hadzhik spoke fluent Arabic. He shared out a packet of Marlboros and soon we were engulfed in companionable smoke. Sadeq was the only one to have been in the fighting during the first gulf war. He was from a village in the Bekme Gorge in Kurdistan near the Iranian border. He told us that he missed the trees, the junipers and wild pear. He joked that his home was no more than a few hundred kilometres from Hadzhik's and one day he would come and visit. It didn't sound very likely.

As they relaxed they revealed more about themselves. Most of them had been in the Zone for two years without leave. As far as I could see they lived like vagrants, without aim or purpose. I didn't say much, content to allow Hadzhik to steer the conversation.

Then one of the younger ones, named Abu Yaseen, asked how I had lost my eye and I explained that I had driven over an anti-tank mine in April 1994 while driving in the no man's land between Catholic Croats and Bosnian Muslims on the outskirts of Gornji Vakuf.

Glances were exchanged and Abu Yaseen asked me which side I had been fighting on. I smiled at his misunderstanding and explained that I had been trying to hold the peace, though the words sounded suddenly hollow in my ears and the smile misplaced.

'We were carrying out a United Nations mandate,' I explained weakly.

'We know about the UN,' said Abu Yaseen. His face was narrow and his chin came to a sharp point. His eyes were small and dark and they made him seem tense and aggressive. He asked me what I thought of the massacre in Srebrenica and I said that it was a terrible stain on the conscience of western Europe.

'It is the way,' said Abu Yaseen. 'Always Muslims suffer.'

I didn't tell them that Naser Oric, the commander of the Muslim guerrillas in Srebrenica, was responsible for massacres of Serbs in Kravica and Skelani in 1993. Or that the Muslim Bosnian government was deliberately disrupting relief convoys to the starving enclave to increase the pressure on the UN and increase the demands for the Americans to intervene with air strikes. I didn't tell them that Clinton's administration had cynically buried the Vance–Owen peace plan; made threats of air strikes that no one, least of all the Serbs, believed they were prepared to enforce. I didn't say that the six hundred lightly armed Dutch peacekeepers were as much hostages as the Muslims with no water or fuel and that as the final Serb assault came down they repeatedly requested and were denied close air support. I didn't say that three days before the town's fall Muslim soldiers shot a Dutch soldier. I didn't tell them because it doesn't matter, because what happened is documented: men, women and children mutilated and slaughtered, thousands of men executed and buried in mass graves and hundreds buried alive. Scenes from hell.

'They were pawns,' I said. 'Everybody used them and then abandoned them.'

Together the Iraqis seemed to reach some form of agreement. Sadeq asked, 'When will the Americans attack?'

'I don't know,' I said. 'Maybe soon. The Americans are angry.'

'George Bush's son will come,' Sadeq said.

'Five years ago my wife died in Basra hospital, giving birth to my son,' said Abu Yaseen coldly. 'My son died forty minutes later. There were no drugs.'

The atmosphere in the tent had changed and I felt Hadzhik shift uncomfortably. Abu Yaseen stared at me.

'I'm sorry,' I told him.

'Hundreds of thousands of women and children have died because of the sanctions. Answer this question: how many of us dead is worth one American? Ten? One hundred? A thousand? I will tell you honestly; when 9/11 happened we were very happy.'

'I don't think that what happened on 9/11 is the answer.'

'You make a big bang and the world sits up and listens,' said Abu Yaseen. 'The west is sending to us its corrosive culture. We are sending something back that corrodes their society. Their society is as wicked as their culture.'

Sadeq asked gently, 'Do you believe that it was the work of *shahid*, martyrs?'

I nodded. 'There doesn't seem much doubt.'

One of them, whose name I did not know, added, 'The Raees, Saddam, says that it was the Jews, so that the Jews could destroy the Aksa mosque while the attention of the world was on America; to bring the Americans to war against Muslims everywhere.'

'You can't keep those kinds of secrets,' I told them. 'I don't believe in those kinds of conspiracies.'

'Bin Laden is a pious man,' said Abu Yaseen. 'He could have been a rich man but he gave it up to fight for the land of Allah, to free the holy places. People in America don't understand how angry we are.'

'Our guest brought us water,' Sadeq said gently.

'We will fight,' said Abu Yaseen coldly. 'And we will die.'

'We will be martyrs,' said the unnamed one.

'We must go,' said Hadzhik, rising to his feet.

'Tell your people,' said Abu Yaseen. 'Tell your pilots who fly over us every day.'

Sadeq walked with us out to the Land Cruiser. 'I am sorry if my companion offended you,' he told me.

'No need to apologize,' I told him. 'I understand.'

He began to speak, stopped and then said, 'Let me ask you a question.'

'Please.'

'Were you here before, in the war?'

'Yes,' I told him. I probably shouldn't have, my security was compromised enough as it was. A pained expression crossed Hadzhik's face.

'There are many ghosts here,' Sadeq said, staring into the desert without showing any sign of having heard me. 'Wherever you have people dying unhappy, you have ghosts.'

Entropic drift

As the afternoon's shadows lengthened we drove north along
the edge of the Wadi al-Batin until we caught sight of the
crooked watchtower away to our right and cut across the
desert, following the ruts of tyre tracks towards the patrol base.

A woman met us at the gate. She was clearly anticipating
a different vehicle and did little to conceal her irritation. 'I
thought you were Patrice,' she said in heavily accented
English.

She was Russian and introduced herself as Ilyena. She
was pretty in a doll-like way with bleached blonde hair and
legs in tight black Lycra leggings. On the top half of her
body she wore a thin brightly coloured halterneck blouse.
Her heels sank in the sand as she walked unsteadily back to
the table under the camouflage netting. It was approaching
4 p.m. and she was obviously drunk.

She was not alone. Her friend Larissa was stockier, in a
pillar-box-red dress with a plunging neckline. Her glossy
black hair was divided into a series of waves dropping to
her shoulders.

Hadzhik spoke to them harshly in Russian and recovered a half-empty bottle of Absolut from the table. Ilyena
pulled a petulant expression, turned her back on him and
pointed the remote control at the television. A moment
later, Michael Jackson was on the screen being interviewed
by a British journalist.

'It doesn't matter where you go,' Hadzhik told me, 'America follows.'

Michael Jackson was attempting to feed a baby on his knee. The baby was veiled in green muslin and the bottle shook spasmodically in Jackson's hand as he spoke.

'God, he's a monster!' said Larissa. 'He's so black.'

When Hadzhik went inside for glasses, Ilyena whispered confidentially that Hadzhik was angry because she had refused to sleep with him the night before. 'He's cheap and mean-spirited. He's always short of cash.'

They began to giggle helplessly, collapsing sideways on the sofa.

Hadzhik emerged with the glasses and went over to sit at one of the plastic tables in the open. I joined him and for an hour or so we played backgammon while the two women flicked between satellite channels.

'What are they doing here?' I asked.

'They're beauticians,' Hadzhik said, crushing a cigarette butt into the surface of the table, 'camp followers who prey on the patrol bases. You want a manicure?'

I couldn't tell whether he was being serious. He rolled the dice with a flourish, a snap of the wrist. I was soon glad we were not playing for money. I watched him slap my stones on the bar with a tedious regularity.

'What's the story with Sadeq?' I asked him.

Hadzhik sat back, poured two shots of vodka and pointed an accusatory finger. 'Your friends, the Americans, buried his unit.'

We downed the shots and slapped the upturned glasses on the table.

'Buried?' I said.

'He was in a front-line unit but not a reliable unit,' Hadzhik explained, pouring another two shots. 'Too many

Kurds and Shias. Before the war he was a shop clerk or something.' He gave a shrug as if to say *What do you expect?* 'I mean, of course these were not soldiers. You saw what they are like. They were not trusted with anti-tank weapons. They were given old bolt-action rifles to fight tanks. In front of his trench was a larger, deeper trench built to stop tanks. They put their trust in it but the Americans came with bulldozers. That's what I mean; I mean they buried his unit. You may imagine: a great wall of sand approaching. He told me that he thought the world was ending: he was a kid from the mountains, not used to the desert. He told me he threw away his gun and ran down the trench. He was lucky to escape; most of his friends were buried alive.'

'I'm sorry.'

'Are you responsible?'

'No.'

'Why apologize? It's war.'

He was right. It was a stupid thing to say.

Hadzhik stubbed out his cigarette and gave me a sad and knowing smile. 'I think maybe there are worse ways to die.'

Around four, another Land Cruiser appeared, trailing dust. There were two occupants, both military observers. The tallest was Patrice, a curly-haired French-Vietnamese man in his mid-forties with a pockmarked face. He wore his camouflage blouse open to the waist. He shook my hand curtly and went over to the rec room, emerging soon after with a tumbler in one hand and a bottle of Red Label in the other. He inverted the bottle as he walked until whisky sloshed over the rim of his glass. He took a swig and greeted Ilyena warmly, putting his arm around her waist and giving her a lip-crushing kiss. The bottle in his hand rested in the divide of her buttocks.

The second man, an American Marine named Toona, was shorter and broader. He was black-skinned with a shaven head and the thigh-rubbing gait of a weightlifter. He went straight over to the ops room.

Patrice set his glass down on our table and combed his fingers through his hair. 'Jonah here has just spent a night in the custody of your friends the Russian peacekeepers,' he told Ilyena. 'Apparently he witnessed a murder.'

I saw a sudden rush of interest in her kohl-rimmed eyes.

'I was there but I didn't see it happen,' I replied.

'Since then you have been mixed up in a riot and been wounded in the arm,' Patrice continued. 'You have caused a commotion here.'

'It wasn't intentional.'

'It is what we expect. You British don't understand anything here. You're rushing towards a war without any thought for the consequences.'

Toona came out of the ops room and walked straight over to our table. 'The Indian guy says that you took water to the Iraqis?'

'That's right,' I told him.

'It's forbidden,' he said. 'You have contravened UN sanctions.'

I looked across at Hadzhik but he was staring intently at the board.

Patrice laughed. 'One minute you dismiss the UN, the next you are its champion.'

'Shut up, surrender monkey,' snarled Toona.

'Why aren't you with your unit in their hour of need, Toona?' teased Patrice.

'You shut up about that too,' said Toona and then

pointed at Larissa. 'What the fuck is that bitch still doing here?'

Patrice laughed. 'I think she is waiting for you to pay her.'

Ilyena rolled her eyes for my benefit, hit him on the chest and said, 'Stop it.'

'It's true,' said Patrice, plucking the bottle of Red Label from Ilyena's grasp just as she reached forward to take it.

'You're a pig!' she said.

'And you are a drunk,' Patrice told her.

'Pig! Pig! Pig!'

The back of Patrice's hand caught her a glancing blow on the side of her head. I felt my hackles rise.

'Give me some of that whisky,' said Toona.

'I was saying that Jonah here was in Umm Qasr with the Norwegian logistics guy who had his throat cut,' Patrice told Toona, refilling his glass. 'He is telling us he didn't see a thing.'

'I'd say the Iraqis cut his throat to keep his mouth shut,' Toona said.

'They say he found the emir's lost gold,' announced Ilyena, nursing her cheekbone.

Patrice sneered. 'Who says?'

'Just people,' she said, with a sulky pout.

'Somebody had a good reason to kill him,' Toona added, swigging at his drink.

Patrice laughed dismissively. 'You think you need a reason to kill someone in the Zone?'

'The guy was snooping around the camps,' Toona insisted, 'opening up containers that have been sealed since the war. You bet he found something.' He switched his attention to me. 'He tell you what he found?'

'No,' I replied.

'There's a lot of folks won't believe that,' Toona said.

'That's why they sent him to this shit-hole,' said Patrice, 'to keep him out of harm's way.'

'No place is safe here,' said Toona. 'You think the Russians are just going to leave it once they figure out he might have something profitable to hide, let alone the Iraqis? I don't have to remind you, we're a long way from back-up. His very presence here is a compromise to our security.'

'You have an overactive imagination,' Patrice told him, before taking Ilyena by the hand. 'Come on, the time has come to cook.'

'You ignore me at your peril,' Toona said and then switched his attention to me. 'I ain't getting in a car with you and I certainly ain't going out on patrol with you, understand?'

'I understand,' I told him.

'I need a piss,' he announced, putting down his whisky and making for the open desert.

I looked across the table at Hadzhik, who shrugged. 'People need to unwind.' He poured two more shots and there seemed little choice but to drink. 'Anyway, Patrice is a good cook.'

A kind of torpor had fallen over the camp and its occupants: only the clink of pans from the recreation room suggested any activity. Larissa was watching MTV with the sound turned low and Toona was slumped in one of the chairs with a bottle of Red Label.

Hadzhik was smoking, sitting contemplating the sunset and the light flaring on the chain-link perimeter fence. As the temperature plummeted Ripley, the patrol base cat, appeared from under one of the Portakabins and began a slow and silent circuit of the camp.

I was squatting, watching something intently.

'What are you doing?' slurred Larissa, looking over from the murmuring television.

'Shhh.' I placed my finger against my lips, motioning for her to be quiet.

Now it had our full attention. The spider was as large as the span of my hand. It had emerged from its burrow under one of the Portakabins some fifteen minutes before and had been standing motionless in the dusk. I was curious, eager for resolution to the events unfolding inches from my feet.

The cricket was similarly large, the size of a mouse. It moved slowly and sluggishly, not jumping, as it should. It walked under the spider, which reared up on its hind legs to expose its fangs as the cricket passed.

'A lucky escape,' said Hadzhik and I heard the sound of him filling our shot glasses with vodka.

'No, wait,' I whispered.

Sure enough, the cricket turned back and approached the spider for a second time, swishing its antennae against the spider's legs.

The spider reacted as if it had received an electric shock, the spasm raking the cricket to its mouth. After the first bite, the fangs moved separately, stabbing down repeatedly like machetes. There was nothing dainty or complex in the method of its killing: the camel spider chews its food like a wad of tobacco, slobbering digestive juice on its prey as it goes.

'It's disgusting,' said Larissa, shuddering.

'No table manners,' I agreed.

I reached behind me for the glass on the table. Its meal complete, the spider reverted to its motionless posture.

'Kill it!' Larissa.

Lifted by the vodka, I took a couple of steps over to the spider and squatted beside it; it was aware of me now, I knew that. It could feel the disturbance in the air that I had caused as tiny shocks in the tips of its palps and its feet and even in the openings on its legs and under its knees. Its entire body was tactile, designed to interpret vibration.

I am threat.

I reached down and placed a forefinger on the spider's sand-coloured thorax, the shell-like cover on the front part of its body. I pressed it against the hard dirt. Then my thumb and middle finger were in amongst the thicket of legs, squeezing slightly and finding purchase. I lifted it and showed it to my drunken audience. It had its legs bundled against its sides, as if trying to make itself unnoticeable.

Its eight small eyes were grouped in two hairy patches. The fangs were folded. They looked like the parings of a thumbnail. The legs and belly looked soft in their coating of dusty ochre hair.

'A female,' I told them, '*Eremobates gladiolus*. Wind scorpion. It's not a true spider. It's something else, something older, an evolutionary precursor to both the spider and the scorpion.'

Larissa looked on in horror. Hadzhik remained impassive and watchful.

The camel spider is doubly misnamed, it's not a spider and it doesn't eat camels. According to folklore it attaches itself to the underside of a camel and, by means of powerful venom, liquefies and digests the unfortunate animal's intestines. In fact, if you see a gang of camel spiders camped out on the bloated carcass of a camel, they are probably there for the flies. As for the myth of the military observer who wakes to find a camel spider on his face, feasting on his ears or nose, it's just that: a myth. The truth is stranger. The camel spider lines its burrow with hair and the observer is in all likelihood receiving a free haircut.

'My father was a bug man,' I offered by way of explanation. Many of my memories of childhood are of hunting for spiders in the dark corners and bends of things, in cellars and breeze-block walls, in storm drains and under manhole covers. There's a knack to catching them: a quick poke and stir with a stick, trapping the spider in its web long enough to catch it in a jar.

Lifting it as if to my mouth, I said, 'They're good to eat.'

Larissa convulsed and I flung it to the ground, where Ripley the cat was patiently waiting. She pounced and seized the spider between her paws and then began to eat it in a leisurely and methodical manner, starting at the head and not even pausing for the thorax. Soon all that remained were eight yellow-brown legs, as long as fingers.

'It never stops,' I said.

'There's something wrong with you,' Larissa told me.

I laughed bitterly. There were so many things wrong with me I'd become frightened of drawing up a list of them, for fear of what I might learn.

'Another drink,' I suggested.

'Of course,' Hadzhik replied.

Dinner

We gathered to eat at the table under the camouflage awning. Larissa laid a tablecloth printed with images from the movie *Titanic*. Two bottles of South African red wine were swiftly uncorked. Sal appeared with a quart of orange juice. Colonel Charles, the Kenyan, emerged from the operations room, yawning and scratching. Catching sight of me, he lumbered over and shook my hand.

'Welcome, Jonah,' he said. He had a row of small, peglike teeth and very pink gums.

Ilyena filled glasses. Per the Swede was the last to arrive.

'Breakfast and dinner are the only meals observed at this base and we try to make the best of dinner,' Colonel Charles explained, with his meaty hand on my upper arm.

The gathering complete, we raised our glasses.

'To our new companions,' said Colonel Charles.

'And American imperialism,' added Patrice, sardonically.

'And French treachery,' said Toona, shaking his head. We drank.

'It's South African,' said Patrice, referring to the wine, 'but here, what can you expect?'

'Please, have a seat,' said Colonel Charles, directing me to a chair. I found myself seated between Patrice and Ilyena.

Larissa brought out the main course: lamb cutlets that Colonel Charles informed me had been bought that morning from the Bedouin and French fries that Patrice announced to the assembled diners as 'freedom fries'. With the help of a third bottle of wine, I started to feel my spirits lift.

'How do you find the Zone?' Colonel Charles asked me.

I considered the question. 'I don't think I've ever been anywhere like it,' I replied.

Colonel Charles let out a deep, rumbling belly laugh.

'This sorry-ass operation has only a few days left,' said Toona, raising his voice to be heard above the sound of Ilyena and Larissa arguing in Russian. 'Then we're going to complete the job we left unfinished in 1991.'

Patrice uncorked a fourth bottle. 'You Americans see everything in such simple terms; you give no thought to what might come after Saddam and the effect it will have on Iraq's neighbours. You get rid of Saddam, believe me you will face an apocalypse. You have no thought for the consequences of your actions.'

'Fuck you,' said Toona, shoving his plate away from him across the table. 'Hey,' he growled.

Larissa stopped talking and looked at him.

'Speak English,' he said.

'We have been hearing about the ambush in Umm Qasr,' Colonel Charles said with a smile.

At first, I wasn't sure what he was talking about, but then I realized he meant the knifing. I was aware that the others had stopped talking and were listening.

'I don't think it was an ambush,' I said for the benefit of the assembled company. 'It was more like bad luck, not deliberate.'

'Of course it was,' Larissa said, leaning forward across the table and waving her wine glass at me. 'You don't know the Arabs. They're disgusting animals.'

Colonel Charles chuckled at her vehemence.

'Larissa has strong views,' he said.

At the far end of the table, Larissa slapped Toona and yelled, 'Get off!'

'Bitch,' Toona muttered.

'I heard you were being followed by the Mukhabarat,' Colonel Charles said.

'That's true,' I conceded.

'The Arabs are like children,' Patrice said. 'They need strong leadership. They don't understand democracy or the nation state.'

'They're devious,' Ilyena added. She crossed her legs and leant towards me. The top buttons of her blouse were undone. 'How old are you?'

'Thirty-two.'

'Are you married?'

'Divorced.'

She studied me closely before removing a cigarette from its packet and offering me her lighter. 'Where is your eye?'

'I left it in a taxi.'

She laughed gaily and I lit her cigarette, aware that Patrice was watching us.

'I like a man with scars,' she said. She held up a bottle of wine to me and when I nodded she poured.

'Give me a cigarette,' Patrice demanded from my left.

Ilyena ignored him, widening her eyes at me. 'Are you here to make money or because you have done something terrible?'

She said it like a challenge.

'What do you think?'

She raised an eyebrow. 'Maybe both?'

'Give me a fuckin' cigarette,' growled Patrice.

She ignored him. 'I bet you did something very bad.'

I glanced across the table to find both Sal and Hadzhik watching me.

Sensing my discomfort, she pressed me. 'Very, very bad.'

'Whore!' Patrice yelled suddenly.

'You bastard,' she screamed at him.

I stood up. 'I'm going to bed.'

'Sit down!' demanded Patrice.

I stared down at Patrice and for a few tense moments he met my stare before faltering. Then he dropped his gaze and scowled sullenly at the table top. Ilyena grinned triumphantly and I sat down again.

After the main course Sal excused himself and returned to the ops room, and as the evening wore on I got steadily drunker. As dessert was served the generator cut out and the camp was briefly plunged into darkness. Amidst the fumbling for lighters and torches there were a series of slaps followed by Ilyena's high-pitched and gleeful squeals. Suddenly the lights came on. Ilyena was topless, with wine splashed on her breasts and her belly and soaking the tangle of her halterneck top.

'Bastard!' she screamed and threw a wine glass across the table at the colonel. As he ducked to avoid it, she spun away from under the awning. The glass shattered against a cabin door. 'You could have damaged my breasts,' she shouted at the colonel. He looked bemused.

Ilyena swayed dopily under the stars. Patrice and the colonel were staring at her equally dopily. She raised her arms above her head. 'Take all my clothes off,' she commanded. 'I want to dance.'

I looked from her across the table to the other diners. Larissa was slumped against Toona with her hand cupped inside his unbuttoned trousers. Hadzhik was staring into the bottom of an empty glass and Per was rocking back and forth with his eyes closed, lost in the music filling his ears.

'Have another drink,' Colonel Charles suggested mildly.

'I'm tired of drink,' Ilyena said.

'We're all tired of something,' Hadzhik observed.

I got up and walked away from the table.

I stood and listened to the thrumming of plastic bags snared on the wire of the chain-link fence. The Bedouin called them desert flowers, the bags that tumbled across the sand from distant cities. Hadzhik appeared beside me, holding a wine bottle.

'Strange to say, but when the war comes and it is time to leave, I will miss this place,' he said.

'Really?' I asked.

'The matter of fact is, Jonah, there's nothing to go back to. There's nothing in Armenia that hasn't broken or been stolen.' He sighed heavily. 'What about you, Jonah? What are you doing here?'

'I'm supposed to be keeping a low profile,' I told him.

'Things are not going to plan for you, I think.'

There was a sudden burst of gunfire from behind one of the cabins; red tracer flew high into the air, arcing across the desert.

When it was over, Hadzhik smiled. 'Sometimes our American thinks he's back in Compton with his home boys.'

'I thought we were unarmed,' I said.

'The desert is full of weapons, Jonah. You'll see.'

The Ethiopian tourist board

That night, in an unfamiliar bed, I dreamt of a cataclysm: the desert surging upward into an immense wall. I woke just as the face went beyond vertical and the crest pitched forward to consume me.

A shadow, silhouetted by the waning moon, was standing in my doorway. I had not heard the door open. I caught a whiff of cheap perfume.

'Who's there?' I called out.

'You were screaming,' Ilyena told me in a flat tone.

'I'm all right,' I replied dully. I felt as if I'd been hit with a bag of cement and my mouth was full of dust.

'I can't stay,' she said, teasingly.

'Go back to bed,' I told her.

She didn't show any inclination to leave. 'Why did you kill Odd?'

'I didn't.'

She paused and seemed thoughtful. 'He found something valuable, didn't he?'

'Forget about it. You'll get yourself killed. Go to bed.'

She advanced across the room and sat at the end of the bed, her hand resting on the tangled sheets next to my thigh. 'Odd couldn't keep a secret. He was an amateur.'

'And you're not?'

'But I am not just a beautician, you know.'

She was wearing a short black robe, embroidered with

Chinese dragons, that was loosely fastened. The robe seemed to hang on her nipples, exposing the curve of her breasts, her round belly and the dark cave of her navel.

'No?'

'Of course, I am nothing official but I keep my eyes open. I think Odd caused a lot of worry with his snooping around. I think people are frightened that he found more than he realized.'

'You know that?' I asked.

'I listen,' she said. 'I watch.'

'You should be careful,' I warned her.

She gave me a sly smile. 'You're looking for the Sheep Market, aren't you?'

'I'm not looking for anything,' I told her but I could tell that she didn't believe me.

She shifted closer to me on the bed. 'When I walked in on you, you looked like a bear.' Her hand slid under the sheet and along the inward curve of my thigh. 'A big brown bear.'

I didn't correct her, when all is said and done a bear is a bear. Her fingers were playing with me, my cock involuntarily thickening and distending in her left hand, while with her right hand she reached into her robe and cupped a breast, inspecting the nipple with a kind of detached curiosity.

'I know you're on your own,' she mused, 'a loner.'

I could feel the foolishness and sheer pointlessness of it but it had been a long time – a long, long time. The sheet slipped away as my thighs flexed and my back arched towards her.

'I can help you,' she said. 'I have contacts.'

She leant forward and cupped me in the hollow of her palm and began licking me with the tip of her tongue, like a cat darting at milk. She glanced up at me. 'We could be a team. Together we could find the container.'

I extended my hands down her broad pale back and she shrugged off the robe and then my hands were in her hair, my fingers knotting in the curls as small surges racked my pelvis and the backs of my legs and I had my eyes closed and I was coming and in my mind I was coming elsewhere.

Afterwards, I fell back and listened as Ilyena spat my come on the linoleum. I felt sad, just as I had known, throughout the slurp and suck, that I inevitably would.

My friend Alex, private security consultant and kidnapper, once told me that men take longer than women to get over relationships. He explained that it's the masturbation that does it; the necessity for porno material makes us cling on long after the relationship is over.

When I opened my eyes Ilyena was tying her robe in a businesslike manner. 'I have to go,' she said. 'We'll talk again tomorrow.'

'Right,' I said.

A few seconds after she had closed the door my mobile phone beeped. I reached across and picked it up. A text message in meticulous longhand from a withheld number, it read, *Where is the bill of lading?*

I didn't reply. I thought about it, though; I pushed the sheet down to the foot of the bed and lay there in the darkened room, with waves of air from the fan travelling up and down my body. I considered texting, *I tore it up*. But I couldn't see any immediate gain in it.

Presently, I noticed that there was a lizard clinging to the outside of my window that seemed to be looking in.

I gave up pacing at around six or six thirty and headed straight out. I ran two miles or so, until the years of cigarettes had their claws in my chest, and I ran on until my second wind came and I kept running. I ran like fury.

Then I stopped and watched the dawn, the sun's first red shaft rushing across the sand towards me. I felt it touch my shins and the backs of my hands and the sweat in my hairline before passing on. I turned and ran back towards the watchtower.

I looped back around the camp, running past the rusty, half-buried steel door of the bunker.

In the shower, I rubbed soap on my chin and then shaved quickly in front of a shard of mirror propped against the timber frame, wincing as the blade scraped across my livid bruises. After I shaved I went back to my room and got dressed.

My room was square; there wasn't much to it really: a linoleum floor tacked to plywood sheets, a small rectangular window with wire-cored safety glass, a metal-frame bed with a pillow and sheet, a raffia-work bedside table and a lamp with a green shade that was partially burnt by the heat of the bulb. On one wall was a poster from the Ethiopian Tourist Board, a cherubic Ethiopian girl smiling out at you from an abundant landscape. The poster was coming slowly off the wall, the edges curling inwards, the paper as dry as parchment. Because I could only think of drought and of famine when I thought of Ethiopia, I couldn't avoid the notion that it was some kind of sick joke. I considered ripping it down. I didn't for a minute believe that she was really a Tigrean village girl. I imagined that she was the cherubic, well-fed daughter of a government minister. The more I looked at it, the more unreal it seemed; the more it seemed to fit the surroundings. I let it stay. It was as much an illusion as the rest of the Zone.

★　　　★　　　★

Colonel Charles was sitting in one of the plastic chairs in the sunlight, watching CNN. He was wearing the same clothes as the day before. He contemplated me sleepily as I came out of my cabin, tucking the tails of my borrowed German camouflage blouse into my trousers.

Patrice and Toona were across the yard doing bench curls in singlets and shorts and Hadzhik was sitting a few feet away in the shade. There was no sign of Ilyena and I was relieved.

'Good run?' Colonel Charles asked, pleasantly.

'Yes.'

On CNN, the Filipino President, Gloria Macapagal, was shown visiting Kuwait and outlining her plans for the evacuation of sixty thousand migrant workers. The Indonesians were already leaving.

'I have always thought that man's abiding weakness is to sit in judgment of his fellows,' said Colonel Charles.

'I try to be tolerant,' I told him. 'I tolerate most things.'

'I saw Ilyena come out of your room last night.'

Hadzhik looked up abruptly. Colonel Charles glanced across at him and then at me. He said, 'It is advisable not to make enemies.'

'I have enough already,' I agreed.

Colonel Charles sat back and considered the television. 'There are reports of shooting last night, in this sector.'

Hadzhik let out a sceptical snort. 'On CNN?'

'I have decided that you will go out together and investigate.'

'It was Toona,' said Hadzhik, raising his chin in the direction of the two observers at the weights, 'shooting at the moon.'

'No,' said Colonel Charles, wagging a finger at Hadzhik. 'I demand an investigation. You must go out on patrol.'

Hadzhik shrugged and looked at me. 'Let's go?'

'Sure,' I said. I didn't want to hang around. 'Why not?'

'There's water in the Land Cruiser.'

'This time, stay away from the Iraqis,' Colonel Charles called after us.

First, we took Crown Route, sliding on the soft sand blown overnight across its surface. Hadzhik had told me that there were road crews that worked around the clock to keep the main routes open and soon we passed a grader coming the other way, its Bangladeshi crew in goggles and white keffiyeh headdresses. They waved as they passed.

Hadzhik reached forward for the cigarette lighter and said, 'Ilyena came to see you.'

'Yes,' I told him. 'She thinks that we can be a team.'

Hadzhik lit the cigarette. He exhaled slowly. 'We'll take a parallel route,' he said.

We turned off Crown and drove out into the open desert.

'Everybody here is dreaming of going home and never having to work again,' said Hadzhik. 'They're all looking for a short cut. It makes people greedy.'

'Not me.'

Hadzhik laughed. 'People think you have found the Holy Grail.'

My head whacked the doorframe and I came suddenly awake. I had no idea how long I had been sleeping. Staring blearily around, I saw that we were driving through an abandoned settlement, a small group of mud-brick huts gathered around a simple well that tapped into one of the underground rivers that burrowed beneath the desert.

I saw the scarred steel cases of cluster bombs strewn like cattle troughs amongst the huts and around them unexploded submunitions, American BLU-63s scattered like tennis balls.

The signs of war were everywhere: Iraqi T-55 tanks ripped open like sardine cans, half-collapsed trench lines and bunkers, huge sand embankments and placid moats of oil ready to be ignited. Twice we came across abandoned weapons caches discarded by surrendering Iraqis. Preserved for over a decade by the scouring wind, the stacks of Soviet-made Kalashnikov AK assault rifles and RPG-7s – rocket-propelled grenades – wore only a superficial coat of rust. Hadzhik filled the back of the Land Cruiser with weapons and tins of ammunition.

'Are you planning on starting a war?' I asked.

'I'm not going to start it, I think,' he replied, 'but I'm planning to be ready when the time comes.'

I changed the subject. 'What do you know about the Sheep Market?'

'You have led a very busy life, my friend,' observed Hadzhik, after a pause, 'too busy maybe.'

'So? Have you heard of the Sheep Market?'

'The further you get from the Zone the more rumours you will hear and the more it will sound like Sodom or Gomorrah.'

'It exists, though?'

'Some call it the Sheep Market and others call it the Flea Market. I have even heard it called the City and the Universal Free Market. Most agree that although it resembles a small town, it drifts like a caravan. At any given moment it may contain the people of a hundred different nations. It is a feature of the Zone.'

'Have you seen it?'

He slammed the rear door of the Cruiser. 'You want to go there?'

'I was told to stay away.'

Hadzhik walked around to the driver's side of the vehicle, his fingers tapping the roof. 'If you have something to sell, then you should go to the Sheep Market.'

'I don't have anything to sell.'

'You keep saying that.'

'Are you watching me, Hadzhik?'

'Everybody is watching you, Jonah.'

'Can I drive?' I asked.

'Sure; why not?'

My arm was still stiff and sore from the knifing but driving was a welcome distraction. Hadzhik eased back in the passenger seat and lit another cigarette.

Damsel in distress

Back on Crown Route, on the borderline, we approached a vehicle pulled over on the shoulder with its bonnet up.

'Unmarked Land Cruiser,' said Hadzhik. Reaching over into the back seat, he produced an AKMS assault rifle from under a blanket.

'Unmarked is suspicious?'

'Not necessarily,' Hadzhik replied.

I checked my mirrors.

'Drive on. Afterwards we'll back up,' Hadzhik advised.

'Sure,' I said sceptically.

As we drove past I caught a glimpse of a dark-haired woman, with her head down under the bonnet. She already had an audience. A few feet away an elderly man in a keffiyeh was sitting on a small donkey with his heels scuffing the ground and beside him there was a woman in a black robe holding a child.

'Damsel in distress,' I said.

'It's very predictable,' Hadzhik warned, watching the track behind.

'Works every time for me,' I acknowledged.

I braked and pulled onto the shoulder, craning to look in the rear-view mirror. The woman came out from beneath the Cruiser's bonnet. She wiped her palms on the back of her jeans and looked back at us, raising a hand to shield her eyes against the sun. I recognized her immediately as the woman who had tried to have me freed from the Russian camp.

'She's beautiful,' I said. 'She needs my help.'

'Maybe she needs a mechanic more than she needs you.'

'Maybe not.'

I turned off the engine and got out. I took several steps away from the car and then the force of the sun hit me head-on and I was suddenly giddy, with my head spinning and my ears roaring like a hurricane. My eye packed in. I crashed to my knees on the sand.

'Great,' I muttered, with my head down between my knees and stray red pixels floating like space invaders down my retina, 'just great.'

With an effort, I raised my head and opened my eye. I felt the whisper of an ominous calm and following hard on it the realisation that I had fallen into an interstice. Focus came eventually but the sun was eclipsed. She was resplendent in a blinding white T-shirt, standing with her feet apart and her hands on her hips in the midday dark.

Nearby, the two spectators, the elderly man on the donkey and the woman in the robe with the child, who I had assumed was the man's wife, shifted and changed. The man's leathery face fissured and cracked and threatening shapes writhed under the woman's black robe. The child's head swelled like a balloon.

I looked back over my shoulder in the direction of Hadzhik, who was standing in the open door of the Patrol, the assault rifle tucked discreetly in behind his right trouser leg. He raised an enquiring eyebrow. He had the range of facial expressions of a pantomime dame and lying there, with demons and space invaders fighting for control of my skull, I decided that it was really beginning to piss me off. I wanted to shout, *Stop it!*

I took long, slow breaths. I opened and closed my only eye. I had a headache that felt like trepanning and just as abruptly I was back.

'*Ribbet*,' I croaked.

I struggled to my feet, rubbed my palms on my face until it smarted and resumed walking towards her. I tried smiling at the Bedou and his wife but got no reaction. The child's head *was* grossly swollen.

I stopped in front of her. I saw the image of my face reflected in her sunglasses. I looked like shit, pale as a ghost.

'Hot?' she enquired.

'Yes,' I said, humiliated.

'You're new here,' she said, offering it as an explanation. There might have been some compassion in her voice but it was difficult to tell.

'Yes,' I said, 'fresh off the boat.'

'You do make an impression,' she said.

'You should see the other tricks I do,' I croaked. 'I'm not just good at fainting.'

She smiled wryly, her teeth bright white. 'Maybe next time.'

'What's your name?' I asked.

'Miranda,' she said.

'I'm Jonah. But you know that already.'

'In the belly of the whale,' she said.

'You got it. My mother's a fortune teller.'

'Really?'

I cackled wildly. 'No.'

She raised an eyebrow. I stopped laughing abruptly.

She asked, 'When did you last get a decent night's sleep.'

'About four years ago,' I replied. I leant towards her. 'What's the matter with the boy?'

'Neuroblastoma.'

'Right,' I said, without comprehension.

'It used to be unusual,' she added. 'These people have five thousand times the recommended level of radiation in their bodies.'

'Depleted uranium?'

'That's what people say.' Then she asked, 'What were you doing at the Desert Palm?'

'We were there to meet a woman.'

'Is that what he told you?'

'Was it you?' I asked her. 'Were we there to meet you?'

She ignored the question. 'What else did he tell you?' Then she gave me the kind of quick meaningless smile that strangers give you in an elevator. 'You don't know me,' she said, under her breath.

Hadzhik joined us.

'What's the problem?' he asked.

'The car died on me,' she answered and then, in an amused tone, 'I'm not dangerous.'

Hadzhik glanced down at the AK and shrugged.

'Let's say it's better not to take a chance,' he said. 'What's the issue with the car?'

'The injectors,' she said.

'Do you want me to take a look?'

'No need,' she said. 'I've fixed it.'

'Really?' Hadzhik asked, doubtfully.

She laughed. 'Really – girls are good at this stuff now.'

'I can believe it,' I said.

'Look, I'm busy,' she said. 'I have to go and find a working hospital. Thank you for stopping.' She smiled at me. 'It was nice to meet you, Jonah.'

'Yeah.'

I wanted to say something more. I watched her slam the bonnet and walk around to the driver's door. The woman with the child got in the back. She looked up to the rear-view mirror for a moment and I found myself standing, with my hand half-raised, as she drove away.

'Who is she?' I asked.

Hadzhik shrugged and turned his attention to the man on the donkey. The Bedou was beak-nosed and unshaven, wearing a dirty dishdasha and a pinstripe jacket threadbare at the elbows.

Hadzhik spoke to him in Arabic, questioning him about the shooting the night before. The Bedou nodded and pointed in the direction of the patrol base. He made a gun by arranging his index fingers one behind the other and shaking them at the sky.

'Da-da-da-da,' he went.

'Sounds like Toona shooting at the moon to me,' I said.

'We have solved the case,' Hadzhik observed, deadpan as ever. He gave the Bedou a packet of cigarettes.

Back at the base, Colonel Charles nodded sagely and said, 'Yes. Yes. It must have been the Iraqis. Don't worry, I will write a report explaining everything.'

'I'm sure you will,' said Hadzhik.

Sal was leaning over the monitor with his fingers on the keyboard and a wash of blue light bathing his face. He looked up as I pulled the door of the Portakabin closed behind me, shutting out the raucous noise from under the cam netting.

'I brought you some food,' I told him, putting the plate down on the desk.

'I was wondering when you'd come to see me,' he said.

'I've been out on patrol,' I told him.

'Yes, I heard. I imagine that you have fully advertised your presence.'

'I'm an observer, it's my job.'

Sal sat back in his chair and propped his chin on his raised index fingers. 'The job's over, Jonah; haven't you noticed? There'll be no medal for you. The UN mission is about to evacuate. It's only a matter of days before the war kicks off. The Americans are determined to charge into battle and change the world.'

'Who sent you here, Sal?' I asked.

'Who sent you, Jonah?'

'I've been swept under the carpet, Sal. Sent into UN purgatory. You know why.'

'People want whatever it is that Odd found.'

'People?' I asked.

'They want to talk to you,' he said.

'I don't have anything for them, Sal.'

'They don't believe that. They say you have something of theirs. They're very serious-minded.'

'Nevertheless.'

We contemplated each other quietly. Sal said, 'By the way, there's a new message for you in your Hotmail inbox.'

'You have my password?'

'Like most people, you use the same password for all your entry points. Some sites are less secure than others. You're vulnerable, Jonah.'

'I'm going to bed.'

'Don't you want to know what it says?'

'I'm tired.'

Sal nodded. 'You don't sleep much, do you?'

'I have problems with it,' I acknowledged.

'You know, they say that people with insomnia have a guilty conscience.'

'Goodnight,' I told him.

Then Sal said, 'I found a story on the news wires.

According to the reports, the CIA are tracking three cargo ships that have been sailing around the Indian Ocean for the last three months maintaining radio silence. The ships were chartered by a shipping agent based in Egypt and are flying under the flags of three different countries. They are steaming around in ever-decreasing circles. They say the cargo might have routed through Syria or Jordan. It makes you wonder what you could hide in a container. Doesn't it?'

'I'm too tired for paranoia.'

'I don't believe in paranoia,' Sal said. 'Not the way you mean it. I see too many connections.'

I slipped out of the door and circled back to my cabin, careful to stay out of the circle of light surrounding the dining table.

My room had been turned over and very little effort made to disguise it. It can't have taken them very long, I didn't own anything that I wasn't wearing and most of what I was wearing wasn't mine. The room didn't have much furniture. It looked more like petty vandalism or an act of deliberate intimidation than a serious search.

They'd ripped a corner of the Ethiopian Tourist Board poster when taking it down and had put it back up at an angle. I straightened it, levering out the drawing pins with the unchewed edge of my thumbnail.

After that I locked the door and sat on the bed with my hands gripping my knees, trying to phase out the noise outside. I let my head slowly roll across my shoulders, feeling the cords of tension running up through my neck. There wasn't much prospect of sleep. Instead, I slid my daughter's drawing out of my wallet and unfolded it on the bed, smoothing my fingers across its waxy surface. I had last spoken to Esme on the day of her birthday. Douglas had answered the phone. 'Yes?'

In the background I remember hearing the thundering feet and raucous unserious screaming of a children's party.

'It's Jonah.'

I'd heard what I thought was a sharp intake of breath, closely followed by a feeling of sudden intimacy, as if I was literally whispering in his ear. I'd said, as I always did, 'I'd like to speak to Esme.'

There was a pause. Three years had passed since the abduction but the night at the steading was always there between us as an unspoken presence. Despite it, he had always been civil in his dealings with me. He had no wish to rake over the humiliation of that night, any more than I did. He set the receiver on the table and I heard him call Esme over.

'Yes?'

'It's Dad,' I'd told her.

She spoke without pause, without recourse to breath, the words tumbling out, a string of little girls' names, presents, games and snippets of other similarly breathless conversations. And then, just as abruptly, 'I've got to go now.'

'Esme.'

'What?'

'I love you.'

'I love you too, Dad.'

I heard the receiver clunk down on the table. I contemplated cutting the connection but something held me back, the sounds of children playing. The yearning for what I had lost. The sure knowledge that there was no way back.

Then somebody picked up the receiver. There was a moment's chilly silence.

'Douglas?' I asked.

But it was Sarah, my ex-wife, not bothering to conceal the anger. 'Where are you?'

'I can't tell you,' I told her.

She ended the call.

I found myself staring up at the cherubic young girl on the Ethiopian Tourist Board poster. Carefully, I folded up the drawing and slid it back into my wallet. If I was convicted of kidnapping and sentenced to a prison term, I had no doubt that Sarah would use it as a pretext to sever all contact – she wasn't going to be standing in line holding Esme's hand outside Barlinnie prison once a week. I would slide unnoticed out of my daughter's life.

Insomnia is interference: a barrage of sheeting, white noise from the shorting circuitry of a broken machine. Mine was delivered by satellite: *I don't love you any more.*

I have combated it in two ways: in the beginning with Valium, anywhere between twenty and sixty milligrams a night, washed down with glassfuls of Scotch to guarantee four straight hours, but more consistently by walking. Like a prisoner, I walked from one end of a room to another. I walked the perimeter of patrol bases and military camps, down the waters of Leith from one end of Edinburgh to another, down Broadway from the Broadway Bridge to South Ferry in the shadow of the twin towers. I walked through the night, through blisters and lightheadedness, and I had it on the run – not beaten, there were still spells that only walking would solve – but three and a half years after the split and I was sleeping through most of each night. I was making progress. But then came the Cowgate fire and Alex across the table at the Tower Restaurant telling me that one of his unattributable friends had turned out to be very much attributable after all and, close on that realization, the crackling noise gathering at the edges of my perception. So I guess that, in this case, Sal was right: insomnia was a product of a guilty conscience. I had it coming.

I stretched out on the bed.

Later, after everything was quiet, Ilyena came to the cabin. She rattled the door and, finding it locked, cursed out loud. She staggered to the window and her face, pressed against the glass, was striated by the wire core and backlit by the moon. She looked like a harpy, a predatory beast. I turned my back to the wall.

'Bastard,' she hissed.

I closed my eyes but sleep would not come. There was no respite from memory.

Glossolalia

There was only one pew without someone stretched out on it and I went to sit at it although it was already occupied. It was the same plain, dark hardwood of all the pews. The Pentecostals didn't seem to believe in prayer cushions. I don't think they kneel. From what I could gather they were fundamentalist in outlook and given to clapping and shouting and even talking in tongues – though it was difficult to believe when you actually met them. The Newfies, the inhabitants of Gander in Newfoundland, were quiet, plainly dressed in check and denim and gruffly polite.

I sat facing the simple altar. I wasn't sure when I had last been in a church – my wedding or the christening of a friend's child? I wasn't much of a churchgoer. As a pre-cocious teenager at a Catholic school I had refused Communion and caused general outrage with my assertion that the Vatican had been complicit in the Holocaust (I made a school history project of the subject). At about the same time, as I recall, my mother was refusing Communion in protest at the Pope's stance on abortion. I don't think we discussed it.

The other occupant of the pew was a middle-aged American lady in a blue dress. She was sitting very upright with an open Bible on her lap. I glanced at her and she offered me a weary smile.

It was four in the morning and no one else was awake. Business-class passengers were huddled up the front, coach-class further back near the doors. Outside the church it was cold and cloudless, the aurora borealis a series of vertical white shafts on the northern horizon. It was September 2001 and I had insomnia.

'Well,' I said, slipping easily into the friendly camaraderie of the last few days, 'it's the right place to read that book.'

Out of politeness, she nodded. 'It's certainly a church.'

'You're not a Pentecostal?'

'No,' she said firmly.

'Do you have trouble sleeping as well?'

The lady frowned, as if mystified by the question. Her skin was grey, smooth and waxy – youthfully preserved in a way that suggested pickling vinegar. When I looked away, she returned to her Bible.

It was all strange.

I had seen Al Gore the day before, on my way to use the Internet at the school. He was walking down Main Street, wearing his post-election beard and looking like an Old Testament prophet cast adrift in the wilderness. Since then a rumour had spread around the church that Gore had made a break for the mainland.

At the school, at the bank of monitors set up in the gym, there was a message from my mother in my inbox (and 237 others in my junk mail box). I had printed and folded it. Now I unfolded it again.

I don't know where you are but I do know that in times of trouble you seem drawn to New York. I can't say that I understand but that's beside the point. Where are you? Are you safe? I know it's ridiculous to worry, given the places that you seem to find yourself in and the situations that you seek, but nevertheless I am your mother and it is my prerogative.

I visited your father today. He continues to deteriorate but I suppose he is spared recent events. He seems more and more childlike. I can't say that I find it easy. There are definitely times when I wish it was all over, which is unchristian of me.

Your sister is pregnant again.

Emotions here are complicated; there is of course a great outpouring of grief and sympathy. We are closer now as nations than we have ever been. But there is also another emotion, not as simple and crude as 'They had it coming', but a feeling that Americans (and I don't include you as one) have at last learned that they are like everyone else, just as vulnerable to envy, spite and revenge. They say themselves they have been expelled from Eden. There are pictures of rejoicing in Arab cities.

My first thought had been that we must be in the grip of some huge cold-war tractor beam, a piece of alien technology, probably recovered from a saucer found under the ice cap and harnessed for use against the Soviets. It was busily malfunctioning, dragging planes out of the sky onto this isolated runway in the Canadian tundra. I counted more than thirty planes, 747s mostly, parked nose to tail on the runway with the wing tips overlapping so that there was no prospect of take-off. Perhaps we were about to be replaced by alien simulacra – like us in every way but each one primed to receive a signal, on receipt of which they would rise up and slaughter the world.

The truth was more terrifying. Initially, the captain blamed it on the traffic-control computers in New York.

At that stage, we could see more planes, in a holding pattern, waiting to come in after us – it seemed oddly plausible. The millennium bug had finally arrived.

As we landed we saw the inhabitants of Gander clustered at the chain-link perimeter fence, staring solemnly at the ranks of planes, as I imagined that ship-breakers had once gathered on the shoreline to stare at floundering ships.

No one's mobile phone could find a signal. We spent twenty-four hours sitting passively in our seats on the runway while they emptied the other planes and the captain slowly fed us the news of the suicide attacks on the World Trade Center and the Pentagon, the heroic fight in Pennsylvania. A female passenger had a brother working for the New York Fire Department and she had to be sedated.

Nobody on that plane imagined that it was a Jewish plot (alien abduction, yes, Israeli espionage – pull the other one!), a few entertained the brief notion that it was terrorists of the home-grown variety, the spawn of Timothy McVeigh, but to be honest it was clear to most from the very beginning that it was al-Qaeda.

A period followed in which we eyed each other speculatively, and inevitably, given my half-Arab looks, a flurry of suspicious glances fell on me. A hostess sat with me for a while and engaged in an over-friendly conversation that we both knew was to establish whether I harboured some fierce and murderous desire. I tried my best to be charming. I showed her my army ID card.

After twenty-four hours we were unloaded onto a yellow school bus and driven to the terminal building. It was huge and hangar-like, a throwback to cold-war vigilance, with vast, open stairways, framed photographs of Superfortresses and B-52s and a row of clocks: New York, London and Moscow. We stood in queues and waited to be interviewed by a group of tired and harassed-looking Canadian Mounties. The passenger with the brother in the New York Fire Department was led away and we never saw her again.

After we had been processed, we got back in the bus and were driven into Gander. By that time, with thirty other planes unloaded before us, the only available accommodation was the Pentecostal church.

I would spend five days in Gander, gathering a few hours' sleep here and there, wrapped up in a blanket on one of the church pews, or walking down Main Street, staring into the windows of the thrift shops and cheque-cashing centres. It was not difficult to tell the passengers from the inhabitants.

I looked up from the printed email.

'Letter from home?' the lady asked.

'From my mother,' I explained.

I read on.

The view here in the House is that the old orthodoxies are out of the window and nothing will be the same again. American policies can no longer be based on the belief that history has ended and with it any threat to peace and prosperity; that free markets will spread inexorably and American democracy is for everyone. It has been a wake-up call. We are all waiting to see what will happen now. Let me know where you are. Love, Mum.

I folded the email. I had not written a reply – I was sure that something similar had been cut and pasted, briefly tailored and sent to scores of others.

'Everything's fine with your mother?'

'Yes, fine,' I said.

She set down her Bible.

'Are you a tourist?'

'Yes, I suppose I am.' I considered the sleeping bodies around us. 'Though I lived in New York once.'

'You're British?'

'I'm an American citizen,' I explained. 'I was born in America.'

'I'm sorry. Your accent.'

'I was raised in Britain. What about you, do you live in New York?'

She seemed shocked. 'No.'

'Just visiting then?'

'Yes,' she said. 'It'll be my first time.'

She smoothed a stray lock of iron-grey hair. She had very clear brown eyes.

'Before she was taken, my daughter worked in Manhattan. She traded in emissions.' She shook her head imperceptibly. 'She told me that she sold people the right to make their air filthy.'

'You can trade in almost anything,' I said, cautiously.

I had a sudden and nagging sense that I was missing something. Taken? There was a formidable and disturbing strength in the rigidity of her bearing.

'Taken,' I asked, 'in what sense?'

'In the sense that I assume she's dead.' She regarded me with her clear eyes. 'She worked for Cantor Fitzgerald on the 104th floor of the North Tower.'

'God. I'm sorry.'

'She was judged.'

'I'm so sorry.'

'Why? It's God's will. You have to accept it.'

'But that's . . . that's . . .'

I struggled for something to say; her calm was deeply unsettling. Eventually, I said, 'Have you spoken to anyone?'

She seemed surprised by the suggestion. 'No.'

'Do you want to? We could speak to the crew.' I remembered the passenger with the brother in the Fire Department who was led away. 'I'm sure that there's counselling available.'

She looked at me pityingly. 'I have God.'

I was unable to conceal my horror.

'Are you Christian?' she asked mildly.

I couldn't bear to say no, so I said, 'I was raised a Catholic.'

She seemed briefly animated. 'We're in the last days now.'

I wasn't sure if I'd heard her correctly. 'You mean the end of the world?'

'We have sinned against Almighty God, at the highest level of our government; we've stuck our finger in His eye. The Supreme Court has insulted Him over and over. They've taken His Bible away from the schools. They've forbidden little children to pray.'

Suddenly I needed to be somewhere else, but there was an unstoppable momentum to her softly spoken words.

'People are in for a surprise,' she said, 'the unbelievers and the idolaters and the murderers, the abortionists and the feminists and the gays, shall have their part in the lake which burneth with fire and brimstone; which is the second death. The unbelievers, who did this, shall be judged every man according to their works.'

I breathed out loudly. 'I don't think we can be sure yet who did it.'

'The battle of America has begun. In the cities of these people, which the Lord thy God doth give thee for an inheritance, thou shalt save alive nothing that breatheth.'

I looked at my watch and stood up.

'Thank you for talking to me,' I said. 'I'm going to go and try and sleep now.'

She looked up at me as I eased away from her along the pew.

'Retribution,' she called out, 'will be terrible to behold.'

I didn't doubt it.

I love you. I might say that of New York. It punctuates so many of my memories. Somehow I was constantly returning – as a young man on the threshold of adult life, later in the immediate aftermath of a marriage collapse and then, by chance, at the time of the attack on the twin towers – riding the bus in from JFK, the ribbons of asphalt through the endless suburbs of Queens, the steel corsetry of the bridges and the cathedral spires of Manhattan.

In September 2001, at the end of a short and unpleasant tour in Sierra Leone and almost a thousand days after the collapse of my marriage, I completed my annual walk across the city, coming to a halt at the barricade on Houston and Varrick. Staring up at the posters of other people's dead plastered there, I wondered if one of the photocopied pictures was that of the grey-faced lady's daughter.

I didn't see her again after that night in the Gander Pentecostal church and in the morning no one else could remember having seen her. It was possible that she was travelling on a different plane and the church had merely offered itself as a temporary refuge. She had chosen the church, rather than having it chosen for her. Those of us who had not made such a choice were loaded back on the plane that morning and flown on to JFK and another marathon processing session, this time at immigration.

At times, I wondered if she was anything more than the creation of my insomniac imagination.

Standing at the barrier, staring upwards into the amputated space once occupied by the towers – buildings that had once seemed as permanent as the twin pillars that score the dollar sign – it was easy to understand how the ideologues would latch on to it as an icon of destruction, of hubris punished and arrogance brought low; a foreshadow of the coming Armageddon. The symbolism was both biblical and Koranic: in the Bible, the people who build the tower of Babel are punished for their presumption; in the Koran the people who fail to heed God's messengers are destroyed in a series of cataclysms known as the punishment stories. Islamism and Christian Fundamentalism were two sides of the same coin: I was convinced that they were going to destroy the world.

The acrid smell and the powder-fine dust caught at the back of your throat.

The Sheep Market

I woke to the rattle of gunfire and found myself sitting upright in my bed, my breath greyhound-quick, grasping around me in the darkness for my rifle, before realizing that the night was silvery-black and silent, the only sounds the soft pad of lizards and somewhere out in the horseshoe of cabins a flapping mosquito screen.

I reached for my G-Shock and squinted at the display. I'd been asleep for two hours and there was no hope of more. I switched on the bedside light and it bathed the cabin in yellow light. The Ethiopian girl smiled down at me from the wall. I swung my feet onto the linoleum. I had spent two days in the Zone and I'd had enough of waiting.

I dressed quickly and walked across the sand to Hadzhik's Portakabin. I banged on the timber doorframe.

'Hadzhik!'

Presently he shuffled to the door and contemplated me sleepily from the far side of the flyscreen.

'Odd told me that he found a container dating back from before the last war,' I told him. 'He said that he found a couple of cars inside.'

Hadzhik snorted and scratched his head. 'More than cars, I think.'

'What do you mean?'

He waved his hand distractedly and shuffled back towards his bed. 'Maybe you have found the smoking gun,

Jonah. A weapon of massive distraction: the Americans will give you a medal and Dubya will be re-elected.'

'What are you talking about?' I called after him.

'I think we should go and look for the Sheep Market.'

'When?'

'In the morning. Go back to bed.'

'I see something,' I said, looking across a scrubby expanse of ore-bearing rocks and thorn bushes on the leeward side of a sand dune, at what might have been a twist of smoke.

'Something?' Hadzhik asked.

The brown wall of the dune grew larger before us.

I pointed. 'There. The other side.'

Pulling off the track, we bounced across ruts and sinks and I kept my gaze fixed on the ground immediately ahead.

'There,' said Hadzhik.

A ruined settlement of drab single-storey buildings came into view. The streets were narrow and the breeze-block houses were small and often roofless. Some of them had blue UNHCR tarpaulins stretched across them for shelter and all bore the marks of fighting, small bullet scars and large shell holes. Many had collapsed or were gutted by fire. The edges of the settlement were dotted with scavenging dogs and battered 4 × 4s the Kuwaitis called *wanettes*. Five empty buses were parked in the sun.

At the entrance to the settlement there was a borehole and beside the pump a line of women standing holding buckets. I slowed as we came up to it.

'Is this the Sheep Market?' I asked.

Hadzhik made no comment. We entered the settlement, driving between rows of fire-blackened houses, the Land Cruiser sliding in the soft sand that had accumulated in the street.

A couple of Bedouin in keffiyeh headdresses and sunglasses emerged from a shadowy doorway cradling AKs. They paid us no attention as we passed.

Down a side street, I glimpsed a square and a throng of people and cars and beyond it a cluster of taller buildings. 'There.'

We turned down a street parallel to the one that we had passed and suddenly we were engulfed by a herd of goats that broke like a bow wave across the front of the Land Cruiser. A small boy sprinted out from under our bull bars.

We took a right turn and just as suddenly the alley was full of migrant workers, Somalis and Pakistanis, swarming around the Land Cruiser, chattering and gesticulating to each other. We inched forward. Men in leather coats whispered into mobile phones from shadowy doorways.

'Take a left,' I suggested.

An open hand slapped the window by the side of my head and I flinched instinctively and then turned in my seat to look. At first I thought the hand was smeared with blood but then I realized that the flesh of the palm was tattooed, painted with leafy spirals and intricate whorls. The patterned skin crawled in front of my eyes.

My own skin crawled.

The owner of the hand was a young dark-haired man with a hooked nose and striking green eyes. He smiled, revealing a line of even white teeth. Unsettled, I did not acknowledge the smile and returned my attention to the crowd ahead.

The hand was withdrawn. The young man disappeared.

We drove slowly down a street of gun sellers, the weapons stacked on blankets and hanging from the eaves of the scarred houses. Grenades were piled up on tables like fresh fruit. The further into the market we drove, the more eclectic the crowd became – these weren't Kuwaiti guest workers – a great thronging mixture of Arabs, Kurds, Turcomans, Tajiks and Nuristanis.

'I don't think they're selling sheep,' I said.

'Let's park and walk,' suggested Hadzhik, indicating an empty courtyard. An eye was painted in blue on one of the yard's walls, a desert sign to ward off evil. I turned into the courtyard and parked. As I was locking the door I heard a hiss. A half-naked boy with thick clots of hair came across the street directly towards us.

The boy said, 'You, give me a dollar.'

I looked at the boy. Half of his face was raw and peeling.

Hadzhik tested the handles of the car doors. 'You can watch our car for a dollar,' he said.

Ignoring him, the boy walked beside us for a while, gesticulating with both hands, flinging out his arms in haphazard gestures. He chanted, 'A dollar, a dollar.'

A man crossed the street and came towards us. He was wearing a threadbare suit and pencil-thin tie, with a pair of dusty leather shoes. His sunglasses and black moustache made him the caricature of an Iraqi plain-clothes man.

'Mukhabarat,' Hadzhik muttered.

I stopped and looked back at the man, already on his way, shouldering purposefully into the crowd.

Behind me Hadzhik stopped and squatted down to speak to a legless hawker on a wooden trolley, the man's bare arms as heavily muscled as a gorilla's. I should have stopped, but for some reason I carried on, brushing shoulders with groups of young Pakistanis.

'Have you come to buy?'

The young man with the tattooed palms had fallen into step beside me. He was wearing a tight white shirt folded back at the cuffs that accentuated the slimness of his musculature.

'No,' I replied.

It was difficult to estimate his age: he could have been fifteen or twenty-five. His gaze suggested something older.

'A shame,' he said. 'You know you can buy anything here, with no consequences.' His mouth was upturned at one corner in amusement. 'Perhaps you are here to sell?'

'To look, only,' I told him.

'An observer,' said the young man mockingly, 'fulfilling his mandate. That too can be paid for.'

'No thanks.'

'You're Jonah, right?'

I stopped. The crowd adjusted and flowed around me. I realized I had lost any sense of direction.

'You have a distinctive face,' he said.

I turned and stared into his unsettling oval eyes. He seemed to have some indefinable awareness of me, as if some instinct in him reached into me.

'Who are you?' I demanded.

'Malak,' he said, extending a long-fingered hand with the palm turned down and his tattoos hidden. He was wearing silver thumb rings and I noticed that he had no fingernails; it looked as if they'd been ripped out at the quick. His hand was cool as snake skin.

'Why are you following me?' I demanded.

He laughed mockingly. 'I thought perhaps I could help you.'

'I don't think so.' I turned back to the crowd.

'Wait,' Malak called out, stepping after me. He put his hand on my forearm and my flesh crawled. I looked down, half-expecting the skin where he had touched me to be stained. 'There's someone here that I know will want to meet you.'

I shrugged him off. 'No thanks.'

We emerged from a street of moneychangers, wads of bills secured with rubber bands stacked on their dirty blankets, and entered a dusty square.

'Legion is here,' Malak said, teasingly.

There was a large tree at the centre of the square and a couple of *wanettes* parked in the dappled shade beneath it. At one corner of the square there was a mosque with its windows and doors boarded up. Several of the buildings facing the square had a visible second storey and appeared less damaged than those on the periphery. The heat was so fierce; it felt as if it was trying to batter me to the ground. My head was reeling.

I heard myself saying, 'Legion?'

'Yes. Legion. He is here. He is interested in your case.'

'My case?'

'We are all interested in you,' Malak said.

'We?'

'We are a fraternity,' Malak explained. 'Legion will explain.'

'Who is Legion?'

'An American.'

I laughed out loud.

'What's so funny?' Malak asked.

I shook my head and looked back and forth, craning to see above the crowd. I was looking for Hadzhik but there was no sign of him. I couldn't work out which direction the car was in or which route we had used into the square. The crowd paid me no attention.

'Legion will speak with you,' Malak said.

'Listen,' I said, 'if you're on some kind of cultist recruitment drive, count me out. I don't want peace, or even peace of mind. I don't love the world.'

Malak studied me carefully. 'We know that, Jonah.'

'Of course,' I said. 'Everybody knows all about me. I probably have a website.'

'We've done our research,' Malak conceded. 'We know the difficulties you are in.'

'Fine,' I said. 'Take me to Legion.'

'Follow me, quickly.'

He led the way, hurrying across the square towards an apparently derelict building. He opened the door. We crossed an inner courtyard to a second door guarded by an armed Bedouin who recognized Malak and stepped aside to let us pass. We ascended three flights of narrow stone steps, taking them two at a time. We strode down a narrow windowless corridor with a door and a guard at the end. Abandoning all caution, I felt something akin to reckless exhilaration. It carried me ahead of Malak down the corridor. The guard opened the door.

It was so sudden, the transition from shade to fierce sunlight, that for a moment I was unnerved. Light flooded in through a skylight and dust motes spiralled like carbonated water in the down light.

Beyond it there were people, though they were indistinct and shadowy. I staggered slightly. I was blinded by the reflection of light on stainless steel, probably a watch face. Then he rose, long and pale like something exhaled by the earth. Three other human shapes rose with him, a woman and two men. They were all cradling guns.

He stepped into the light and his long sinewy fingers closed on my upper arm and were followed by a voice with an American accent, hoarse and unhurried.

'This way . . .'

I was steered across the room, over piles of cushions that slipped and sank beneath my feet, and I stepped on what I think was a chessboard, scattering the pieces. I got the impression that people around me were leaving, their hurriedly gathered robes disturbing the dust motes. We passed through a doorway into a large and empty room with a door at the far end.

I looked up at my companion. He was taller than I am and he had a long loping stride that I struggled to keep up with. His face was tanned bronze, hollowed out and etched with two vertical lines that stretched from the harsh triangles of his cheekbones and framed his chin. He had a high forehead and close-cropped hair that was thick with dust. Everything about his stride spoke of action and certitude.

'You're the new Brit, right?'

I found myself staring at the stranger, at his mouth, its weirdly voracious aspect and his teeth – they were impossibly white and regular. I guess thousands of dollars' worth of reconstruction.

'Hey, kid, cat got your tongue as well as your eye?'

He steered me through the door and up a flight of steps, through another door and out onto a large flat roof. The settlement was spread out beneath us.

'Here,' he said, stepping back to look at me.

He was wearing a grey T-shirt with *Ranger* printed across the chest and a pair of dusty jeans pulled over suede cowboy boots; he had a matt black SIG Sauer 9mm pistol in a holster on his belt. I guessed he was in his mid-fifties. The short-sleeved shirt revealed the bunched, corded muscles in his arms.

Either side of us, two swarthy men wearing desert camouflage moved in a disciplined choreography of tacking moves. Their skin was the same olive hue as Hadzhik's and they wore their hair long, curled against the collar of their camouflage smocks. They were holding modular, aluminium M4A1 carbines with reflex sights and M203 grenade launchers on the mounting rails, and the black plastic loops of receivers were visible in their ears as they scanned the surrounding desert.

They didn't seem interested in me.

The woman was black, with tight-cropped hair, wearing a blue linen trouser suit and a Kevlar body vest. She was carrying a compact black MP5K 9mm machine pistol. She had positioned herself at the far side of the roof where she had a view of both the square below and the entrance to the roof. She bent a hand to the side of her head, listening to someone speaking into her earpiece.

'You're the new Brit? Jonah, right?' he said.

'Yes,' I replied. 'Sir?'

He laughed. 'Call me Legion.'

The woman spoke softly into a concealed mouthpiece in her lapel. She looked up. 'The Kuwaiti police are inbound and the Mook know you're here. I'm calling in the heli-copter.'

Legion shook his head in a gesture that conveyed both mild frustration and bemusement. 'My posse: Wendy and the Chechens, Ruslan and Magomed. I have to take them every damn place.' There was a pause while he gazed speculatively at me. 'How are you getting on?'

'Fine,' I said.

'Just fine?' Legion said, leading me, gently this time, to the north-western edge of the roof. 'What's your secret?'

'I'm sorry?'

'Everybody has a secret,' he said. 'You were in the Desert Palm with the Norwegian guy who got his throat cut.'

'That's right.'

'Why?'

'Why was I there?'

'Sure. I mean you arrive in Kuwait out of the blue, nobody's expecting you, you get off a plane, you look strange, an hour later you are in the most dangerous bar in the Zone, the only bar in the Zone, engaged in an illicit deal with persons unknown that goes all wrong and results in this Norwegian guy getting his throat cut. I mean, who are you? What were you doing?'

'I got in a car with Odd. He took me to the bar. I drank vodka. I passed out. When I came to he was dead.'

'He give you anything before he died? Any kind of paperwork.'

'No.'

Legion stuck his boot up on the low stone balustrade that ringed the roof and studied me sceptically. 'You sure about that, tiger? I mean, nobody ever tells the truth here. You get them all, everything from bottom feeders to land sharks, and every one of them a liar. There are times I think it's impossible, like even the dust in the air is full of lies.'

I met his gaze squarely and said, 'I'm sure.'

I was right in a way. I mean, I hadn't been given. I'd taken.

Legion nodded abruptly and turned to look away across the settlement at the desert beyond. He looked chiselled, like some kind of monumental sculpture. 'Take a look,' he said. 'What do you see?'

I did as I was instructed. There was nothing but a blanched and empty landscape as far as the horizon.

'Nothing.'

'Fifty million bucks a year is what it costs to keep the UN kicking their irrelevant heels here; one thousand three hundred military personnel and two hundred civilian staff. You call that nothing? You should look harder.'

I shrugged and glanced at him, at the fierce angularities of his face. Everything about him was fierce. 'A border?'

'You can call it a border if you like, but the Bedou would laugh in your face and they've been here longer than anyone.'

'So what is it?'

'Good question – the Mesopotamian plain is a frontier. It's overlooked on one side by the Iranian plateau and on the other by the mountains of eastern Turkey. It has no natural defences and has always been the prey of the states surrounding it. Iraq is full of battlefields, everywhere you step you're tripping over bones. Old bones and new bones. What you've got is a bunch of vengeful tribes and faiths and sects and autonomous city-states and the only thing holding it together is Saddam and his secret police. And the law in Iraq is anything Saddam writes on a scrap of paper. And remember, in Iraq Islam does not unify, it divides. It divides a ruling Sunni minority and an oppressed Shia majority. In Iraq it's a lot safer to depend on your tribe than on government and Saddam understands that better than anyone, which is why he surrounds himself with his own tribe, the Tikriti. But even within his own tribe there are factions fighting for prominence, and even within his family there are divisions, cousins against cousins, brothers against brothers. Now look the other way.' We turned and stood with our backs to the balustrade. 'What do you see?'

'The American military?'

'And beyond that?'

'Kuwait?'

'Sure. Kuwait. Back in '59 Allen Dulles called it the most dangerous spot on earth – I'd say it qualifies again. In 1922 your fellow Brit Percy Cox took a drive out into the desert. I don't think he liked the desert much because he didn't drive too far. When he stopped the car he drew a line in the desert and declared it Kuwait. Britain handed control of it over to a bunch of pearl barons, who are now oil barons and more interested in building hotels than a state. They enjoy the protection of the holders of God's own franchise, the USA – the most powerful nation on earth, Get this: "Through its partitioning of the Arab lands, western imperialism founded weak mini-states and installed the families who rendered it services that facilitated its exploitative mission." You know who said that?'

'No.'

Legion grinned, his teeth impossibly white in the sunlight. 'The big guy: Saddam Hussein.'

'That's what you call an impartial view?'

'It's the truth. Between us we chopped up the Caliphate into parcels: Iraq was just a province of the empire, nothing like it is now. Syria, Palestine and Libya are names from ancient times that hadn't been used in the region for a thousand years. Algeria and Tunisia don't even exist as words in Arabic. Persian Gulf security? It's a fiction. Listen, here's another: "Since God laid down the Arabian Peninsula, created its desert and surrounded it with its seas, no calamity has ever befallen it like these Crusader hosts that have spread in it like locusts, crowding its soil, eating its fruits and destroying its verdure; and this at a time when the nations contend against the Muslims like diners jostling around a bowl of food." You know who said that?'

'No.'

'OBL. Osama bin Laden. We cradled an evil zealotry, Jonah; we created totalitarian regimes that ruthlessly expunged the pluralism and diversity from Islam. We nurtured Wahhabism in Saudi, which in turn gave birth to the super-Jihadi, Osama bin Laden. The Agency's Op Cyclone trained and armed 35,000 zealots, who became the Taliban and al-Qaeda. We were so eager to sow shit in the Soviet backyard back in the eighties we encouraged the Saudis to match our funding in Afghanistan dollar for dollar. We wanted the Reds out and the Saudis wanted a Stone-Age hole they could drop their delinquent sons into. We beat the Reds but now nobody can stop the sons – they climbed out of the hole meaner and nastier than they went in and they're getting stronger.'

'Mook are inbound,' said the woman.

Abruptly, he turned to look at me. 'Let me ask you something. You like the desert?'

'Sometimes I like the silence,' I told him.

Legion pressed the tip of his index finger against his right temple, as if he was thinking, and then he pointed it at me. 'I don't have a bead on you yet,' he said.

'Mook are inbound,' repeated the woman.

'All right, Wendy, I heard you the first time.' Legion leant over the edge of the balustrade and stared down at something below. His eyes narrowed. 'Which side do you think he's on?'

Below us in the enclosed courtyard Hadzhik was standing against a wall, smoking a cigarette. 'Hadzhik? I don't think he's on anybody's side.'

Hadzhik opened his eyes and, seeing that we were watching him, he waved diffidently.

'Wendy?' Legion asked.

The woman stared back impassively. 'A recent payment into an account in Limassol.'

'Source?'

'One of our accounts.'

Legion gave me a sympathetic look. 'I'm afraid you're wrong.'

I didn't say anything.

'And you?' His gaze came to rest on my face. We were only inches apart. 'Wendy?'

'The subject of further investigation,' she replied.

A huge white Russian Antonov 12 cargo plane with UN emblazoned on the fuselage came in low from the direction of Iraq and banked steeply, heading for Doha.

Legion grinned savagely and called out, 'You ever see a carpet fly?'

'No.'

He gestured towards the aircraft. 'It's a lesson, a testament to the feverish pursuit of further riches. I could run you up to UN Sector headquarters Umm Qasr and they'd sit you down in an air-conditioned briefing room and tell you that you're going to be clearing $350 a day tax-free, that's before they show you a map or try and explain the geopolitical situation. That may not seem like the earth to you but let's just say you're an observer from Ethiopia or Uganda, Bangladesh or even China, it's a fortune. It extinguishes any other considerations.'

He paused with two fingers raised as if he was about to jab them into my chest.

'But it's not enough. It's never enough. It merely creates a climate for the pursuit of further riches. Take that plane, for instance. Our exalted leader, Major General Soloman Jipe Kisukumu, Chief Military Observer, tinpot UN generalissimo, controls it. Every day a plane flies up to Baghdad carrying "vital" medical supplies allowed under a UN-brokered deal. The plane is met by one of Saddam's boys, Uday Hussein; he stockpiles it and sells it on to the

Gulf States at a mark-up. Viagra and stuff, the kind of pills the tired-out Emirs are screaming for to put blood back in their dissipated peckers. Soloman has a deal going with these guys. The plane comes back down full of antique carpets, family heirlooms that Iraqi families are offloading so they can buy some bread. In a few days' time the carpets will be on sale on Fifth Avenue. When he's done here, Soloman will be able to go back home to darkest Africa and buy some fucked-up pygmy country held together with Scotch tape. It's asset stripping, zonal-style. Vulture capitalism.'

'I was also told to stay away from the Sheep Market.'

Legion nodded. 'People don't like the idea of young Turks pushing the prices up. Don't be fooled by appearances. You can buy just about anything in the Zone. You can transfer any amount of money to anywhere on the earth. You want a seriously fuckable whore with mile-high legs fresh out of Latvian high school? You want oil vouchers? You want a couple of keys of pure Afghan heroin? Enriched uranium? Blood diamonds? A Stinger missile? Enough weapons to equip your own army? You want to put down a deposit on an artefact from the national museum in Baghdad?'

'What are you buying?' I asked him.

'That's simple. I track the value and provenance of weapons. I buy anything that poses a clear and immediate threat. And you? What are you selling?'

'I'm just a tourist,' I told him.

'Tourist or an exile?'

'Something of both, I guess.'

'Kuwaiti Police are here,' said Wendy.

'Well, Wendy, what are you waiting for? Tell the flyboys we're ready for them.' Legion ran his hand across the

back of his neck. 'You believe the Norwegian guy died for
no reason?'

'I don't know why he died,' I replied.

'Care to find out?' I heard the *thud-thud-thud* of an
approaching helicopter. Legion shaded his eyes with his
hand and scanned the horizon. 'Tell me, do you believe in
conspiracies?'

'I'm more inclined to the random fuck-up theory,' I told
him.

'I'll bear that in mind,' Legion said and indicated for the
bodyguards to join him. He gazed speculatively at me.
'Come on, I'm going to show you something.'

'What about Hadzhik?'

Legion held out his arms. 'What about him? He's done
his job. We paid him a thousand dollars to deliver you
here.'

The helicopter was an old Bell Huey, painted white with
UN in black lettering on the side of the open cargo doors. It
might have been forty years old. It circled us twice, the
pilot's bulky helmet and darkened visor ducking back and
forth in the cockpit as he sought a better view of the ground
below.

'You work for the UN?' I asked.

Legion laughed at the expression of disbelief on my face
and said, 'Sure. I'm the new military adviser to the UN
general.'

'The general needs a military adviser?'

'General Kisukumu's bag is thievery. Warfare he leaves
to others.'

'You have a cellphone?' Wendy asked.

'Yes.'

'Hand it over.'

I gave her my Nokia.

She switched it off and slipped it into a pocket. Behind them, the Huey barely touched the surface of the roof.

'Come on,' said Legion. 'Step into my office.'

He turned and ran for the open door with his body-guards following.

I stood for a few seconds in the furious draught caused by the rotor blades and then I ran for the helicopter. I dropped into a bucket seat beside Legion and Wendy climbed in after me. The Huey took off immediately, banked steeply and behind us the desert swallowed up the settlement, as if it had never existed.

Azzam Holdings

Legion reached up and unhooked a headset from the rack above our heads. He thrust a pair into my hands. 'Put these on.'

As I snapped the muffs over my ears the thud of the rotor blades receded and Legion's voice sounded nasal and metallic in my ears.

'You've met my data analyst,' he said, indicating Sal, who was sitting facing the rear in the jump seat behind the pilot. 'He tracks the markets.'

Sal was drinking coffee through a plastic straw from a Starbucks cup. He nodded to me between sips. I nodded back.

'How is it, Sal?' Legion demanded.

Sal smiled. 'AKs are through the roof,' he said. 'It feels like Kashmir did eighteen months ago. You remember that? The signs are all there. Even mass issue of free weapons to the Fedayeen isn't dampening market confidence.'

'WMDs?'

Sal shrugged. 'Rumour and speculation only.'

Legion jabbed a demonstrative finger at me. 'People used to believe that a monopoly on organized violence was the defining characteristic of the modern state. That view is obsolete now. Capital and crime have gone global, governments have rolled back, the monopoly of violence has broken down and weapons of mass destruction are leaking out. Hundreds of millions of people live in nothing even resembling an effective modern state. And it's not only states that wage war now. The protagonists are flattened networks, irregular militias, Armageddon cults, virtual corporations and cellular organizations. Terrorism has followed crime into the global marketplace.'

Sal sucked noisily on his straw, the sound like reverb in our headphones.

'And containers?' Legion asked him.

'Are bullish,' Sal replied.

Legion grinned, revealing the dark crevices in his gums. 'Give me more.'

'Word has been put about amongst all the usual people that the Iraqis will pay good money for the contents of a forty-foot container and so "container fever" is officially with us,' Sal explained. He flung the cardboard cup out of the open doorway and pushed his glasses up his nose. 'The Russians are dismantling the container wall around their compound and down at Camp Doha the Brits and the Americans are checking all traffic going in and out. Across the rest of the Zone it's open season. We've got observers, policemen, traders, nomads – anybody and everybody randomly cracking open containers. But none of them know what they are looking for. The Iraqis are wiser than to reveal the contents.'

Legion leant forward in his jump seat so that his mouth was only inches from my own. 'However, word is getting out about the existence of a short cut, an electronic treasure map that, given the right password, will spit out the golden goose. Isn't that right, Sal?'

Sal nodded.

'What's on the Norwegian's database?' Legion asked him.

'The location, plate number and date on over 3000 containers across the Zone and associated logistics areas,' Sal explained. 'That's Camp Doha, Umm Qasr port and the three sectors of the Zone. The system was devised to allow UN Department of Peacekeeping to keep track of the number of serviceable containers in the expectation of a rapid deployment of UN forces in the aftermath of a US victory in Iraq. We all know the Americans are going to storm into Iraq; Department of Peacekeeping was attempting to plan for what came after. It's a simple database: it flags services dates and spits out the plate number and location. But provided you have got the plate number, you can use it to find a container.'

'Where do we find the plate number?'

'On the bill of lading.'

'So?'

'If you've got the BOL you've got the container,' Sal explained.

Legion was looking at me.

I twisted the microphone stalk towards my mouth. 'Do you have the database?'

His eyes narrowed. 'Do you have the bill of lading?'

We flew through the desolation of late afternoon, the helicopter's shadow running over the debris of the shoreline and the low and muddy breakers. After the broad mouth of the Tigris and the Euphrates, we crossed a maze of dilapidated concrete canals on the edge of the wetlands and turned away to follow the shoreline, over shallow creeks the colour of rust and exposed thickets of mangrove roots that were hung with shreds of slime.

Eventually, Legion reached across and grabbed my arm. 'There's almost nothing left of the marshes. Nothing.'

We saw the bloated carcass of a camel in a yellow-green pool. It was a primeval wasteland of sun and slime, heat and decay.

'There are only about 20,000 Marsh Arabs left,' Legion was saying, leaning out of his seat and scanning the horizon. 'Saddam has systematically dammed the main tributary rivers and poured chemicals into the remaining swamp. He displaced over a quarter of a million people who are now sitting in refugee camps in Iran.'

He tapped on the pilot's shoulder and, chopping with his hand like a spade, pointed inland.

'I'm going to show you something,' he said, 'something instructive, an indication of who and what we're dealing with here.'

We followed a muddy olive-coloured river across a parched landscape of cracked mud and dried-out reed beds, which became drier and more desiccated until we were flying across an open dusty plain.

'For eight years this was a battleground between Iran and Iraq, one of the most inhospitable on earth.'

From a distance the trench lines looked like meandering knife scars gouged in the dust, running as far as the eye could see. Closer, the ochre-washed rags of burst sandbags and the sepulchral white concrete bunkers were visible. In places the opposing trench lines were no more than a few hundred metres apart. The ground was churned up and broken apart by shell craters.

'Hundreds of thousands of people died here. Eventually Saddam used tabun, sarin and soman as well as mustard gas to force the Iranians to the negotiating table.'

We followed a trench line. The bottom of the trench was invisible, cast in shadow. I wondered what hidden danger lingered there.

'Will they use gas this time?' I asked.

'I don't know the answer to that any more than you do. You have to try to cast yourself into the mind of a cornered psychopath.' He smiled. 'Would you?'

'I might,' I said. 'I guess I'd want to keep it as an option.'

'That's the answer we're all struggling with.'

I asked, 'Are we still in the Zone?'

Legion grinned. 'We're in the no-fly zone.'

'The no-fly zone reaches all the way to Baghdad.' It seemed likely that we had left the Zone and that we were flying deep into Iraq.

'You think too much.' Legion waved off my expression and returned to the horizon. 'There!'

First I saw the thick oily black smoke from the pile of rubbish lit to draw our attention, and then the Gujaratis' Tatra crane with its perpendicular boom fully extended and the rest of their motley collection of vehicles fanned out around it.

Legion spoke curtly to the pilot. 'Put us down.'

We landed a hundred metres from the crane, beside a battered dun-coloured Nissan Patrol. As we sprinted out through the swirling sand kicked up by the spinning rotor blades, a man emerged from the Nissan. He was dressed in a spotless white keffiyeh, a dishdasha and tennis shoes. Over his robes he was wearing a polished Sam Browne belt with a holster and a stainless steel revolver with a wooden grip.

'The man!' Legion shouted. He gripped him by his shoulder and squeezed. 'Jonah, meet Abu Hattem.'

We shook hands. He was bearded with a prominent hooked nose and eyes the hard, shiny brown of apple seeds.

'Jonah's the new guy,' Legion explained. 'Hattem lives over in the Iraqi wetlands.'

He was a Marsh Arab and I knew enough to know that he was from an ethnic group bitterly opposed to Saddam.

'Saddam's army can poison the marshes; they can drain them dry and bombard them with artillery. They can reduce them to a parched wasteland roamed by wolves. But they'll never conquer them. Isn't that right?'

Hattem nodded. 'Eloquently put,' he said, in clear English.

'How goes it?' Legion asked him.

'*Hudu'nisbi*,' he replied, 'a day of relative calm.'

'Only the most violent events receive attention, isn't that right?' Legion said, slapping him on the shoulder.

'Of course.'

'You done with the sea can?'

Hattem smiled, his expression offering neither menace nor comfort.

Legion winked at me. 'Come on, Jonah.'

We strode towards the crane, leaving Hattem standing by his Nissan.

'Hattem is a practical man, not an ideologue,' Legion told me. 'He is a local patriot, not an internationalist. For us it's a question of trying to find a place in his plans.'

'Is that "us" the UN?' I asked.

Legion laughed. 'Let's just call us the good guys.'

'The good guys?'

'No leader in the Middle East can afford to be openly on America's side any more. Everybody hates us; but they still want to buy Reeboks and Michael Jackson CDs and Office XP. They want to clear out the corrupt old autocracies that rule the Middle East and they understand that we are the only power with the ability to do it.'

'So now we're supporting the Shias?' I said.

'Sure.'

'I had always thought that *we* weren't interested in a democratic Iraq? That's why *we* didn't support the Sha uprising after the ceasefire in '91. That's why we sat back and watched Saddam slaughter 50,000 people.'

'Maybe we were wrong,' Legion said. 'In case you hadn't noticed, the world has irrevocably changed. We used to think that either the world would evolve to the point at which it mirrors America or it could be safely left to its own devices. But we've discovered there's no such thing as peaceful evolution. We're no longer talking about forgettable events in distant countries: we're talking about an attack on the heart of America.'

'What does 9/11 have to do with Iraq?'

'This is total war, Jonah; anyone who doesn't believe what we believe is our enemy. The era of containment and deterrents is over. All this talk of Afghanistan then Iraq: it's bullshit; it's the wrong way to look at it. There are no stages. We're waging total war in forty to fifty countries. You know how many fracture lines there are where the Islamic and non-Islamic worlds meet? I'll tell you: Israel, Nigeria, Sudan, Bosnia, Kosovo, Macedonia, Chechnya, Sinkiang, Kashmir, Timor, Mindanao et cetera et cetera, the list goes on. The American people are demanding that we impose worldwide order. They have spoken and made it clear what they want.'

'Would that be unlimited access to cheap fuel?' I enquired sarcastically.

'You're a bright one,' he sneered. 'I think you mean freedom, democracy and free enterprise. You believe 9/11 exploded a myth but you're wrong. It strengthened us.'

Aziz, the Brummie Gujarati, approached from the direction of the crane. 'All right, Jonah,' he said and, falling in to step with Legion, explained, 'we're ready, you just give the say-so and we'll lift her up.'

Legion ducked under a loop of hawser hanging loosely from the crane's hook and the soft crunch of his footfall on sand was replaced by the thud of boot heels on metal. He lifted his Oakleys onto his forehead and stared down at the partially exposed lid of the sea container beneath his feet. He stamped his feet.

'Shazam!' Legion tipped back his head and yelled. 'Holy fucking Moses! Look what we found. A sea can!'

He rolled his eyes in my direction and drawled, 'You care to comment?'

'What do you want me to say?'

Legion grabbed me by the arm. 'Come on.'

At the far end of the container a trench had been excavated to expose the bolted doors.

Legion glanced across at Aziz. 'You had a look?'

Aziz shrugged.

Legion returned his attention to me. 'You want to see what's inside?'

'Sure,' I said.

One of the Gujaratis standing at the edge of the trench handed Legion a torch.

'Brace yourself,' Legion said.

We slid down the bank to the doors with our ankles sinking in the soft sand. The doors had already been forced opened but the backsliding sand had built up against them and we had to squeeze sideways to get in.

Inside, standing beyond the swirling motes of dust in the slice of light from the doors, it was absolutely black. I could feel Legion's presence beside me and hear the slow certainty of his breath but that was all. Legion did not turn the torch on immediately.

'This container left Southampton docks twelve years ago carrying machine tools for Baghdad. Umm Qasr port was full, ships were backed up in the Khawr 'Abd Allah water-way, so it was offloaded in Shuaiba port in Kuwait instead and cleared customs a few days before the Iraqi invasion. You know how much air there is in a forty-foot container?'

'No.'

'Two thousand three hundred cubic feet. You know how long it would take eleven people to use up that much air?'

'No.'

'Me neither but I keep thinking about it.'

He flicked the Maglite on.

I suppose I was expecting the cars but the container was full of bodies. The aridity had preserved the skeletons, the bones held together by strings of dried ligament. The torch beam skimmed across gaping skulls and the shadowy caves of ribcages.

Legion put his hand on my chest and I fell back before him against the wall of the container with the torch in my eye, blinded by dancing prisms of purple and green.

'The consignee on this container was Azzam Holdings, a company owned by a Saudi businessman called Bakr Abd al' Aswr. That name mean anything to you?'

'No.'

'The shipping agent was a Russian company called Samizdat that regularly cleans its money in the Limassol Laundromat. Samizdat mean anything to you?'

'No.'

'The *Eloise*, a Panamanian-flagged container ship; ring a bell?'

'No.'

'Agricultural equipment? Machine tools?'

'No.'

'A couple of Range Rovers?'

I didn't reply.

The torch beam left my face and flicked back across the bodies.

'Hattem's boys have already identified a couple of them from personal effects,' he said. His voice was calm and evenly modulated again. 'We've matched their names with those of Kuwaitis missing since the war that are posted on the web. We think they made a break for the Iranian border about a week after the invasion, hidden in the back of this container. The Saudi border was closed by that stage. Bakr Abd al' Aswr unloaded the machine tools and filled the container with people who probably paid a lot of money to ensure their safe passage out of Kuwait. Then he loaded the container on the back of a flat-bed, drove it out here and dropped it in a hole. It seems to me that they suffocated. What do you think?'

'Sounds about right to me.'

'Tell me, Jonah, what else do you think a man like that would be capable of?'

'I don't know.'

'Is there anything a man like that wouldn't sell to the Iraqis?'

'I don't know.'

'Where are the cars?'

'I don't know.'

'Get out!'

I stumbled out through the narrow gap and then he was on me, pinning me up against the sand bank. I heard the distinctive click-clack of guns being made ready by the Chechens somewhere above me.

'You want to know what I'd do if I was Saddam? I'd fight a scorched-earth withdrawal up the Tigris and the

Euphrates; I'd sabotage the port facilities in Umm Qasr and blow every oil well and bridge from the Kuwaiti border back up to Baghdad. I'd turn day to night. I'd embed units in hospitals and feeding centres and when the coalition breached the Red Zone I'd unleash the lot: gas, germs, dirty bombs . . .'

I spoke slowly in a measured tone, eye to eye, our faces inches apart. 'Are you planning on knocking out my teeth? Poking out my remaining eye?'

'My Chechen *boyeviks* will fuck you faster than a mouthful of razor blades.'

'I'm already fucked.'

He looked away and I found myself staring at the hard line of his jaw and the crow's-feet, like striations in rock, that branched from the corner of his eyes.

He looked back. 'What's your price, kid?'

'I'm not selling and I can't be bought.'

He nodded sympathetically. 'Nice speech but a little too vociferous. We know you're troubled, Jonah. You don't sleep. You have fits of anger and sadness.'

'Fuck you.'

There was a pause while we stared at each other.

'Who sent you?' he asked.

'Nobody sent me.'

There was a further pause and then he nodded and smiled, his teeth bright white in the shadow of the doorway. 'All right. Let's get you back to your patrol base.'

We climbed the sand walls in silence.

'Hoist her up,' Legion told Aziz at the top of the trench. 'Let's get this over with.'

Aziz muttered into his handheld Motorola and squatting figures stood up and sprinted in every direction.

We retreated fifty metres. There was no sign of Abu Hattem or his battered Nissan.

'There's a war coming,' said Legion. 'And when it's done, believe me, nothing will be the same again.'

The hawsers attached to the container abruptly tautened and groaned. The crane juddered and yanked the container upwards, lifting it out of the trench it had been buried in and swinging it across the sand.

'What will happen to the bodies?' I asked.

'The issue will be handed over to the ICRC's technical subcommittee on mortal remains and they'll identify the bodies and repatriate them to their families. End of story, no need for us to become further involved. Let's get out of here.'

As we approached the helicopter, the drooping rotors began an ungainly first turn and behind us the Gujaratis climbed into their vehicles.

We flew back across the hot and dusty plain, over the drained wetlands and the rubble of smashed irrigation systems and re-entered the Zone, crossing the Tigris and Euphrates at Umm Qasr. We flew over the hulks of sunken ships scattered in the harbour and the port complex with its rows of bombed-out warehouses and buckled railway tracks and at its heart, the container wall surrounding the Russian base.

Below us a crane was lifting one of the containers from the wall. At Legion's instruction we circled briefly. He said, 'Someone's going to find that container, Jonah. You better pray it's not the bad guys.'

I pressed my face to the glass and he made no further comment.

The helicopter flew on across the desert. Eventually the dogleg of the watchtower appeared on the horizon.

'Don't talk to anyone,' Legion told me. 'Trust your instincts. Nobody is worth shit here.'

Wendy handed me my phone.

As we landed I asked him, 'What am I worth?'

'You? Who knows? Maybe something. You remember anything about those cars, you let me know.'

'Message received.'

'Watch out for yourself, tiger.'

I pulled off the headphones and jumped down onto the hard-packed sand and ran from the helicopter. A few seconds later it lifted off behind me and I walked over to the nearest picnic table under the camouflage netting. Hadzhik was sitting, gently swaying, with his eyes half-closed and an empty bottle of vodka on the table before him.

'Find what you're looking for?' he asked; his voice slow and slurred at the edges.

I walked over to my cabin.

Monsters

I was staring into the sky, watching the contrails of Predator drones, when there was a knock on the battered steel wall of the crow's-nest.

'Word has reached us that you are sitting here doing nothing. Therefore you must be a very wise man.'

'Not me,' I replied.

Spicy clambered up the last few rungs into the crow's-nest and stretched out against the floor. He was drenched in sweat from the climb and there were dark stains under the armpits of his red shirt. It was the day after the helicopter ride with Legion and no one would speak to me, let alone get in a car with me. I'd only been in Kuwait a few days but it seemed like longer. I'd made myself into a pariah in double-quick time.

'Christ! Aren't you afraid of heights?' he asked.

'No, it's the depths I fear,' I told him.

'I come bearing an invitation to a dull and lurid party,' Spicy announced and rolled over onto his back. 'An end-of-the-month do at the British Embassy.'

'I have a job to do here,' I told him. 'I've only just arrived.'

'Your drab patch of sand is not going to get up and walk. And if the Americans invade, well at least you got out of their way.'

'I'm not a pretty sight,' I protested.

'Jesus. You obviously haven't met what remains of the expat community. Besides, I have something for you.'

He rolled back onto his front and produced a small parcel from his pocket. 'If this is what I think it is . . .'

The parcel contained my eye, wrapped in a thick wad of tissue paper.

'Bless black cab drivers,' I said, 'and a special thank you to Mary Moriarty.'

'I thought it would be round,' said Spicy.

I knew what he meant; my faux-eye, an asymmetrical sliver not an eyeball, has always caused surprise.

'It works, though,' I said and slipped it in. I blinked twice. 'I can see!'

'*Thattaboy!*'

We were rattling along Crown Route in Spicy's Land Cruiser, listening to Nine Inch Nails, when Spicy said, 'Do you believe in monsters?'

'Yes,' I replied without hesitation.

'Whoa Tonto!' said Spicy, in response to the vehemence of my reply.

The world is full to the brim with monsters. I've come to the conclusion that you only have to step outside your door and it's not long before something awful happens. And it doesn't stop at your door. There's nothing you can do, the fires that consume your neighbour's house will soon leap the gap and engulf your own.

Spicy said, 'Did you used to watch *Doctor Who*?'

'Of course I did,' I told him. 'I used to hide behind the sofa.'

When I was a kid I had this carefully worked out night-time fantasy, a piece of childhood solipsism. I was the only person left on a post-apocalyptic planet conquered by Daleks. I'd alter the perspectives under the covers of my bed, creating a cavernous space out of dizzying blackness. I floated as weightless as space debris, imagining that it was a life-support pod encased in igneous rock and not even the collective brilliance of Dalek minds could figure out a way to break in. Perhaps unsurprisingly, since the break-up of my marriage the Dalek dream has on occasions returned, or a form of it; this time there is nothing beyond the pod, the world has ended but I have not ended.

'Which do you reckon for the all-time best? William Hartnell, Jon Pertwee or Tom Baker?'

'It's close,' I said.

When I was ten my parents settled in a small town in the Home Counties on the suburban periphery of London, not so much a town as a railway station with a town attached. I felt misplaced. I looked misplaced. As soon as I was old enough I upped sticks and moved to Edinburgh to study Arabic at the university. But it wasn't enough. And after three years and with a mediocre degree in my pocket I upped sticks again, this time to New York. I alternated between dosshouse hotels packed with gibbering winos and the one-room apartments of aspiring actresses. I worked in bars and clubs and I never saw daylight. I hoovered cocaine off toilet seats at Save the Robots. And during the course of a year, I realized how shallow and mediocre I had become. I wanted something more, something visceral.

'Jon Pertwee,' Spicy announced.

'Doctor Who and the Green Death,' I conceded, though I'm fond of Tom Baker.

There was a hiatus, then all in a rush he said, 'I wanted to be one of the Doctor's companions.'

I also wanted to be one of Doctor Who's young and energetic companions. It seemed like a window on a more exotic world. I wanted to climb into the unassuming little box and travel who knows where through time and space and face monsters, anywhere away from Surrey.

'Which one?' I asked.

'Sarah Jane Smith, the journalist.'

'She was sassy,' I said.

In 1988, right after the Tompkins Square riots, I took the first available standby flight back to the UK. The following day I borrowed a friend's suit and walked into an army recruitment centre. I joined up on the spot. I'm not sure what it is about army discipline that attracts so many rebellious characters: perhaps it is the challenge of an unyielding wall to pit yourself against or perhaps it's the anonymity, the opportunity for a respite from yourself. Whatever it was, and I'm not clear myself, I can say that I got what I must have secretly wanted. I can say that I have faced real monsters.

'I have an unspeakable secret,' Spicy announced.

'Don't we all?'

'Spicy was sent here to protect him from the temptations of the flesh.'

I have given in to so many temptations, to lust and envy and pride and sloth and gluttony and greed and rage. I'm not even sure that an intimate acquaintance with human frailty makes you any more tolerant of your fellow man.

Spicy said, 'I have been gluttonous and indiscriminate. Boys, girls, they're all the same to me. It's not as if I've a predilection for young guardsmen by the name of Wayne or Darren. I mean, that is no longer forbidden. Nothing quite so pedestrian; my failing is to have been indiscreet with some rather senior officers, and their wives for that matter.'

'I could see how that would land you here.'

'It's rather unfortunate that the army takes such a dim view,' Spicy agreed.

I snorted. 'You want me to follow that with some kind of confession?'

'Don't be paranoid.'

'Can't help it,' I said.

'Clearly,' Spicy retorted.

Spicy came and went throughout the Zone apparently at will, answerable to no perceivable authority. I never saw him in a uniform, or displaying any form of military deference or protocol.

'How do you get away with it?' I asked.

'My father's a general,' he replied.

'My father's a vegetable,' I said.

'I guess you must take after your mother?'

Now, that made me laugh; the last time I heard from my mother she'd been invited to join the Parliamentary Intelligence and Security Committee.

We stopped at Camp Doha on the way down, at the American gate. Outside the guardroom was a small skip used as an honesty box for soldiers to hand in any inadvertently discovered ammunition. We spent ten minutes emptying the contents of Spicy's Land Cruiser into it – AK assault rifles, 82mm mortar tubes and RPG-7s – while the sentries stared open-mouthed.

'Save one,' I suggested. 'You never know.'

'Good thinking,' said Spicy. 'RPG?'

'Fine.'

He winked at the guards and retrieved a warhead and launcher.

'Right,' said Spicy, flicking his hair out of his eyes, 'let's sally forth and party.'

Roaring like a warlock

Inside the embassy, I stood in line with Spicy to meet the host and his wife. The ambassador was a short barrel-shaped man in a Prince of Wales check suit. He had a rubbery face and close-cropped greying hair. 'Name's Padgett, a Blair appointee,' Spicy said, rolling his eyes in mock weariness. 'A man of the people, he looks like a fucking *Spitting Image* puppet. Fellow's got a moneyed wife that's too good for him, goes by the name of Alice. Fucks like a piston.' He shook himself. 'Oh God! Hurry up, that's us.'

The ambassador gripped me by the hand and said, 'Come on. Have a beer; you're on British soil now. There are a few seasoned hands to avoid if you don't want to end up in the bottom of the pool.'

His wife, a tall, blonde woman with a spray of light freckles, said, 'We're all very proud of the job you're doing.'

I replied without thinking, in a sceptical tone, 'Really?'

She snorted, stifling a giggle, and waved a hand in front her face. 'I'm sorry,' she said.

'Don't mention it,' I said.

She turned her attention to Spicy, who was behind me in the queue. He took her hands in his and kissed both cheeks. 'Alice, darling, you look gorgeous.'

'Don't be ridiculous, Titus. I look like a diplomat's long-suffering wife. You look like an upended mop.'

'No, Alice,' Spicy replied, 'I look like a dissipated aristocrat and, as you well know, there's a world of difference.'

'I shall speak to you later,' she said, mock-sternly.

The next in line was the Deputy Head of Mission, an overweight Yorkshireman who introduced himself as Tony Hatton and made as if to punch me. 'How's the arm?'

'Getting better, thanks.'

'We should talk sometime. I like to be kept abreast of events at the front line, or in between them, so to speak.'

'Sure.'

Walking away from the line, Spicy linked arms with me. 'Something fierce for pleasure is loosed,' he said. 'Now let's find a drink.'

We were edging our way through the crowd when I sensed a presence beside me. Turning, I saw that it was Malak, the young man from the Sheep Market with the unsettling green eyes. His tattooed fingers brushed the fabric of my shirt.

'Jonah,' he said.

I almost flinched.

'Hey, Malak.' Spicy reached across, looping an arm around Malak's shoulders. They kissed on the mouth, Spicy's thin lips compressed against the flesh of Malak's.

After gently pushing Spicy away, Malak fixed me with an amused stare, 'Welcome, Jonah.'

'Everybody is a Brit, it seems,' I said uncomfortably.

'Your country has a fine tradition,' he replied.

'Let's drink buckets,' Spicy said, waving at the back of a passing waiter.

'Spicy's not convinced by you,' Malak said. 'Spicy thinks you might be a plant, a creature of Five or Six.'

'Don't talk rot,' said Spicy, on tiptoes, craning this way and that.

'What's there to spy on?' I said.

Malak smiled. 'Spicy feels threatened.'

'Why are you here, Malak?' I asked him.

'Your government very kindly gave me asylum; I retain a fondness for your country.'

'Malak's the local prodigal,' Spicy added, 'an Iraqi exile from the marshes returned to confound and astonish.'

'You're a Marsh Arab?' I asked him.

'No. Not originally.'

'Malak's origins are even murkier than yours,' said Spicy.

'I was raised in the north,' he explained, 'in the Kurdish mountains by the Yezidi sect. It was only later that I lived in the marshes.'

'Malak's a devil worshipper,' Spicy added.

Malak laughed lightly. 'It is true that the Yezidis believe that the devil was shown forgiveness by God and that he manifests himself on this earth in the form of a peacock. The Yezidis have been persecuted by the Arabs for centuries.'

'Not keen on the Arabs, are you, old son?' said Spicy.

'I'd be happy to see them all burn,' Malak answered.

I frowned. 'Burn?'

'Sure.' He shrugged. 'Why not? Remember Dresden? Hiroshima? You were not so punctilious about the Germans or the Japanese.'

'At last, a waiter!' yelled Spicy.

I caught sight of her alone at the back of the room, a head taller than those around her, at the centre of a palpable exclusion zone. She was standing beside a long table draped in cloth that served as the bar, wearing a white T-shirt that exposed her long brown arms and a pair of faded jeans. She was drinking gin and tonics poured for her by a white-liveried waiter, with what appeared to be a single-minded determination to get drunk. Beyond her were French windows that led out into a tiled courtyard and the embassy swimming pool. The party had already turned raucous. A number of oil people had been thrown in the pool. I felt suddenly heavy and ravenous, the sight of her enough to break one mood and bring on another.

I extended two fingers from the whisky glass in my outstretched fist, pointing. 'Who is she?'

Spicy leered drunkenly. 'You really are a glutton for punishment.'

'She's . . .'

Malak interrupted, 'She defies definition.'

'Oh yes,' came Hatton the Yorkshireman's amused drawl from Spicy's shoulder, 'she hits most people that way. She can't help it. Doesn't know how to switch it off.'

The ambassador's wife joined us and laid a pale hand on Spicy's shoulder. 'Whom are we talking about?'

Spicy pointed.

'Who is she?' I said.

'A loose cannon that needs to be tied to the deck,' said Alice.

'She's one of ours,' Hatton added. 'Diaspora. Her name is Miranda Abd al' Aswr. She's a Brit, a fully fledged passport holder, though by what route it was acquired is anyone's guess. According to local rumour, her father was some kind of Somali dissident. Her mother was Dutch Surinamese, with a squirt of Chinese. It's an agreeable combination. They say that if you stir the races together you get the most beautiful people.'

Spicy could hardly contain himself. 'Jonah is something of a mongrel too.'

'Ah, well . . .' Hatton said. 'There are always exceptions.'

'Jonah got hit with the ugly stick!' Spicy exclaimed.

I said, 'She's married?'

'Separated, divorced maybe, possibly widowed. Nobody knows.' Hatton shrugged. 'Her husband Bakr was a businessman who ran the import/export end of a family conglomerate called Azzam Holdings. Saudi by nationality, he came out of the Hadhramaut, the same Yemeni province as Bin Laden. They say he was in Afghanistan with Bin Laden. He disappeared into Iraq a few days after the tanks rolled in. She stayed.'

'Miranda was in the city throughout the occupation,' Alice said. 'She refused to leave. Ostensibly, she's a heroine. She harboured the British Ambassador for a while in one of the air vents in her house. There are, however, darker rumours.'

Malak was watching me with an amused and knowing smile.

'Tell me,' I said.

'Her husband was a business associate of Uday, Saddam's son,' Alice said. 'She knew Uday, some say intimately. There are rumours that he exercises a sort of droit de seigneur over his business partners' wives.'

'Are you saying she slept with Uday Hussein?' Spicy demanded.

'I'm passing on a rumour,' she said. 'That's what bored diplomats' wives do.'

'Not all they do,' said Spicy, meaningfully.

She reddened. 'You're drunk.'

'Uday was here during the occupation, supervising the systematic looting of the emirate,' Hatton added.

'Throughout that time she remained in the city and although the street she lives on was blockaded, her house was never searched. It's easy to see how the rumours got around. On top of that, a couple of days before the liberation she vanished with her son, only to resurface alone during the prisoner exchanges that followed the armistice. She claims to have been kept in Abu Ghraib prison. Isn't that right, Malak?'

'She was there,' Malak agreed.

I found myself staring at Malak's hands, his missing fingernails, and a slow, almost imperceptible shudder travelled down my body.

'Yes, Jonah,' he said, reading my expression. 'I have been a guest of Saddam's prison system.'

He watched me, amused.

'What is she doing here in Kuwait?' I asked.

'She manages the nomad museum down in Hawalli,' said Hatton. 'Ethnic stuff, Arab/Islamic artefacts – swords, rugs and manuscripts, you know; some Greek and Bronze-Age pottery from Failaka island. It's a fine collection, by all accounts.'

'There's a couple of Regency-era portraits and some David Roberts prints,' Alice explained. 'Her taste in men may be suspect but in other matters it is impeccable. I believe she does some work for a private human-rights organization in the Zone. She fights her corner. Perhaps you've seen her there?'

'I don't think so,' I said.

'She's mercurial,' said Hatton, in admiration.

'She's an axe murderer,' said Spicy.

'They say she gets drunk every Wednesday,' said Alice.

'They hang women in Abu Ghraib on Thursdays,' Malak explained.

There was a pause. Spicy said, 'And?'

Malak smiled, his teeth sharp and very white. 'The story, told by those that have survived, is that the Raees, Saddam, holds a party for the women at the prison every Wednesday night. He sends bottles of liquor, sometimes arak but sometimes French wines. The women do not know which one of them will die in the new day.'

'I'd get plastered,' Alice said.

'If a prisoner is particularly attractive she might be taken from the prison and driven to an apartment downtown, one of his hideouts away from the palace, where beauticians with hairbrushes and make-up kits prepare her before a guard leads her to a room with a bed and makes her strip naked and lie down. As she is lying there she feels drowsy and immobilized. When she can no longer move her limbs a door opens and the Raees enters from an adjoining room, naked. Without a word he climbs on top of her and satisfies himself.'

'More detail than necessary, Malak,' said Alice.

'I haven't finished, hear me out: there is a story that on one occasion he did not wait for the hangman. His doctor, who later defected and told the tale, was summoned one night to deal with one of Saddam's emotional disturbances. He arrived to find the Raees naked and blood-splattered, muttering incoherently. With the help of a bodyguard he managed to get the Raees onto the bed to administer a sedative. When he went to the bathroom to wash the blood off his hands he found a woman in the bathtub with her throat slit.'

There was a pause. I couldn't help but remember Odd, slumped in a stall, with his throat cut and an expanding lake of blood around him.

'I think I'm going to go and look for a drink,' said Alice.

'You should tell that story to our dissenting MPs,' said Hatton.

'Go and talk to her, Jonah,' said Malak, staring at me with his disturbing green eyes.

'Maybe that's not such a good idea,' said Spicy, a note of caution in his voice.

'Of course it is,' said Malak. 'Unforeseen consequences are what make life interesting.'

Sometimes you know, a spark leaps from eye to eye. It's inexplicable chemistry, you just know. Her irises were walnut-coloured and running at the edges like broken yolks and her skin was lucent, copper and bronze. There was an unbroken line of silver rings stretching from the top of her ear to her lobe. Just looking at her made me contemplate a lifelong relationship.

'Do you always drink on your own?' I asked her.

'They're frightened of me,' she replied. There was the suggestion of deep lines around her eyes, either laughter or sorrow, I couldn't tell. Her parted lips revealed even white teeth, an easy smile. 'Anyone with a mind and a vagina scares them witless.'

I had the sudden sense that any control over the situation that I had blithely assumed had fled. I found myself looking at her feet. She was wearing sandals that exposed her toes and she had painted her nails a deep mauve colour that complemented the darkness of her skin. Her toes were the ugliest part of her, large and flattened. For some reason I imagined that she had spent her teenage years with horses stamping on her feet. I had a vision of how drunk I was and looked up from her feet at her face.

'Somebody kissed you,' she said.

'No, nothing so dramatic; I recovered my eye.'

'It suits you. You look good now the bruises have gone down. You have a kind of asymmetrical beauty.'

'Thank you,' I said. 'What are you doing here?'

'That's easy: I'm a Brit.'

'That's not really what I meant.'

'I needed a drink,' she said. 'It's difficult here sometimes, unless you distil your own. I don't.'

'And tonight is bad?'

She took a second to answer. 'You've been listening to gossip.'

'It turns out you're a celebrity,' I said.

'D-list maybe. Once. The truth is I needed a drink and there isn't anywhere else to get one in this town. Don't you have bad nights?'

'Plenty.'

'You chew your nails,' she observed. 'You look worse for wear.'

I looked down and considered the seamed scar tissue and callused ridges, the revealing autobiography of my hands.

She said, 'I thought you'd be dead by now.'

I looked up from my hands. 'Why?'

'You seem to have a habit of being in the wrong place.'

I laughed. 'Story of my life.'

'How did you lose your eye?'

'I got blown up by a tank mine. In Gornji Vakuf.'

'I was in Zenica for a while,' she said, distantly. 'It was a tough time.'

'What were you doing there?'

'Looking for someone.'

'Someone?'

She frowned. 'I heard a rumour that my husband had

been fighting with the Muj against the Serbs and I went looking for him.'

'Did you find him?'

She looked at me. 'No. And I didn't find him in Peshawar, or Kandahar or Grozny, either.'

'I guess you must have really wanted to find him.'

'Are you mad? I wanted to know he was dead. Shit. That way I might get my son back.'

She lit a cigarette. Her eyes closed as she drew the smoke into her lungs – she radiated anger like heat from a fuel rod. 'They'd been gone for years by then but there were always rumours. When you live with uncertainty like that it can drive you crazy.'

'I suppose,' I said.

After a pause, she said, 'Why did you come here?'

I looked around me, searching for Spicy. He was over in the corner of the room, engaged in animated conversation with an airline steward. There was no sign of Malak. Spicy was laughing and with the fingertips of one hand he was stroking the steward's forearm. 'A friend invited me.'

She smiled, the anger banished. 'I'm not sure I can offer what he can.'

I smiled wryly. 'That's not what I'm looking for.'

She lifted her eyebrows and said, 'So what are you looking for?'

'You know, a full night's sleep,' I said lightly. 'Tenderness. Riches. Shit like that.'

She raised a sceptical eyebrow. 'Really?'

I shook my head. 'Actually, I want to roar like a fucking warlock.'

She laughed at me. There was something riotous and satisfying in her laugh; the ill-disciplined laughter of love-making.

'Amen to that.'

'The truth is I don't know,' I said, laughing myself. 'I've been out in the desert.'

We stared at each other and there seemed to be some monster of knowledge, both alluring and repellent, in her beautiful eyes. I felt a very strong desire to place my thumbs on the stark outline of her nipples and splay my fingers, cupping her ribcage. I felt the same riot of emotions that I had felt when I first saw her back in the Russian base. I wanted to lift her up and enfold her.

'Let's drink a toast,' she said.

'What shall we drink to?'

'Three a.m. No.' She shook her head, her teeth in her lower lip, suppressing laughter. Then she looked at me again and raised her glass. 'To the darkest hour.'

'Do I want to drink to that?'

'Of course; after this it starts getting lighter.'

We drained our glasses and there was a silence between us while we continued to stare at each other.

'I guess I wanted to say thank you,' I said eventually, 'for trying to rescue me.'

'Why? I didn't get you out.'

'You tried.'

'Sure.'

'Why?'

She shrugged. 'Word went around the souk in Umm Qasr that you were being held. I was at the souk. Human rights are my thing.'

'Really? I thought you were after the cars.'

She stared back neutrally. 'Cars?'

'Yes. Two Range Rovers imported by your husband's firm. Azzam Holdings? Lost at the time of the Iraqi invasion. About the same time as he buried eleven

Kuwaiti businessmen in a container out by the Iranian border.'

She tilted her head slightly and said, 'Big ones eat little ones here.'

'Law of the jungle?'

'Desert,' she said, emphatically.

'Yeah. Right.'

'Either you're very stupid or you're powerfully protected.'

'Stupid. Definitely stupid.'

She didn't like that. 'I should leave,' she said.

'Don't.'

She sighed. 'No choice, sugar.'

She brushed past me as she left, her thick black hair running across my shoulder.

I was in the bathroom staring at myself in the mirror, the alien and unfocused movements of my glass eye and the gaunt and unfamiliar outline of my face already burnt by the desert sun. Four framed prints of the English countryside were hanging on the wall. I suppose they must have been Constables. Thinking of Miranda, I felt an inexplicable euphoria. I mean, she had just walked out on me, but it didn't feel that way.

I was about to turn on the tap when Hanbury, the British colonel with the taste for solo golf, came in. He stood facing me with his back to the closed door.

'What are you doing talking to that whore?'

'I'm very well, thank you, sir. I find the desert suits me.'

'She's up to her neck in this, isn't she? Of course, I should have known.'

I turned on the tap and splashed water on my face. I

shook out my fingers and reached for a towel. Hanbury came over and sat on the edge of the row of sinks.

'I've been on the secret telephone,' he said. 'I hadn't realized what a sad story you are. Tell me, I'm interested, why did your wife leave you?'

'I don't think she liked the people I mix with.'

'Perhaps she had a point.'

'Perhaps,' I conceded.

'The police want to question you further in connection with a statement made by a military policewoman they have in custody. She says she helped kidnap your wife's lover.'

It was bound to happen. The police had made it clear in the immediate aftermath of the abduction that the case wasn't closed.

'You really are an interesting piece of work,' Hanbury said.

'I don't know what you are talking about.'

'Don't fuck with me. I could have you on the next plane back and the police waiting on the tarmac to meet you.'

'What is it that you want?'

'I want to know what Odd found.'

'Why?' I asked.

'I beg your pardon?'

'It's a simple question. Why are you so interested?'

'You're in league with that woman, I know it.'

'Then you know more than I do.'

'Don't play the innocent with me,' Hanbury growled. 'I was at this game when you were still a snotty-nosed kid.'

'Exactly what game is that?'

Hanbury sneered. 'Listen, I've met a few of you boys and I haven't met one of you without a venal streak. You think I don't have sources? You think I haven't heard what they are whispering on the streets? Whatever it is your friend Odd found, the Zone is full of people looking for it. Why would that be?'

'You tell me.'

'Because whatever it is, it's valuable to the Iraqi regime, which means that it is even more valuable to us.'

'Us?'

'I have resources, authority and access,' Hanbury said.

'And retirement coming up?'

'You're an impudent prick.'

'Yes I am,' I replied. 'What do you want, sir?'

'I want my share.'

'You'll get what's coming to you,' said Malak, so softly that the words were almost inaudible. He advanced across the white-tiled floor, one hand raised as if in warning, displaying the intricate tattooing on his palms.

'Get away from me,' Hanbury hissed, backing towards the stalls.

'What are you frightened of?' asked Malak, teasingly.

'Don't touch me.'

'Go,' said Malak, inclining his head in the direction of the door.

With his back to the wall and keeping as much distance as possible from Malak, a terrified-looking Hanbury slid out of the room.

'Interesting technique,' I commented. 'You'll have to show me how you do that.'

Malak winked. 'I have a reputation for hocus-pocus.'

He leant against the row of sinks, in almost exactly the same position that Hanbury had occupied a few minutes before. 'What did you say to make Miranda leave so abruptly?'

'I think that she has a pretty low tolerance for fools.'

'She's a very single-minded woman,' Malak said. 'She knows how to survive.'

'You were in prison together.'

'Exactly,' he said.

'How can I help you, Malak?'

He sighed.

'Spicy's drunk. Take him home to bed.'

The Emir's basement

I listened to the sharp twang of bed springs and a papery scuffling noise that was followed by a low and guttural moan. I was lying fully clothed on a made-up bed, shivering in the claustrophobic air-conditioned chill of an apartment in Salmiya, one of the seafront suburbs of the city that was popular with expatriate workers. The apartment was provided as transit accommodation for the British contingent to the Observation Mission and with its bare walls, cheap rattan furniture and frayed white sheets, it bore all the hallmarks of military occupation. In the next room the moans grew ever louder.

Spicy and Robin, the airline steward, were having sex; somehow I had imagined that it would sound very different, but it didn't. It sounded the same. I got up off the bed and padded across the white-tiled floor to the window at the farthest corner of the room and opened it, hoping for some respite from the noise.

Away from the desert there was no escape; hot sluggish air bathed my face like a warm, wet towel. Out in the Gulf, stars shone dully on a flat metallic sky. Another night that would eventually become morning and leave me wondering how I had spent the time. But I knew how I wanted to spend the time, I wanted a drink, more than one in fact; I had a ravening desire for drink – but I'd been through every drawer and cupboard and there wasn't a bottle in the place.

My mobile gave a single beep, a text message. The number was withheld. The message read: *Open the door.*

I went out into the hallway and stood listening by the door for a few moments but it was impossible to hear anything. I contemplated knocking on the door to Spicy's bedroom and telling them to pipe down, but what was the point?

My hand hovered over the front-door handle. I looked down at the display on my mobile.

I opened the door.

Malak was standing in the corridor. He raised a forefinger, wagged it gently in admonishment and then pressed it to his lips, commanding silence. Either side of him were two large men with beards. They were wearing the unmistakable uniform of the religious police. One of them wedged his large, flat foot in the door.

We stared at each other.

'Trick or treat,' said Malak softly, raising his eyebrows in an expression that seemed to say, *What can you do?*

'I'm all out of sweets,' I replied flatly.

Malak cupped his hand to his ear and together we listened in uncomfortable silence to the panting from Spicy's bedroom. The policemen frowned.

Malak fixed me with an intense stare. 'Jonah, if you call out or alert your friends, it may cause . . .' he paused and rolled his eyes in the direction of the policemen, 'complications.'

'What do you want?' I asked.

'To show you something.'

'And if I refuse?'

Malak shook his head. 'Your friends are engaged in an illegal activity. It will not go well for them.'

'I don't have any friends.'

He opened his hands. 'You have nothing to fear.'

In the time that it would have taken to hesitate we had gone down the stairs and out onto the street amid the rows of gleaming new cars and we were heading towards a Kuwaiti police car with darkened windows.

'You don't have any shoes,' said Malak.

Looking down, I saw that he was right. 'Do I need shoes where I'm going?'

Malak held the door of the police vehicle open for me. He didn't reply.

In the dark tunnels below the prison, the police captain and Malak walked arm in arm. I followed a few steps behind and with each step I became more fearful. Malak had told me, as we crossed a bleached white courtyard towards the low concrete block that we were now beneath, that this was the prison where the Kuwaitis had imprisoned collaborators after the liberation.

'Ten years later and there are still Iraqis and Palestinians missing inside,' said Malak. 'They can hold you for months, sometimes years, simply on suspicion of crime. You know, our friends are not so very different from our foes.'

'Friends?' I said.

'Allies,' countered Malak. 'You fought a war for them.'

'Did I?' I said.

The police captain met us at the entrance to the block holding a bamboo cane. He kissed Malak on both cheeks and dismissed the two policemen, who turned around and walked away without comment.

'This way,' said the police captain, indicating politely with his free hand.

He led us down several flights of an iron spiral staircase

and the air became cold and stale as we descended. At the bottom two guards in Sam Browne belts relieved me of my belt.

'No shoelaces,' I said, determined to show a brave face. It wasn't easy.

Malak and the captain set off down a passageway and I followed a few steps behind. They spoke to each other in low, indiscernible voices. The captain's cane swished regularly at the top of his polished boots.

I contemplated whistling.

'Will I have my own cell?' I asked.

Malak glanced back at me briefly before resuming his conversation with the captain.

At the end of a passage with green-stained concrete walls, we came to a barred gate beside which a Bedou in a drab and dirty dishdasha was lounging at a desk. Before him was a large book like a hotel register with sepia-coloured pages and spidery black lettering.

The captain instructed the man to open the door. The Bedou in the dishdasha considered Malak and me impassively and said, 'The name of the prisoner?'

The captain dropped a buff envelope on the desk and said angrily, 'Open the door.'

The Bedou pursed his lips, slowly opened a drawer and removed a bunch of keys. With his other hand he swept the envelope into the drawer. Then he pushed back his chair, careful to show that he was not in a hurry, and got up to open the gate. Standing, he was tall and stooped, with a prominent paunch. It occurred to me that not appearing in the register might be considerably worse than appearing within it – *disappeared without trace* was the phrase that sprang to mind. I was convinced that I was in serious trouble.

We followed the Bedou into a corridor lined with solid steel cell doors. It smelled of shit and vomit and as we passed one of the cells a mad howling started up from within. Everything seemed designed to magnify the sounds of misery.

'Nice place,' I said, struggling to keep my voice even.

Malak glanced across at me. 'I've seen worse.'

It seemed believable that he had.

The Bedou stopped by the open door of the last cell and motioned for us to enter. The room was bare concrete, a box twelve feet by twelve with porous grey walls; the only feature a stinking hole in the corner of the room, its rim streaked with faeces, and at the centre of the room a length of chain hanging loosely from a pulley.

A man was trussed naked on the floor, with his hands and feet tied behind his back and attached to the chain. At the sight of the captain he began to shake. His eyes were almost closed; both sides of his face were bloated beyond recognition.

The captain squatted down beside him and shouted, in English, 'Death to all infidels!'

'Please,' the man whispered hoarsely. He started to weep, the tears squeezed out between the swollen flesh, leaving streaks on his bloody face.

The captain stood and spoke softly, again in English, 'Where is the bill of lading, Colonel?'

I frowned. 'Colonel?'

'Don't you recognize him?'

I didn't at first. Not with the bruises and his face pressed against the shit-stained floor and the sparse tufts of hair above his ears wet with vomit. But when his eyes registered my presence and widened with outrage, I saw that it was Hanbury, the English colonel. Less than three hours had passed since I'd seen him at the embassy party. They'd made fast work of him. I wondered whether they were about to do the same to me.

'You . . . you . . . bastard,' he choked, bloody drool running out of his mouth onto the concrete. 'You . . . fuck . . . fucking . . . bastard.'

'He recognizes you, Jonah,' said Malak. 'The police have been talking to Hanbury about missing shipping documents. It's interesting how many times your name came up.'

'I don't know him,' I protested. 'I met him once on a golf course.'

The captain retired to the far side of the cell and lit a cigarette.

'I'm trying to get you out of here,' Malak murmured. I wasn't sure if he was talking to me or Hanbury. He knelt down on the floor and reached out to lay his tattooed hand on the crown of Hanbury's head. Hanbury squirmed. Malak sighed and withdrew his hand. He looked up and glanced around the cell. 'Believe me, I know what you are going through,' he said, 'but there's no need to be frightened. Not really.'

'Leave him be,' I said.

Malak frowned and assumed a pained expression. 'You think I'm enjoying this, Jonah?'

'Tell us where to find the cars,' the captain demanded between puffs on his cigarette.

'I can't help you,' I told him.

'Very well, Jonah,' said Malak. He began stroking the slick, wet hair behind Hanbury's ears and although he was addressing Hanbury his words were clearly directed at me and his eyes never once left mine. 'You see, Colonel, I have been told that the whole matter can be resolved, without unnecessary embarrassment for either side and no requirement for you to leave the country under a cloud. The police have even smashed up your car so you'll be able to explain the bruises as a result of the car accident. You know how badly they drive here in Kuwait; nobody pays attention to the road. You can say that you were talking on your mobile. It will be easy for you. And with my connections in the religious police, even the other issues, the illicit alcohol and the underage girls, can be put to one side. It won't cost you a thing. It couldn't be simpler. They just want the bill of lading.'

'I don't have it!' Hanbury screamed.

'We are negotiating,' Malak answered smoothly, with a raised eyebrow for my benefit. 'I've been authorized by the police to offer you a way out of the predicament that you have got yourself into. You've made a mistake but all you've lost is a little dignity. And we can all afford to lose that, can't we, Jonah?'

'I misplaced my dignity a long time ago,' I told him, grimly.

'I'm trying to be reasonable,' Malak countered. 'I'm trying to get the two of you out of here. The police just want to know where the bill of lading has got to.'

'I don't have it. I've told them a thousand times I don't have it,' Hanbury pleaded.

The captain said, 'So who does?'

'He does,' yelled Hanbury. He was looking at me. 'He's hidden it.'

'Is this true?' the captain said.

'No.'

'Are you sure? Perhaps you have forgotten?'

'I don't have it,' I told him.

The police captain reached over to the steel control unit

mounted on the wall and pressed a button. The chain jerked once and became taut and then hauled Hanbury up by his wrists and ankles. He screamed, mouth agape, his eyes bulging out of their sockets, and then fainted.

'How about now, *Englishman*, do you remember now?' the captain asked me.

Hanbury was hanging suspended with dislocated arms and a line of drool stretching from his mouth to the floor.

'Let him down,' I said.

Malak nodded to the captain. 'Please.'

Irritated, the captain grunted and punched the button. The chain reversed direction, depositing Hanbury in a heap on the floor.

'They've known about him for some time,' Malak explained. 'Buying alcohol in bulk at the Sheep Market and selling it to clients in the city. They even claim to have information that the same thing has been happening with Shia girls from poor families in Basra. Next to these crimes, selling the content of misplaced containers found in the Zone and the foreign military bases was viewed as a minor crime, beyond the jurisdiction of the police. But this container is different; the timing of the shipment and the identity of the consignee are issues of national security.'

'Why are you telling me this?'

'You killed the Norwegian,' the captain growled. 'Why did you cut his throat?'

'I didn't kill anyone.'

Malak assumed a sympathetic expression. 'I might as well tell you, Hanbury has admitted that he found shipping documents for a forty-foot container containing two armoured Range Rovers and, thinking that he could sell the vehicles for personal profit, he passed the documents to one of his staff, a logistician who was engaged in cataloguing containers, and instructed him to look for the container. This is the man who was with you at the Desert Palm bar. This is the man who had his throat cut.'

Hanbury opened his eyes again and started moaning softly.

'What do you think, Jonah?' Malak continued. 'Why did Odd go to a bar that is off-limits to UN personnel? Do you think that Odd found the cars? Perhaps he decided to cut Hanbury out of the deal? Maybe he got greedy?'

'I don't know.'

'Is there anything that you can tell them that will ease the suffering of this man?'

'No.'

'Tell them that you have the bill of lading.' His fathom-less green eyes stared hard at me. I held the stare until my eyes began to water. Then I looked away.

I said, 'If you are looking for something that Odd had, maybe you should speak to the people who killed him.'

'I have. They say they don't have the bill of lading either. They're animals – they want to break you on a wheel. They don't have the same sense of fair play as the Kuwaitis.'

'They?'

Malak sighed and shook his head. 'You don't want to know who they are.'

'Who are they?' I demanded.

'You don't ask the questions,' the captain said and broke his cane across my back.

I slid down to my knees, excruciating pain sheeting through my kidneys and lower back, lights flashing in my brain. The fuckers didn't have anything on me; I knew that – I knew that for sure.

'Are you all right, Jonah?' Malak stooped to ask.

'I tore it up,' I said, through gritted teeth. 'I tore it up into a thousand fucking pieces.'

'Are you serious?'

I gave him my best shit-eating grin, fighting through the pain to give him every tooth. 'You can torture me all the fuck you like.'

Malak straightened up and I had the same feeling I had when I first met him, of some instinct in him reaching into me. 'We might just do that,' he said.

Rolling onto my stomach, I crawled over to Hanbury and started to clumsily untie the knots on his ankles and wrists. I paused to catch my breath and looked across at the police captain, who had moved away from the control box and was now standing in the doorway, one broken half of the cane hanging loosely against his thigh. He made no move to stop me. 'Where are his clothes?' I demanded in Arabic.

The police captain merely shrugged and moved out into the corridor with Malak following. The screaming from the other cells seemed to have abated. I imagined that everyone was listening.

I cast aside the last of the rope, turned Hanbury over and dragged him by the armpits across the cell to the wall. I propped him up and scooped blood and saliva out of his mouth. He coughed.

'Get me out of here,' I called out.

'I'm trying,' said Malak, walking back into the cell. He squatted beside me, glancing once over his shoulder to see that the captain was not watching, and whispered, 'It's going to be OK.'

The police captain appeared in the doorway. He stroked his beard. 'Now, before it's too late. Give us the location of the cars.'

'I can't.'

He flung the end of the cane to the back of the cell in disgust. 'All right then. You can go.'

'It's over?'

'Oh no. No. It's not over for you until we find the container.'

Malak helped me to my feet and led me down the corridor past the man in the dirty dishdasha, who had returned to his desk by the door and was studiously ignoring our departure.

At the top of the stairs, Malak said, 'I'm going back down for Hanbury.' Then in a lower voice, 'Go back to the apartment.'

He lingered for a few moments, with his tattooed hand gripping my upper arm.

'We need to find that container, Jonah. Lives depend on it. Millions of lives.'

He called a guard, who escorted me across the courtyard to the entrance to the prison. It was still dark outside; barely an hour had passed since they had texted me in the apartment. I walked and about a half a mile from the prison I found a taxi.

I sat up straight in the back of the cab, to avoid pressing my skin to the seat.

A walk on the beach

The internal light on a car parked opposite the entrance to the apartment block flicked on as I passed it and I recognized Miranda sitting in the driver's seat, half-disguised by shadow. I walked over to her.

'How did you find me?' I said, leaning in the car window.

She had her forearms resting on the top of the steering wheel. 'Where else were you going to go?'

I laughed bitterly. 'Story of my life: stalked by beautiful women.'

'Make the most of it, sugar.' She reached up and flicked off the light.

'You want to come in?' I asked.

'It's not safe for me to be seen with you.'

'Safe for me or safe for you?'

She dismissed the question with a shake of her head. Her long fingers drummed impatiently on the top of the steering wheel. She looked up at me, the whites of her eyes bright in the darkened car. 'For your information, I didn't kill Odd.'

'He went to the Desert Palm to meet you.'

'I was never to going to show up.' She gazed into the road. 'I sent him to scare him.'

'You certainly did that.'

'He read my ex-husband's name on a piece of paper. He did some homework and got hold of my mobile number –

like you said, I'm a celebrity in this town. I didn't want anything to do with it so I sent him up to the Desert Palm.'

'He got more than a warning.'

'I'm sorry,' she said. 'I was trying to protect him.'

'From what?'

'Not here.'

I laughed at the irony of that as a lure. 'You expect me to go somewhere with you?'

'Well, I was thinking – will you come for a walk?'

It was unexpected, and for some reason that made me smile. 'Sure.'

I stepped back to allow her to get out of the car. She slid out of the seat and stood facing me with her hands tucked in the back pockets of her jeans. She was such a strange mixture of grace and gracelessness.

'Are you OK to walk like that?' she said, looking down at my feet.

'Like this?' I scuffed the soles of my feet back and forth on a paving stone. 'I could cross the empty quarter.'

She reached over her shoulder and the hazard lights flashed once on the wings of the Patrol as the locks clicked shut. We set off walking side by side towards the seafront.

'Did they take your shoes?' she said.

I laughed. 'No. I just forgot to wear any.'

'I used to walk on hot coals,' she said.

'You were in the circus?'

'Oh yeah. I was on the travellers' circuit from the age of seventeen, doing festivals. I've also been an artist's model, a bit-part actor, a stone-thrower, a dutiful wife, a has-been, a drunk . . .'

'I've thrown stones,' I told her. 'And I've had stones thrown at me. I've been both sides of the riot shield.'

'You don't seem like a soldier,' she said. 'You look like one, though.'

'Thanks.'

'Why did you join the army?'

'Everybody I knew was doing smack. I thought it was a way of not doing smack.'

'It's an extreme measure.'

'Sure. I'm not suggesting that it bears close examination.'

'Are you a good soldier?'

'Not really.'

She smiled. 'You know what this feels like – out after dark?'

'What?' I replied.

'Running away from school.'

'I think that we went to similar kinds of schools.'

We walked across a concrete intersection and down a slipway onto the sand. It was still warm, the heat of the day rising through the soles of my feet.

'Where are you from?' she asked.

'My family?'

'Yes. You do have a family?'

'My mother is from Guyana and my father is a Palestinian. I was born in the States.'

'You're an American?'

'Not really, I have citizenship, a passport – but not really. My parents were doing their doctorates at Berkeley. It was an accident of birth. I grew up in England, at boarding school in the Home Counties, and for some years – and for no reason that I can put my finger on – I've lived in Scotland.'

'You don't have a place,' she observed. We stopped at the water's edge and looked out at the Gulf. There was no surf. The running lights of tankers lay on the still water like drips of paint. It could have been a vast lake of oil.

'I've never really understood the grip that places have on people. And you?'

'My father was a Somali,' she replied. 'He was an exile, a political opponent of Siad Barre. He came from the most ethnically homogenous country in Africa. My mother was the opposite: she had a slice of everything; Scotland, Holland, Surinam, China, you name it. They lived in north London and that was my place, for a while anyway.'

I took a few steps into the warm, sluggish water. Lifting my foot, I half-expected it to come away black with oil.

'They died in a car crash when I was small,' she told me. 'After that, I was at a convent school run by nuns.' She lit a cigarette. 'I ran away at the first opportunity.'

I turned to look back up the beach at the yellow rectangles of light dotted on the apartment blocks. 'I've always found it difficult to understand people who believe in things.'

'You mean God?'

I nodded. 'Amongst other things.'

'You don't claim to understand very much,' she observed.

I laughed. 'It's true. I get more confused every day. What about you?'

'I have a mission,' she said.

'To find your ex-husband?'

'To get my son back,' she replied.

My mobile chirped like a cheerful sparrow. I took it out of my pocket and stared at the display – *number withheld*. I never recognized the caller these days.

'Don't answer it,' she said. 'People are listening.'

But I did. It was Alex, calling from an unknown location to tell me that a warrant had been issued for my arrest.

He said, 'It's all over, mate. The whole fucking thing is crashing to earth. What are you going to do?'

'I think I'm going to throw my phone in the sea.'

There was a lengthy pause. Alex said, 'Are you all right?'

'I'm in denial,' I said, lightly.

'Are you going to run?' he asked.

'Run?'

'You have a few hours.'

'Where would I go?'

There was a pause.

Alex said, 'I'm sorry, man. I didn't anticipate this.'

'No worries.'

'I won't call again.'

'Right.'

'You're a good man, Jonah – a man to rely on in a scrape. You've been a friend. Goodbye.'

The phone clicked dead. I stared at the display.

Miranda was watching my face. 'Run?'

'As in running away from school,' I explained. I flung the phone as far out into the sea as I could and it hit the water with a dull *plop*. 'Everybody is offering advice: run, hide, confess . . .'

'Don't trust anyone,' she said, emphatically.

There was a silence between us.

'You're not the only person to have told me that.'

'I can imagine,' she said.

'What about you?' I said. 'Should I trust you?'

A shade of something that might have been regret crossed her face like a passing cloud. 'I don't have a great track record.'

'Me neither,' I said. 'Me neither.'

She lit another cigarette. 'You don't smoke, do you?'

'Not any more. Listen, I need you to help me.'

'What?'

'Help me take my shirt off.'

She smiled. 'I thought that you were going to ask for something difficult.'

I unbuttoned my shirt and she helped peel it off my shoulders and back.

'Nasty,' she said.

'Looks worse than it is,' I told her.

'How do you know?'

'I'm guessing.'

'My father used to say that a bad beating can do you a world of good. He had enough of them to know what he was talking about.' She balled up my shirt and dipped it in the seawater. 'This is going to hurt.'

She started dabbing at the bruise with the dampened shirt.

'*Fuck!*' I breathed.

'Hold still,' she said, laughing. 'I'm almost done. There. You want to come back to the museum? Maybe we can find you a shirt.'

The museum

The heavy Indian door to the museum faced straight onto the road. She produced a set of keys attached to a strip of red ribbon from her back pocket and opened it after turning the tumbler in three separate locks.

'We used to have a night guard who lived here,' she explained. 'Now we have an alarm wired to the police station.'

The walls on either side of the steps were lined with nineteenth-century orientalist paintings and pieces of Arab furniture. At the bottom were two large glass-fronted show-cases, one containing ornate swords and daggers and the other small inlaid boxes. The lighting was low and discreet. There was something heavy and sensual about the place.

While Miranda was disabling the alarm, my attention was drawn to a large portrait of a striking-looking western woman wearing Bedouin costume, with Roman columns behind her.

'Who is she?' I asked.

'Lady Jane Digby el-Mezrab,' Miranda said. 'She married a sheikh from Palmyra in the Syrian Desert and stayed with him for thirty years. She lived with the tribe in their tents and adopted their customs.'

'Is that your story?'

She smiled. 'Something like that. You want me to tell you?'

'Sure.'

'Come on,' she said. 'Let's go up to the roof.'

She pointed out the nearby Iranian school and, across the ring road, the mushroom-shaped water towers that the Iraqi Republican Guard had used as gun positions during the occupation in the first war.

'You could see the men manning the guns. We gave them regular Iraqi names, Nathem and Kathem we called them. Like Jack and John.'

I was wearing one of her husband's expensive silk shirts, which she'd pulled off a rack at the back of a store room full of crates and held up against my chest.

'You're about the same size,' she said.

His initials were monogrammed above the breast pocket. On the rooftop, I asked her about him.

'Bakr loved to talk.' She glanced across at me, her face inches from mine. We were standing side by side, with our elbows touching, at the edge of the balcony that ran around the roof. 'He trained as an architect, in Houston; he was a devotee of Frei Otto but he never built anything. I guess I loved him when I believed he might deliver. I was young. Did you ever fall for somebody like that?'

'I was somebody like that,' I replied.

'So what happened?'

'Trouble came.'

'And now you're somebody else?'

'I suppose so,' I said, unconvincingly. It occurred to me then that there is no such thing as change in people; my marriage was never going to work. It was inevitable that I would let Sarah down.

'Where are you?' she asked.

I smiled grimly. 'Nowhere. Here.'

'Your face gives you away,' she said.

'I was thinking that, no matter how hard we try to change, every one of us returns to our true self in the end.'

'You got it.'

'What happened?' I asked.

'I married a pauper, who turned out to be a prince,' she explained.

'Sounds like a fairytale.'

'I preferred the pauper. In Afghanistan it was the struggle for freedom. When I first met him he was so fired up. We were in Peshawar, in Pakistan, I was doing volunteer work for an NGO and he was mobilizing the Mujahideen to fight the Soviet occupation. We met in the courtyard at Greens Hotel. He just walked up to me. It was exciting. I was eighteen years old. A runaway.'

'And here?'

She shook her head. 'Family money.'

'What happened?'

Miranda folded her arms and hunched her shoulders and I found myself studying the shadows play in the hollow of her neck. 'Simple. The Jihadis won. They beat the Russians. And then it was time to go home. I mean, I thought I was the one playing the war tourist but in fact it was Bakr. It had been his small rebellion against his family, his gap year. I had no idea how wealthy his family was and how persuasive that could be: he wasn't exactly candid with me. I learned about him in fits and starts, depending on what he decided to dole out. We got up one morning and he just said come to Saudi. They welcomed him back with open arms; they were even OK with me. Of course, they wouldn't give him any responsibility, not at first. We drifted from palace to palace around the kingdom, getting bored and stoned. I got pregnant. Eventually they threw

him a bone. He had an uncle up here running an import/
export offshoot of one of the holding companies, buying
and selling goods, mostly in Iraq. The old man was diabetic
and the business was dropping off but Bakr was convinced
that it had potential. He was right. He made a lot of money.
We had a baby. I suppose we were happy.'

'But he fell in with a bad crew?'

She smiled, her teeth bright white in the darkness. 'Sure.
It's a cliché. What do you expect?'

'Who were the cars for?'

'Uday.'

'Saddam's son?'

'Sure.' She laughed. 'You really want the story?'

'I'm waiting.'

'OK. I imagine Uday saw a film or read a comic and
suddenly he had it in his head to have a customized fleet of
armoured Range Rovers for his bodyguards. He probably
asked for a lot of leather and chrome. Bakr found them for
him in Kazakhstan on a trip. He bought them from a
wealthy Russian businessman who'd picked them up at
auction back in Britain. Uday could have bought a convoy
of armoured Mercs brand new – I mean he already had a
fleet of the latest Mercs – but these Range Rovers had been
used by the Royal Protection Squad to escort the British
royal family. You could see how it would appeal to Uday. I
mean, if you're a first generation dictator's son, the notion
of dynastic succession upheld through successive gener-
ations is irresistible. On a simpler level I think Uday was
turned on by the idea that Princess Diana might have
parked her immaculate butt on the cream leather seats.
Let's face it. Thugs love Diana, the world over.

'The cars were shipped in a forty-foot container and
cleared the docks at Doha two days before the invasion.

My husband and son disappeared on the day of the invasion and so did the container. That was the last I heard of the container until the Norwegian guy called me.'

'And you sent him up to the Desert Palm, where somebody killed him.'

'That's about it, sugar.'

'So why kill Odd?'

'I don't know,' she said. 'It's a mystery.'

'You were close to Uday Hussein.'

'You've been listening to gossip.'

'Yes.'

There was a moment of perfect stillness and quiet.

'What do you want?' I said.

'I want to find my son and I want to get him the hell away from this awful place.' She turned so that she had her back to the balustrade and she was facing me, with her ageless walnut eyes searching mine. 'What are you doing here?'

I thought for a while. 'All my life things have happened to me. I've fallen into things.'

'And?'

I shrugged. 'Why change?'

She paused and turned her face towards the city and beyond it to the desert, its vast blackness.

'There's a storm coming,' she said.

'You can tell?'

She looked back at me. 'You think I'm a witch?'

'I don't know.'

'Oh, sugar, I saw the weather forecast, that's all.'

I felt as though I was plunging to earth. I reached out with my fingers until they came in contact with her hair. I gathered it in a thick bunch in my hand and leant forward, drawing her lips to mine.

The thin coat of lipstick melted under my tongue, a

murmur of sweetness and she opened her mouth wide and a stream of air from her lungs raced inside me.

Some time later I told her, 'I tore up the bill of lading.'

'I know,' she said. At least I think that's what she said.

I straddled Miranda, the tip of my tongue running down the cord of her spine. Her skin gave off a warm and musky smell. We were lying naked on a pile of haphazardly strewn Bedouin rugs, with the museum's exhibits on the shelves around us and our hurriedly discarded clothes in crumpled piles on the stairs.

I kneaded the skin of her shoulders and ran my thumbs down the ridges of her backbone, following the line drawn by my tongue. There was a small purple bruise at the base of her spine from where the stiff denim of her jeans had rubbed against the nub of bone. I nipped at her skin with my teeth and she squirmed beneath me.

I slipped my fingers back and forth along the divide of her buttocks until I felt the wrinkled opening, warm and moist like a sea anemone, throb against my gently circling finger. I pushed one into the opening, which at first constricted and then opened to meet me like a flower.

She gasped and raised herself on her elbows, gazing at me over her shoulder. I looked up and our eyes met. She murmured, 'Yes.'

I felt a shiver pass through me, a moment's sudden pause.

'Please,' she said.

I moved my hands up her flanks and rested my forearms on her hip bones and pressed my fingertips into the small of her back. Slowly, I pushed into her.

A sharp intake of breath, then she relaxed and exhaled and I pressed as far into her as I could go and she sighed softly beneath me, her face turned down and pressed into the geometric patterns, her fingers clawing at the edges of the rugs. I put my lips down to her hair and whispered: 'Are you OK?'

She murmured, 'Don't stop . . .'

I lifted myself up onto my knuckles and looked down at her smooth and muscular back to where our two bodies were joined, my hips pushing her buttocks into a heart-shaped mound. Energy surged through me and I pushed again. I could feel my heart pounding.

I reached across her belly, my fingers sliding into the dampened fold of flesh beneath and the sounds issuing from her throat became hoarser with each passing moment.

I started kissing and softly biting her neck and then my lips were against the metal of the rings that ran through her ear and I was whispering in her ear. She had her hair thrown back, her rolled-up eyes as pale as old ivory. I had no idea what I was saying.

She gasped in her throat and then thrashed and yelled. And as she came I let myself go, let the tempo of my thrusting run out of control until a jolt like mains electricity went blasting through every cell of my body and I came deep inside her.

I collapsed onto her slippery back and buried my face in her hair, panting, with my chest heaving.

'Mmmmm,' she murmured into my neck.

I rolled off and lay on my side with my arms wrapped around her. I could feel her heart pounding against her ribcage.

After a while, she said, 'You want a drink?'

'Sure.'

She got up off the rugs and walked across the room. I

watched her shoulders move, her back, buttocks, legs and
the mane of tangled hair like spun sugar reaching down her
back.

'Ice?'

'No.'

We lay with our faces pressed together. In the museum the
only light came from the glass cases holding the exhibits
and the candle that she had carried with her down from the
roof. It fell on her hair and on her shoulders, the puckered
areola of her vaccination scar, the angular curve of her
thighs and the soles of her hennaed feet.

She was remarkable; I wanted to give her my life.

She slid her hand along the sweat of my belly,
through the curls of hair and, starting at my shoulder,
ran the tip of her tongue along the scab of my recent
knife wound.

'What are you doing?' I asked sleepily.

'Didn't you ever have a thing for wounded animals?'

'Not me,' I replied. 'I had more of a thing about throwing
shopping trolleys off the top of multi-storey car parks.'

She smiled and shook her head. 'Didn't you ever have a
pet?'

'I kept spiders.'

She wrinkled her nose. 'I guess I should have known. Do
spiders get sick?'

'Not often. I had a tarantula once, a big female; she fell
off a table and split her abdomen.'

'Did she die?'

'No. I fixed her.'

'How?'

'I superglued the wound.'

'That's not a solution.'

I laid the back of my hand against her cheek. 'For spiders it is.'

She raised herself on one elbow and looked down at me. 'You could help me get my son back.'

'Could I?'

'Maybe.'

The flesh of her breasts had been softened by feeding, by her missing son; my kneading fingers drew the skin upwards towards her large, purplish nipples. They swelled beneath the pads of my fingertips.

She sighed and shifted her legs, parting them slightly. My fingers traced her mid-line, reading the signs of childbirth sinking into the post-natal groove that separated the walls of muscle.

'We'll find them,' she breathed, but I wasn't sure who she meant by *we*.

She leant into my shoulder, her teeth sinking into the meat. Later, I felt the blink of her lashes on my shoulder. I closed my eyes to sleep.

I smelled coffee and after it a sharp streak of sulphur. She was sitting, angular and bony, at the edge of the cushions, her hennaed feet free of the tangle of the sheet. She was wearing a short blue dress and had one knee drawn up with her chin resting on it and the other leg tucked under her and the flesh of her sex displayed. She winked at me and blew out the match in her fingers. The contents of my wallet were spread out on the floorboards, my daughter's wax drawing and the picture of the polar bear cut from the magazine.

'What time is it?' I asked, yawning and scratching.

She took a long slow drag on the cigarette, turning her face away from me to exhale.

'It could be morning or night,' I said, bunching the sheet in my lap.

She turned back to me, smiled indulgently and combed her fingers through my stiff hair. 'It's morning.'

'I slept,' I said. 'I mean, I really slept.'

She passed me a mug. 'Here, drink this.'

The coffee was black and unsweetened, a jolt to the brain. She handed me the wax crayon drawing. 'Who did this?'

'My daughter; she's six.'

'You're married?'

'Divorced.'

She took another drag on her cigarette and shook her head. 'Hell, I've never seen a face go in so many different directions.'

'Sorry.'

'Don't apologize, Jonah. Where are they?'

'Scotland,' I told her, 'on an island.'

'I've never been to Scotland,' she said and folded up the drawing again. Next, she passed me the picture of the bear. 'I read somewhere that the polar bear will be extinct in the wild in sixty years.'

'Sixty years is a long time,' I said.

'If you stay here, I'd be surprised if you made it to next week.'

'I don't have anywhere else to go,' I said.

'You have a daughter,' she chided me. She was right. I had every reason to live.

She filled the resultant silence by resting the meat of her thumb against the side of my face. 'Soon we have to go,' she said. 'The staff will come to open the museum.'

'I tore up the bill of lading,' I said.

'I know, you told me,' she said. She stubbed out the

cigarette in her mug and stood up. 'I'll drop you in town, near a taxi rank. You'll have to make your own way back to Salmiya. It's better if you're not seen with me.'

We moved about the room and up the stairs towards the roof, rolling back the arc of our passion, picking up our casually discarded clothes. Dressed, we walked downstairs together. She brushed against my shoulder and at some point we joined hands. She opened the main door, pointing to where the car was parked and holding the car keys. I stepped cautiously into the gritty heat.

I took several faltering steps before returning to the museum door, strangely reluctant to go out into the light. We kissed.

'You poor boy,' she said, touching my face with her fingertips. 'You better take care of yourself.'

'I'll do my best,' I said.

'Go on and get in the car. I have to set the alarm.'

I lingered in the doorway; she looked across at me from the keypad and smiled. I contemplated a speech – an explanation, an expression of commitment beyond ordinary meanings. But there was a simpler answer.

'GZ5003004NR,' I told her.

Yes, I tore up the bill of lading – but not before I'd memorized the numbers.

'I'll help you get your son back.'

Shamal

I felt the shaking as a vibration, distorted as if I was submerged in thick fluid. It seemed to have been going on for a long time. The shadow of someone was leaning over the bed, a hand gripping my bicep. I squinted upwards and a bird seemed to strut above me with its emerald-blue neck outstretched and its tail feathers fanned and on each feather a single iridescent eye.

'Rise and shine,' said a soft and familiar voice.

'Malak,' I croaked.

He was perched on the edge of the bed, wearing a sarong wrapped around his skinny midriff. On his hairless chest was an elaborate peacock tattoo.

'What are you doing here?' I managed.

'Didn't you get my messages?' he said, his tattooed fingers gently stroking the flesh of my upper arm.

I sat up abruptly and swung my legs off the bed, setting the soles of my feet on the cold tiles. I scratched my hands across my scalp. 'I threw my phone in the sea.'

'After your friend Alex told you that the police have issued a warrant for your arrest?'

'Yes.' I staggered about naked, picking up my clothes. 'You've been listening in.'

'That's an expensive shirt,' Malak said. 'Did Miranda give it to you?'

'Yes.'

'Did you tell her anything?'

I rounded on him, angrily. 'That's an interesting tattoo, Malak. Did the Yezidis give you that?'

'No,' he replied, calmly. 'This was done to me later. In prison.'

There was a pause.

'You know I remember her, from Abu Ghraib; from the prison,' he said. 'I know who she is underneath.'

There was a further pause.

'What do you want?' I asked, repeating the question that I had asked him the night before.

Malak smiled. 'Don't worry, your secret is safe with me.'

'What secret's that?' enquired Spicy from the doorway.

'It's time we took Jonah back to the desert,' Malak said.

'We'll all go,' said Spicy. 'After breakfast we'll take a drive out to the Zone. Bacon and eggs, anyone?'

'Bacon?'

'Yes, old chap, the forbidden swine. Robin has rather thoughtfully smuggled a few rashers in. Like it crispy?'

'We'll be along in a minute,' Malak told him. Spicy raised his eyebrows and headed back towards the kitchen whistling.

Malak was still staring at me.

'What is it that you want?' I demanded.

'We're all on the same side,' he said.

'Are we?'

We drove across the city to the oilfield road and out across the shimmering asphalt, into the closed military areas. We worked our way up a convoy of over a hundred US vehicles, tank transporters and container lorries interspersed with Humvees. CH-53 Sea Stallion helicopters roared overhead.

The morning was clear but there was a stark and brittle quality to the air. The sunlight was reflected off the dunes like a sheet of polished metal. Dust devils snaked across the sand and spent themselves on the edges of the expressway. Exhaust fumes rolled in through the windows and the heat boiled out of the sun, scorching the plastic seat covers and curling the paint on the mottled bonnet of the Land Cruiser. The asphalt road was wet-black and rippling in the distance, distorted by heat waves. The straggly thorn-bush verges were blackened with fire and in some places still burned. Sometimes above the noise of the car's engine, we could hear the snap and crackle of the flames.

'Burning bushes,' Spicy mused. He pulled a face. 'A sign?'

'There's a storm coming,' I told them.

Malak regarded me with curiosity. 'How do you know?'

'I heard it.' And now I could feel it, in the stark imminence of the copper-coloured sky and the claustrophobia of the Land Cruiser, and in my sinuses, which were gummed together in a lump.

I sank low into the seat and, closing my eye, thought of Miranda. I felt exhausted and exhilarated and, like someone clinging on to the last moments before waking, I tried to hold on to the memory of the texture of her skin and the warm and musky smell that rose off her hair.

'Jonah doesn't sleep much,' observed Malak.

I opened my eye. Spicy frowned and looked across at me.

'I just haven't woken up yet,' I replied.

Malak returned his attention to the desert, the trace of an ironic smile on his lips. I wondered how much he knew and whose side he was on and indeed who the hell he was.

We were driving through an area of oil refineries protected by high wire fences, the gantry scaffolds and stainless-steel pipe work alone in the emptiness, alone, that is, until you looked closer and started to see the armoured personnel carriers and tanks hidden under camouflage netting.

'That's why we're here,' Spicy announced, 'to protect the oil.'

'That's not why Jonah's here,' Malak said. 'Jonah kidnapped his wife's lover.'

'I was angry,' I said, watching a passing Humvee, trying to make light of it, hoping that it might be sufficient explanation.

A crackle of distant thunder echoed across the desert. It sounded as if the earth was being torn and moved.

'Jonah may be right,' said Spicy.

'Will it rain?' Robin asked.

'I don't think it's that kind of storm.'

'What other kind of storm is there?' Robin said.

'Storms,' said Spicy, 'come in all shapes and sizes.'

We left the oil refineries and military convoys behind and when we turned off the asphalt onto Crown Route there were no other vehicles to be seen. We were back in the Zone.

'Home,' said Malak, taking a large and ostentatious breath.

There was a distinctive rippling movement on the track ahead. At first I thought it was leaves on the track, but there were no trees.

Dry lightning revealed them crossing the cinder-dry
track – more than could be counted – with their sleek
brown bodies slung low amid the multiple arches of their
legs. At first it seemed that you weren't seeing right, that
ragged webs of sand and lightning and motion and filthy
glass had cooked up an illusion, a nightmare from the
cinema. But then the headlights showed them more
clearly, in the middle of Crown Route, an exodus of
spiders.

We stopped to watch and I got out of the Land Cruiser.
Looking back, I saw two of them convulsing on the hard-
packed sand behind us, wounded by our tyres.

'What are they doing?' Spicy asked.

'They're all going the same way,' I said.

At first I wondered if it was some form of mating hunt. I
picked one up, a female. I briefly imagined packs of
sexually ravenous females hunting males.

Another emerged from the side of the track. It walked
taller than the one in my hand; its legs were longer but its
body was smaller. As it crossed the glare from our headlights, I saw that its hair was darker, almost black.

'Male,' I said, 'both sexes.'

The spider's entire body is a tactile ear. Some of the hairs
are specially built for vibration; they know the direction of
any disturbance.

'They're running,' I said, thinking aloud.

There was a sound, a sigh that became a soughing, a
gentle whistling.

'The horizon is lost,' said Malak.

'Jonah,' said Spicy, and there was something in his voice
that made me look up, into the flat immensity of a storm
that rose into the cloudless brilliance like a wall.

'Oh boy,' said Robin.

The whole surface of the desert appeared to be rising in obedience to some supernatural force. A solid wall that hurtled towards us. No longer a whisper, it rose to a howl.

'*Shamal*,' said Malak.

'That kind of storm,' I said.

'Get in the car,' commanded Spicy, stumbling backwards towards the Land Cruiser, his voice rising to a yell.

Turning, I saw that Malak was grinning, with his eyes tightly closed and his nose tilted upwards to the roiling wall of sand and his arms outstretched.

'Malak!' I screamed.

'You called up the storm, Jonah!'

At first it was like flurries of hail, tiny pebbles rising and lashing my shins, knees and thighs, and then the ground buckled like hot plastic and the storm's cargo struck and the sky was shut out and the Land Cruiser was picked up and rolled over.

'Jonah! Malak!'

I staggered blindly with my arms flailing in front of my face. I didn't know whether to curl up into a protective ball or keep moving. I tried to keep moving but with every step the force of the storm grew stronger, the sand giving way beneath me as it was sucked into the air. I was sinking and the ground was rising. Everything was spinning, as if I was caught in a whirlpool. The sand ran like water. I lost all sense of direction. Panicked, I opened my mouth to yell and it was instantly filled with choking sand.

I realized that I was drowning. I dared not open my eye.

I heard a voice out of the darkness that I thought was Legion's voice saying, 'You can't win against the sand, not against nature.'

Then a vicelike grip closed on my upper arm and I was dragged into the crumpled cab of the upturned Land Cruiser. Malak reached across my body and pulled the door shut.

I was doubled up in the cramped cab with my shoulders against the steering wheel, retching into the upturned roof while clouds of sand swirled around my head. Outside, the storm was relentlessly scouring the outer surface of the car, turning the splintered windscreen milky and opaque.

We shifted and scratched and with every movement the sand rose in clouds around us, forcing its way into the cab of the Land Cruiser.

In the back, Spicy was holding Robin in his arms. 'How long will this last?'

'A storm can last for hours,' said Malak, hoarsely, 'perhaps days. Entire armies have disappeared in the sand.'

'We're going to run out of bloody breath,' gasped Spicy.

'Give it a rest,' I said, between dry heaves.

'All right for you, love. I've got reasons to live.'

'Maybe Jonah has too,' said Malak, winding his keffiyeh around his head. 'Cover yourself. Keep your eyes closed. Breathe through the cloth, a sip at a time.' He reached out and gripped my shoulder. 'We will survive.'

I wrapped a cloth around my head. 'Cars have tried to kill me before,' I croaked.

'What's the best Iraqi job?' asked Spicy. After that I think he said 'foreign ambassador'.

The storm raged without ceasing or relenting. The air around us became fetid and stale. We were entombed in the roaring darkness.

After a time I tried to move my legs but I couldn't. I tried to move again, this time with all my strength, and managed to move my feet and toes a little. The sand came up to my waist. We were slowly being buried alive. I reached up with one hand and touched the foot well above my head. I ran my fingers across its rough surface.

I didn't want to die. Just as before, standing over Odd's bloody corpse, when the time came and given the choice, I desired to live. With my bare hands I started to scrape at the sand, shifting it away into the darkness so that, for a few precious seconds, I could move my legs. I felt the others working at the same task in the cramped space around me, fighting back the sand that trickled into the gap created by each movement.

The storm raged on, hours passed. During this time I managed to keep the sand back just enough to move my head and arms but I wasn't able to do any more. There was nowhere to move the sand to.

Then the thirst came: the hot, dry sand sucking the moisture out of our throats. I felt my tongue cleave to the roof of my mouth. Then it began to swell, so my breathing became almost impossible because of the huge spongy blockage that filled my mouth.

I could no longer tell whether I was still breathing. I felt myself drifting into a dark stupor, into haunted dreams of water, the cool blue expanse of a great body of water; my body plunging into the water, the air bubbles from my mouth rising out of the depths, spiralling towards the distant surface.

I was dying. I saw my daughter's face floating in the water before me, her hair gently stirring in the current. Her gap-toothed smile.

I wanted to reach out and hold her.

*   *   *

Something changed. I tried to fathom what it was but my mind was numb and unresponsive.

I listened. I heard nothing. There was no sound. I wondered if I was dead but only for a second. Perhaps I was deaf. Then I realized: the wind had stopped. The storm was over and I was alive.

I struggled to work my way out of the sand. I managed to free my right arm and reached out to touch Malak's covered head. I tried to speak, to tell the others, but when I opened my mouth no sound came out, my tongue was too swollen.

A handful at a time, I scooped away at the sand, pushing it into the darkness around me. Then I felt the sand abruptly cascade out from under my fingers. Painfully I pulled the cloth away from my face.

Sweet, fresh air seeped into the car. I opened my eye and was dazzled by the light. The windscreen had shattered and I had opened a tunnel to the outside.

I started frantically digging at the hole, widening it and taking great gulps of air. I pushed the sand around and behind me like a swimmer, packing it into the spaces that I created with every movement. I felt the others stirring. I could move my legs; there was a rush of tingling blood followed by involuntary contractions as strings of cramp knotted my sinews. I twisted and heaved, struggling through the rushing sand as through a waterfall.

'*Push!*' I heard myself say.

Yes, again a turbulent rebirth: I slithered out through the windscreen onto a pristine sand slope, rolled over and lay belly-up, with my mouth open but no sound coming out. Spasms shot up my legs.

Malak emerged a few seconds later and we slid together to the foot of the dune. He rolled over, arched his back and clawed his hands as if electricity was surging through his body. Beside him, I kicked off my boots and socks and started moving my toes. A few seconds later Spicy emerged in an explosion of sand and sparkling shards of windscreen, with his arms windmilling frantically.

For a minute or so, we flick-flacked like fish. Then we faced each other, crouching on our hands and knees, heaving and panting. Our lips were so swollen that when we tried to speak they split like ripe fruit.

'Robin,' croaked Spicy, gripped by sudden panic. He crawled back up the dune and disappeared into the hole.

I climbed unsteadily to my feet. I had started shivering uncontrollably.

I shielded my eye and looked out over the desert but did not recognize it. The landscape had changed completely. I looked upwards, beyond the unfamiliar horizon, at the dome of the sky and couldn't help noticing how clear and beautiful it was.

I took a few slow, stiff steps. Small eddies of wind twisted across the surface of the desert like after-shocks. There was still a fine haze of sand at about knee height in the still air.

Suddenly hundreds of jam-jar size plugs of sand popped like champagne corks and a horde of spiders emerged, shook the sand off their legs and scuttled away.

I glanced to see if either Malak or Spicy had seen the spectacle but both of them were inside the vehicle. I looked back but there was no sign of the spiders.

A plastic bottle of water was flung out of the hole and after it an RPG-7. I stumbled over to the bottle, grabbed it and snatched off the cap. I took small sips, the tepid water running down my parched throat. Malak slid out of the hole and held out his hand for the bottle. I passed it to him and he gulped at it hungrily.

'Robin?' I croaked.

Malak shook his head. I slung the rocket launcher over my shoulder.

Spicy climbed out of the hole soon afterwards, dragging a pack of water. He slid down the slope and stumbled away, the cardboard carton leaving a shallow groove in the sand behind him. He was muttering angrily and when I caught up with him there were tears running down his cheeks.

'*Fuck*,' he said. '*Fuck. Fuck!*'

'Slow down,' I said.

He suddenly collapsed. I knelt beside him, tore the plastic packaging on the six-pack, opened one of the bottles and let water trickle between his lips. After a while he opened his eyes and looked up at me.

'Sorry, old chap,' he whispered.

'There's nothing to apologise for,' I told him.

'He wanted to see the desert for real; he'd only ever seen it from the air.'

There was no consolation I could offer. We passed the bottle back and forth.

'What now?' I said.

'The radio's out, the sat phone's out. Nobody knows we're here. So we walk.'

'Which direction?'

Spicy produced a GPS from his pocket and switched it on and a minute or so later the LCD lit up and he pointed and said, 'That way.'

We ruffled our hair and shook the sand out of our pockets and the seams of our clothes. Spicy lit a cigarette and immediately broke into a coughing fit that left him retching on his hands and knees. When he had recovered we lifted him up and started walking.

We trudged slowly across the desert, our feet sinking into the freshly deposited sand. Within minutes our eyes were burning and sore. We had a bottle of water each.

'Where are we going?' I asked eventually.

'The patrol base,' Spicy said.

The battle of Patrol Base Three

In the distance there was a coil of yellow smoke and as we approached we saw the distinctive dogleg of the watch-tower and the new and unfamiliar dunes that surrounded it.

'Maybe they're signalling,' said Spicy, without much conviction.

A gust of wind came up and glowing cinders swirled like ragged fireflies around the tower.

'The camp's on fire,' I said, filled with sudden foreboding.

Then there was the distinctive crackle of small-arms fire and I knew that the camp was under attack. I started to hurry, shambling through the ankle-deep drifts, the RPG rattling against my shoulder.

'Jonah,' Spicy called out in warning. I stumbled forward heedlessly.

At that moment a dozen armed men rose from behind a dune to my left and advanced towards the buckled ribbon of the perimeter fence. Russians: I recognized their voices and shabby green uniforms. They drove each other on with sharp cries and shouts and occasionally one of them would drop to his knees and fire a shot in the direction of the cabins. Answering fire was sporadic and poorly aimed. I followed them, keeping low against the sand.

Coming around the side of a dune, I saw from a distance that the ops cabin was burning and beside it there was a half-buried Land Cruiser. There was a dead man in a black uniform lying in a tangled heap beneath one of the picnic tables, thick black blood oozing out of his keffiyeh onto the sand.

A sudden burst of automatic fire from one of the cabins forced the Russians into cover behind the generator shed and sent me scurrying in the opposite direction, along a newly formed ravine between sand dunes. I was moving away from the cabins in the direction of the watchtower. As I ran down the ravine, a man stood up on the crest above me. With a raised AK he began firing, shooting at the Russians amongst the dunes.

Looking up at him, I recognized Sadeq, the Kurd from the Iraqi police post.

'Sadeq,' I called, without thinking.

Sadeq turned and searched the stark shadows below him. He seemed to recognize me but levelled his rifle at me all the same.

'Go back,' he shouted hoarsely. He fired randomly in my direction and I crouched down, slipping the RPG off my shoulder.

Colonel Charles appeared from the direction of the cabins, shambling head-down along the ravine towards me. His meaty arms, bound at the wrists with white plasticuffs, swung back and forth as he ran. Raising the rifle, Sadeq fired. The bullet struck him smack between the eyes and I saw his face sucked in backwards so that he looked suddenly like a Cyclops.

Balancing the stalk of the rocket-propelled grenade on my shoulder, I slipped off the safety catch and raised the aiming sight. I rested my cheek against the block.

Sadeq fired again in the direction of the cabins. I stood up and shot him in the chest.

I was kneeling over him when another group of Russian soldiers appeared over the crest of a dune. Lying down, they began to fire at the dunes beyond the cabins.

An officer crawled over to me. It was Nikitin, Korobko's deputy. He glanced down at the body and grimaced. The warhead had travelled less than thirty metres before hitting its target and failed to arm. Unexploded, it stuck out of Sadeq's shattered ribcage. 'An Iraqi?' he asked breathlessly.

'A Kurd,' I said, thinking that it made a difference. Nikitin looked around and then jumped to his feet and ordered his men down the slope of the dune towards the cabins.

Nikitin forced Sadeq's AK into my hands. He shouted, 'If they come your way, shoot at them.'

The Russians moved off and I slid back down the dune to Colonel Charles. Spicy was kneeling over him. 'He was a nice old codger,' he said.

Two figures raced along the ravine towards us. I lifted the rifle to my shoulder but they kept coming. It was Patrice and Toona. They were both cuffed. They saw me kneeling beside Colonel Charles with the rifle in my hands but ran on towards the open desert.

'You had better get out of here,' Spicy told me.

Disgusted, I threw down the rifle and headed towards the cabins.

Per came over the crest of a dune, cradling an AK, his face blackened with gunpowder soot and his wrists bloody and raw. He found me standing amongst the cabins.

'Jonah,' he said, quietly. 'You're late for your own disco party.'

'Looks that way.' I turned my attention to the body a few feet away under the picnic table. 'Who were they?'

'Palestinians. Saddam uses them sometimes; it is convenient if he wishes to issue a denial.'

'And Sadeq?'

Per shrugged. 'One less Kurd, who cares?'

He went over to the kitchen and returned a few minutes later with a bottle of vodka. He unscrewed the cap as he walked and took a large gulp. He sat down on the doorstep, propped the gun against the doorframe and offered the bottle.

'No thanks,' I said.

'There was a Saudi with them. An English-speaker.'

'Did you get his name?'

'No.' He shrugged. 'They called him *hafiz*.'

He started scratching under his socks, at the flesh chafed by his boots. 'You look like shit,' he said. 'What happened to you?'

'Got buried,' I replied.

'If you had been in your tower, perhaps they wouldn't have surprised us,' Per said. 'We might have, how do you say, put up a fight.'

'What did they want?'

'You.'

The Palestinian gunmen had come in the hours before the storm, when most of the occupants were struggling with hangovers. They handcuffed them and herded them into the recreation room. Upset to find that I was not amongst the prisoners, the Palestinians had smashed the radios and computers in the ops room and set fire to the cabin. They had been preparing to withdraw when the storm struck and drove them back into the recreation room with the prisoners.

After the storm the Russians had sent out patrols to re-establish communications across the sector. It was one of these patrols that had come across the Palestinians and started the firefight we had stumbled into.

'What's going to happen?' I said.

'You think your Tony Blair is going to use this as a pretext to start the war?'

I said, 'Where's Hadzhik?'

'He went off that way.' He nodded in the direction of the old bunker.

'What are you going to do?' I asked him.

'They broke my iPod,' Per said. 'I don't know how I'm going to deal with the silence.'

I ducked into the low, dark entrance of the bunker. A draught of cold air broke across my face and I was taken back suddenly to a steading in northern Scotland, to a man's body lying on cold concrete and the crude and unnecessary act that had exiled me here to this lawless and violent place.

Hadzhik was slumped against the far wall. Someone had covered him with a blanket. It was wet with blood. He opened his eyes and gave me the same sad and hooded smile as when I first met him, thawing a can of beer over in one of the Portakabins. His arms were black, bloody to the elbows, and there were daubs of blood on his face.

'Come near,' he said.

I bent over.

'I'm going to die.'

'No,' I said, unconvincingly. 'You'll be all right.'

'They came for you,' he whispered. He sniffed and

wiped his nose with the back of his hand, smearing his face with further blood. 'You can't hide, Jonah. Not even here. You know, I think it's in your nature to attract trouble, as it is in mine.'

'I've often believed that,' I agreed.

'You choose your life, Jonah. We all do.' He sighed. 'We are shaped by these choices.'

'I understand,' I said.

'I didn't expect this,' he said suddenly. 'I didn't expect to . . .'

A sob racked his hunched frame. Gently, I lifted the blanket. They had gutted him and the glistening whirls and loops of his intestines flopped in his lap. I felt the bile rise in my throat. I let the blanket fall.

Hadzhik stared at me wide-eyed. 'Everyone is frightened of you, Jonah. They think you're going to destroy the world.'

'I'm not going to destroy the world,' I told him.

'Jonah?'

'Yes.'

'Jonah, what am I going to say, on the other side?'

'I don't know,' I said. As I reached out to him he gave a look of surprise and died.

A shadow had fallen across the door and I looked up. A man was standing silhouetted in the doorway, the sunlight flaring on the tarnished muzzle of a gun barrel that was pointing straight at me.

'Stand up,' he said, his voice soft but authoritative.

I did as I was instructed.

'Show me your hands.'

I held them out, palm upwards.

He was tall and he had to duck his head as he stepped into the bunker. His dark face seemed to consist of a series of flintlike points, the cheekbones almost piercing the hard, unshaven skin. There was a single streak of grey running the length of his beard. His face was unfamiliar to me but I felt immediately that there was some affinity between us.

'Step outside.'

He backed up and I followed him out, momentarily blinded by the fierce sunlight.

'Where is the container?' he asked.

'Safe.'

He frowned. 'You are wearing my shirt.'

There was a pause while we both considered this information. I was the first to break the silence. I said, 'Your wife wants her son back.'

'She told you that?'

'Yes.'

He said, 'She wants to negotiate?'

'Possibly.'

'You have the packages?'

'We have them,' said Malak, from the top of the bunker. He'd been squatting just above the entrance, with the sun behind him. He stood up, casting a knifelike black shadow between us.

Miranda's husband raised his hand against the sun and squinted up at him.

'Who are you?' he asked in Arabic.

'You don't know me,' Malak replied, 'but I know you, Bakr Abd al' Aswr.'

'You are offering the packages?'

'Yes, we are in a position to offer them to you.'

There were shots from the direction of the patrol base.

'Come to Baghdad,' Bakr said. 'Bring the packages with you.'

He turned and ran, disappearing over the crest of a sand

dune. I looked up at Malak, who was staring into the desert, an unreadable expression on his face.

'Packages?' I asked.

Malak gazed down at me. 'You'd better run, Jonah,' he said. 'The Russians are coming.'

'What are you going to do?'

Malak laughed. 'They won't catch me.'

The oldie moldie

Gogol cursed and kicked the left-side drive sprocket on the BMP, 'Piece of shit!'

He had long, pale hair, combed straight back from his shiny forehead, almost no eyebrows and a pair of orange-tinted Oakleys. I've noticed that since the 2001 Afghan campaign all spooks and secret warriors are wearing Oakleys.

We squatted in the shade cast by the hull of the personnel carrier with our backs to the road wheels and our hands cuffed in our laps. We were a bruised and sorry crew: Spicy, Per and myself.

'My father worked at the Kurgan factory,' Gogol barked. 'Twenty years ago he was building these heaps of shit. Where the fuck did you get this?'

'The Kuwaiti army,' Nikitin explained.

'What?'

'There was no money to freight our vehicles.'

Gogol pushed his sunglasses up his forehead, revealing the mottled red pouches under his eyes. He looked as if he was struggling with a phenomenal hangover. 'Are you fucking serious?'

Nikitin shrugged. 'They lent them to us. It was either that or walk.'

'You let the Kuwaiti army lend you a piece-of-shit twenty-year-old coffin built by alcoholics east of the Urals! Didn't they have anything American?'

'They thought we'd know how to fix them,' Nikitin said disconsolately.

A huge Russian with streaks of oil across his shaven, cannonball-shaped head squeezed his upper body out of the driver's hatch at the front of the vehicle.

'The transmission's fucked,' he announced.

'Hit it with a hammer,' suggested Gogol.

The driver ducked back into the hatch and a few seconds later a sledgehammer was tossed out. It rattled across the louvres and dropped onto the sand. The bald Russian stuck his head back out and growled, 'I've already hit it with a hammer.'

Gogol rolled his eyes and looked over at me. 'Sarcasm is lost on these airborne boys.'

Gogol wasn't wearing a uniform and it was pretty clear that he wasn't conventional Russian military. His ankle-length black leather coat, his haircut, his sunglasses and his watch were way too expensive.

'We need to move, now,' said Gogol. 'This place will be crawling with Americans soon.'

'How?' asked Nikitin.

Ignoring him, Gogol took a packet of Marlboro from the pocket of his coat and put a cigarette between his lips. He lit it with a gold-plated lighter.

'Marlboro,' Gogol said, taking the cigarette out of his mouth and considering it. 'American brand.'

'They make them in China,' said Spicy.

The edge of Gogol's steel-tipped cowboy boot struck the side of Spicy's head. He sprawled on the sand.

Businesslike, Gogol said, 'We'll take the Cherokee.'

'Is that safe?' Nikitin asked.

'Correct me if I'm wrong, comrade, but the Iraqi army uses BMPs. We are sandwiched between the most heavily

armed force assembled in history on one side and the
Republican Guard on the other, just a few days away from
a war and probably the heaviest aerial bombardment in
history, and you are trying to tell me that it is safe to sit in a
BMP?'

Niktin looked at his feet.

'Bring Jonah,' said Gogol.

'And me,' gasped Spicy.

'Very well,' said Gogol, 'bring him as well. And tape his
mouth. Leave the others.'

'You have been expelled from Eden, I think,' said Gogol,
contemplating the passing desert, the flat ground pucker-
ing and dilating in the haze. 'There is no safety for you any
more in shopping malls, fast-food restaurants and theme
parks. For us it is no surprise. For years we have had
people who hate us in our own backyard: Afghanistan,
Chechnya, Tajikistan . . . Russia will be sixty per cent
Muslim by 2015. They breed like fucking lab rats.'

Nikitin drove along Crown Route, sitting tense at the
wheel, studying the gravel surface, in places buried by
drifts of sand. The sunlight was yellowing as the afternoon
progressed.

'I never thought we had a right to Eden,' I said. Spicy
and I sat in the back seat, with our hands tied. Spicy's
mouth was taped.

'You want to know what is the real weapon of mass
destruction?' Gogol said. 'I'll tell you: people. Population
growth. You think it is some kind of funny coincidence that
fifteen of the nineteen 9/11 hijackers were from Saudi
Arabia?'

'I guess not.'

'They have one commodity only. Oil. And they can't

stop having babies. In the Persian Gulf the women can't get contraception. When oil prices were rising, population grew; now oil prices are falling it is growing just as fast. The population is doubling every twenty years. The populations of the Gulf need high or rising prices. The US, Europe, Japan, China and India need stable or falling prices. It's irreconcilable.

'Per capita income in Saudi has fallen by three-quarters over the past twenty years. As the population doubles over the next twenty years, per capita income could drop by as much again. There's no work. Large numbers of young men face a lifetime of unemployment. The rat cage is now too small. Rising population and falling income fuel anti-western movements: couple that with Islamic fundamentalist Wahhabism and you have a time bomb. That is the true threat.'

'I'll bear it in mind,' I said.

'You *should* bear it in mind,' said Gogol. 'Can't you go any faster?'

'At times like this, after a storm, one must drive carefully,' Nikitin replied.

From a distance, I saw the light flashing on Elephant beer cans strapped to iron stakes. Then we were in the cleared route through the minefield, the stakes flashing by on either side of us.

Gogol craned his head out the window, looking into the sky above. 'We've got company,' he said.

The helicopter swooped low over the Cherokee, raced ahead and set down several hundred metres ahead us. One of the Chechens leapt out carrying the unmistakable shape of an RPG. He sprinted forward and dropped to his knees, training the weapon on us.

Nikitin slammed on the brakes, looked over his shoulder

at the road behind and reached for the gear lever. Ahead, the helicopter lifted off, the nose close to the ground, circled and flew directly over us.

We accelerated in reverse, churning clouds of dust.

'Stop!' Gogol shouted. Nikitin braked.

The helicopter had deposited the other Chechen to our rear. He was also carrying an RPG. We were hemmed in, stuck between Chechens pointing rockets at us with a minefield on either side. I reached across and ripped the duct tape off Spicy's mouth. He sucked in air as if he'd been deep underwater.

'I expect you wish you'd taken the BMP,' he gasped.

The helicopter swooped over the car and set down in front of us again. Legion jumped down onto the sand and Malak and Wendy stormed out after him carrying assault rifles. He strode straight through their covering arc and up to our vehicle and rapped his knuckles on the bonnet, 'Come on out, little piggies!'

Gogol glanced at me.

'I'll huff and I'll puff and I'll blow your house down!' Legion roared.

Nikitin grunted angrily, 'Your mother.'

Legion stepped back a few paces and wagged an admonishing finger at the windscreen. He looked over his shoulder and nodded. Malak and Wendy brought up their weapons and we watched in silence as they made ready, levelled at a point a few feet above the roof of the Cherokee and pressed the triggers in unison.

We cowered in the back seat.

Legion held up his hand and they stopped firing. The ensuing silence reverberated through the vehicle. There was a general sense of contemplation.

'Open the fucking doors,' Gogol ordered furiously.

The locks popped open.

'Get out.'

We obeyed, sliding along the back seat and tumbling out onto the sand. Legion acknowledged our presence with the slightest nod. His greeting for Gogol was more exuberant.

'Yevgeny,' he said warmly, 'it's been a long time.'

'You're crazy,' Gogol said.

Legion smiled. 'You'd be amazed,' he said, 'how many of you people feel it's your duty to tell me that. I wonder why it is – wishful thinking, perhaps. I heard you died in a car bomb in Grozny.'

Gogol's eyes flicked away to the nearest Chechen, whose RPG remained trained on the vehicle, and back to Legion. 'Maybe you visit the wrong chat rooms.'

'It's possible,' Legion conceded.

Gogol lit a Marlboro, his fingers shaking.

'You still smoking?' Legion asked.

Gogol hissed out blue smoke. 'I'm a Russian. This is not California. Not yet.'

'Soon will be,' said Legion cheerfully, 'a shining sea of blacktop; shopping malls, theme parks, cinemaplexes and multi-lane freeways from Medina to Irbil. We're most of the way there already. Soon you won't be able to imagine what it was like before the Americans arrived.'

'Your culture is a virus.'

'A fiercely pathological one at that: it's got you, Gogol. Look at you.'

'The last I heard,' Gogol said, 'you were handing out cash to hoodlums in Afghanistan; like a missionary for global capitalism, I think. Did you bring your suitcase of escrow money here?'

Legion smiled indulgently.

'You Americans can't buy everything,' Gogol said,

pointing the lighted end of the cigarette at him. 'If you could you would have Bin Laden in Guantanamo Bay by now.'

'You're so right, Yevgeny.'

A fawn-coloured dog, ribbed and sharp-faced, appeared out of the minefield and stood and watched just beyond the iron stakes. The Chechen hissed at it and it slunk away. There was a pause while the two old adversaries contemplated each other.

'What are you doing here?' Legion asked eventually.

'The same as you,' Gogol replied.

'You believe the hype?'

'I trust your instincts, Legion, if not your judgment. Besides, we know that Bakr Abd al' Aswr was buying more than just second-hand cars in the late eighties.'

'It was a long time ago,' Legion said.

Gogol acknowledged the self-evident truth of this with an almost whimsical shake of the head and stared down at his boots. 'You knew who you worked for in those days. Government meant government.' He looked up. 'Who are you working for, Legion? Who's the contractor?'

Legion gave him the brazen refusal of a smile.

Gogol pressed him. 'Is this Pentagon work – the Office of Special Plans – does your government know that you're here? Is it approved by Congress?'

There was a further pause. Legion wasn't giving anything away.

Gogol said, 'You know that they make yogurt at Vector now?'

'I'd heard,' Legion replied.

'They use the same vats they once used to make killer germs.'

'I don't really have time to hang around exchanging pleasantries.'

'You don't want me to say it out loud, do you?'

'Let's say I prefer a degree of constructive ambiguity,' Legion acknowledged.

'The *known unknown* – like your Mr Rumsfeld says?'

'Sure.'

Gogol turned to me. 'Do you know what's in those cars, Jonah?'

'No,' I replied.

'But you are wondering why Legion and his gang are devoting so much attention to the location of two used cars? You want to know the truth?'

'Do I have a choice?' I asked.

'I don't think so, not in these circumstances,' he said. 'We do not have the luxury of ignorance any more, not since 9/11 – the world is a more dangerous place. We're all Indians now.'

Legion raised his hands. 'Fuck it, tell him.'

'Smallpox,' said Gogol.

He seemed to wait for a reaction. I really couldn't think of one – I wasn't surprised particularly. There had to be something of greater value in the cars than a tenuous connection with the Princess of Wales. I'm slow, but I'd worked that out.

Gogol continued, 'It is possible that some of our former distinguished scientists, who have unfortunately fallen on hard times, sold a kilogram of freeze-dried smallpox to Uday, Saddam Hussein's son.'

'Not just the regular oldie moldie,' Legion added. 'The way I heard it, your people beefed it up first – gave it more bangs for the buck.'

'They used a mouse to fell an elephant,' Gogol

explained. 'They took the worst thing in the world and made it even worse. The scientists inserted a gene from a mouse that controls the production of a signalling molecule called interleukin-4, which helps the immune system fight off invaders. I think maybe sixty million people would die. Atishoo, atishoo – we all fall down? We could sail back into the Stone Age on the wings of science.'

'Very poetic,' I said.

'We would sell our fucking souls for two fingers of vodka. And don't look at me like that; you were the first to use it. You used it to conquer America. Your puritan zealots exterminated the Red Indians with infected blankets, isn't that right, Legion?'

'God's truth,' he said.

'I'm telling you, it's fucking ironic,' Gogol said. 'Just as the son was about to hand to his father the most potent weapon ever invented, his father launched an ill-conceived and ultimately disastrous war on Kuwait. And in the confusion the container slipped through the cracks. It disappeared.'

'Until recently,' Legion said.

'What are you going to do with it when you find it?' Gogol asked. 'Is it going to be like with the Indians: a grand metaphor to make the non-American peoples recognize your inevitable victory? Are you going to thin the herd?'

Legion sneered. 'I don't know what you are talking about.'

'Come on, Legion, I can guess how this thinking goes. Your Pentagon experts think terrorists are mosquitoes, which need a swamp to breed in. You think that you can drain the swamp, clear the waters and eliminate the threat. You understand that this question is of some considerable significance to the interests that I represent.'

'How are the oligarchs?'

'Frankly, they are concerned.'

'You can tell your employers that their interests are best served by aiding ours,' said Legion. 'Now, if you'll excuse us, we have a world to save.'

'I'm not finished,' said Gogol. 'The interests that I represent are offering a stable source of oil, Russian oil from the Caspian Basin. They have responded to the fact that Saudi oil does not seem so secure since 9/11. I'm sure you can understand that the situation right now is good for a change in the flow of global capital. They do not want this positive change jeopardized by further world-changing events. They don't want a clean slate or free-flowing oil. Therefore, they want to know what you are going to do with the packages.'

'We're going to take them to Mordor and throw them in the fires of Mount Doom,' said Legion.

'I can tell you for sure this answer will not reassure them. There is no clarity in it.'

'It's the only answer they're going to get, Yevgeny.'

'I'm warning you,' said Gogol. 'I will be watching, every step.'

'Don't get in my way, Yevgeny,' said Legion. 'I will not hesitate. You understand me?'

'Yes, I understand you,' Gogol said. 'And it makes me very frightened.'

'Don't worry so much,' said Legion.

The villa in the desert

The helicopter flew east, away from the setting sun, following the skeletons of the blackened power-line towers that marched in single file across the desert. With a crackle the pilot's voice broke in over the headsets.

'Straight ahead.'

I saw an isolated building on the horizon and beside it the unmistakable blue rectangle of a swimming pool. As we came closer I could see that the building was a white cube and the whole west-facing wall of the top floor was glass. A large drift of sand had built up against the north side.

Legion's voice broke in. 'Helluva house, huh? Sort of place you could plan world domination in – we call it Dr No's. The glass is an inch thick, steel shutters come down and seal it up in the event of a storm; same with the pool. The Kuwaiti who built it hightailed it out after the invasion and hasn't set foot back in the country since. Now, it's the UN General's place, his little secret hideaway in the Zone. He flew in a 60kVA generator, powered the place up again and filled the pool with drinking water.' He winked at me. 'The general's in Cyprus planning the great withdrawal and we've taken it over for a few days.'

The pilot turned the stick in his hand; the helicopter banked and started down. Some way off I spotted a corral of vehicles that I recognized as the Gujaratis' collection of recovery trucks and cranes.

'First time the team is all in one place,' said Legion as we set down.

One of the Chechens reached out and slid back the door. It was like opening an oven. Legion jumped down and strode out towards the house and we ran after him, doubled up beneath the spinning blades. Behind us the pilot lifted off.

'Show him his room,' Legion said to the Chechens, 'and then bring him out to the pool. I'm going for a swim.' He pulled his T-shirt over his head and flung it away. I'd never seen a torso so scarred.

I paced, as I always do in a new and unfamiliar room, back and forth like my avatar, the polar bear in the picture. I opened the curtains on the dusk. I lay stretched out on the indigo bedspread listening to the growl of the air conditioning. I leapt up and pulled the curtains closed again. I felt frustration and anger in equal measure.

There was a pale blue shirt and a pair of cargo pants hanging in the wardrobe and a pair of white plimsolls in my size in a shoebox on the floor. In the bathroom, a wash kit was lying on the marble surface next to the sink and beside it a pile of thick white towels on a rack. I gulped water from the tap.

Returning to the bedroom, I tore off my old clothes and flung them into the corner of the room. Seeing the imprint of my body on the bedspread and the litter of sand that I had left behind, I tugged it off the bed and threw it after my clothes.

I stood under the shower, spun the dial as far into the red as it would go and stood under the scalding jet watching the grime pool around my feet.

I towelled myself dry, dressed in the clothes provided

and stepped out into the corridor, where the Chechens were waiting. They escorted me down a corridor and out to the swimming pool.

'Listen to me, Jonah. There's no public service, there never has been; all there is, is money and power and those who have it and those who don't. The people here live as people have throughout history, as the cattle of stronger men. Government exists solely to benefit the governors. The enforcement of law is force only. There are no duties, only taxes to be avoided and no freedoms, only privileges to be grabbed.'

I was standing by the pool. Legion had climbed out of the water and was towelling himself down. The water behind him was impossibly blue. The two Chechen body-guards were squatting some way off, out of earshot.

'You read Marx?'

'No, not really,' I said.

'You should. I mean, if you really want to understand. Marx had a theory that money, left to itself, reduces all human values to an index that is measured by money.'

My only experience of Marx was that my ex-wife kept a copy of the *Communist Manifesto* in the downstairs toilet of our army quarters, mostly I imagined, to antagonize my colleagues. She hated the army for all the right reasons, for its sexism and racism, its rigid class structure and its obvious dislike of me; and for what for me were the wrong reasons, for the exhilaration of battle and its crude and glorious gallows humour. I wondered what she'd make of the Zone. Would it arouse in her the same sense of moral outrage?

Legion noticed my gaze and spread wide with his arm, taking in the pool, the cluster of sun chairs at the far end and the woman lying there, reading.

Miranda.

My hands involuntarily curled in on themselves, my ragged nails sinking into the meat of my palms. It's a nasty experience having your worst suspicions confirmed. I can't say I was surprised to discover that Miranda was one of Legion's crew, but the anger twisted in my gut all the same. I'd been hoping I was wrong.

Legion treated me to an unnerving and voracious grin. 'Let me ask you a question. Do you believe that living well is the best revenge? Are you listening to me?'

'What?' I said dully.

He flung the towel away.

'Hey baby, look who's here!' he called out.

Without a glance, Miranda set down her book and walked to the pool side. As her arms lifted to dive, her white swimsuit was drawn tightly across her chest and the shadows of the sun defined her nipples and the dip under her ribcage. Her body rose, pivoted and slid into the water with barely a splash.

'You met, right – at the embassy?' he said, with his back to me, padding barefoot across to a sun lounger.

She crawled for a length, her arms effortlessly scything through the water. She reached the end, twisted smoothly under the surface and launched into breaststroke.

'Yes,' I said carefully. 'We met.'

He stripped off his shorts and pulled on a pair of jeans. He scooped in his balls and buttoned the fly. He gave me a look, almost jeering, that seemed to say, *You have nobody to blame but yourself.* 'I know you fucked her.'

I hated him then, with a kind of visceral and humiliating hatred that rushed through me like sulphurous wind, like the desire to rip my ex-wife's lover's tongue from his fleshy mouth.

'I've always been a bad judge of character,' I told him in a deliberately neutral voice, 'particularly when it comes to women.'

'She just wants her son back.' He buttoned a plain white shirt. 'I guess that must have struck a chord?'

'It did.'

'Don't judge her too harshly,' Legion said. 'We've all done things that are doubtful. Isn't that right?'

'It is.'

'And you chose to tell her that you know the numbers of your own free will.'

'I did.'

'I know it's difficult sometimes, simply to keep the secrets in.'

'That's true,' I acknowledged.

'What sustains you, Jonah? Work? Love? Service? Rage – is it rage?'

I didn't answer.

Legion said, 'You like horses? Jonah? Are you listening to me?'

'What?'

'Horses?'

I snapped back, I'd been in a glide. I didn't know what he was talking about. I said, 'My ex-wife keeps horses.'

'That doesn't mean you like them.'

'You're right there,' I said, though I did, once.

'Come on,' he said.

I followed him as he strode towards the house, with the two Chechens keeping a watchful and proprietary distance. 'As a teenager in Arizona, I used to break mustangs,' he said.

'Breaking and entering was more my line.'

'You're a wild thing, Jonah.'

We were walking towards the wooden steps that led up to the terrace.

A thought occurred to me. I said, 'You think you're going to break me?'

Legion laughed. 'No, but you're right in a way; I'd like to harness all the aggression. Stop you jumping around like a scalded cat. Give it an outlet, some direction.'

'What kind of direction?'

'We're going to rip the Iraqi regime apart and, if we're quick, do it without a war.'

I stopped mid-stride. 'Are you serious?'

'Deadly. Plunge in the whirlpool, Jonah.' He paused at the foot of the steps, turned back towards me and snapped his fingers under my nose. 'I'll ask you another question: have you ever done something to be proud of? I mean something that really grabbed you by the balls and made you want to shout out loud. Have you?'

'No.'

'More importantly, do you want to?'

'Yes,' I said.

He smiled and motioned for me to go first and I started to climb the stairs. He followed me, a step behind.

'You hold the fate of nations in your hands, Jonah.' I glanced back at him and he seemed to read my mind. 'I'm not bullshitting you,' he said. 'Do you understand what people would do for that kind of power? What they would pay, who they would kill? They'd tear each other limb from limb.'

We emerged onto the terrace. Sal and Malak were standing behind the sliding doors in the huge living room, with their backs to us. They were relaxed and laughing.

'Is everybody on your side?' I asked.

He shrugged.

'You've been watching me since I arrived,' I said.

'We deliberately left you at large,' Legion explained. 'You were an identified but unknown element. *A known unknown*. We wanted to learn more. We listened, we watched, we hoped to find your conspirators, identify their conspirators.'

'I must have been a disappointment.'

'No, Jonah, you were more than we could have hoped for.' He put his hand on my shoulder. 'Come. Down to business. It's time for a war council.'

The living room had bare white walls. The temperature was icy, the floor a vast expanse of bleached wooden floorboards swept by tides of chilled air. It held an eight-seat dining table, a computer station and three sofas corralled around a Persian gabbeh, the pile half a finger deep.

Aziz, the leader of the Gujarati salvage team, came up the spiral staircase from the lower floor and perched on the end of a sofa with his dirty elbows resting on his oil-streaked knees. After him, Miranda appeared, wearing a short black dress over her swimsuit. She took a seat on the farthest sofa, as far from me, it seemed, as she could get. She tucked her legs under her and absent-mindedly smoothed the fabric across the upward curve of her thighs. She wouldn't meet my eye.

Sal settled into one of the dining chairs and opened his laptop. Malak leant against a far wall. Wendy seemed, as usual, to have found the spot with the best view of the room.

Legion ran his fingers along the surface of the dining table. 'Listen up, everyone,' he said. 'We have a new addition to the team. Jonah Said. He was in the bar with the Norwegian when he got his throat cut. He has shown both determination and an ability to keep himself alive. Some of you may have mixed feelings; put them aside. This is my call and as you know all the calls are mine. Jonah, I think you've met everybody.'

Legion sat in a dining chair, put on a pair of gold-rimmed spectacles and contemplated the sheaf of satellite photographs spread across the table. 'First, the worst-kept secret in the Zone: the myth of the golden container.'

While he was speaking I heard the sliding door close and glanced around to see Spicy standing inside the room like a beckoned henchman.

Malak said, 'The Norwegian Odd Nordland went up to the meeting in Umm Qasr with the bill of lading for a container shipment that arrived in Shuaiba port on the *Eloise* a few days before the Iraqi invasion. The container's point of origin was Poti in Georgia. The freight company now defunct was called Samizdat. There were two cars in the container, former British Royal Protection Squad vehicles that were originally bought at auction in the UK by a Kazakh entrepreneur, who later sold them on to Bakr Abd al' Aswr, who was working on behalf of Uday Hussein. The Mook are still looking for the bill of lading, which means that they didn't find it on his body, which means that they don't have the container . . . and they really want that container.'

'Over to you, Jonah,' Legion said. 'We need that bill of lading.'

I said, 'What's in the cars?'

'If our intelligence is correct, and we have every reason to believe it is, then it's just like Gogol said. Smallpox. A couple of vacuum packs of freeze-dried smallpox stashed in the cars' upholstery.'

'What are you going to do with them?'

Legion smiled. 'You're not as stupid as you look.'

I ignored his mocking tone. 'What are you going to do with them?' I demanded.

'The answer's simple: bait.'

'Bait?'

'The gun may smoke, Jonah, but we need a motive and intent. A gun by itself means nothing; it's got to be in someone's hands. The world needs to see things as they are, right now – America is haemorrhaging allies and drowning in transatlantic vitriol. In order to establish irrefutable guilt, we have to prove that someone is interested in buying WMDs.'

'Someone? You mean Saddam?'

'Saddam.' Legion removed his glasses and laid them on the table in front of him. He pushed back his chair and looked up at me. 'Or Uday.'

'Uday?'

'Sure. Uday: the bitter, passed-over son; the emasculated cripple whose only thrill is torture and watching other people fuck. We know that Uday dreams of being a martyr. Who better?'

I said, 'How?'

I waited in vain for him to elaborate. I didn't really need him to elaborate. The answer was sitting on the sofa. Miranda. What was it that the ambassador's wife had called it – droit de seigneur?

Eventually, I said, 'And with that you expect me to jump on board?'

'What do you expect? This is a false-flag operation, Jonah. Deniable. Unaccounted for. The finance is routed through shell companies that aren't worth the paper they were written on. Simply put, it doesn't exist. And believe me when I say that at the end of it nobody is going to give you a medal.'

'I'm not interested in medals.'

'There aren't many people with the stamina for what we do. We are a fraternity and even though it is a fraternity, men are not rated by their outward appearance or rank, country or creed. For us, the world is divided into those who have it and those who don't. It is the absolute resolve to achieve the end, the strength to discard all scruples in the choice of means and the vision to understand that what we do is in the service of humanity.'

'Is it?'

'Yes. Absolutely. Believe me, it doesn't matter what's in the cars; what matters is who it delivers into our laps. And if we've got it right, I'm talking about the worst guys: the profiteers who live off the sanctions, Saddam's own clan, the Tikriti, and his ever-so-nasty family and the terrorist groups that he sustains.'

'And then?'

Legion said, 'Listen, I know where you've been, what you've seen; you know all about the beasts of the earth. I'm telling you that you're not alone. There's not a single person in this room who hasn't seen terrible things. There are people here who have done time in Saddam's prisons, who have been tortured. And we understand better than anyone that there are people out there who will not listen to reason; who only understand the language of violence; who must be stamped on to make them listen.'

'Stamped on?'

'We're talking the first in a long line of perfectly aligned dominoes, Jonah: the end of the tinpot dictatorships, the House of Saud, the al-Sabahs, the Assads and Arafat and his cronies.'

'You want to remake the Arab world?'

'Sure. Why not? Let's invade their countries and kill the leaders, get rid of every last rotten one. I feel a strong sense of personal affront. This is the first step, Jonah.' His smile grew sharper. 'But we need the bill of lading.'

'I tore it up.'

'Sit down, Jonah.'

He indicated the chair opposite him and I sat down. He leant forward so that I was held in the grip of his implacable stare.

'You wanted us to think that you had walked away from it,' he said, softly.

'I did walk away.'

'No, Jonah, you just wanted everyone to think that. Sure, you destroyed the evidence – you convinced everybody you didn't give a fuck. But it wasn't true, was it? I mean, you could have just forgotten the numbers, thrust them out of your mind. But you didn't. Why do you think you did that, Jonah?'

'I remember numbers,' I said.

'You were curious, Jonah. Don't tell me you weren't.'

'I don't know,' I protested. 'I wasn't thinking straight.'

'Curiosity is a survival trait.' Legion's hand closed hard around my wrist. 'The truth is you've been with us since the beginning, since you took the bill of lading from Odd and since you memorized the numbers. You came here, you wanted it and now you've got it.'

'It wasn't like that.'

'How else was it, Jonah?'

'It's not that simple.'

'You don't have anywhere else to go, Jonah. There's a warrant out for your arrest. There's no home to go back to, only prison.' He paused. 'We're all you've got.'

And at that point I let them believe that I was tired, so tired that I could hardly hold my head up. You could see that they expected me to rest it on the table. I'd been in a sandstorm and a firefight; I'd been knifed, whipped and beaten up. I'd suffered four years of insomnia. I didn't have anything left in me.

Abruptly Legion let go of my wrist and sat back in his chair. 'So? Are you in or out?' His voice rose to a manic yell. 'Don't keep me waiting.'

I lifted my head and looked around the room at the expectant faces. Softly, I said, 'I'm in.'

'Give us the numbers.'

I repeated the string of letters and digits and Sal's fingers rattled across the keyboard.

'You've done the right thing,' Legion assured me.

Sal stopped and looked up. 'It's Camp Doha.'

A moment's silence followed.

'We'll need a massive distraction,' said Malak.

'You know who to call,' said Legion.

Lifestyle management

I had another shower, crouching on the floor of the stall with the scalding water pummelling me.

When I came out, with a towel around my waist, I found Miranda standing in the middle of the room. We stood blinking at each other. She was wearing the same short black dress, but she had removed her swimming costume.

'We can't find the cars on our own,' she said. 'We need Legion. He has the database. Believe me when I say that I wish we could do this by ourselves.'

'Please don't treat me as if I'm stupid.'

'I'm not.'

'You've got what you wanted,' I said.

'No.'

'I gave you the numbers. Legion has the database. What else could you possibly want?'

'You.'

'Forgive me for being sceptical.' The resentment leapt unbidden in my voice.

'I'll never forgive you for that,' she said defiantly.

'So, what? It was love at first sight? Do I amuse you?'

'The only remotely amusing thing about you is the thought of that bear,' she said and then, gripping the hem of her dress, drew it over shoulders and discarded it in a single, fluid motion. She stood in front of me naked, with the back of one hand against her flexed hip.

'I don't have anything else to give you,' she said. 'I don't have anything else to convince you.'

And there wasn't anything else to say.

I went to her and she pressed a finger to my lips as she loosened the towel. I picked her up by the waist and carried her to the bed. She put her arms around my neck and lifted her smooth legs to wrap them around my back, drawing breath as I entered her. I felt myself spinning, enfolded in her limbs. I was at the centre of a whirlpool, going down, taking her with me.

She was crying, tears running into her hairline. I was shaking, my whole body in spasm, swollen with a sound that was beyond the capacity of my voice to express.

Afterwards, we lay on the bed, catching and controlling our breath. I couldn't see her face but I could tell that she was smiling. I could not claim to understand her need. She stretched her limbs and I put my hand in the thick mass of her hair.

'I didn't imagine that it would be like this,' she said, looking up at the ceiling, 'in these conditions.'

'Me neither,' I said, softly.

She turned to me abruptly and cupped my face in her hands, the tips of her fingers at my temples, at the vein, as if she was verifying my existence. Her expression was grave, intense. 'What do you hate most?'

'Betrayal,' I said without hesitation.

'She really hurt you, didn't she?'

'Does it show?'

'Oh, baby, it shows.'

'So?'

She shook her head slightly, the tips of her fingers sliding across my temples and into my hairline, along the rims of my ears. 'Would you believe me if I said I was trying to protect you?'

'Do I have "gullible" tattooed on my forehead?'

'It's difficult to read through the frown.'

I didn't seem to be able to stay angry with her. 'I saw your husband,' I told her.

She stiffened. 'My husband?'

'He led the attack on the patrol base.'

She let go of me and rolled onto her back, her gaze travelling across the blank white ceiling.

She sighed. 'It's all bad things.'

'I told him that you wanted your son back. He took it as an invitation to negotiate – he invited us to Baghdad.'

'Everyone wants us to go to Baghdad.'

'Why?'

'I'm the only one who can get close to Uday.'

'And me? How do I fit into this?'

'Legion wants you to keep watch over me,' she said.

'Why?'

'He doesn't trust me.'

I laughed.

'It's true,' she said. 'He trusts you. You have qualities that he admires. He talks about you as if you're his son or something.'

'Did Legion send you?' I asked. 'Now, I mean.'

'That's not why I came.'

'That doesn't answer my question.'

'Yes, he sent me.'

'He doesn't know me,' I told her.

'I think maybe he does. I see it myself.'

'What is there to see? I don't see it.' I stared at the blank, white ceiling. 'Come with me.' I said it without thinking, without regard for the consequences. It felt as if something dead inside me had been revived. At that moment I realized I had given myself to her utterly. 'We could turn ourselves in. We could try and stop this.'

'I can't. I'm sorry. I have to find my son.'

Then she slipped out of the bed. She reached down and picked up her discarded clothes and, balling them in her fist, turned her back on me and, without a backward glance, strode naked out of the room. The door closed softly behind her.

I slept without dreaming, without interruption, and woke with the dawn. I went running, slipping unseen out of the quiet house and wearing only a pair of shorts, I ploughed barefoot across the sand towards a bruised purple horizon. Gusts of cold wind stirred the surface of the sand. It looked as if it was about to rain. I felt a strange euphoria.

Returning, I saw Spicy standing in the shadows by the entrance to the villa. I stopped opposite him and stood for a while with my hands on my hips, catching my breath. It was clear that he had been waiting for me to return.

'What do you think you're doing?' Spicy asked quietly.

I look long slow breaths, breathing in through my nose and out through my mouth.

'Is that too difficult a question?'

I looked at him then; the mask of effeteness had fallen away and there was a hardness in his pale eyes that I had not seen before. It was not unexpected.

'What do you think these people are up to?' he demanded.

'I'm not sure,' I replied, truthfully.

'Jesus, they must think you're manna from heaven.'

'How so?'

'A criminal suspect on the run and in need of shelter, we practically delivered you into their laps.'

'We?'

'Come on,' he said. 'Don't be bloody daft. You don't believe for a minute that this circus is officially sanctioned, all that bullshit about false-flag operations and smoking guns.'

'What are you saying?'

'It's not a set-up, Jonah. They're not agents provocateurs. This isn't deep cover. It's the real fucking McCoy. They're a criminal gang. They mean to devastate the world in exchange for cash.'

'And what do you think you're going to do about it?'

'I'm going to stop them and you're going to help me.'

'Am I?'

Behind us the door opened and Malak stepped out. He was wearing a short-sleeved T-shirt, the tattoos snaking out from under the sleeves and spiralling across his forearms.

He looked from Spicy to me and back again and his eyes narrowed and he inclined his head to one side in a strangely birdlike gesture. Spicy lit a cigarette and flicked his hair out of his eyes. He smiled wanly. 'Catching a lungful of air, old bean.'

'Is that so?'

'God's truth.'

Malak nodded, as if confirming some prior suspicion. 'Chief says breakfast, nine o'clock.'

'I'll be there,' I told him.

I stepped past Spicy and into the house.

I allowed myself to stand for a moment at the top of the stairs and let my gaze travel the length of the table to where

Legion, surrounded by retainers, bodyguards and contractors, filled the room with his presence. He was sitting relaxed, wearing half-lens spectacles and reading a copy of the *Wall Street Journal*. But nevertheless he commanded his surroundings: by his stillness and by the harsh planes of his warrior's face; by the fact that everything on and around the table, from the plates to the litter of guns, the buff files and radios and the faces of his bodyguards, seemed to be ranged towards him or away from him. The Chechens, Ruslan and Magomed, lounged on either side of him with their guns on the table. Wendy was standing directly behind him with her hands behind her back. Miranda sat facing him across the table. At the far end Aziz was watchfully shovelling eggs into his mouth.

No one spoke.

Eventually Legion looked up, fixed me with his lazy and voracious smile and said, 'Eat, Jonah. Fill your stomach. Get your strength up.'

I helped myself to salmon and scrambled eggs and buttered toast from the sideboard. I was hungry. I couldn't remember when I had last eaten.

Sal emerged from the spiral staircase and flopped down in a chair. He opened his laptop. I watched him reel out a black cable and plug it into the telephone jack in the wall.

Malak came up the stairs. He didn't sit; instead he drifted distractedly around the periphery of the room, picking things up and moving them. Just having him in the room made me feel uneasy.

I listened to a drawn-out series of modem bleeps.

Eventually, with everyone gathered, Legion looked up from his paper. 'Well?'

Sal nodded, running a finger across the mouse pad.

'The Orlov brothers have accepted the contract for a conveyance vehicle,' he said.

'I need spares,' said Aziz.

'Give me a list,' said Sal. 'I'll forward it to the Orlovs.'

Aziz pushed his plate aside. 'I need hub seals, transmission input and output seals, seals for the brake and clutch systems, two clutch kits, rubber cooling-system hoses, drive belts, fuel pumps, service filters for each vehicle, replacement pads, brakes and shoes, two ECUs, fuses, bulbs, wheel bearings, shock absorbers, suspension bushes, pins and bolts. And you better throw in a couple of new fuel tanks.'

'Write it down for me,' Sal told him.

Legion grunted, 'And the in?'

'It's set up,' said Malak, 'a Lagos.'

'Scale?' Legion snapped, folding his paper.

'Like I said, a Lagos. It'll be like Nigeria. The whole place will go up.'

'Response?'

'They have been running exercises all week,' Sal explained, 'and their response times are slow and mostly geared to a suicide bomber at the gate. We have roadblocks going in north and south to produce gridlock. The Orlovs' crew have the road south from Umm Qasr, my friends in the Kuwaiti police have the road northbound.'

'The guard force? Comms?'

'The guard force are mostly shelf-stackers, Territorials, part-time soldiers. We have their Motorola fleet map, IDs, the lot – we'll send out a kill signal a few minutes before the balloon goes up and their radios will be useless. We have the video feeds and cellphone network. We're talking a full systemic attack.'

The sliding door to the outside opened and I looked up

from my eggs to see Spicy enter the room on a wave of cold, sand-clogged air.

'Bad weather is coming,' said Ruslan.

Legion sighed and set the paper to one side. 'I've been thinking, Titus, I believe that you should take Jonah with you.'

'Is that a good idea?' said Spicy.

'I think so,' said Legion. He regarded me impassively. 'Don't you?'

I shrugged. 'Whatever.'

'Take him down to Camp Doha, Spicy. Buy him a coffee. Watch the show.'

Spicy frowned. 'Show?'

Legion smiled menacingly. 'We'll join you down there. Sparks will fly.'

Raiders of the lost pox

There was a stationary queue of trucks loaded with containers leading out of the chicane at the entrance to the camp and backed up all the way onto the expressway. Drivers and soldiers stood in bored-looking groups down the line.

We showed our army ID cards to the sentries at the British gate and ducked between two trucks heading for the NAAFI canteen.

In the canteen, Spicy sauntered over to the counter and ordered two mugs of tea from the Russian contract worker at the till. She scowled, set down her lipstick-stained cigarette in an already overflowing ashtray and shuffled behind the glass counter towards an urn.

'You used to get ash with your tea,' said Spicy in good humour, 'then somebody complained. Now she has to put the cigarette down before she serves the customers.'

He leant back against the counter and surveyed the room. There were two military policemen at one end of the room and two army nurses in combat fatigues at the other.

'The Feds,' Spicy said and, making his finger and thumb into a gun barrel and cocked striker, fired off a silent shot at the policemen. They deliberately ignored him.

'It's the most heavily policed pie shop in the Middle East,' he said.

The Russian woman banged two cups down on the counter, spilling tea across the surface.

Spicy contemplated the milky white puddles.

'You take milk?' he asked.

'Not usually,' I replied.

'Sugar?' she asked.

'Two,' Spicy said. I shook my head.

'Any pork pies?' Spicy asked.

She rolled her eyes, sat back behind the till and resumed smoking her cigarette.

'Always worth asking,' Spicy said. 'Come on.'

We went over to the table where the military policemen were sitting. The one facing us looked up without visible expression. His colleague stared sullenly at the table top, nudging a foil ashtray across the scratched Formica surface of the table with the tip of a cigarette.

'Corporal Daws,' Spicy said warmly, 'it's always a pleasure.'

'Likewise,' replied Daws.

'Shot any deserters recently?'

'I think that's the Iraqis you're thinking of, Mr Rhodes-Spicer.'

'Oh really? I must pay more attention.'

'Are you on duty, sir?'

'Observing, old chap, for Kofi Annan; I've got my eyes peeled.'

'Eyes peeled but a deficit of attention, is that right, sir?'

'You've got me there,' Spicy admitted.

'Shouldn't you be wearing a uniform?'

'At the dry cleaners, Corporal Daws. You can't just wash a uniform like mine, old chap, too much gold braiding. By the way and talking of chaps out of uniform, have you met Major Said?'

Corporal Daws looked up sharply. 'No, sir, I don't believe that I have.'

'Major Said has been having a rum old time.'

'Has he?' said Daws.

'Yes,' said Spicy. 'Knifed, sandblasted, shot at, you name it.'

'Really?'

'Oh, yes,' said Spicy. There was a pause. 'Well, if you'll excuse us.'

We took a seat on the far side of the café by the window.

After a few minutes, Corporal Daws's colleague stood up and left the café without looking in our direction.

'He's gone to make some calls,' I said.

'Sure to have done,' Spicy agreed cheerfully.

'You want them to arrest me,' I said. 'Is that as good as your plan gets?'

'Look,' said Spicy, ignoring my question. 'Watch the man with the clipboard.'

I turned my attention to the queue of vehicles outside. A lance corporal in smartly pressed combat fatigues and wearing a Logistic Corps beret was walking down the line of trucks holding a clipboard. He stopped briefly beside each vehicle to speak to the driver.

'That's Orlov,' said Spicy.

Orlov stopped beside the cab of a truck, consulted his clipboard and rapped on the door. After a brief exchange at the window the driver climbed down to talk to him. There was something in Orlov's posture and gestures that suggested an easy confidence. He pointed to a squat, bull-necked man in oil-stained coveralls who was coming down the line and started waving his clipboard to gain his attention. The man in overalls stopped briefly to chat to a group of drivers and then, acknowledging the waving corporal, hurried towards them.

'That's the "shunter". He shunts the cargo to and from the loading bays.' Spicy wagged a finger at me and lit a Silk Cut. 'Of course, he is also an Orlov.'

The driver handed his keys to the shunter, who climbed into the cab. The Orlov with the clipboard ground a cigarette beneath his boot. He tucked the clipboard under his arm and pointed to the café. The driver nodded in agreement and together they headed towards us. Behind them the shunter manoeuvred the truck out of the line.

'He'll get a smile out of Olga,' said Spicy. 'He has the kind of face that inspires confidence. You'll see.'

The Orlov nodded to Daws as he entered and guided the driver to the counter. He joked briefly with the Russian girl at the till who, as Spicy predicted, smiled and poured two coffees.

The Orlov offered the driver a seat facing the counter and sat down opposite him, facing the window.

'What are we doing here?' I asked.

'Ssssh,' said Spicy. 'Just wait.'

Presently, the Orlov stood up and, leaving his clipboard and beret on the table, headed towards the toilets at the back of the café.

Spicy slouched in his chair, a satisfied smirk on his face.

A pause followed. Eventually I said, 'Is that it?'

Spicy nodded. 'Bar the shouting, that's it.' He leant forward again. 'Let me ask you a question, Jonah, how far into this world of subcontracted illegality were you planning on immersing yourself?'

I considered the question and followed it with my own. 'Who do you think you work for, Spicy?'

'To be honest, I'm not exactly sure. I imagine that it's

some faceless government department full of data analysts recruited via the Internet. It does seem rather mundane, doesn't it? Somewhat out of character.'

'I guess so.'

'Well, put it this way, I wasn't given a lot of choice. Caught with my pants down, so to speak, and offered an ultimatum by a rather nasty former public schoolboy who, I imagine, was subcontracted for the job. So now I look in boxes and open mail. I turn over logs and see what scurries out from beneath. I sniff panties.'

'You must be pleased, then,' I observed.

'Over the moon, old chap,' he said and then became very serious. 'Look, I'm sorry, Jonah.'

'Sorry?'

'Campbell will be back in a minute and then he and Daws will arrest you. You'll have to go back to Blighty, of course. It was inevitable. The mission here is coming to an end, Department of Peacekeeping in New York is pulling the Russian battalion and all contract staff out of the Zone. The observers will follow soon after – your official job here is over. There isn't going to be a second UN resolution: Chirac has said that France will vote against a second resolution regardless of the circumstances. Bush and Blair are meeting for a council of war in the Azores. The war is about to start.' He gave me a sympathetic look. 'I'm sorry about this business with the kidnapping. I can't make it go away but I've been told that if you cooperate they may be able to lessen the amount of time you serve. I'm told that you have allies back in the Ministry of Defence.'

'I do?'

'There are people who speak highly of you, Jonah. They attribute qualities to you: determination, resourcefulness.

They say you used to be very promising, once. But you went over to the dark side.'

It was typical of General Monteith; he just couldn't help but express his belief that good and evil struggle in us all. And I liked Spicy's description of Alex, a nasty former public schoolboy through and through.

I leant forward across the table. 'I'm going to let you in on a little secret; quite a big one, in fact. You see, I'm one of Monteith's little men . . .'

There it is. My secret finally revealed: I'm not what I seem.

Spicy fell back in his seat. 'Jesus!'

Yes, I'm a spook: separate from others, a secret warrior with a streak of rebellious obedience; my activities governed by the 1994 Intelligence Services Act. My earliest childhood memories, ones that pre-date the spider hunting that logically followed, are of long afternoons listening to my sisters' calls as they searched for me – watching from hiding places and refusing to be found – relishing the power that concealment brings. I've done it all since, all the courses run by the Defence Intelligence and Security Centre at Chicksands – close observation, conduct after capture and resistance to interrogation – and while I'd rather believe that it's possible to live a life without deception and lies, a life without concealment, the fact is I'm a professional deceiver.

The truck driver was beginning to look impatient. He consulted his watch and then glanced over his shoulder at the queue. He looked back at the clipboard and beret on the table and comprehension dawned.

'Shit!' He stood up abruptly, knocking over his chair, dashed out of the café and sprinted towards the gate. The truck was long gone. A few tables across, Corporal Daws looked up from his paper.

'It's an old, old scam,' Spicy observed quietly.

'They suspect you,' I said quickly. 'They're stringing you along.'

'Why would they?' he said.

'They want to know who you report to. You need to be careful.'

The driver burst back into the café and rushed up to Corporal Daws, who set his paper down beside him.

'They stole my truck!'

The shock came up through the floor. I experienced a moment of sudden and terrible recognition but found that I was not, as I expected, flying through the air. Unusually, everything else was moving.

'Incoming,' screamed Corporal Daws as he ducked under the table.

There was no window. I shook the glass off my shoulders and arms. I stood up and inspected myself for injury, but I appeared untouched. I looked across at Spicy, who appeared similarly untouched. We stared at each other in mute surprise.

Across the café the driver was rolling on the floor screaming, his hands clamped over his face and blood running out through his fingers. Corporal Daws crawled across to him.

The M77 DPICM submunition has a shaped charge with a convex copper cone that, on detonation, is converted into a slug of molten copper that will punch through up to 102mm of armour on a tank. As well as the shaped charge there is a sheath of prestressed steel wound around the explosives that instantly becomes approximately two thousand pieces of omni-directional shrapnel. It would fit in your hand.

A Multiple Launch Rocket System, a tracked weapons platform with a full complement of 7,728 M77 submunitions in twelve M26 warheads, had detonated in the American camp on the north side of the tank park adjacent to the helicopter landing site and beyond it the British camp.

It was surreal carnage. People were running in every direction.

I went down the steps from the NAAFI and ran through the veined grey smoke that was rolling out across the camp like volcanic ash, while further explosions rocked the camp behind me and depleted uranium projectiles came arcing across the sky.

The Gujaratis' assorted armoured vehicles were parked in a line out on the expressway beyond the dragon's-teeth chicane at the entrance to the American camp. I ran towards them, aware of Spicy running beside me.

Sal pushed open the passenger side door on the Casspir and yelled, through the keffiyeh covering his mouth, 'Get in.' I swung myself up into the cab next to him and Spicy followed. Aziz, who was in the driver's seat, grinned manically at me. Sal was staring intently at his laptop. He said, 'Let's go.'

We swung into the chicane while human shapes staggered past us out of the smoke onto the expressway. We made for a rent in the flames and smoke, slaloming between the debris strewn across the tarmac, and followed a line of Abrams tanks. The ammunition inside the Abrams had cooked off in the intense heat; they looked normal from the front but as we swung around the line we saw they had a half-melted look with the back ends hanging off.

We headed towards the chopper park. A fuel bowser went up off to our right in a massive explosion and

suddenly rotor blades were sailing through the air in a
flurry of other debris.

'That way!' Sal shouted, pointing straight ahead.

Fire burst in the air above the Casspir. Flames washed
down the windscreen. I closed my eyes – fake and real.
There was another explosion.

Something struck the outside of the hull. I opened my eyes
and found that I was still alive. The cab of the truck was full
of smoke and dust. Sal was swearing, hunched over the
laptop. He rubbed furiously at the screen with his sleeve.

The perimeter fence on the north side of the American
camp had a gaping hole blown in it and beyond it, on the
British side, the prefabricated hangars and the NAAFI
Portakabin were burning. We went straight through the
hole and across the parade ground towards the camp's
transit accommodation.

We plunged back into flames, driving between rows of
burning Portakabins and churning melted plastic furniture
and flaming rags of camouflage netting under the wheels.

We hurtled out from the Portakabins into a narrow
avenue between floodlit containers stacked four high,
marked with names like Sealand, Nedloyd and Maersk.
The left side of the Casspir scraped a container with a
teeth-jarring grinding.

'Stop!' Sal yelled.

Aziz braked and we slewed right, skidding to a halt with
the headlights pointing down the long avenue of containers. A few seconds later the steel door was yanked open and
Legion was standing on the hard-packed sand beneath me
with a grin on his black-streaked face and a stockless
shotgun in his hand. Behind us in the American camp
more ammunition was cooking off, sending projectiles
screeching into the sky.

'Some diversion,' I said.

'Best we could do at short notice,' Legion replied. 'You got a fix on the container?'

'Give me a couple of minutes,' Sal said, his fingers dancing on the keyboard.

'You've got thirty seconds,' Legion growled.

'Got it,' Sal said triumphantly. He looked up. 'Let's go.'

Legion slammed the door shut and ran back towards the vehicles behind.

We emerged from between the containers and entered a landscape of cranes, cargo extensors and abandoned forklift trucks cross-lit by arc lamps and over by the quayside the dark outlines of ships and metal catwalks. We entered a maze of dusty alleyways of stacked containers, each marked with a letter combination and seven digits. The alleyways were gloomier, the only illumination coming from occasional fluorescent tubes suspended from the top of the stacks above our heads and the flash of explosions beyond. We drove on, from pool to pool of the bleak, unnerving light.

'Right here,' Sal said.

We turned right under the boom of a yellow crane, into an even narrower alleyway.

'Now left. Here.'

We turned left onto a broad tarmac road, bumped over railway tracks, skirting a row of half a dozen moored military supply ships.

'Stop,' Sal ordered.

Outside, the air was hot, the smell of oil and the sea mingling with the reek of burning drifting across from the American camp. The occasional explosion still sent billowing flames into the air.

'Hey presto,' said Sal, pointing at a dusty container at the bottom of a stack. 'Get out.'

We hurriedly dismounted and approached the container. Examining it, I saw that the customs seals on the container had been cut with bolt cutters and a crude attempt had been made to disguise the fact, the steel pins banged back into each other. I felt a brief stab of pity for Odd the Norwegian, who had simply been in search of a few thousand dollars to pick himself back up after his divorce and instead had stumbled on this container. Opening it had cost him his life.

'What is it?' asked Spicy.

'I was thinking how things snowball.'

Two of the Gujaratis dropped to the ground from the back of the Casspir and ran forward with crowbars. Within seconds they had sheared away the broken pins and thrown the levers, releasing the doors with a dull thud.

I started forward but Ruslan and Magomed shouldered purposefully past me and slid into the space between the Range Rovers and the container wall.

I followed.

The cars were white. When I lifted my fingers from the hood they came away caked in a film of decade-old sand as fine as talcum powder. Glossy black metal, sleek as the gleaming elytron of a beetle, shone from beneath. Two identical 4.6-litre armoured Range Rovers that might once have carried Princess Diana's bodyguards but that now contained, we had been told, a much more insidious cargo.

Ruslan had chosen the passenger-side door on the nearest vehicle, Magomed the one behind it. They were both carrying strips of white plastic that they slid into the doorframes, popping the locks.

'There's no way they are going to drive them out of here,' Aziz muttered from behind me.

'I don't think they mean to drive them,' I said.

Ruslan unsheathed a knife and slashed downwards across the leather upholstery of the passenger seat. He reached into the stuffing and, after a few seconds of reaching around, pulled out an aluminium foil package. He held it up.

'Go,' Legion shouted from the doorway.

Ruslan darted out of the container. Seconds later, Magomed followed, clutching an identical package. The smallpox.

'We'll lift the container and take the cars,' Legion said, calmly and firmly. 'Stick it on the flat-bed and drive it straight out through the front gate. Bring up the crane and break down the stack. Come on!'

The Orlovs' stolen truck pulled alongside the Tatra. Aziz started yelling in Hindi and stepped into the crane's hook and was lifted away to the top of the stack. I backed into the shadows and watched as Gujaratis scaled the container walls, hauling chains and hawsers after them. The containers were lifted one after the other off the stack while beneath them Legion paced back and forth on the tarmac, checking his watch.

We watched as the final container, the one with the cars, was lifted onto the back of the flat-bed. The Gujaratis turned the twist locks to secure the container and slapped the steel sides, stepping away as the truck lurched forward a few metres.

'Go,' yelled Legion.

The truck accelerated away, followed by the crane, in the direction of the British gate.

Nobody moved for a few moments. Legion turned to look at me. Distant flames made sharp outlines of his face.

'It's done,' he said.

I glanced at Spicy, who was watching me from a few

steps away, his mobile pressed to his ear. He frowned, looked down at the phone in his hand and said, 'I'm not getting a signal.'

A few steps beyond him stood Malak, holding a black Makarov 9mm pistol, the barrel resting loosely against his thigh. Aziz was squatting by the door of an adjacent container stack, poking at the sand with a stick.

Events had slowed radically – even the explosions seemed muffled and distant. It occurred to me that I was no longer of any use to them. I glanced across at Wendy and she returned my stare – it must have been the first time I had seen her when she did not appear to be engaged in some unseen conversation. The time for discussion had passed. I assumed my cover was blown.

'I'd certainly rather have a bullet,' I told them, 'than have my throat cut.'

Legion chuckled and nodded to Malak, who stepped up to Spicy and shot him in the back of the head. The shot echoed back and forth down the narrow canyons between containers. Spicy crumpled. Malak stood over him and fired two more shots, to the head and chest.

'He was a traitor,' Malak explained casually.

'We can't afford to be forgiving,' Legion told me, with his hand on my shoulder. 'We can't let anyone get in our way.'

'No,' I said, dully.

'Let's go,' Legion yelled.

We ran for the Casspir.

Hard rain

Rain spilled in through gashes in the corrugated aluminium roofing, the falling water catching and reflecting the light from the scattered bonfires as it fell, striking the concrete floor of the warehouse in a relentless pounding like a drumbeat.

On the far side of one of the fires, Ilyena was gyrating topless with her hands pressed together and pointing upwards.

A group of the Gujaratis were passing a chillum back and forth, their matted heads engulfed in clouds of bluish hashish smoke. One of them was actually playing a set of drums, the rhythm of the beat morphing in and out of the downpour, their nodding heads accompanying Ilyena as she moved. Larissa staggered out of the darkness in her pillar-box red dress and slumped into an Orlov's lap.

Malak swigged at a bottle of vodka and flung another length of timber on the fire. He was bare-chested and the firelight made iridescent eyes of his tattooed peacock's fan and a devil of his face. He was talking and joking, though I couldn't hear what he was saying.

Spicy was dead. It felt as if the one person who'd shown me any kindness – the one person that I actually had some responsibility for – had died for it. I had no idea what I was supposed to be doing or what to believe; I didn't know whether Legion's gang were selling smallpox or not, whether the operation was officially sanctioned or not. I didn't know whether to try and help them or to try and stop them. My instructions were vague. Penetrate. Listen. Observe. Maintain cover. Wait for something to happen. It felt as if I was tipping back into a dark trough, a miles-long storm drain, and that once I was submerged and caught by the current, there was no telling where it would lead. It made my head reel.

I needed some air. I carefully eased myself backwards out of the circle and stood up slowly, shaking my cramped muscles. It didn't seem as if anyone at the fireside was going to miss me.

I skirted the wingless carcass of a Predator drone (on the TV the Iraqis were claiming to have shot one down – I didn't waste my time wondering how it had got here, nothing about the Zone surprised me any more). I kept to the edges. The walls of the warehouse were marked with smoke and dust and graffiti – *Down USA, Fuck Bush: you are come here for petrol not for freedom* – and the scars of open fires.

We were somewhere in Umm Qasr; either on the Iraqi or Kuwaiti side, I wasn't sure which. I wasn't sure that it made any difference. Wendy was standing beside the nearest exit, whispering into her lapel. She paused as I approached and held out a torch.

'He's out beyond the cars,' she said.

I held the reassuring weight of the Maglite in my hand and stepped out into the rain. The workshop was on the far side of the yard, with its doors hanging open and cascades of blue-white sparks coming off the cars mounted side by side on hydraulic lifts inside. I sloshed through the mud towards it, the rain plastering the clothes to my body.

Inside, I held up my hand to shield my eye from the

striking arc and dodged through a scrum of Gujaratis holding welding masks like shields above their heads. I passed within a couple of feet of Aziz, who was holding a stopwatch in one hand and gesticulating furiously with the other. He was shouting, though it was impossible to hear a word. At the far side of the workshop, I slipped through the narrow gap between two doors and into a pitch-black space beyond.

I flicked on the torch and followed the ellipse of light across a rough concrete floor until I reached two crates made of wooden planks bound by steel hoops. One of the crates was open in two halves and there was a rocket inside. It was a drab grey colour, about two metres in length, with flared venturi – nozzles used for the dispersal of liquid – in the nose cone.

'Find what you're looking for?' asked Legion from the darkness beyond the crates.

I turned and pointed the torch in the direction of his voice.

'Get that light off me!' he snapped.

I dropped the light back onto the crates.

'We were the first to seed clouds in warfare,' Legion explained casually. 'Back in Vietnam we attempted to flood the Ho Chi Minh Trail.'

He stopped at the edge of the light and leant forward so that the beam lit up the harsh triangles of his cheekbones and made horns of his eyebrows.

'They're Sov-era weather rockets. We found them abandoned in a warehouse in Karabakh. They have a problem there with hailstones damaging the grape vines. The rockets were used for dispersing silver iodide to seed the clouds with rain and prevent the formation of hailstones.'

He tipped back his head, revealing the pale length of his

neck and took a swig of a bottle of Jack Daniel's. He wiped his mouth with the back of his hand.

'They use these babies and, provided the clouds are tall enough and they get the dilution and dispersal right, then the vector will fall as rain across the city and . . . POP!' He smacked his lips together. 'Everybody's infected. Seven to seventeen days after that and everybody's contagious. After that it's impossible to contain. It'll spread like wild-fire.' He leant forward and winked. 'They're worthless pieces of shit. They'll burn up in the atmosphere.'

'What is happening here?' I asked.

He held up the bottle in a gesture that might have been a salute. 'We're having ourselves a party.'

'It feels like we're deliberately drawing attention to ourselves.'

He paused, with the bottle at his lips. 'You don't miss much, do you?'

I said, 'You want the Iraqis to believe.'

'We're advertising,' he conceded. 'We're a crew, lashed together for a one-off job and now publicly enjoying the spoils. Tonight the subcontractors get paid off – and as they spread out they'll leak information. Soon everyone will know . . .'

'That you have something to sell,' I finished for him.

'That we have something to sell,' he confirmed. 'That's right, Jonah. We've set up a stall in the marketplace.'

'And you're selling death.'

'Sure. It's a commodity in demand. It's believable, therein lays its strength. You can sell it. Blair believes. Bush believes. Uday believes, maybe Saddam does too. The west believes that it is worth going to war over – it's a *known unknown*. You half-believe it yourself.'

'Spicy called it the real McCoy.'

'Spicy was Hanbury's boy. He would have sold you to the Iraqis for coins.'

'I only have your word for that.'

He leant further forward and looked me straight in the eye. 'It's up to you what you believe, Jonah.'

'So what am I doing here?' I said.

He stepped away into the darkness. 'Well, let me ask you a question. Do you trust Miranda?'

It wasn't a question I wanted to answer. I said, 'You think I'd be a fool to, don't you?'

'I know why you like her, Jonah,' he said, from somewhere off to my left. 'She's fearless, beautiful and bloody-minded. There's nothing half-hearted in her. It's clear what your taste runs to . . . but she has a son that she hasn't seen in over twelve years and for the first time, maybe the only time, the means to secure his release. Let's put it this way: on one side a single life and on the other millions. What would you choose, Jonah?'

'I don't have to make that decision.'

'You have a daughter,' he said, softly. 'You have some idea.'

'Some,' I acknowledged.

Then he was standing at my left shoulder. 'You know where she's going, don't you.'

'I have an idea.'

'I can't go with her, Jonah. I can't expose the operation.'

'So?'

'That's where you come in. I need someone bold, brave and perhaps a little foolhardy, someone who can think outside the box. Let me put it this way: Americans don't like spying very much, it's an intuitive and messy business that is at odds with the American quest for the exact, factual truth. That is why we place so much faith in high-tech intelligence reconnaissance and electronic eavesdropping, what Lyndon Johnson called "patient reading", but it can't make up for the lack of human intelligence, for sources on the inside. I sat in a congressional committee hearing last year, after 9/11, and listened to the Director being asked how it was that John Walker Lindh, the so-called American Taliban, had managed to get close to Osama bin Laden and al-Qaeda and the CIA had not. The question was fair; we stuck our hands in the air and admitted it. We fucked up.'

'What does that have to do with me?'

'I need a penetration agent.'

'Penetration?'

Legion stepped up close, so that our faces were just a few inches apart. He looked me straight in the eye. 'I want you to go with her, Jonah.'

Wendy rapped on one of the warehouse doors with the butt of her pistol. 'We have to leave. NOW. The threat is imminent.'

'I want you to go to Baghdad,' Legion said, 'into the Red Zone.'

He paused as if to give me a chance to reply. But I had nothing to say. In my head I was watching clippings, repeats of the lousy soap opera that was my life so far. How could it fail to lead to Baghdad? They say that when a man is sentenced to be executed a kind of contentment descends on him and he acts with precision and diligence. I smiled politely. Maintain cover; that's what I'd been told.

Legion sighed. 'You need some sleep, Jonah. Things may seem clearer in the morning.'

'Now, why don't I believe that?'

'She's prepared a bed for you,' he said. He took me by

the arm and squeezed my shoulder. 'Come on, the chopper's waiting. I'll take you to her.'

The helicopter plunged into the darkness, the rotor blades thudding unseen above.

'There's no real evil in the world,' Legion explained, his voice crackling in my headphones. 'It's just the world, full of people. Only there is not enough water, not enough jobs, not enough agricultural land and not enough space.'

I watched the pilot in the seat in front of me, the black insect carapace of his helmet lit up by the green light of the instrument panel. I had come to a realization. Spicy was right. Legion really did mean to devastate the world. And I was the one that had handed him the smallpox.

'In America, we have fifty per cent of the world's wealth,' Legion said, 'but only six per cent of its population, and because our lifestyle with its cultures of secularism, consumerism, celebrity and hedonism is not up for negotiation it falls upon people like us to work hard to maintain the disparity. To do this we have to dispense with all sentimentality. I think you understand the degree of doublethink involved. The moral ambiguity. To achieve our aim we have to cease thinking of human rights, the raising of living standards and democratization. These people are incapable of running a democratic society; they have neither concern nor capacity for human decency.'

His voice changed pitch and I realized that he was quoting, though I did not recognize the source: '*When all the world is overcharged with inhabitants, then the last remedy of all is war; which provideth for every man, by victory or death.*'

Ahead of us in the distance, the villa was lit up like a beacon.

'I'm not so naive as to believe that conquering Iraq and relocating our troops from Saudi is going to solve our problems, Jonah. Israel isn't going to pull back to its 1967 borders, the suicide bombers won't stop, the Iranians aren't going to give up their nuclear weapons programme and the dictatorships won't fall. Democracy isn't waiting in the wings. An occupied Iraq will be a magnet for every Jihadist in the Islamic world. Iraq was a cesspool for the British when they occupied it in 1917 and it will be a cesspool for us as well.'

The helicopter banked and began to descend.

'Saddam's Ba'athists understand this and they have prepared a follow-on plan: a guerrilla war, manned with troops drawn from trusted forces, with an installed infrastructure of arms caches, safe houses and secure non-electronic command and control systems. We can't let it happen, Jonah. We can't let this turn into another Vietnam.'

The helicopter touched down in a storm of swirling dust and I tore off my headphones, unwilling to listen to any more. I jumped down onto the sand but Legion called me back, grabbed me by the shoulders and shouted in my ear.

'We're going to build a new world, Jonah,' he said.

I turned my back on him and ran through the rain to the villa.

We stood facing each other across the broad wooden worktop in the kitchen. Outside the rain beat against the panes of glass. We were bathed in bright white light.

She held out a large brown manilla envelope and I took it from her. Into it I emptied the contents of my wallet, the protective and the mundane: credit and debit cards, driving licence, my daughter's wax crayon picture and the magazine cutting of the polar bear. I threw in my watch.

'What about my eye?'

'Keep it,' she said, with a wry smile.

She handed me a black felt-tip pen. I sealed the envelope and wrote my daughter's name and address on the front. I slid it back across the worktop towards her.

Her long brown fingers rested on the envelope. 'You have to put this behind you now,' she said. 'If you mean to survive.'

I'd given them the smallpox and now I was going to have to find a way to stop them using it. I was in deep waters, with no recourse but to keep swimming.

BAGHDAD –
THE RED ZONE

*'My brother and I against my half-brother, my half-
brother and I against my father, my father's household
against my uncle's household, our two households
against the rest of the kin, the kin against the clan,
my clan against other clans and my nation and I
against the world.'*

Traditional nomad saying

Inside the threat's decision cycle

Entering the city, we saw Saddam's huge cast-iron fore-arms grasping crossed scimitars that rose from the ground like fangs. They towered over the jumble of flat rooftops and washing lines. Beneath them, embedded in the con-course were the rusting helmets of thousands of Iranian soldiers killed in the Iran–Iraq war. It was a city of monu-ments with no public spaces, a giant sepulchre.

Miranda said, 'The arms were cast in Basingstoke.'

'I went to school near Basingstoke.'

'You know there's a line in the Hadith: "Paradise is in the shadow of swords."'

'Not in Basingstoke,' I said.

'Nor here,' she added.

And she was right: if paradise had once resided in the flat, dirt-packed plain of the Tigris and the Euphrates it had long since been squandered. All I could see was squalor: the whole city was filled with dust and a sense of fin-de-siècle weariness. It was browned out, with the voltage falling further by the day. Over in the east, beyond the Tigris and the Qanat al-Jaysh canal, a thick pall of smoke rose from a thousand street fires in the sprawling Shia slum officially named Saddam City, but known to its inhabitants as Sadr City.

'People are looking for a way out, making contact with the world outside to find a way to survive when Saddam is

ousted. You can feel the texts humming in the air.' She
leant eagerly forward on the front bench of the bus, her
face animated, her walnut eyes shining in the midst of pale
green circles of exhaustion. Her lips were in constant
motion, compressed and gnawed. I hadn't seen her like
this before. 'It tastes like static. The regime is fraying and
unravelling before our eyes, collapsing under the weight of
its own venality. Everyone except Saddam's immediate
family are liquidating their assets and exporting the capital.
No one wants to get caught out by Saddam before the
Americans arrive and no one wants to be the last man
standing fighting for Saddam when the game has been lost.
Military commanders and Ba'ath party officials are leaking
their positions to the Americans, declaring that their soldiers and paramilitaries will not fight. The country is
fragmenting into neutralized zones and pockets of threat.
It's a question of timing.'

   You couldn't help but wonder what it must be like for
Saddam, a bloated spider at the centre of a web gone
ragged at the edges. A massive and violent secret state
designed and built for no other function than to ensure his
own survival: the constant and deliberately random movement, the two dozen beds simultaneously turned down in
two dozen palaces, the bunkers and under-city tunnels, the
fallback locations, the shellfish and steak flown in from
Paris and filtered through nervous poison tasters; in every
room a newscast, CNN, Sky, al-Jazeera, World Service;
bottles of Blue Label and tubs of Rohypnol; the tightly
orbiting bodyguards of the Amn al-Khas, the decoy mo-
torcades and body doubles and beyond them the satelliting
battalions of the Special Republican Guards. The ever-
decreasing room for manoeuvre and finally – at the end –
the bullet in the gun at your belt. I couldn't help but

wonder how it would end for Saddam: a missile attack on a motorcade, a collapsed bunker or a shoot-out in a spider hole. A final choice. A single bullet self-administered or ignominious capture.

We crossed the drab and dilapidated city, driving down wide boulevards that were packed with beaten-up cars, trucks and red-and-white taxis. We circled palm-lined roundabouts. We drove past a sequence of unlovely concrete buildings that Miranda named the Ba'ath Party HQ, the Ministry of Industry and Military Production, the Ministry of Propaganda, the Republican Guard HQ and the Olympic Committee Headquarters. She paused as she considered this last building. I knew enough about Uday Hussein to know that he was the chairman of the Olympic Committee.

She said, 'It's the only Olympic Headquarters in the world with its own basement prison.'

'Were you there?' I asked.

'No.' She shook her head. 'Not in that basement.'

I let my fingers catch in the thick mass of her hair, lifting it away from the line of burnished steel rings that framed the hollows of her ear.

She ducked her head and gave me a contemptuous sidelong glance. 'There's no glamour in it.'

'I didn't think there was,' I said.

'I hate this place,' she said fiercely.

Enough to kill everyone in it? The question hung unspoken.

I said, 'I guess I think you're brave to come back.'

'Don't make it sound as if I had a choice.'

I stared out of the window into a squall of dust.

'Look, I'm sorry,' she said, her voice softening. 'My head is in a bad place.'

And your heart? I wondered silently.

We sat on the upper deck of the Peace Bus, surrounded by the black canvas bags and aluminium flight cases of our newly acquired craft, and tried not to listen to the booming cant of the unashamedly socialist Member of Parliament that drifted up from the lower deck. The MP was convinced that the Raees was going to grant him a televised audience and that he would, by the power of his deep understanding of the Iraqi people, deliver peace on a plate. It was bullshit, though we refrained from telling him so – after all, he had given us a lift across the western desert from Amman in Jordan.

The thing about us that clearly irked him the most was the fact that not once on the sixteen-hour journey had we shown any inclination to interview him. I'd thought about getting the camera out and pointing it at him to placate him but beyond switching it on and loading a tape, I didn't really have much of a clue. Instead, we'd retreated to the top deck where the most overweight of a gang of Ba'ath party minders picked up at the border was stretched out on a bench alongside an equally dead-to-the-world peace activist-cum-human shield with a shaven head and tattooed tears below his right eye. They snored loudly as we lumbered in and out of the endless convoy of oil tankers moving along the two-lane ribbon of blacktop, while cars and vans darted around us and lengths of shredded tyre tumbled towards us out of the dust. Everywhere there was wreckage, buses crushed like tin cans and the hulks of burnt-out tankers and people coming out of the dust and picking over the remains.

'What is there left to bomb?' I mused.

'They'll pile wreckage on wreckage,' she said. 'They'll find things to bomb. They'll bomb the desert.'

Getting into Iraq had been pathetically easy: we'd slipped through the obvious opening, ironically enough a door created by Saddam's own vanity, his desire to publicize his defiance.

We'd checked into the Intercontinental Hotel in Amman and obtained our ten-day visas down the road at the Iraqi Embassy, after handing over letters of introduction from a fictitious Dutch-based English-speaking cable TV station. We were both carrying UK passports, worn and well stamped, and with them the paraphernalia of believable identities; IDs, debit and credit cards. My wallet even contained a membership card for an Amsterdam video-rental shop. But I couldn't escape the knowledge that these preparations were a long way from a convincing cover story and I didn't much rate our chances under questioning. But then what did I know? We were media. We could go anywhere.

We had a room in the Palestine Hotel on the east bank of the Tigris. The Palestine was the temporary headquarters of the world's floating press pack. If the mass of the populace did not expect Saddam to survive, it was surely lost on the crowd of journalists, minders, drivers and human shields that milled around in the hotel foyer.

The parking area in front of the hotel's shopping mall was jammed with cars and clusters of Ba'ath party operatives and overweight, mostly middle-aged Fedayeen with AKs, in a tight corral resembling a siege. Periodically a rat would drop out of an overhanging palm and strike the bonnet of a twenty-year-old Chevy Caprice, then pause briefly to watch the action before scurrying off in search of richer pickings.

Dogs drifted back and forth licking this, tasting that. The

water came out of the taps a dirty brown colour and the
rooms stank of petrol, which was cheaper than disinfec-
tant.

I hadn't seen anything like it since the Grand Hotel in
Pristina in June '99. I couldn't see how our cover stories
were going to last more than a few minutes.

Every couple of hours a group of police cars circled the
roundabout beneath our balcony, the occupants waving
flags and chanting slogans. Meanwhile the tanks and
equipment of the US 4th Infantry Division were bobbing
in the waters off the Turkish coast. Later they'd call it
Tommy Franks's feint.

Across the hotel room the curtains stirred in a lacklustre
breeze that carried on it the smell of burning rubbish.
Outside, the police cars circled again, chanting, as if by
rote, *Saddam! Saddam! Saddam!*

The bedside light dimmed and flared. My seed leaked
slowly out of Miranda onto the tangled sheets. It was dusk
and we lay with our legs entwined, contiguous objects
bounded by a line of sweat. I slid my hand down the curve
of her belly and pressed my thumb into the damp well of
her navel. She leant back into me, her shoulder blades in
my chest, her cheek sliding across mine.

'What's the next step?' I said, resting my chin on her
shoulder.

I felt her eyebrows furrow against my temple.

'They make contact,' she whispered, speaking softly into
my ear.

'How?' I felt the movement of her eyelashes on my skin.

'I don't know. A phone call or a tap on the shoulder.'

'Where?'

The hint of a shrug. 'Here, anywhere.'

'Then what?'

She whispered, 'I'll go to Uday.'

'And then?'

'We negotiate a price. I give him the location for the exchange of goods. We arrange a handover. Uday gets the packages of smallpox, Legion gets the money and I get my son back.'

I slid my fingers across her belly. She became very still, her only movement the gentle, rhythmic rising and falling of her chest.

'And when Uday gets the smallpox?' I ask her.

'You know I have to,' she said.

I could hear the sound of gunfire, somewhere away to the east in Sadr City.

'Why did he lock you up?'

'Uday?' she said, staring over her shoulder at me. Her eyes narrowed. 'Because it gave him pleasure.'

I ran my hand up her sternum and over the stubs of her nipples, until the tips of my fingers brushed a raised, coin-shaped scar just below the curve of her collarbone.

'What's this?'

'Cigarette burn.'

'Who did this to you?'

'Stop it,' she said.

'Why?'

'It doesn't help.'

'Doesn't help who?'

'Me, Jonah. I'm the one I'm worried about. I have to be strong for this. I don't think you have any idea.'

There is vividness in anger. I said, 'I have an idea of how crazy someone would have to be to hand over a kilo of weaponized smallpox to a psychopathic tyrant: crazier than a sack of cats.'

'Stop it,' she said.

'How do you know your son is even alive?'

She twisted and slapped my face.

'What's the location for the exchange of goods?' I demanded. 'When does Legion hand over the smallpox?'

There was a pause while we contemplated each other.

'I'm sorry,' she said. She turned her back on me again and we lay for a while.

'There was a time when I prayed,' she said softly, 'after I was released from Abu Ghraib. When I thought I would never see my son again. I prayed that God would cause someone to find the container and open it and spread the germ everywhere and to everyone, adults and children. So we'd stop needing so much. Needing love and needing money and happiness.'

'And now?'

She didn't say anything for a moment. 'I don't pray any more.'

She took my hand and drew it down her sweat-beaded flank and across her lower back into the groove at the base of her spine. She tipped her forehead into the pillow and shuddered against my hand.

I woke suddenly and she was sitting at the edge of the bed, smoking.

She said, 'The world must seem very ugly to you.'

'It's how I know I fit in.'

'It's the wrong weather for polar bears.'

I rubbed my palms across my face and eased myself up on my elbows. 'Does he have a name?' I asked.

'Who?'

'Your son. That's all you call him. All you ever call him. Does he have a name?'

'Fuck you,' she said.

We stared at each other.

'Why can't you trust me?' she asked. 'Or is it just that you don't trust women? Have we let you down, Jonah? Am I the new villainess in your life story?'

I stared at the ceiling. 'Legion doesn't trust you.'

'And you're Legion's boy in Baghdad?'

'That's not why I'm here.'

'Why are you here?' she demanded.

'Because of you.' There, I'd said it and with it came understanding. I saw it clearly: falling in love, in the circumstances, was utter madness.

'Then you have to trust me,' she said.

'I trust you,' I told her. *But should I,* I asked myself. 'Give me a cigarette.'

Rough guide to Baghdad

The first is the most difficult, it messes with you and makes your head reel, but after that it gets easier, so easy in fact that after only a few puffs you're hooked. You're a smoker again.

We walked in the mid-afternoon heat past a broken-down fire engine and dropped down onto Mutanabi Street, with its crumbling brickwork and rotting Ottoman balconies strung with washing, joining the desultory crowds drifting past the pavement stalls and barrows of the Friday book market. The street was older and lower than those surrounding it and, Miranda explained, prone to flooding. There was something tenuous and foolhardy about it, a street of books that floods when wet.

There weren't that many books on sale. Those books that were available were spread on trestle tables, their covers faded from too much time in the sun. They were dated, motley and vaguely pathetic. I browsed a few titles at the first trestle: *The Glory of Amsterdam*, *The Anglo-American Threat to Albania*, *Advance Training Course for Customs Officers in African Countries*.

Our Ba'ath party minder, a twenty-something named Abdel who had been provided for us by the Ministry of Information, said, 'Not one English-language book has come into the country since the start of sanctions. In

1985 the national literacy rate was eighty-nine per cent; by 2000 it was fifty-eight per cent.'

Abdel did not talk about 'before Saddam', or 'before the war' but about 'before sanctions'. It was the prime event that punctuated his relentless advocacy of the regime. There was something about him, his thin neck and bad teeth, his cheap suit and a certain brittleness of character, that reminded me of Odd, the Norwegian, and looped me back in time to that first evening when I'd got off the plane and allowed myself to be taken to the Zone. I had the same sense of hilarious prescience that I had experienced in the potholed forecourt before entering the Desert Palm, the sure knowledge that whatever happened, the consequences would be unexpected and most probably unpleasant. It was difficult not to feel sorry for Abdel.

We'd been doing the markets, the tourist circuit. 'Seeing and being seen', Miranda called it. We'd seen the dog market at the Souq al-Gazil, a stretch of wasteland beside the road that echoed with the sound of several hundred barking dogs, where traders sold guard dogs to combat the daily increase in robbery and theft.

'He will tear a piece from your enemy,' said a man when I stopped in front of a skinny German shepherd. The man had his arm locked around the dog's neck and from the way it lunged at me, it seemed unlikely that it would bother much with distinguishing between friend and foe.

And after that we walked through a milling crowd of people buying and selling goldfish in clear plastic bags, while Abdel told us in the same punitive tone of voice that the sanctions were responsible for the collapse of the national immunization programme and that polio, tuberculosis, meningitis and measles were common again. Goldfish were not in short supply.

A trader dropped a bag and the smack of the explosion as it struck the pavement retorted across the market like a gunshot and everything stopped for an instant and then with a sigh of relief resumed. A dirty child scooped up the fish and ran, disappearing into the thicket of legs in the moving crowd.

I wished them both luck.

We walked through the vast flea market in Liberation Square, past blankets spread with household bric-a-brac: plumbing fixtures, postcards and old magazines, plastic sandals, piles of Pokemon stickers, anything with even vestigial monetary value. It seemed as if the city had already stripped itself bare and was now selling the leavings.

We took two taxis. The first broke down and the driver left us by the side of the road and headed for the Shurjah market in search of a fuel pump.

'No car parts, huh?' I said to Abdel.

'It is important that people understand our suffering,' he said. 'Sanctions have killed more people than the bombs dropped on Hiroshima and Nagasaki. You must make a film.'

'We're just looking for locations,' I explained. 'The filming will come later.'

'I know,' said Abdel indignantly. 'I have hosted many TV crews.'

Another taxi pulled up.

'Take us to the book market,' said Miranda.

I found a copy of George Orwell's *Nineteen Eighty-Four*, an orange banded Penguin edition, printed in Suffolk, in

1954. On the back, below the biography it said: *Not for sale in the USA.* I let the book fall open at random and read a sentence: *When you make love you're using up energy; and afterwards you feel happy and don't give a damn for anything.*

As I was standing reading the passage, a man in rags with dishevelled shoulder-length hair drew close and started muttering as if he was begging for coins. He was just one more of the hundreds of homeless people that roamed the streets. He tugged at my sleeve. I glanced towards Abdel but he was engaged in conversation with Miranda. I winced apologetically and put down the book, to the obvious disappointment of the vendor, who shot the beggar a doleful look.

I moved on to another stall but the beggar followed, trailing a few steps behind, jabbering incoherently. Reluctantly, I pulled a couple of thousand-dinar notes out of my pocket, balled them up and pressed them into his hand. As I did so, I noticed that he had no fingernails. I looked up sharply.

He leant in close and whispered in my ear. 'Be at the National Restaurant at the al-Rashid Hotel at nine o'clock.'

Then he seemed to take fright and backed away into the crowd, clutching the money to his chest.

Miranda joined me with Abdel in tow. She said, 'Find anything?'

I shook my head. Something about my expression must have put her on her guard because she gave me an enquiring look.

'What now?' I said.

'Tea.'

We sat in the al-Shah Bandar café opposite the old

Ottoman administration building and sipped at glasses of vanilla tea and watched the nagileh pipe slowly circuit the room. I lit another cigarette.

'You look like you're making up for lost time,' Miranda observed.

Eventually Abdel excused himself and headed for the toilets.

I leant across the table and said, 'They've made contact.'

She gave me an evaluating look. 'And?'

'Nine o'clock in the restaurant at the al-Rashid.'

She laughed and shook her head.

'What now?' I asked.

'We lose the minder. I was getting bored with him anyway. Of course, you'll have to find somewhere to hide the body.'

I stared at her.

She shook her head, an expression of consternation on her face. 'I'm joking. It was a joke.'

Abdel rejoined us.

'Let's go to a different part of town,' she said.

'I need to buy some more cigarettes,' I told her.

It was on Arasat, standing on the pavement, that I remembered Malak's words at the British Embassy party down in Kuwait City just a few days before. His cold, unsettling aspect and softly spoken words: *I'd be happy to see them all burn*.

There was an entirely different kind of fin-de-siècle impulse at work in Arasat, something closer to Nero's heedless fiddling, in the brittle and feverish hedonism of the nouveaux riches and the overstocked shops and gleaming car showrooms

'It's a steal,' said Miranda gaily as she stepped out of the taxi onto the kerb, 'it's a cancer run wild, a sarcoma, a Cheerioma.'

We strolled arm in arm up the wide tree-lined boulevard past shops selling swimming pools and Hugo Boss and Belgian chocolates, while the sons and daughters of the profiteer elite cruised past in reptile-bright Mercedes and BMWs.

Abdel, his first time in Arasat, struggled to keep up with us while simultaneously fighting off the clutch of impoverished widows in tatty black robes and grimy shoeshine boys that pursued us and tugged at our shirtsleeves. We walked past a restaurant called Castello's that was a little castle complete with turrets, a small moat and a wooden drawbridge.

'Isn't that beautiful?' Miranda announced.

Abdel scowled.

'Let's get a drink,' she said and pointed. 'There. The Scales.'

There was a fountain at the centre of a shallow pool with soft underwater lighting at the entrance to the al-Mizan Restaurant. Bow-tied waiters wearing red-and-white striped waistcoats threaded swiftly between tables packed with sleek, well-fed Iraqis and their Jordanian business partners. As we approached, a flurry of waiters diverted towards us and chairs were pulled back and napkins flourished.

Miranda called for the wine list and said, 'Let's drink something expensive.'

She sent back the first bottle, calling for something even more expensive. The second bottle was more to her liking and after the waiter had uncorked it she waved him away and took charge of pouring herself.

'Drink?'

I nodded. 'Always.'

'Abdel?'

Abdel placed his hand firmly over the wine glass. Ignoring him, she tipped the wine into his water glass, filling it to the brim, and without raising the neck of the bottle continued pouring as she reached across the table to fill my glass and then her own.

'Silly me,' she said.

A trio of waiters rushed to the table and whisked away the wine-soaked tablecloth while a fourth brought on a new one. Oblivious to the commotion around her, Miranda raised her glass and announced, 'Let's drink to the vulgar new rich.'

Dutifully I raised my glass. Abdel stared stony-faced at the table top.

'Come on, Abdel,' she urged. 'Treat yourself. There's a month's salary in every mouthful.'

Abdel reddened.

'Isn't that right, Abdel? Ten to twenty dollars is the average monthly salary for a civil servant?'

Abdel said, 'I don't feel well.'

Miranda gestured expansively around the restaurant. 'What do these people do, Abdel? I don't remember the Arasat strip being like this before the embargo. I mean, let's face it, these guys are not punching holes in their ration cards.'

'It's a gangster business,' he said, his face getting redder and redder.

'Say again, Abdel?'

Abruptly, he stood up and threw his napkin on the table in disgust. 'I'm leaving,' he said, a noticeable tremor in his voice.

'But we've just arrived,' protested Miranda. 'We're going to have a celebratory drink. We're going to drink to the new rich: to the sanctions.'

'You can stay,' he said, 'but I am leaving.'

He hurried out of the restaurant and disappeared down the street. I noticed that none of the beggars bothered to pursue him.

She reached across and we clinked glasses.

'Cheers.'

She took a sip of wine and contemplated me over the rim of the glass. 'Do you think that was over-harsh?'

I shrugged. 'I guess it was necessary.'

'You know how to be harsh,' she said.

'Yes,' I conceded.

'It's time to put on our glad rags,' she told me.

I dropped my cigarette butt in my wine glass. 'Let's go.'

Back at the hotel we made our preparations. Unusually, the water was scalding hot and we took a shower, and with it the first steps towards a transformation that had in it some glamour but also a shade of self-conscious espionage.

After the shower, as I buttoned a white dress shirt, folded back my cuffs and attached cufflinks and cummerbund, I watched her perched naked on the edge of the bed, painting the nails on her fingers and toes.

Then she returned to the bathroom and worked on her face: foundation, eyeliner, mascara and lipstick. She rubbed the blade of her palm across the mirror and worked quickly and deftly. I'd never seen her wear make-up before – no, that's not true: there had been the hint of it before – but now it looked strange on her. It made a smooth oval of her face and rendered her eyes enormous.

Next, she stepped into a black dress with a halterneck and, lifting her hair, allowed me to tie the straps in a bow before sashaying away and slipping her feet into heeled black mules.

Finally, she stood at the centre of the room, brown-skinned and bare-shouldered, with world-swallowing eyes and a shiver of molasses hair. The exhaustion was gone from her face and she looked magnificent.

'Are you ready?' she asked, by which I think she meant are you ready to be brave.

And all I could do was smile sadly and hold out the hourglass ends of my tie. She laughed and, with an expression of mock concentration and her tongue pressed into her cheek, she tied my bow tie. Then, taking a step backwards, she smoothed the silk lapels of my jacket.

'You look good,' she conceded. Her hair fell across her face and I could only make an ill-informed guess at what she was really thinking.

'You sure about this?' I asked.

She nodded and would not meet my eye. 'Yes, I'm sure.'

She reached for the pashmina that was draped over the back of a chair and gathered it around her shoulders.

'Let's go,' she said.

I remembered Spicy's line on the night of the embassy party: *'Let's sally forth and party.'* Spicy was dead. Then I remembered Winston Smith's words from *Nineteen Eighty-Four*: *'We are the dead.'*

I put on my best smile.

We emerged from the elevator to a flurry of audible gasps and craning heads and strode through the foyer. Journalists, peace activists and Mook fell back before us like a bow wave. Somebody started taking photos, the flash bulbs popping.

'It's Posh'n'Becks,' a journalist called.

'More like Beauty and the Beast,' said another.

We were impervious. I lit another cigarette.

The ace of hearts

We arrived at the hotel just before ten and strode in through the foyer across the tiled floor mosaic of George Bush senior.

The restaurant had the gaudy over-ornate décor of the Kasbah. The walls were covered in gold leaf and black lacquer. We weaved amongst the crisp white cloths of crowded tables following the smartly dressed Sudanese maître d'. We were given a table in the corner, at the far side of the room from the stage, where the house musician was playing a sitar.

The maître d' pulled back Miranda's chair for her, frowned and then broke into a wide grin as he recognized her.

'Miss Miranda,' he said and shook his head. 'Where have you been?'

'I've been travelling, Johnny,' she said, with a smile.

'Now you're back,' he said. His gaze flicked across to me and I saw a hint of cautious enquiry behind the fixed smile. I gave him a tight-lipped nod.

'What's good, Johnny?' she said, gaily. There was a childish, unnatural quality in her voice and in the highly strung brightness of her smile that I had not witnessed before. It was as if she'd been ratcheting up an emotional level with each location, from Mutanabi to Arasat and now finally the al-Rashid.

'I recommend lamb kebabs and grilled Tigris fish,' the maître d' told her.

'Then that's what we'll have.' She looked up at me from her chair. 'Sit down, Jonah.'

I sat. Johnny shook out my napkin and laid it across my lap.

'And wine, Johnny; bring lots of wine. I feel like celebrating.'

'Whatever you say, Miss Miranda.'

'What are you doing?' I asked her as soon as he was out of earshot.

'This isn't about you,' she snapped. 'Not everything is about you.'

She drank twice as fast as I did and Johnny brought a second bottle with the food. I watched her as she chattered about nothing, waiting for something that would take her away from me, possibly for ever.

The lights of the motorcade swept across the ceiling and were followed by a perceptible shift in the level of background noise in the room. Seconds later, bodyguards with lupine faces and bulky leather jackets barely disguising Skorpion machine pistols fanned out across the dining room. Two swiftly disappeared through the swing doors into the kitchen.

Seconds later, he entered. The scorned elder son.

His Excellency Uday Hussein, Speaker of the National Assembly, Chairman of the Iraqi Olympic Committee and the Iraqi Football Federation, Commander of the Fedayeen Saddam. The thirty-nine-year-old eldest son of Saddam, one-time heir apparent, now the mentally unbalanced prodigal with his star eclipsed by his younger brother Qusay.

Uday was at the centre of a pack of the sleek new rich, casually well-dressed smugglers and profiteers who had grasped the boundless opportunities offered by sanctions and shortages. They moved with the grace of parasitic fish picking at a wounded shark's maw.

He stood out from them. His face was bloated, his thick black drooping moustache surrounded by five or six days of stubble. He walked with a noticeable limp, the mark of an assassination attempt in December 1996 when gunmen had riddled his Porsche with bullets and left him partially paralysed on his left side and, if you believed the rumours, impotent.

Miranda had told me that as a child he had been encouraged to torture political prisoners.

He snarled something and the sitar player scurried from the stage. Five gypsies clutching guitars were ushered out of the kitchen by the waiters and edged fearfully towards the stage.

Uday pointed to a table and its occupants fled.

Other tables were being thrown together and tablecloths shaken like sheets. Terrified waiters hurried out of the kitchen carrying bottles of Black Label and Hennessy on trays.

Within minutes the room was transformed. A sea of deserted tables stretched across the room littered with half-eaten dishes and hastily discarded cash.

I looked around for a waiter but Miranda's hand gripped my wrist.

'You have to trust me,' she said and I saw something in her eyes that I had never seen before: fear, visceral and raw.

We were the only other people left in the room.

'You don't have to do this,' I said, the hurt and anger coming out unbidden in my voice. 'There must be another way.'

Then he looked up from his glass of cognac and surveyed the room with his brooding, mud-brown eyes. His gaze came to rest on us and I felt the sudden brittleness in Miranda's posture.

'Don't look straight at him,' she said. 'Never meet his eye.'

'This is crazy.'

'He'll eat you alive,' she said.

'Jesus.'

'Go and wash your face.'

'No.'

A beat.

Then her face relaxed and I knew I'd lost her. 'You know, Jonah,' she said. 'I've realized that you're missing a certain saving stupidity. You have no discretion.'

'I love you.'

'It was just a couple of fucks. Don't read too much into it. It's over now. I needed your help to get here, that's all.'

'Stop it,' I said.

'I needed the numbers and I needed to get into Baghdad without being raped or locked up. I needed some expendable muscle. You've done your job. Walk away. You might live. You might even be forgiven.'

'What are you trying to achieve?'

'Jesus, Jonah, don't you ever think that maybe your wife was right?'

I got up and walked away from her.

At the sink in the washroom I bathed my face in cold water and discarded the ridiculous bow tie, popping the studs in my shirt. In the mirror my eyes were intensely bright, both of them, sighted and blind, catching the light from above the sink as it reflected off the water. I ran my fingers through the stubble of my scalp, leaving droplets in my hair and on my lapels.

Of course my wife was right.

Angrily, I stuck my head back in the sink, right under the tap, immersing my whole head. Bubbles of air rushed from between my lips. I flung back my head, spraying water everywhere and sucked at the air to nourish my infuriated mind. Briefly, I searched my bruised and battered face in the mirror, seeing there the bull-headed beast, savage and impetuous.

I could hear the gypsy band through the walls.

A wave of sudden and heedless fury had lifted me from my seat and carried me out of the dining room and as I stared at myself in the mirror I reasoned it could just as easily carry me back again.

The shooting started soon afterwards, the bullets slamming into the wooden panelling of the stage – thock thock thock.

Looking in the mirror, I tipped my right hand to my right eyebrow in mock salute. 'You will be dead before the night is out,' I said.

Then I strode back into the dining room, into the stench of cordite. Johnny the maître d' intercepted me a few steps later.

'May I suggest a drink at the hotel bar?' he said, in a measured tone.

'No.'

'It's not safe.'

I stepped past him. Two of the bodyguards blocked my path with their handguns raised and pointing at my head, so that I was staring into the silvery zero of each muzzle.

Across the room Miranda was sitting on a chair at the far side of the centre table. Uday was a few steps behind her.

He was standing opposite the stage with a machine pistol in his hands. The gypsy band had their trousers around their ankles and one of them was urinating copiously, the liquid running down his shaking leg. The whole stage was pock-marked with bullet holes and the restaurant floor was scattered with empty casings.

One of his bodyguards whispered in Uday's ear. He sucked on his overbite and turned to look in my direction. His eyes were enormous. Everybody was looking in my direction. Only Miranda's eyes chose not to see me.

The bodyguards drilled the barrels of their guns into my neck and circled slowly with exaggerated steps so that they were behind me. A third bodyguard with slicked-back hair and a dyed moustache placed a hand on my chest. He reeked of cheap eau de Cologne. With his other hand he patted me down.

Uday carefully removed the cellophane and paper ring from a cigar. Someone passed him a match and he bored a hole in the curved end. Then he lit it. He waited until it was burning evenly and then fixed his gaze on me. 'Who is that?'

'My date,' said Miranda, lighting a cigarette.

He regarded his cigar thoughtfully. 'Have you slept with him?'

'Not yet,' she replied and exhaled. 'Usually I sleep with handsome men.'

He limped towards her with the machine pistol hanging loosely by his side. He grabbed a chair and turned it around so that he was sitting right in front of her with its backrest against his chest. Then he leant forward and grasped under the table for her. His hand slid under her dress and she seemed to slump against him, with her hair falling over her face and her head dropping on his shoulder.

I stiffened, the tension making rigid strings of my arms and legs, and the bodyguards behind me ground their handguns further into the back of my neck. The bodyguard with the slicked-back hair splayed his fingers on my chest and opened his mouth, releasing a draught of fetid breath from between his gold-capped teeth.

My senses felt heightened, the information flooding in from all sides. Around me there was a commotion of breaking glass and falling chairs. The decks were being cleared. On the stage an overweight man in a leather coat was pressing fistfuls of cash into the hands of the gypsy singers and shoving them towards the door. A bodyguard was herding the waiters back into the kitchen and another had a video camera and was advancing on Miranda.

Uday lifted his black, stubbled chin and blew smoke over Miranda's shoulder. She groaned softly. He tapped ash on the floor.

The camera zoomed. He worked his hand inside her.

Abruptly, he stood up and the machine pistol clattered against the side of the table and the chair went skimming away. He limped towards me. I was careful not to look straight at him, to let him approach peripherally. I concentrated on the bodyguard in front of me and his slicked-back hair, copycat moustache, gold teeth and fetid breath.

Then Uday's fingers were smeared against my lips and nose so that my head was pressed back against the muzzles at my neck and my nostrils were filled with the unmistakable smell of Miranda.

'Is that what you want, ugly man?' he hissed.

He stepped back and nodded to the bodyguards, who kicked my feet out from under me. The bodyguard with slicked-back hair stamped a Cuban heel on my head and pointed his gun between my shoulder blades and another trussed me with plastic cuffs at the wrists and ankles.

I watched as Miranda was escorted towards the doors, with Uday limping after her. His last words were, 'Bring him.'

His cigar sailed in a burning arc across the room. They grabbed me by my collar and dragged me across the floor.

I lay curled up in a litter of burger cartons and discarded cigarette packets in the foot well of a black Mercedes. I had slicked-back hair's Cuban heels at the small of my back and every now and then he stamped on me. Each groan from me elicited a satisfied grunt from him.

By my calculation we drove for ten to fifteen minutes. We passed briefly through a darkened tunnel and the car juddered as though passing over a series of ramps and came to a halt. I heard the sound of a metal gate closing behind us. The doors were flung open and I was grabbed by bodyguards and dragged out of the car onto the concrete. They used a knife to cut the tie around my ankles and the blood rushed painfully back into my feet. I was lifted up.

We were in a courtyard surrounded by high perimeter walls with a warehouse in front of us. Two off-duty bodyguards in suits lounged by the entrance to the warehouse. They regarded me with minimal interest.

Slicked-back hair shoved me from behind and I hobbled a few steps and fell. The other two lifted me by the armpits and frogmarched me towards the warehouse.

Inside there were rows of aluminium racking loaded with boxes of cognac and champagne and cigars and cigarettes. Some plastic chairs were arranged around a card table and a television sat on some boxes. Pin-ups from magazines were taped to the wall.

I was dumped a few feet from the table and my legs were tied again. Slicked-back hair bent over me and said, 'Keep quiet. Watch the film. Learn what is coming for your armies.'

I lay for an hour or so while they played cards and in the background *Black Hawk Down* played on Youth TV, the channel owned by Uday Hussein. American Rangers, mostly it seemed played by Scottish actors, blundered haplessly from ambush to ambush in the mazelike warren of Mogadishu, emptying magazine after magazine – thousands of high-velocity rounds – into hordes of anonymous, hate-filled Somalis.

Slicked-back hair leant back in his chair, removed the cigar from his mouth and said, 'You like?'

'It's like *Zulu*,' I said, 'but without the close-harmony singing.'

I got a kicking for that. At the end of the film the names of nineteen dead Americans scrolled up the screen and the thousand or so Somalis got barely a mention.

A bulky, briefcase-sized mobile phone rang. Slicked-back hair answered it. He grunted and looked my way.

'Yes,' he said, nodding. 'Yes.'

He stood up and addressed one of the other bodyguards, a large man with a weightlifter's shoulders, an imitation leather coat and a pencil-thin tie.

'Cut him loose.'

Pax Americana

Slope. Dark. Light-stripe. Dark. Light-stripe. The lone car sped down the tunnel, plunging through shafts of electric-blue light, the dripping brickwork shimmering like metal. Twice we scythed through standing pools, black sheets of water that engulfed the car.

I rubbed my swollen wrists and listened to bodyguards speaking Arabic in the front seat. According to them, the tunnels were steadily filling with untreated sewage and the deeper the pools became the more the chance of a vehicle stalling. This far under the city there were no communications and the electricity was increasingly unreliable. They did not relish the prospect of becoming stranded in a car with the Raees's volatile eldest son. They'd rather take their chances above ground.

We eventually emerged in the lower storeys of an underground car park. Motorcycle outriders had closed the road ahead of us and we drove up the ramp and out onto the street without pause. For a time we drove parallel to the Tigris and I recognized the lights of the Palestine Hotel on the far bank.

We swept through a tiled archway, framed by date palms and decked with manned AA guns, into a high walled compound and down another ramp into another underground parking area.

The bodyguard with the imitation leather coat held the

door open for me and I stepped out and was guided to an elevator, while behind me a man in overalls advanced on the Mercedes with a hose.

In the sudden, bright light the bodyguards ignored me and stared at the elevator ceiling.

'Who is this guy?' said imitation leather coat.

'Salesman,' answered slicked-back hair.

'What is he selling?'

'Weapons.'

'Of course, weapons. Does the Raees know?'

'Why do you think we are using the tunnels? This is Uday's secret.'

Imitation leather coat's nostrils flared. 'I don't like it.'

The elevator stopped and we stepped out into a corridor, our heels ringing on the marble tiles. There was no other noise. Down another corridor we went through a door that opened onto a balcony overlooking an enclosed courtyard. The balcony ran around all four sides of the courtyard and was divided by marble columns supporting a row of arches. The marble was chipped and stained by running water.

Below us, at the centre of the courtyard, a skinny-looking lioness paced listlessly around a drained fountain.

'Why doesn't he feed her?' said slicked-back hair to the other.

Imitation leather coat shrugged. 'He's got other things on his mind.'

On the far side of the balcony Miranda's husband, Bakr Abd al' Aswr, was standing, barefoot on a woven mat with his back to us. Beside him on the ground was a scratched olive-green prismatic compass.

We stopped about twenty feet short of him and waited silently as he performed the rak'a, a series of physical movements, standing, bowing, and kneeling. First he raised his thumbs level with his earlobes and then crossed his arms at waist level. He reached down and placed his hands on his knees and finally knelt down on the mat and prostrated himself, pressing his forehead to the floor.

I listened to him recite the Fatiha and then a portion of the Koran: '*He is God, One, God the everlasting Refuge, who has not been begotten, and equal to Him is not anyone.*'

Finally he stood and after a moment's calm reflection turned to look at me. His face was all prisms and sharp flintlike points.

'Does it seem threatening to you, this act of devotion?' he asked, not unkindly, in clear English with the soft, authoritative voice that I remembered from the bunker at Patrol Base Three.

I shook my head. 'No.'

He stroked the white streak in his beard. 'Your countrymen believe that all human beings are Americans under the skin, that we all want the same thing.'

'That's not what I believe.'

He nodded to himself. 'What do you believe?'

'I believe that *there is nothing but our present life; we die, and we live, and nothing but Time destroys us.*'

He seemed pleased. 'You know the Koran?'

'A little,' I said.

'You are an Arab,' he observed.

'Of sorts,' I replied. 'My father is a Palestinian.'

He held out his hand in invitation and led me over to the edge. Together, we contemplated the animal below. The lioness ignored us and continued to pace.

'She is called Zeena.' He looked across at me. 'We are prisoners, you, Zeena and I. A tame Islamist, a tame lion and . . . what about you? How did they tame you?'

'They took everything that meant something to me.'

He tilted his head slightly in a predatory hawklike gesture. 'They?'

'You're right,' I said. 'I have no one to blame but myself.'

He nodded, apparently sympathetically. 'You are sleeping with my wife?'

A pause. Slicked-back hair and his companion were lolling against a pillar. It didn't seem like they were about to kill me. 'Yes,' I replied.

'Do you love her?'

'Yes,' I said.

'Is she happy?'

'She says that she wants her son back.'

'She sleeps with you and she sleeps with Uday. What do you think she whispers to him?'

I kept my voice level. 'That she wants her son back.'

He returned his attention to the courtyard. There was a further longer pause. He looked sad.

'She is pregnant.'

After a moment I realized that he was talking about the lioness.

'I have tried to persuade Uday to return her to the zoo but he will not listen.' He looked across at me again, his gaze searching my face. 'Uday rarely listens and he knows nothing of consequences. I could attempt to warn him about the consequences of this transaction. I could tell him that for him it is the worst folly. Smallpox was a cold-war weapon: it offered the security of mutually assured destruction. Ten years ago Saddam could have used this germ as a credible threat, a means of dissuading the west from retaliating after he liberated Kuwait from the al-Sabah family, but times change. Now you have a mass-produced vaccine and we have none. The majority of

people that would die now would be the poor, the oppressed and the ignorant – the very people that you believe
threaten America – and so the tables have turned and
because you have decided that poverty foments terrorism
you have conceived a slum-clearance programme that is
gigantic beyond imagination. Now you want Saddam to
have this power of mass death because you want him to
cross the threshold and use it. It is perfect for you: a Year
Zero solution to your problems. We liquidate our surplus
populations, wipe out the ludicrous boundaries of petty
nations such as Iraq, Saudi Arabia, Egypt and Sudan and
remove any disturbance to the flow of gasoline.'

'I was under the impression that we were here to stop the
weapons of mass destruction, not spread them.'

'Does Iraq have a chemical weapons programme today?
No. Does Iraq have a long-range missiles programme
today? No. Nuclear? No. There is no threat, so your
neocons have conjured one out of thin air, out of a tired
old story.'

'More than a story.'

'A gift. A dream come true for your evangelical funda-
mentalists, the fulfilment of the prophecy of your Book of
Revelation. The end-time. A new world hastened by a
spectacular act of destruction. Having created a myth, you
want to know what it is capable of and after that you cannot
resist the temptation to try it out.'

'Do you mean the neocons or Saddam and his sons?'

'They are the same: one is the product of the other. The
Americans – your Mr Rumsfeld – built up Saddam to fight
the Iranians, just as they built up the Mujahideen to fight
the Soviets. Uday is the delinquent son of a modern myth.
These are the most dangerous kind of sons. They think
that they can change the world, so there is no limit to what

they will try to do. Uday will buy this weapon no matter the cost and at the end he will use it, and unlike his father he is not concerned with how history will judge him. He will throw himself willingly into an abyss and imagine that it is victory.'

'Like Bin Laden?'

He smiled indulgently. 'I met him once at Jaji in Afghanistan, during the war against the Soviets. There was so much spirituality on his face. This is the effect of Jihad. It is a very noble state to be in. It keeps you young, gives you a great purpose in life.'

'Tell that to the families of the victims of 9/11.'

'You create a political slum from Riyadh to Islamabad, you expect people not to be angry?'

'I understand anger,' I told him, 'but spirituality? I'm afraid that's lost on me.'

'Of course it's lost on you. You have no purpose. You treat your life as if it is yours by choice, as if it's a suit off a rack. You wear it as if you have a right to it.'

'Don't I? Don't we all?'

'No.' He clapped his hands and the bodyguards approached. 'They will take you back to your hotel, Jonah. I am giving you your life.'

Shock and awe

There was someone in the room. I heard the door open distantly as if I was submerged in water and then footsteps, the tap of stilettos on floor tiles. I struggled to lift my head but I was paralysed, my body mired in sleep. A few seconds later the bathroom light came on. Startled and blinking, I flinched against the headboard. After a brief interval the light began to flicker continuously, like muscular fibrillation. I looked down at the twisted sheets. Around me the vandalized hotel room glimmered, the floor strewn with debris. I'd come back to find the room ransacked but it didn't surprise me; as far as I could recall, every room I'd slept in since I'd got off the plane back in Kuwait City had ended up this way.

I hadn't meant to sleep. I remembered some notion of staying awake until she returned. But my body had betrayed me. I'd lain on the bed and my eyelids had drifted inexorably down.

At the bathroom door, Miranda crumpled up her dress. It wasn't the one she'd been wearing when we parted. She used it to wipe the sweat from under her breasts and armpits and flung it into the farthest corner. Naked, she stood pale as a wraith in the flickering light.

At the sink she soaped her hand and used it to wash her vulva. To rinse, she scooped handfuls of water over her abdomen and thighs. She wiped a thick cake of make-up off her face. She looked up suddenly and turned in my direction. Her face was bruised and shiny. I didn't know what to say. She seemed to assume that my silence was anger, because she said, 'Do you want to hit me as well?'

I shook my head sadly. 'No.'

'I have to sleep now,' she said, 'for a short time.'

I nodded.

'I don't want you to touch me.'

We lay like cellmates, electrically aware of each other. I faced the slender, shadowy bulwark of her back. Her skinny frame huddled against the far wall, the sheet slicing across her buttocks, the pillow folded over on itself beneath her head. I contemplated the soft hairs at the nape of her neck. I wanted to press myself down on her, imprint myself – take her back from Uday.

'They know they're not going to win a conventional war,' she whispered.

I didn't say anything. The silence hung in the air.

'A hundred million dollars and my son back,' she said. 'That's the deal I made.'

'Is that a good price?' I asked, hoarsely.

'I'm not responsible for what they do with the money or the germ.'

I was silently boiling.

'It's done,' she said. 'The exchange is set up. There's no point agonizing over it.'

I groaned.

'Can't you think of anything but fucking me?' she asked.

I buried my head in the pillow.

*   *   *

Tremendous noise. Smart weapons rained down upon the city: 2,000lb penetrator bombs and Tomahawk cruise missiles tunnelling out of the darkness. Our eyes opened simultaneously and, staring wide-eyed at each other, we acknowledged the obvious: the war had started. I looked at the dial on my unfamiliar new watch. It was 5.35 a.m.

Then the sirens and flak started.

She slipped out from under the sheet and walked over to the window. The billowing orange of the explosions washed across her naked body, the shock waves throwing up a massive plume of smoke and dust high into the predawn sky.

'Come away from the window,' I told her.

She ignored me, and the curtain, thin as a shift, wrapped itself around her naked body.

'It's not safe.'

'They've hit Dora Farm,' she said softly. Her voice sounded strangely disembodied. She ran her hands through her hair. 'Oh, my God!'

I bunched the sheet in my lap. 'What?'

'Fuck! Fuck!'

'What?'

'They've tried to take them out. Saddam and his sons.' She pointed out of the window. 'That's where I've just been, over there near the university at Dora Farm. Shit!'

'What is it?' I demanded.

'Somebody must have given up the location,' she explained, pacing back and forth across the room. 'If Uday's not already dead, he'll disappear. Soon they'll be so far underground that we won't get anywhere near them. Fuck!' She stopped abruptly and looked at me. 'We need to get out of here. We can't go out of the front entrance; where's the fire escape?'

'What are you going to do now?'

She stopped and looked at me. 'What do you mean what am I going to do?'

'Where's Legion?'

She shook her head. 'We don't have time for this.'

'We?'

She clenched her fists in exasperation. 'Yes: we! They'll come for us, Jonah. They'll kill anyone who could have given up the information. You don't get to be an innocent bystander here. Get dressed.'

'Where are the goods being exchanged?'

'There is no fucking deal, Jonah! It's too late. The war's started.'

'That won't stop Legion.'

She went over to the chair and started dressing, pulling on a pair of jeans and a T-shirt. She looked back at me.

'I love you,' she said. She closed her eyes, paused for a few beats and opened them again. 'I can't talk to you about this now. What I need you to do is get out of bed and get dressed. Please.'

We ran across a labyrinth of flat roofs, jumping from one to the next, over low palisades and through thickets of washing lines and multi-pronged TV aerials that snagged at our sleeves. We cut left and right, skirting the open spaces and stairwells and the burning embers of rooftop fires, as the stream of tracer hurtled fruitlessly into the sky and the warren of streets below us seemed to divide and merge in a continuous maze.

She was all muscle and sinew and sure-footed running, while I stumbled in a fever of fatigue and strove to keep up but fell ever further behind. I tripped against a broken balustrade and went over in a roll that carried me across the roof below.

When I caught up with her she was pulling a black robe off a washing line. She thrust a dishdasha into my hands. 'Take this.'

She started jogging, but more carefully now. I judged that we were heading north and east.

'Where are we going?' I gasped.

Abruptly she stopped and pulled the robe down over her head and shoulders. She shook out the black folds.

'We need to split up,' she said.

I stared at her. 'Are you serious?'

'They'll be looking for two people.'

'We're in the middle of a bloody war!'

'It's over.'

She was right. The air assault had ended and even the flak had tailed off. The sirens had stopped. Below us the streets were quiet, eerily becalmed.

'We have to stop Legion,' I told her.

'And I have to find my son,' she said, quietly.

There was a pause. I realized that she was going to look for her husband.

'I'm not a monster,' she said.

'I know,' I told her.

'Legion's heading for Sadr City. That's where he plans to launch the rockets from. That's where you'll find him and the smallpox.'

'Then that's where I'm going.'

'When you get there ask to be taken to Moqtada al-Sadr at the al-Hikma mosque. Tell him about the smallpox and tell him that you intend to stop it happening. He'll know what to do.' She reached out and laid the palm of her hand against my cheek. 'We'll meet at the Jamila souk in Sadr City.'

'The Jamila souk,' I repeated.

'Keep going in this direction. Stay off the main roads and don't talk to anyone.'

She lingered for a moment, staring at me. 'You should have told me earlier.'

'That I'm a spy?'

'Yes.'

'I'm sorry.'

'Stay alive,' she said.

'I'll see what I can do,' I told her.

She ducked under a washing line and strode away, departing with as much determination as she had arrived in the Russian base down in Umm Qasr, in a whirl of raven-black cloth and a black hood. Within a few seconds she had completely disappeared. I remembered that the first time I saw her I had mistaken her for death approaching.

I contemplated the dishdasha in my hands. It wasn't much of a disguise but I put it on. I walked. For the first time since I had got off the plane in Kuwait I felt as if I had a clear objective. I was going to Sadr City to stop Legion.

I walked eastwards into the early morning light, moving from shadow to shadow until I found my way barred by the open expanse of the Qanat al-Jaysh canal and I was forced to abandon the rooftops.

The first person I saw on the street was a man leading a pony harnessed to a paraffin tank. Then a group of veiled women heading for the central Baghdad markets with plastic buckets filled with fish. They appeared oblivious to the attack that had happened just hours before.

I had lived through the night. It was morning and the sun was about to come up. On the outskirts of Baghdad lakes of oil had been set on fire and a dense black pall was already drifting across the city.

Two battered old Mercs came slaloming up Port Said Street towards me. I stopped by the steel shutter of a closed shop and turned my face from the street, but they didn't pass. They screeched to a halt on either side of me. A gang of Fedayeen led by a Mook with a pockmarked nose jumped out and surrounded me. The Mook was a squat man in a shiny suit with the obligatory Saddam moustache and a pair of mirrored sunglasses. He told me in Arabic that I was wanted for questioning. I told him I was a journalist investigating a story. He smiled indulgently. His teeth were filled with gold.

I explained that I had papers from the Ministry of Information.

The Mook turned to the soldier next to him and took his AK. He casually smashed the butt into the side of my head. What I felt first was not pain but nausea, an overwhelming need to vomit. As I crumpled forward, the sky careered away and my legs collapsed. To my ears, the sound of my body hitting the ground was like a rotten melon dropped on concrete. I slid down. Blinking, I looked up at the circle of leering Fedayeen and the sky above.

The Mook stooped over me. My eye was not working as it should. He came in and out of view. He was holding something shiny in front of my face. It was my glass eye. He must have knocked it out. It seemed to blink. The Fedayeen were laughing.

'Where is Miranda?' he demanded.

My ears were working at least.

'Where are the cars?'

I shut my eye. The boots came in, each kick punctuated by a sharp pain. My lungs were empty. I couldn't breathe.

I felt myself being dragged to my feet. I could hear them laughing. I kept my remaining eye shut.

GBH

They came in without a word. I heard the click of the padlock and the bolt sliding and they came straight in and grabbed me under the armpits. I was dragged out of the cell and along a corridor that was hardly wider than my shoulders.

They took me to another room and sat me down. Blindfolded, I listened to the sound of a chair being scuffed across a floor and the stamp of boots in the corridor outside. I leant forward with my back straight and my forearms pressed together to ease the pressure on the handcuffs.

A strangely familiar voice, speaking in English with a distinctive Scottish accent, said, 'We are not savages, we look after our prisoners.'

Suddenly, the blindfold was pulled off. I kept looking at the floor. I strove to project exhaustion and dejection, the impression that everything was too difficult to understand. It was the time for saving stupidity.

'Look up, it's all right, you can look up,' he said soothingly. I listened to a long, loud bronchial rumbling at the back of his throat.

I looked up. He spat in my face. The saliva ran down my cheek and trickled into my mouth. Everybody was laughing. I let my head fall to make a smaller target of myself, once again masking my alertness. There had been enough time. I had seen the room.

There were four of them: two behind, two in front. The Iraqi that I had named Scots was sitting facing me; he was holding a man's black lace-up shoe. I had not been in this room before. There was a meat hook in the ceiling and two rubber tyres stacked against the far wall. An electric cable with exposed wires poked out of the wall to my right and there was an enormous bloodstain on the plaster in front of me. There was an unlit paraffin heater in the left-hand corner of the room. It was very cold. The air was musty and stale, as if we were far underground.

They were not wearing watches.

Scots slapped me around the head with the shoe. 'We are very worried about America,' he said. He sprang out of the chair. I kept my head down and watched his feet going back and forth. It sounded like he was tapping his palm with the shoe. 'You have election irregularities in Florida. You have flouted the Geneva Convention in Guantanamo Bay. You commit genocide against Arab peoples.'

He came over and slapped me again, harder than the first time.

'You do not come in uniform. You have forged papers. You are CIA assassin.'

'I'm not.'

'You come to kill Uday at Dora Farm.'

'No.'

He came and put his face up close as if studying me and then paced up and down and came back and hit me again. I kept my head down.

'Where is the woman?' he demanded.

'I don't know. I'm sorry.'

'Where is she?'

'I don't know. She left me.'

'Where are the cars?'

'I don't know.'

He kicked the chair over, dropping me on the floor.

'We do not have to keep you nice for a video,' he said, standing over me. 'You are not prisoner of war. Nobody knows you're here.'

One came up behind and kicked me in the back. I crawled into a ball, my knees tight up to my chin. I closed my eyes and clenched my teeth and let them kick me in my back and shins. Scots was kneeling over me, punching me in the head. I started to bleed as new and old wounds reopened.

Eventually, they lifted me up and straightened me out. My nose was pouring blood. I spat out a tooth.

'You are in the shit now,' said Scots. He nodded to the two men holding me. They blindfolded me again and dragged me back down a corridor. I couldn't tell if it was the same corridor. I listened to a metal door being scraped open. Then there was a gagging smell of shit and my shoulders were being wedged down against two ridged porcelain footpads and my head was being forced into the hole. It was as if I was being forced down into some deeper and darker dungeon. An oubliette.

From time to time I heard the sound of footsteps moving along the corridor outside. Sometimes I heard whispers and knocking, even loud voices, though I did not know who was making themselves heard.

It was cold and I had started to shiver. There was a taste of metal in my mouth. My lips had been split in several places during the beatings and the wounds kept trying to congeal. The blood from my wounds had thickened and my clothes and hair were matted with it. It was sticky and unpleasant and as it clotted it got colder.

The room was tiny. I had manoeuvred my body so that I was lying on my side, bent around the toilet pan, with my cheek resting on the concrete and my cuffed hands wedged between my thighs.

My nose was blocked with solid blood so that I had to breathe through my mouth. At least I could no longer smell anything.

They came for me again, pulling me out into the corridor by my wrists and grabbing me under the armpits. My feet dragged beneath me and the scabs on my toes scraped off on the rough concrete floor.

In the room, they hung me up on the meat hook. Someone threw a bucket of cold water over me. I gasped with the shock of it.

They removed the blindfold.

Scots was standing on the rubber tyres, wearing elbow-length black industrial rubber gloves. He was holding the electric cable from the wall. He grinned savagely. 'There is pain coming,' he said, 'a new kind of pain.'

I pissed myself as I have seen frightened dogs piss themselves on a veterinarian's consulting table.

'Where is Miranda?' he demanded.

'I don't know,' I said, my voice cracking. 'Please.'

'Where are the cars?'

'I don't know.'

The wires stroked my skin and for a fraction of a second I felt a tingling and then the hammer blow. I thrashed as the electricity jellified my musculature and blinding white light arced up and down my brain stem. When my eye regained focus it felt as if there was a large hole in my head, as if part of my brain had been removed.

'Fish supper,' said Scots, 'salt'n'sauce. Where is Miranda?'

I shook my head. I was deprived of my faculties of reason. I didn't understand the question.

Again the electricity convulsed me.

Darkness. Darkness for a long time. I opened my eye and closed it again. There was darkness inside and out.

I was confined in a space that I estimated to be at least a millionth of the size of the roaming ground of an adult polar bear.

An animal I couldn't see sniffed me. I felt a wet nose on my skin. A rat. It had come up the soil pipe. Of course there was a rat. I read somewhere that there are now more rats on the planet than humans. I shook myself and the rat fled back down the pipe.

Twice, the door was dragged open and someone stepped into the toilet and pissed on me.

It was cold. I was in a deep, dark place.

The neoliberals believed that globalization would fill the world with liberal republics, linked together in peace and trade. They declared the end of history. But you can't second-guess history. History has responded with a flowering of war, tyranny and empire. Torture is widespread.

I read once of a man who had been subject to torture – victim is the wrong way to describe him – who claimed to have been strengthened by the experience. He said that the problem for his torturers was that he held beliefs and principles based on reason and universal rights and these never left him in the dark confinement, and although his health and body were tested, his spirit grew in adversity.

I have these beliefs, they are close at hand – they were

given to me by my parents and by the schoolteachers who struggled to teach me. It was claimed that they under-pinned the society I was brought up in. But I have been around the block since then. I have been to some of the worst places in the world. I have stood on the edge of pits filled with the bodies of women and children. I have not seen any empirical evidence of universal rights. I simply do not believe in reason.

I did not have idealism to sustain me. But I had some-thing else. I had sheer bloody-mindedness. I had all the rage and shambles of my screwed-up life. They could not humiliate me any more than I had already been humiliated. They could not humiliate me any more than I had already humiliated myself. I could not be debased by the mechan-ical actions of a body I had no respect for. It was just pain. And when it was gone there would be no lasting memory. Not of the worst of it, anyway. It would fade. I knew that. Our minds aren't made to hold the particulars of pain.

But they can hold purpose. Slowly, I lifted my leg, flexed it and held it for a few seconds suspended above me and then let it gently drop. I repeated the exercise. Again and again in the darkness.

There was something else. A fragment finally recovered from my memory. Finally, I had recognized my torturer.

Again a bucket of freezing water woke me. The blindfold was removed. Scots stood on the rubber tyres holding the exposed wires of the electric cable. The others left the room and we were alone again. It was the third or fourth time – I wasn't sure.

'How are you?' he asked. It was the same question every time, the opening line in a formal ritual.

'I'm hurt badly,' I told him, truthfully.

'Perhaps we can get you some medical attention?'

'Please,' I said. 'Please help me.'

'We need to help each other,' he explained, 'so that things may run smoothly.'

'I've told you what I know.'

He shook his head. 'You are lying, Jonah. You are a Jew.'

'Please don't hurt me,' I pleaded.

'Where is Miranda?' he shouted. He brandished the wires in front of me. I wasn't even sure that he was interested in the answer.

'You were a waiter at the Phenecia Restaurant in Edinburgh,' I told him in Arabic.

He stopped and stared, the cable forgotten in his hands.

'Your name is Ali Shuaib,' I told him. 'I had two eyes then. We spoke in Arabic. You were studying civil engineering. You lived with the other Iraqi students in a small flat off the Newington Road. I used to tip you well, don't you remember?'

'Yes,' he said, softly. He looked suddenly small and frightened. I felt something like euphoria.

I hauled myself up a few inches on the hook, letting the dead meat of my hands hold me and allowing my secret store of rage to empty itself into my feet.

'I was poor like you.'

'Yes,' he said.

I lashed out, kicking him in the centre of his chest. He staggered backwards off the tyres, slipped on the wet concrete and went down with the cable in his hand. There was an explosion of sparks and arcs of lightning cracked to and fro across the floor. His body thrashed and bucked.

I hung there, a few inches off the floor, while the tides of electricity snapped back and forth and coils of smoke gently rose from his body. I'd only used a fraction of the rage that I contain.

There was a smell of roasting meat.

In the cemetery

A hand came and put a date in my mouth. I sucked on the smooth, sugary pulp. My lips were still bleeding and my mouth was filled with the mingling tastes of sweetness and iron.

Bakr said, not unkindly, 'You are in a sorry state.'

The flesh of my wrists had swollen so much that it covered the cuffs and I had lost all feeling in my hands. There was pain but it was located in unidentified parts and I experienced it distantly, as if once removed.

'You have been here for four days,' he told me. 'You are lucky to be alive.'

It didn't seem proper to talk of days; there had been only darkness and beatings and electricity.

'Where am I?' I croaked.

'You are in Baghdad, in the air-raid shelter beneath the Jadriya Equestrian Club.'

'How's the war?' I croaked.

'The Americans have reached Nasiriyah and Najaf. They are only 150 miles from Baghdad.'

'Where's Legion?'

'Here, somewhere in the city. There is not much time left.'

'Time left for what?'

'Come on,' he said, refusing to answer my question. 'Let's get you out of here.'

'I can't move,' I told him.

He called out to persons unseen. They lifted me up. I couldn't walk properly on my feet and I was half-carried and half-dragged down the corridor while they held me upright.

We went through a steel door and up a concrete spiral staircase, my feet slapping painfully against every step, and through another steel door that opened abruptly onto the world above. Outside it was permanent dusk, with black clouds of burning oil and swirling sand obscuring the sky. In the near distance bombs fell and the explosions rumbled like thunder.

I saw that we were in a stableyard. I was dragged past a cluster of grooms grappling with a huge black stallion. Beyond the stable, terrified-looking ostriches sprinted back and forth across paddocks that were fringed by rocking date palms and wind-blown brambles. In the car park there were three identical enamel-black Mitsubishi Shoguns with their engines running. A group of tall, sharp-featured Somalis carrying a mixture of AKs, PK machine guns and RPGs were standing in a loose protective circle around them. They were all wearing bulky white chemical-protection suits with gas-mask pouches at their hips.

My legs still wouldn't function, so I stumbled and tripped as I was carried towards the cars. I was bundled into the back of the nearest one and Bakr eased himself in beside me.

'Drive,' he instructed.

Looking back through the rear window, I saw that at the entrance to the club there was a mural of Uday, Qusay and their father carrying rifles and galloping on horses like an Arabic version of *Butch Cassidy and the Sundance Kid*.

★   ★   ★

We drove north-west across the burning city.

My hands hung uselessly in my lap. They hadn't bothered to uncuff me, so it seemed unlikely that my departure from the air-raid shelter counted as a rescue.

The inside of the car reeked with the sour battery-acid smell of fermenting sorghum rising off the skin of the Somalis. Bakr reached across me and wound down the car window and I felt the cool breeze hitting my skin. I turned my bruised face to it and it tingled. My body was aching all over and I was falling asleep, nodding off with my head lolling on my chest.

When I woke up we were driving down palm-lined streets in a quiet residential district on the northern side of the city. The streets were empty and there was hardly a sound.

The convoy of Shoguns parked in front of a wooden door set in a high brick wall topped with broken glass that extended for a block. The door was banded with iron and studded with nails.

Indicating for the Somalis to follow, Bakr got out and strode across the pavement to the door. I was lifted out of the car and dragged after him. Bakr pounded with his fist.

After a lengthy pause, a small hatch was pulled to one side and a paraffin lamp raised to the metal grate. Beyond, I glimpsed a face shrouded in black – a woman's face – what could be seen of it impassive but with striking turquoise eyes.

She said, 'Who's there?'

'You know me,' said Bakr.

'Step closer,' she said. He stepped up to the hatch. 'I recognize you,' she acknowledged.

'I'll break down the door if I have to,' he told her.

There was a pause followed by the sound of bolts being

thrown and the hollow clunk of the latch coming off. The door opened. I was lifted over the threshold into an unlit chamber with uneven flagstones, while behind us the woman set her shoulder against the door and pushed it shut. She slammed the bolts and turned to face us, holding the lamp aloft.

I think I knew what she was immediately, but it didn't click on a conscious level for a couple of seconds. It was the black habit and headscarf. I was thinking in terms of Islam, but the woman was a nun. I realized that we were in a convent, in the heart of Baghdad.

'You mock this place with your presence,' she told us.

'Just take us to the cemetery,' Bakr snapped.

'This way,' she said, indicating for us to follow.

She led us down a corridor with walls of lath and plaster and then along one side of a cloister and down a flight of steps. Clouds of plaster dust rose as we descended, my feet flopping uselessly on the steps.

I was dragged past a row of cells with closed doors. At the end of a corridor was a small door that opened out onto a small courtyard full of gravestones. The nun stopped at the doorway.

'I will not go any further,' she said. She turned her back on us and walked back up the corridor, taking the lamp with her.

'The last man to gain admission to this cemetery was Scott Ritter, the weapons inspector with UNSCOM,' Bakr said softly, when she had gone. 'He followed a rumour of me. He spent an hour going back and forth between the gravestones with a metal detector. He didn't know what he was looking for. He couldn't know.' Bakr looked at me. In the darkness it was difficult to read his expression. I was trying to work out what was coming, some kind of terrible revelation. 'She's not going to get her son back, Jonah.'

He set off across the cemetery, weaving between haphazardly arranged grave slabs, and the Somalis dragged me after him to the far side of the cemetery against the outer wall.

Beneath the wall was a solitary wooden cross and beside it the silhouette of a human form, a kneeling woman in a black robe.

'I did not know my wife and son were in Abu Ghraib prison,' Bakr explained. 'I thought they were still in Kuwait. I was stranded in Basra. The war had just ended and the Shias had risen against Saddam. Nobody knew what the Americans would do. I'd been branded a traitor and I couldn't go back to Kuwait or Saudi Arabia. Everything was confused. Bush called for an end to Saddam but a few days later there were Iraqi army helicopters in the air and the rising was crushed. After that, I returned to Baghdad. There was nowhere else for me to go. By the time I learned that my wife and son had been put in prison it was too late. Miranda had been released and the child was dead.'

The Somalis lowered me onto the hard-packed soil of the grave. As I leant forward to relieve the pressure on my wrists, my fingers grazed the desiccated stems of a clutch of dead flowers.

'It is the most difficult thing, to lose a child. He was five years old.' There was no hint of self-pity in his voice. 'It was a punishment for me to have my son buried here in a Christian burial ground. Uday was angry with me, the cars were lost and with them his best hope of recovering his father's favour.'

I half-crawled, half-dragged myself over to her and flattened my cuffed hands against her back. She seemed to shrink further inside herself. I let my head hang down against her shoulder. I didn't have any words. I didn't have any way of breaking through the barrier that she had erected against the pain.

'Uday sent her back to Kuwait at the same time as the prisoner exchanges. I don't know how long our son survived alone in that place. Not long, I think.'

'I'm so sorry,' I whispered. 'I'm so sorry.'

'Bring them,' Bakr said.

The Somalis grabbed us and dragged us away from the grave.

Salman Pak

We drove south-east out of the smoke-filled city, over the Tigris and out into desert.

Miranda sat beside me on the bench seat but I was unsure whether she was even aware of my existence. Her face was a mask. She stared blankly into the foot well.

Eventually we turned off the tarmac and bumped along on a dirt track alongside a barbed-wire fence and a row of collapsed and smoking bunkers. We drove through an unmanned gate and passed the wingless fuselage of a Boeing 707 and then circled an area with a small lake that was fringed by a row of trees stripped of their leaves. There were rows of barrack-like housing blocks and in front of us, beyond a huge bomb crater filled with orange-tinted water, there was a partially collapsed building.

Inside, it was like a bank vault after a raid, with the vault door lolling open and swirling motes of dust issuing out of the corridor beyond. There were fresh footprints on the floor.

I was dragged past a row of ten-foot-high metal tubs. Hanging beneath the ceiling there was a tangle of ducts and conduits and a network of mesh walkways and we had to duck repeatedly beneath the low-hanging pipes. There was no sound. Nothing was working.

At the end of a corridor we went through a steel door into an airlock. Gogol, the Russian I had first encountered in the aftermath of the battle for the patrol base, was standing just the other side. He was wearing a white protection suit with the hood down and a gas-mask pouch strapped to his leg. He had his sunglasses pushed up into his long, pale hair and the bags beneath his eyes were if anything darker and more mottled than the last time I had seen him, in the aftermath of the sandstorm down in the Zone.

Beyond him was a bare concrete room, with as its dominant feature a glass window that took up the entire far wall. It looked onto another room, a laboratory with a row of tables and workbenches that seemed larger than they should, owing to the distortion caused by the thickness of the glass. There was a body lying face down on one of the tables.

Gogol acknowledged our presence with the briefest nod and walked over to the window. My helpers carried me to him and left me propped against the glass. On the other side Ruslan, one of Legion's Chechen bodyguards, lay motionless on the table. His clothes were soaked in blood.

Gogol leant his forehead against the glass. 'On the twenty-first of February this year, a man sneezed in the lift of the Metropole Hotel in Hong Kong, There were seven other people in the lift and the following days they travelled to four other countries, Canada, Vietnam, Germany and Singapore. Just over a month later and more than two thousand people in seventeen countries had been infected with the virus SARS. One sneeze. You understand the significance of what I am saying? You understand how quickly these things can get out of control? You understand what will happen if the smallpox is released?'

'I understand.'

'Legion is wrong when he says that only Arabs will die.

Millions will die in the west also. Borders would close. The global economy would shut down. Starting up a global vaccine programme on short notice is like trying to turn a tank on a coin. Your own country, for instance, has only enough vaccine for a third of the population and the vaccine itself carries a huge risk of serious side effects: fevers, sores, blindness, encephalitis and gangrene.'

Gogol returned his attention to the corpse on the table. I let myself slide gracelessly to the floor.

'You have to admire their nerve,' Gogol said. 'It's a cowboy foray. Legion and his crew drove straight over the Iraqi border and up Route Six with Tikriti number plates on their vehicles. Tikrit is Saddam's home town, so no one dared question them. They got as far as al-Qurnah before they were stopped at a checkpoint. There was a gunfight. Several Iraqis and this Chechen died. The rest escaped.'

'Who is the corpse?' demanded Bakr.

'His name is Ruslan Maslenkov,' Gogol replied. 'He was wanted by the FSB for murder and kidnapping committed in Chechnya, Ingushetia and Dagestan. He was a known associate of the Chechen separatist leader Shamil Basayev. This is not government work, Jonah.'

'Is he infected?' Bakr asked.

Gogol snorted. 'Who knows? In case you haven't noticed, nothing works here. It's fucked. All of it: microscopes, the lot. I don't know if it ever worked. Your scientists, if you ever had any, have run off or defected. They're living in condos on Palm Beach. Their wives are having tit-jobs and face-lifts.'

Gogol stopped talking. He blinked and stared at Bakr who was pointing a pistol at him. The Somalis looked on amused.

Bakr appeared unruffled. 'I asked you a question.'

Gogol breathed out heavily. 'There's no physical sign. There won't be. The infected show no sign of contagion for up to two weeks after infection. I need that mobile lab.'

'It's coming,' said Bakr. 'We have to know where Legion is now.'

'A population centre,' Gogol told him, 'somewhere crowded. He will want to maximize the potential for infection. You think he'll sell to us?'

'Legion intends to survive this,' Bakr said. 'For that he needs money.'

'If we can get to him soon enough and buy the virus then we can destroy it before its release,' Gogol said.

Bakr looked down at me. 'You must tell us.'

'How do I know you're really going to try and stop him?' I asked.

'Where are they heading?' Bakr demanded and, turning to Miranda, he pointed the pistol at her. 'Where is Legion?'

She looked up and stared hollow-eyed into the barrel of the gun.

'I'll count to five; then I will shoot her: one . . . two . . . three . . .'

'Sadr City,' I told them.

The motorcade roared down the streets through the rolling smoke from the oil fires, the speedometer well past one hundred. A pedestrian was run over, dragged under the tyres of the lead vehicle and each successive vehicle. Given a choice of killing someone or chancing an ambush by slowing down, it was easier just to floor the pedal.

Miranda and I were wedged in between two red-eyed khat-chewing Somalis swathed in bandoliers of ammunition over their protection suits. Sweat ran out of their hair and down their faces in glistening beads. The khat churned in their mouths. They had removed my handcuffs and shooting pains were emptying out through my bloated hands and crumpled legs. Miranda continued to stare blankly downwards.

We were in the third vehicle, behind a Shogun towing a box-shaped olive-drab trailer. I guessed it was the mobile lab that Gogol had demanded.

The road to Sadr City passed the Oil Ministry, which was conspicuously untouched by the bombing, then the Ministry of Education, followed by the cracked sphere of the Martyrs' Monument, then the festering Qanat al-Jaysh canal, its water covered in thick, oily scum.

'The world of Sunnis, of Christians and Ba'athists, is behind us now,' Bakr explained from the front passenger seat. 'We are travelling into a world beyond Saddam's control.'

We entered a desolate industrial zone with the shell of a sewage-treatment plant and the darkened mass of a power station. We drove more slowly, the vehicles nose to tail down a dark street of warehouses.

'First they called it the City of Revolution,' Bakr said, 'and then Saddam City and more recently Sadr City, after Muhammad Sadiq al-Sadr, leader of the Shias, murdered by Saddam in 1999 for daring to criticize Saddam during Friday prayers. Sadr's son Moqtada controls it now. The city was designed for five hundred thousand but already there are two million and a hundred and twenty mosques. The sewage system packed in years ago and now the electricity system has collapsed. They will have to drink from the Tigris. It is lethal. One swallow will give you dysentery.'

There was a traffic circle at the entrance to the slum with a horde of dirty children wielding rags and buckets. We slowed. Three girls, beggars under the age of eight, launched themselves at the still-moving car and clung on to the door handles and wing mirrors and allowed themselves to be dragged along the road until we stopped.

Four armed militiamen with green headbands stepped off the pavement and approached the cars. The children scattered. Two of the militiamen blocked the lead car's way while a third leant in the driver's side and the fourth walked up the line talking into a handheld radio.

'Give them some money,' Bakr suggested.

I listened to the electric whirr of the window descending. The nearest militiaman leant in the driver's window and looked us over. He was young and bearded with dark brown eyes.

'We have business here,' said Bakr. He nodded to the driver, who handed over a roll of dollars.

'I want to get out of the car,' said Miranda in Arabic.

Bakr spun around in his seat and glared at her furiously. The militiaman craned his neck to see past the driver's head.

'You don't need me any more,' she said. 'Let me get out.'

'Not now,' snapped Bakr.

'I want to get out of the car,' she said to the militiaman.

Then she looked at me and burning through the mask of her face came a bright shaft of pure determination. Outside the car the militiaman stepped back and lifted his AK, aiming it at the car. The other militiamen did the same. The Somalis were packed so tightly in the cars there was no way for them to respond.

'Let the woman out of the car,' the militiaman ordered.

'She's my wife,' protested Bakr angrily.

'He's lying,' she said. 'I request sanctuary in the al-Hikma mosque.'

I didn't have much to work with, given the state of my face, but I gave her my best approximation of a smile and, after a pause, she gave an answering smile.

'I'll see you shortly,' she said.

'Let the woman out of the car,' the militiaman repeated.

'Yeah, shortly,' I croaked.

'Get out,' spat Bakr.

She opened the rear of the Shogun and got out. The militiaman nodded to his companions, who moved aside to allow us to proceed.

The convoy resumed and I watched her receding through the rear windscreen, standing beside the militiaman, her expression unfathomable. Within a few minutes we were in a warren of brick huts and small squares, weaving between piles of rubble, taking lefts and rights in narrow slum alleyways and side streets running with raw sewage. Children flitted in and out of blackened arcades and floated plastic cups in open drains.

Armed men watched us from doorways.

All against all in the Jamila souk

The stretch of sloping medieval wasteland that was the Jamila souk was illuminated by refuse fires. At the centre of the square a cluster of stalls were selling piles of rancid tomatoes and cucumbers. Women in black robes searched for food on expanses of festering rubbish surrounded by swarms of flies and mosquitoes.

The cars wallowed and bounced on the rutted tracks that criss-crossed the square.

'Stop,' said Bakr.

The convoy halted. We waited a few minutes.

The Range Rover emerged from a side street and advanced slowly across the square perpendicular to us, towing a trailer mounted with the rocket launch tubes. A hundred feet short of us, it turned broadside on and parked. The purple-black armoured panelwork of the vehicle was dented and scarred with glittering bullet marks. Magomed, the remaining Chechen, got out of the driver's side of the first car. He was wearing a chemical suit in forest-green camouflage with a flak jacket over it and had his rifle slung across his back. He strode around and opened the back door.

After a pause, Legion got out. He was the only one not wearing a chemical suit. He was in jeans and a T-shirt, holding a matt-black SIG Sauer pistol in one hand and a vacuum-sealed aluminium foil package in the other. He looked up at the blackened, smoke-filled sky with exultant carelessness and then turned back to the car to Wendy, who slid out after him. Sal got out of the front passenger side clutching his laptop and Aziz the Gujarati climbed out of the back. They were carrying assault rifles and wearing flak jackets over their chemical suits.

There was no sign of Malak.

Legion looked around and fixed us with his clear blue eyes. Without waiting for the others, he splashed through the rubbish to the centre of the ground between.

'Get out of the car,' said Bakr.

Outside, the smell from the open sewers was overpowering. The Somalis slung their arms round my shoulders for support and I let my weight hang on them as they hauled me out of the car. I flopped like a rag doll.

Eight more Somalis cradling bulky black PK machine guns and RPGs emerged from the row of Shoguns. They fanned out along the length of the cars with their guns cocked, so that there were two parallel picket lines divided by a strip of no man's land a hundred feet wide.

'Good day to you,' Legion called out. 'You must be Bakr.'

Bakr advanced on Legion. 'That's right,' he replied. 'You are Legion.'

The Somalis holding me edged onto the strip. I slumped between them, my arms still clutched round their shoulders. Legion considered the line of armed Somalis and finally he looked at me. 'You're all smashed up, Tiger. You're all out of luck.'

I didn't reply.

'So what are you offering?' Legion asked Bakr in a businesslike fashion.

'A hundred million dollars,' Bakr replied. 'The same agreement you had with Uday.'

'How is Uday?' Legion asked. 'Did he make it out of Dora Farm?'

'He's alive.'

'But no longer in the driving seat for this particular deal?'

'The Hussein family is not central to future resistance,' Bakr explained.

Legion shrugged matter-of-factly. 'It makes no difference to me. Method of payment?'

'Direct bank transfer, as originally agreed.'

'I'm amazed you people still have unfrozen assets. Are we using Hans?'

Bakr nodded. 'Yes, Hans.'

'Good old Hans; he may be a sonovabitch but he's our sonovabitch.'

'Do you have a phone?'

'Wendy,' Legion barked. She came forward holding a Thuraya satellite phone. Legion stuffed his pistol in the back of his jeans. 'Sal, fire up the laptop.'

Sal opened his laptop on the bonnet of the Range Rover and connected it by data cable to another Thuraya.

Legion dialled a number.

'Hans,' said Legion. 'How are you? This is your old friend Caspar from Phoenix. I hope we didn't get you out of bed. Yeah, we're back on track. All systems full ahead. Friend of mine wants to say hello.'

He passed the sat-phone to Bakr who read aloud from a piece of paper. 'This is your friend Ali speaking,' he said. 'I have news from your friend Assad. Wait, please.'

He handed the phone back to Legion and nodded to one of the Somalis, who banged on the side of the trailer with the butt of his AK. There was an abrupt rattle as the side door of the trailer snapped open and Gogol emerged from its shiny laboratory interior wearing a hooded white isolation suit and gloves, bright-yellow rubber boots and a gas mask.

Legion grinned. 'Kind of brings it home to you. Guess we're all glad we had our injections, huh?'

Gogol stopped in front of Legion and held out a gloved hand to receive the package. Legion passed it over and immediately reached for the pistol from the back of his jeans. Gogol walked back across the square and climbed into the trailer, closing the door behind him.

We waited. I slumped still further and the Somalis stooped and grasped me more firmly. Nobody was paying any attention to me. Why should they? Slowly, carefully, I was marshalling my rage, flexing my bruised muscles.

The door on the trailer rattled open again. Gogol climbed out and closed the door behind him. He stood for a few moments and then reached up and pulled off the mask. His long white hair was plastered against his skull and his forehead was running with sweat.

'Well?' asked Bakr.

Gogol nodded. 'It's good.'

'So do we have a deal?' Legion demanded.

'We have a deal,' Bakr agreed.

Legion passed the phone back to Bakr. 'Tell Hans the good news.'

'Your godchild is five today,' Bakr told the listening banker.

Bakr handed the phone to Legion who listened and laughed before ringing off.

'Where's the other?' Gogol demanded.

Legion raised his eyebrows comically. 'The other, Yevgeny?'

'The other package,' Gogol insisted. 'There were two

packages. Two cars. Two packages, each one five hundred grams. Where's the other package?'

Legion grinned. 'Not part of the deal, Yevgeny.'

'What do you mean?'

'You didn't think we were just going to waltz straight up here and hand over the lot, did you?'

Gogol was staring at Legion. 'What are you going to do with it?' he demanded.

Legion tossed the phone to Wendy and reached for a second pistol from the back of his jeans. 'Jesus, Yevgeny, when are you going to stop whining? The end result is the same. You release your stuff and we release ours. It doesn't matter who kicks it off. I mean, you were going to go the whole way, right?'

'You crazy fucking bastard,' Gogol told him.

'Difficult times call for radical measures, Yevgeny,' Legion told him. 'Bakr understands that. The cycle of history is again on the brink of barbarism. If over the next few decades the human population increases by half again, then over half the world's organic matter will be human. The only possible result of such a concentration of human activity is war, pollution and disease. There is a very real danger that the human race will become extinct. You understand, as responsible custodians of the planet's welfare we can't let this happen.'

I allowed myself a grim wince.

'We selectively cull animals,' said Legion. 'Homo sapiens is not so different. Pre-emptive control measures are required.'

Gogol was outraged. 'Control measures?'

'Open your eyes, Yevgeny. Much of the human race is, frankly speaking, not obviously worth preserving.'

'Particularly not the Arabs?'

'Sure. Why not? We destroyed communism, you think we couldn't do the same to Islam? Islam is the aggressive ideology of an unfree and dangerously deluded people. Take Bakr, he thinks that he's going to build an army of Jihadists out of the ashes of the plague. Isn't that right, Bakr?'

Bakr smiled.

Gogol spun around on Bakr. 'What are you doing?' he demanded, furiously.

Bakr shrugged. 'Legion is wrong. You can't kill everybody, because even with the smallpox you can't change the world as you wish. The strongest will inevitably survive. And when the dust clears and the boundaries of your rotten client states are gone for ever, what will remain is the Caliphate, one Islam stretching from Morocco to Indonesia.'

'Millions will die!' Gogol shouted at him.

'Martyrdom is all that we have,' Bakr replied in a soft voice. 'It is our strength.'

Sal looked up from his laptop and said, 'The transfer's been made.'

'And we have linkage,' Legion was triumphant. 'We have motive, intent and finally proof. Thank you, Assad.' He slapped a hand down on Bakr's shoulder. 'You're a generous man. You want a receipt?'

'You won't get away with this,' Gogol said.

'We just did,' Legion said, 'me and my crew got rich beyond our wildest dreams. In a few seconds the money will be dispersed to offshore accounts across the globe. Isn't that right, Sal?' But Sal didn't reply, he was frowning, hunched right over the laptop, his fingers racing across the keys.

'Sal, disperse the funds.'

There was no reply.

'Sal?'

'I can't.'

'Don't fuck with my pension, Sal.'

'It's frozen.'

'What do you mean it's frozen?'

'They've frozen the account.'

'They?' Legion yelled. 'Who are they?'

'I don't know!'

'I do,' I said, because there are certain times when circumstances compress you into a moment of truth. I wasn't sure at first if my voice had carried.

A beat, then all eyes swung my way.

There was an awkward moment while the assembled company contemplated me, with my mouth hanging open and my head slewed sideways, and they seemed to ask themselves whether I could possibly have spoken.

'Hans is no longer your sonovabitch,' I croaked.

Which is an approximation of what General Monteith had told me in a windowless basement beneath Whitehall before he put me on a plane bound for Kuwait: it seemed that Swiss confidentiality wasn't what it had been and even Hans, who had brokered some decidedly unsavoury deals in his time, was beginning to worry about his level of exposure in the new post-9/11 world order. Which is why, instead of getting to throw rocks at penguins in the Falklands, I got sent out here on yet another of Monteith's 'tricky assignments'.

'And if I refuse to go?' I remember asking.

Monteith's reply, when it came, was characteristically succinct. 'Do not pass Go. Do not collect two hundred pounds. In all likelihood, a dishonourable discharge and off to prison for kidnapping.'

'And if I go?'

'Witness formally retracts her statement and the police go back to chasing ordinary decent criminals.'

And so I accepted the mission, not just because they were blackmailing me (they've been doing that for four years) but also because, as I am painfully aware, like so many who constantly find themselves on the wrong side of authority, I am also in love with it.

Legion was having a hard time of it. His face was rent with fury. I suppose it must have been a blow to realize that he hadn't been able to see far enough into me to recognize the truth. He thought he'd found a protégé.

'Sal?' he demanded.

'I went through everything, Legion. I looked in every corner. I'm telling you he's dirty. There's no way he's a spook.'

But I'm a new generation of spook. I've been professionally laundered – put through the mangle – and it doesn't matter how far back in the records you go, others have hacked in first. Read the reports of my progress through school and the military: brave, timid, solitary, charismatic, inward, outgoing. You won't learn a thing. Even the stains are artificially manufactured. The fact is I ceased to be in the army for all practical purposes years ago.

There was something offhand in the manner of Sal's death, in the way that Legion simply lifted his right arm and squeezed off a shot without seeming to take aim, without even looking at him. The bullet's impact snapped Sal's head back and carried him a couple of steps before he crumpled. The laptop slid off the car's bonnet after him.

'You're not going to let me down, are you, Jonah?'

Legion growled and he pointed the gun in his left hand straight at me. He wasn't the only one. Bakr was also pointing his gun at me. The Somalis holding me shifted skittishly and exchanged terrified, khat-enhanced glances. The tension was rising second by second.

'You're not going to rain on my parade, are you, Jonah?' Legion demanded.

But I was used to disappointing people. You get numb to it after a while.

'The parade's cancelled,' I managed with the last of my voice.

He jabbed both ways with his pistols. 'I don't see any fat ladies ready to sing, Jonah.'

And right on cue, the fat ladies. There was movement on the edges of the square, a phalanx of young black-clad Shia men holding AKs, streaming at speed from doorways and out of alleyways, with expressions of grim purpose. They fanned out as they approached, swiftly encircling the opposing groups. Then I saw Miranda striding across the wasteland towards us. She stopped a couple of metres short of Legion.

'This is the Mahdi army,' she told him, 'this is their town.'

'So now the Whore of Babylon speaks!' he yelled.

'The people here will not let you leave,' she told him.

Legion pointed both barrels at her. 'Fuck you!'

She shook her head. 'Put down your weapons. Surrender while you have the chance.'

There was a pause, with eyes sliding this way and that and sweat rolling freely off foreheads and fingers hooked in trigger guards, gently stroking.

'The Mahdi army!' Legion sneered. 'Are you fucking serious?'

'Where is Malak?' she demanded.

'I'm going to kill you,' Bakr said and took two steps towards her.

Which was my cue and at last I let loose all the rage, all the stored-up self-hatred and humiliation, summoned up out of the deepest, darkest shit-hole oubliette of my soul. Yeah, the lot: losing my eye, my wife, my self-respect. The whole shebang. Now! It roared up out of me like vomit, a wave of electricity crackling across my shoulders and down my arms into my hands and I drove the Somalis' heads together, skull against skull in a thunderous clap. I thrust them away and hurled them onto the ground.

Then I stepped forward and snatched the gun from Bakr's hand. I took a few shambling paces towards Legion, who was shouting orders. I wanted to shoot him dead. But the rage was draining away. I wavered, my eye slipping in and out of focus; the gun held with both hands, one swollen finger stuffed in the trigger guard.

Legion had grabbed Miranda by the hair with one hand and with the other he was holding a pistol to the back of her head.

'Stay back,' he growled, forcing her onto her knees.

I staggered a few more steps, not sure which direction I was heading in. My eye focused again and I was pointing the gun at Bakr.

I fell flat on my face.

Then the shooting started. The air was filled with supersonic crackling, a terrible maelstrom unleashed. Bodies fell, glass burst, tyres exploded, metal screamed. The ground hummed and the sky shimmered and swirled, vapour trails streaking overhead.

*   *   *

Balanced at the centre of the crack and swirl, Legion flexed and swayed, his arms outstretched at ten and two with a SIG pistol in each hand and the veins in his forearms as taut as hawsers and his trigger fingers squeezing out a staccato: *left hand . . . right hand . . . left hand . . .*

Muzzle flashes like firecrackers.

Somali . . . Shia . . . Somali . . .

He pumped shot after shot into their scattering ranks. Thirteen rounds a magazine. Nothing touched him. There was no way he was going to die in the Jamila souq.

Abruptly he stopped, ejected his spent magazines and turned and ran. He rolled across the bonnet of the Range Rover and into cover.

I turned my head and crabbed sideways through drifts of paper and rotting vegetable matter. All around me bullets ricocheted off the ground and scraps of shrapnel whizzed through the air like firecrackers. Miranda was spread-eagled and Wendy lay collapsed on top of her. Wendy's mouth was opening and closing, with foaming pink blood leaking out of it. A round had struck her in the chest and penetrated her body armour, tearing through her chest cavity. Pieces of shrapnel scythed through her clothing as I watched, releasing explosive mists of blood. I saw Magomed go down and a few seconds later Aziz.

Miranda's eyes were closed. I reached out and touched her, my fingertips stroking her forehead. She opened her eyes and looked at me and there was an implicit challenge in her gaze: *Who are you?*

I grabbed her hands.

'Follow me,' I yelled.

I swivelled on the slope and started crawling downhill at any angle to the cars, with my elbows and knees flat against the ground. I heard the metallic cork pop of a rocket-propelled grenade going off and the rocket sailed above my head, its warhead exploding against the side of the trailer.

Gadarene

It was difficult to judge how quickly time was moving, each second stretching to fill a howling vacuum. Although my senses had been stunned by the concussion of the grenade, they were paradoxically more acute than ever. I could separate one thing from another, each individual sound: the swarming weight of flak; the slow slump of impacted cars; the living crouching and firing; the dead falling; the wounded screaming; and beside me, inches away, the steam of Miranda's breath like a blow-torch.

We came to the lip of a trench and slipped down into a drain and for a second I was fully submerged. Then I was on my knees, hands and elbows gripping the sides of the trench.

'Fuck,' I said, wiping muck from my face.

Miranda surfaced and I reached out and grabbed her. We clung to each other, in a break in time, desperately needy, extinguishing the world beyond. Then the wind blew, gusting suddenly, and a sheet of flame washed over the trench and our cowering bodies and an instant later came the ear-splitting detonation of a fuel tank exploding and after it the smell of burning flesh.

'Come on,' I said. I grabbed her by the hand and led her after me, sloshing down the trench and out of the mael-strom.

Eventually, somewhere out on the edge of the square with the sound of gunfire behind us, I levered myself out of the trench and reached down and helped Miranda up after me. There was a sudden rent in the clouds and the sun bore down on us and our clothes steamed.

'Are you OK?' I gasped.

'Do I look OK?'

'No,' I said. I stared around, looking for cover. A few feet away I saw the entrance to an alley.

'This way,' I told her.

I climbed to my feet and staggered clumsily into the alley, a narrow street hemmed in by breeze-block huts with zinc roofing. I motioned for Miranda and she followed. A gust of wind stirred the dust, picking up scraps of paper and plastic bags and spinning them around, forming miniature tornadoes in the centre of the street. From a doorway a young boy beckoned to us.

'Come,' he called.

At the entrance he indicated for us to take off our robes and for Miranda to remove her shoes. There didn't seem to be any reason not to. He took two fresh robes from a rack and passed them to us.

Inside, it was a mosque. We edged along the bare white walls, Miranda gathering the shawl of her robe around her head.

An old man with a grey Sufist's beard and eyes white with cataracts led the prayers. One of the young bearded men flanking him produced a small linen bag and emptied a heap of smooth white pebbles onto the frayed rug in front of him. His hands were guided to the pebbles and as he prayed the imam tossed them from hand to hand, occasionally dropping one and then arranging them in complex patterns on the floor.

Nobody paid us any attention. Beside me a young boy was nursing a baby with a dummy in its mouth. A few feet away there was a wild-eyed man who, when not asleep, muttered angrily.

The prayers continued. I felt desperately tired, my hands and feet throbbing with dull pain. Miranda stared blankly at the carpet, lost in her own private grief. We had reached our own end-time.

After the prayers came the chanting.

'*Hu, hu, hu,*' grunted the congregation, on and on, louder and louder for several minutes until they reached a deafening peak. There was a short pause and then they started again.

'*Hay, hay, hay,*' they chanted, their voices rising in a call to forget the world, each crescendo higher than the one before. There was rapture in it, a kind of fierce and cleansing elation; in it you could disappear and become nothing. I wanted nothing more than to become nothing, to find the mind's tune and lose myself for ever in the hypnotic chanting.

The voices eventually fell into silence. People were shaking and drained. I felt empty of everything and suddenly I could think again, clearly enough to understand. There was an opportunity to right my various wrongs and for the first time I felt urgency and purpose.

'Malak has the other package, hasn't he?'

She nodded.

'We have to stop him,' I told her.

She looked up at my face and it was as if she was seeing me for the first time.

'Come on,' I told her.

We staggered outside into the narrow alley, followed by the wild-eyed man. He muttered incomprehensibly and then shuffled away down the street.

From the mouth of the alley I could see the length and breadth of the square. It was eerily silent. The shooting had stopped and between the lines of smoking cars and the burnt-out trailer nobody moved. We took off the robes.

'We need a vehicle,' I told her. We limped across the square.

Three of the tyres on one of the Shoguns were still intact and we stepped over piles of corpses to reach it. There were bodies everywhere. I relieved one of the Somalis of his boots, sunglasses and keffiyeh. From another I took his AK, from several their magazines.

Miranda knelt beside her husband's bullet-ridden body. 'I don't know him,' she said. 'I hardly recognize him.'

'There's no time,' I told her and my voice sounded harsh even to my own ears. 'Find some body armour. And look for Legion. I want to know he's dead.'

She gazed up at me.

'Hurry,' I said.

She nodded and climbed to her feet.

I turned my attention to the Shogun. The bodywork was riddled with bullet holes and the dashboard and upholstery were carpeted with glass from the shattered windows, but the damage was superficial. The key was in the ignition and the engine turned over on the first attempt. It sounded fine. I brushed off the back seat and loaded it with weapons, an RPK-74 machine gun and an RPG and cans of 7.62mm ammunition. I had to pause often, resting my head between my knees. The pain came in waves, the throbbing in my wrists and ankles and in my ribs and my face increasing in intensity then falling off again. I tried to change the wheel. I got the jack out of the back of the Shogun and managed to manoeuvre an intact spare out of the back of one of the other Shoguns. I rolled it over to the one that needed replacing but when I stamped on the wheel brace to loosen the nuts my jaw fell open in an involuntary scream and the pain overwhelmed me. I blacked out.

When I came to I was slumped against the side of the car and Miranda was standing over me holding two Kevlar vests.

'Legion's not here,' she said.

'Then he's alive,' I groaned, my head spinning, 'somewhere nearby.' I expected him to appear from one of the surrounding alleyways at any moment. I struggled to focus my mind. I had to get a grip, to keep my actions orderly. 'Put that body armour on,' I told her.

'You look as if you could do with some help,' she said.

'You're the one who's good with cars,' I acknowledged.

'You want a cigarette?' she asked.

'I want you to change the wheel.'

'Have a cigarette,' she said, gently.

I accepted one, the flame from the lighter trembling in her hand. I dragged hungrily at the nicotine.

'They were stopped at a checkpoint in al-Qurnah,' I told her, as she loosened the nuts on the wheel. 'One of the Chechens died in the shoot-out. That's what Gogol said.'

'Malak must be in the marshes,' she said. 'He knows the marshes. He was there before. He has allies there. From al-Qurnah it's easy to get into the marshes.'

She jacked up the vehicle, pulled off the old wheel and rolled it away. Then she lifted the new one onto the bolts.

'So that's where we're going,' I told her.

She nodded grimly. 'That's where we're going.'

I watched her tighten the nuts, spinning the brace in her palms. Then she let down the jack and stowed it in the back of the vehicle. When she was done she held out the other vest. I put it on, wincing as I tightened the Velcro straps across my bruised ribs.

'I'll drive first,' I told her.

Miranda sat beside me in the Shogun. She folded her arms and turned her face away from me, pressing her forehead to the glass. I glanced at her; she radiated exhaustion.

'Are you strong enough for this?' I asked.

'I'm strong enough,' she replied wearily. 'What choice do I have?' She looked back at me. 'Anyway, you don't look so hot yourself.'

'Legion was right,' I said, 'I'm all done in.'

We backed up and crossed the square, threading through the wreckage and taking the first route out of the ghetto.

On the scarred and blackened road out of Baghdad we watched immense ladders curve down out of the sky and as each rung struck the ground there was an explosion and a rippling, thunderous booming.

The bombs were falling from B-52s flying unseen, far above the haze. The Americans were demolishing the heavy armoured divisions of the Republican Guard, the Medina and the al-Nida, in their holding areas on the outskirts of the city.

We passed the burnt-out hulks of Russian-built T-72 tanks and oil tankers and desultory groups of soldiers squatting in the reeds on the banks of the Tigris. We passed mile after mile of brutalist electricity pylons, stretched out to the horizon, looking like broken-necked giraffes.

Three hours from Baghdad, on the road beyond al-Kut, we swapped places so that Miranda could drive. I sat in the passenger seat and fed bullets into magazines.

The police cruisers came over a rise behind us, advancing three abreast with the spinning blue lights of their roof arrays pulsing in the rear-view mirror.

'Put your seat belt on,' I told her.

I climbed over the seat into the back, extended the legs on the bipod of the PK and set them on the top of the bench seat. I fed a belt of link ammunition in the breech, locked and loaded.

'Stand by,' I called.

I opened fire and a streak of ball and red tracer arrowed towards the target, the recoil kicking into my shoulder and a cascade of searing brass cartridges tumbling out of the weapon onto the seat and the foot well and onto my exposed skin. The cars broke left and right, scything across the desert and trailing comet's tails of dust. One of them rolled and disappeared in an explosion.

The second wave came on. I spotted the familiar outline of one of the Range Rovers. They were gaining on us. I emptied the last belt of link and threw the machine gun out after it and it tumbled away along the tarmac. The Range Rover swerved to avoid it and slalomed along the road verge.

'Put the pedal to the metal!' I yelled.

'We can't go any faster,' she screamed.

The first of the police cruisers pulled alongside us, roaring across the desert. The others jockeyed for position on either side of us, the occupants firing wildly, the streams of fire snapping like bullwhips, converging and diverging around us. The remaining windows shattered.

I scooped up the RPG, removed the nose cap and the safety pin and set it against my shoulder. I pressed my torso into the bench seat and braced my leg against the back of the driver's seat. I glanced back to make sure the rear nozzle was aligned with the opposite window and, setting my eye against the optical sight, I aimed it out of the side window.

I fired and the rocket streaked across the gap, hitting the nose of a police cruiser, the molten copper slug slicing through the engine block. The car seemed to pause and an instant later the nose dug into the sand and it somersaulted, over and over, unravelling like orange peel.

The Shogun was filled with smoke from the back-blast and the snap and crackle of bullets and ricochets and spinning flakes of steel. We left the road, the tyres thudding and rattling along the sand. I threw the RPG stalk out of the window and climbed into the front seat and grabbed the AK. We veered back onto the road. We were taking fire from every direction, the bullets puncturing streaks of light through the bodywork.

The armoured Range Rover was alongside us now, its panelling scored and burnt, its blackened windows a crazy paving of glittering bullets and striated armoured glass.

I strafed it back and forth, emptying a magazine into it without visible effect.

'Jonah!' Miranda screamed.

There was a burnt-out truck in the centre of the road. 'Go left!'

We slammed like a dodgem into the side of a cruiser and it veered away, unpeeling like a sardine can, the metal screeching like chalk on slate. We stormed out into open desert, away from the Tigris, flanked by pursuing vehicles. I emptied five magazines, shooting left and right in multiple bursts out of every window. Another car rolled.

I was out of ammunition. It was the Shogun and the Range Rover now. Miranda glanced across at me, her face a mask of fear. I did up my seat belt.

'Just drive,' I said.

One of the tyres burst and the whole vehicle started to shudder, strips of rubber shredding and flailing away behind us. The Range Rover pulled alongside again. Then the front passenger window glided downwards and I was faced with Legion's lupine grin and his eyes like furnace doors ajar. He bared his bright white teeth and opened his mouth.

Another tyre burst and another. The Shogun was dragging itself forward now, with the engine screaming in rage and pain, the bodywork flying off and a jet of searing black oil spraying from the bonnet.

Legion was speaking, his mouth and tongue moving in a complex incantation with flecks of spittle on his lips and teeth.

Miranda was screaming. I was screaming. We were covered in oil and enfolded in clouds of billowing steam.

Then we were in the minefield, in the grip of a bestial turbulence. There was a flash and a thunderclap and the first mine picked up the Range Rover – the armoured cladding seemed to bulge and contract – and flipped it on its roof and in the blast wave the Shogun slewed sideways, the back sliding out in a spray of dust and gravel. The rear left-side wheel hit another mine.

The Shogun opened like a flower. Then, casually, it was happening: I was flying through the air.

THE MARSHES

'Thou hadst cast me into the deep, in the midst of the seas; and the floods compassed me about: all thy billows and thy waves passed over me.'

The Book of Jonah

A turbulent rebirth

A vulture is slouching towards me – it's maybe ten or eleven feet away – swinging its black ruff of feathers and its bald death's head from side to side. Then it leaps, spanning the distance, the scarlet insides of its mouth parting in a screech as loud as a thousand mourners.

Finally, I find my voice. After all, why come so far to die? I'm not done yet. 'Fuck off!' I roar.

Startled, it lands at my feet and hops sideways and then takes ungainly flight.

I didn't do it. Don't get me wrong, I accept full responsibility for it and I am forced to accept the consequences of it, but I didn't agree to it. Douglas Barr, my wife's lover, was lifted without my knowledge.

It was the autumn of '99 and I was fresh back from Kosovo, between missions and once again attached to an infantry regiment. Once again in command of an ungovernable platoon, which viewed me with the innate suspicion of any pack to an outsider. I was never confronted, not face to face, but words like *wog* or *raghead*, *paki* and *nigger* had a habit of drifting across the parade square, the range testament to the level of confusion about my ethnic origin. They didn't know what to make of me and I don't think they were much interested. Certainly nobody had me down for a spook.

When the call came and Alex asked me to meet him out by the perimeter of the camp, I didn't give it much thought. I dressed in black as instructed. I took the secret way out of the camp. There was a certain familiar routine – Monteith had a habit of using Alex as a cut-out to communicate with me. It's not that I'd forgotten Alex's offer of revenge. I'd struggled with it, sure. I'd even dreamt about it. But I'd never taken the offer seriously. In fact, it wasn't until I was standing outside the steading and the woman, with her deliberate and teasing resemblance to my wife, lit up her face with a lighter flame that I realized what had been done in my name.

I'm not trying to deny that I felt that sulphurous heat inside the steading, the visceral desire to rip out Douglas's tongue at the root. And the remorse that I felt afterwards was just as genuine. But I'm not to blame.

The question, the one that I repeatedly turned over in my mind as I walked back down off the moor and in the car on the long silent drive back to Edinburgh, was why. Why had he done this? I had quickly discounted the notion that Alex's actions had been prompted by some brotherly sense of male solidarity. Alex's chumminess had its limits. He rarely took unpremeditated action. Whatever it was, there was something in it for him.

It was only when we were back in Edinburgh, parked in a lay-by alongside the woods surrounding Dreghorn barracks, that Alex indicated that he was ready to speak.

'Oh come on,' he replied in answer to my question, 'don't tell me you didn't give my offer some thought.' He sighed and reached up and switched on the car's interior light. 'Please, don't take it personally. I have to make a living, after all. Your people saw an opportunity to consolidate their stake in you and took it.'

I was incredulous. 'This was an approved operation?'

'You know yourself that you have a wayward streak. You can't keep coming and going, Jonah; once you are in their world, you are in for keeps. Your wife recognized that. That's why she left you. I was contracted to formalize the arrangement.'

There was a pause while I considered this information. 'So how does this work?'

'The police will want to question you. Everyone is going to know you did it. But there's no proof. No evidence. You deny everything and no formal charges will be brought. The police will find something better to do.'

'And after that?'

'It's very simple. You show any signs of waywardness or, for instance, an inclination to publish your memoirs, and your controller will tip the police a nod and a certain young policewoman, a former member of an undercover unit working in Northern Ireland, is arrested and offered immunity from prosecution in return for testimony. She tells them that you appeared at the cottage on the second night and that she got a good look at your face. The service dismisses you as a psychopathic fantasist and you go to jail for kidnapping and probably never see your daughter again.'

For the second time that night I could have killed someone with my bare hands. I felt the sulphurous heat wash through me again and a fierce tingling in my hands and my gums. Alex, who was experienced in reading such signs, nodded to someone unseen and there was a brief flare of reflected light on the windscreen and a small red point of light hovered just above my sternum. Alex had always had a taste for the melodramatic.

'Don't get any ideas,' he cautioned.

I concentrated on my rising and falling chest, the cadence of my breath, and let the moment pass.

Eventually, I asked him, 'And if I behave?'

'Life carries on as normal, you continue to work at arm's length and everybody gets along swimmingly. I mean, Christ, I've just given you the perfect cover! You're disgraced. They could send you anywhere.'

Even here.

I'm alive and unmasked, flat on my back, covered with blood and dust and shit, but alive. Again. Twice now a tank mine has whipped me raw and catapulted me into the sky. Twice now my life with all its lousy decisions, events both banal and tumultuous, lies and concealments, artifice and bad faith, has flashed before my eyes. Twice, against all the odds, I have survived. This is me talking, in the here and now. And I am glad.

The buzzing in my ears is lessening.

Miranda.

I stamp the ground with the flat of my hands and use the impetus to lever myself up onto my elbows. I look around. Twenty feet away the wreck of the Shogun is burning. Beyond it, the Range Rover, held together by its armour, lies upside down like a stunned cockroach.

I swivel around.

She is huddled in a ball and covered in a white sheet of dust. I roll over on my stomach and crawl towards her, dragging myself forward on my elbows and with each heaving movement, with every exhalation, I groan out loud . . . *breathe . . . breathe!*

I make promises: deliver her alive and I will make amends for all my various wrongs. I will be an honest

man, non-violent, faithful, a good father. I will quit spying.
I will do my best.

I grab the nearest part of her and it is as if a jolt of
electricity passes through her: her whole body tightens,
wrapping in on itself, and then there is an explosive
racking. She coughs and splutters and gasps like a ship-
wrecked survivor surfacing for the first time.

She is alive. My heart soars. Who says prayer does no good?

She opens her eyes and for a fleeting moment smiles.

'You're crying,' she says.

'Got something in my eye,' I say hoarsely.

Then she remembers and the grief brims up in her and
overflows, rising from a tightly furled pit, from that deep
place where she has kept her love for her son alive for over
twelve years.

We rest our grimy foreheads against each other and tears
run freely down her cheeks.

'I thought you were dead as well,' she sobs softly. 'I
dreamt I was looking for you among the piles of dead in a
vast battlefield.'

'I'm here,' I tell her. 'I'm not going anywhere.'

'I love you,' she says.

'I love you too.'

She rubs the tears from her eyes with the back of her
hand. 'What do we do now?'

'It's not finished,' I tell her.

'It's not,' she acknowledges, 'Legion?'

I glance back at the Range Rover and the mass of
vultures clustered around the windscreen and windows
tugging at strips of carrion.

'I'd better take a look.'

'Be careful,' she warns.

*　　*　　*

I drag the buckled door open and the flies rise like a wave. Legion is suspended upside down from the harness with his mouth hanging open and blood spooling out.

He's alive.

I squat down beside him. He is still talking, the words barely intelligible through the wreckage of steel and porcelain that is all that remains of his teeth. There is no sense in the words. No meaning that I can discern. But then he becomes aware of my presence and his eyes roll in my direction.

'You had me fooled, Tiger,' he slurs, 'I didn't take you for an errand boy.'

'Somebody had to stop you.'

He closes his eyes and opens them again. 'Did you volunteer for this, Jonah? Did you leap at the chance?'

'Not exactly.'

'You'll never belong,' he says and despite everything, there is gloating in his voice. 'They'll never let you in, Jonah. No matter how hard you try. You're the wrong kind.'

'You're dying,' I tell him.

'And the oceans will run with blood,' he intones. He coughs up some darker, fibrous matter. 'Did she tell you she loves you?'

'Go to hell.'

'Hell is on this earth, Tiger, and we are in it,' he whispers and his mouth forms the terrifying rictus of a smile. 'You're going to destroy the world, Jonah.'

Then the blood starts to pour like a waterfall from his mouth. I reach out and pinch his nose between my thumb and forefinger and he starts to choke and I hold on as he thrashes and gasps while his blood pours onto my chest and lap.

Finally, he is dead.

I stand up and stagger back to the road and behind me the vultures swoop down on the car again.

Miranda looks up at me and I don't have any comfort to offer her.

'Let's find some shade,' I say.

I help her to her feet and we walk slowly, supporting each other, across the sand towards the road. We find shelter in the shadow of a burnt-out truck, strip off our body armour and flop down exhausted on the tarmac. Above us vapour trails rise like pieces of lint stretched to their limit. We are all done in.

'He said I'm going to destroy the world,' I tell her.

Hours pass.

A distant drum roll rumbles across the surface of the desert towards us. My first thought is that it is the Americans, a column of tanks on the road. The rumbling gains in volume until it resolves itself as the fearsome clattering of loose metal tracks on tarmac and the roar of a single, straining diesel engine.

I risk a glance from the shadows and look first south and then north towards Baghdad. A bulldozer is bearing down on us. It's an old, battered D6 that is flecked with orange paint and there is an Arab, with his face tightly wrapped in a red-and-white keffiyeh, hunched at the controls and a white flag on a bamboo pole flying above the open cab.

I step out of the shadow of the truck and hold my arms out to show that I am unarmed. I walk forward towards the bulldozer with a packet of cigarettes in my hand.

The Arab spots me. The bulldozer judders and seems to rear with the blade rising and then settles back on its tracks.

The engine idles noisily. The Arab loosens his keffiyeh and leans forward over the tracks to take a look at me.

'*Salaam aleikum,*' I shout, standing beneath him.

He switches off the engine. The silence is startling.

'*Salaam aleikum,*' I repeat. Miranda steps out of the shadows behind me.

'*Salaam aleikum,*' the Arab replies, regarding us impassively.

'*Khayfa-l Haal?*' How are you? I ask.

'*Khayfa-l Haal?*'

'*Alhamdulillah. Allah yubaarikfi. Allah yubaarikfi.*' Allah be praised. May Allah bless you. May Allah bless you.'

'*Alhamdulillah. Allah yubaarikfi. Allah yubaarikfi.*'

'Take some cigarettes,' I say, climbing up on the tracks and passing the packet up to him.

He helps himself to several, lights one with cupped hands, flicks away the match and then disperses the others amongst the pockets of his dirty dishdasha. Then he sits back and exhales. He is a lean man, with an austere face and dark eyes. 'You are lost,' he says.

'What makes you say that?'

He looks around, as if the answer was too obvious for words.

'Where have you come from?' I ask.

'Ramadi,' he replies, 'west of Baghdad.'

'Where are you going?'

'To al-Amarah.'

'When will you get there?'

'*Insh'Allah, bukra.*' God willing, tomorrow.

'May we travel with you?'

'Are you in a hurry?'

Miranda and I glance at each other. 'Yes,' she says.

'I am also in a hurry,' he says, without any detectable trace of irony. 'Climb aboard.'

We ride huddled together on the floor of the cab and share water from a scratched plastic container while above us the Arab grips the levers and the bulldozer rattles and clatters down the road towards the distant city of al-Amarah.

We camp that night away from the road and spend an hour or so cutting reeds and camouflaging the bulldozer in preparation for the coalition night patrols.

Afterwards we sit beneath a tree and share some flat-bread and dates and the man prepares tea, transferring it back and forth between a set of shot glasses and an enamel teapot lodged on a bed of coals in the sand. We drink three draughts of tea. The first, he explains, sweet like love, the second bitter like life and the third soft like death.

We smoke cigarettes and he tells us his story.

His name is Hashim Hunein and he is a Marsh Arab, born in the marshes in 1929 when lions and hyena roamed free. He was raised in a house built of latticed reeds on a floating reed platform in the Hawr al-Hawizeh marsh. For over two hundred years his family had fished, kept buffaloes and grown rice and millet in the summer and wheat and barley in the winter. He was resettled to a breeze-block settlement west of Baghdad following the uprising in 1991. Now he was going home.

'How far are we from al-Amarah?' I ask.

'A comfortable distance,' he says. 'You will see it to-morrow.'

He shares with us the news broadcast on the radio that

the Marsh Arabs led by Abu Hattem, the lion of the marshes, have risen up and captured al-Amarah and al-Qurnah. I remember the Arab in a spotless white dishdasha and Sam Browne who had been introduced to me by Legion beside the buried container full of bodies.

'Where is Abu Hattem?' I ask.

'In al-Amarah,' he replies.

'Will you take us to him?'

'Of course.'

'Is this your bulldozer?' Miranda asks.

He laughs. 'It is now.'

'What are you going to do with it?' she asks.

'The tyrant is gone,' he says. 'It is time to flood the marshes once more. For years I have dreamt of casting my net in the marshes again; now I am going to make it happen. I'm going to destroy a dam, as many dams as I can. You cannot hold back the water for ever.'

In due course he stubs out the last of the cigarettes. 'Come, it is time to sleep.'

He gives us a blanket and we huddle beneath it, holding each other as the desert rapidly cools around us. Out on the horizon, decoy flares thrown out by American planes flash like distant lightning.

We meet the first roadblock outside al-Kumayt, just north of al-Amarah. A group of Marsh Arabs emerges from the shadow of a wrecked T-55 tank to watch the slow progress of the bulldozer towards them. They are wearing black-and-white chequered keffiyehs and holding a collection of AKs and RPGs. They hold up their hands for us to stop.

'Where are you going, old man?' they call, their voices filled with amusement.

'I've come to break the dams.'

They laugh. 'Help yourself. And the foreigners?'

'They come to speak with Abu Hattem. Where is he?'

'In town,' they reply, 'at the Governor's office.'

'I'll go with you,' one of them offers. He climbs up into the cab and squats beside us with his AK clutched between his knees.

We continue to clatter down the road.

We find Abu Hattem standing, surrounded by body-guards, on the steps of the administration building in the dusty square at the centre of the town. Hashim parks the bulldozer on the edge of the square and we dismount and walk towards Hattem. As before, he is wearing a spotless white dishdasha and polished leather Sam Browne and he is holding a black satellite handset to his ear. He listens in silence but his eyes swivel in our direction to acknowledge our approach. He nods almost impercept-ibly. A small boy is kneeling at his feet holding the small, square satellite dish at a shallow angle.

'Americans,' he says, cutting the connection, as if the word explained every stupidity. 'Are you Americans also? Have you also come to tell me to get back into the marshes?'

'No,' I tell him.

'I remember you,' he acknowledges and switches to English. 'You were with Legion. Are you CIA?'

'No.'

'Where have you come from?'

'Baghdad.'

He laughs. 'On a bulldozer?'

'Some of the way.'

'Where is Legion?'

'He is dead.'

His hard, shiny eyes do not register any emotion. 'What do you want?'

'We are looking for someone.'

He gestures around him. 'Everyone is searching for lost ones. This country is full of graves. What makes you think I can help you?'

'We are looking for a Yezidi,' Miranda tells him, 'a young man named Malak who bears a peacock tattoo on his chest.'

'Do not repeat his name here,' Abu Hattem growls.

'We believe that he is hiding in the marshes,' Miranda insists.

'We know this man,' Abu Hattem says. 'A few years ago he sought shelter with us in the marshes. We believed that he was an escaped prisoner. We trusted him. But he was a spy working for the Iraqis. He betrayed our refuge to the Iraqis and many of my people were killed. He is no friend of ours.'

'He is back,' Miranda says, 'and he has with him a weapon that will kill your people and not just your people; across the world it will kill many millions of people.'

He shakes his head sceptically. 'A weapon of mass destruction?'

'Yes,' I say, 'the real thing.'

'What are you going to do if you find him?' he asks.

'We are going to stop him.'

He considers our bedraggled condition. 'How?'

'We need your help,' I acknowledge.

'He came this way in a convoy of vehicles with Tikriti plates,' Miranda explains. 'He was travelling in an armoured Range Rover.'

'There is the wreck of a car that fits that description in al-Qurnah.'

'We need to get there.'

He deliberates for a minute or so and then nods. 'Come then.'

The tree of the
knowledge of good and evil

Slewed sideways in the middle of the road and up on blocks, stripped of anything valuable and surrounded by the corpses of Iraqi soldiers killed in the ambush, the Range Rover resembles the scorched shell of a monstrous black beetle brought down by industrious ants.

Opposite it, in a small square surrounded by single-storey breeze-block houses is Adam's tree – a dead cedar tree – its silvery-white branches like gnarled, arthritic fingers. Behind it is a low brick wall and beyond that the broad, shallow flats where the Tigris and the Euphrates converge.

We get out of the Land Cruiser and a crowd soon gathers around Abu Hattem. There is a heated exchange. Hands wave and fingers point. We hang back, aware of our status as outsiders.

Eventually Abu Hattem extracts himself from the crowd and comes over to us with a skinny, hollow-faced man at his side.

'You are right, Malak is alive,' says Abu Hattem. 'He stole a canoe and went west into the marsh alone.'

'We need to find him,' I say. 'There isn't much time.'

Abu Hattem indicates the skinny man beside him.

'This is Dhauba. He is a Mandean. He will be your guide. He says he has reason to hate the Yezidi.'

I nod in greeting but the Mandean seems unwilling to meet my eye. Miranda is staring at the dusty earth.

Abu Hattem unbuttons the holster at his waist and offers me his handgun. It is a stainless-steel Smith & Wesson 0.38 revolver with a wooden grip – practically a museum piece. I weigh it in my hand and open the cylinder. There are only three bullets.

'Kill him,' he says.

'I will,' I tell him.

The still surface of the water sparkles as we glide across it. Dhauba stands at the stern of the canoe with a bamboo pole in his hands and a knife in his belt, propelling us forward. The canoe is narrow, only three and half feet at her widest beam, the prow and stern sweeping upwards in curves to form tapering stems. The seams are caulked with bitumen and sheep's wool.

We sit on movable boards near the bow. I look into Miranda's eyes; it's obvious she's bone-weary and her face is so thin that it has contracted to sharp planes and etched lines. I dread to think what I must look like. 'Try to sleep,' I tell her and she rests her head on my shoulder. I shift the revolver from hand to hand. I realize that I am happy to be here with her even though we are putting ourselves in harm's way. It feels like a gift.

She looks into my face and her fingers lightly stroke the back of my head. 'What are you thinking?'

'I was thinking that I'm glad that you're here,' I tell her. 'And you?'

She is searching my face. 'Do you trust me? Do you?'

'We're out here in the marsh together,' I say. 'What choice do I have?'

'I don't think they intended you to survive Baghdad,' she tells me.

'What do you mean?' I ask.

'They have your passport. When they killed Odd and stripped his vehicle they stole it and now Malak has it. The Orlovs altered it.'

'And?'

'He's going to pretend to be you, to get back into UK. He plans to carry the infection there. That's what Legion meant when he said that you're going to destroy the world. You were going to be Typhoid Mary. In the aftermath, you were going to take the blame. It's a set-up.'

We pass an Iraqi artillery piece, sinking beneath the rising waters; it is clear that the dams are already being broken and the marshes reclaimed. A kingfisher, as bright as a jewel, flits between the reeds. The landscape is transformed.

'When this is over, if we get out, is there any hope for us?' she asks.

We pass a fitful, restless night on an island in the ruins of an old settlement, in the carcass of a reed mudhif, the piers of bound desiccated reeds like the remains of a bombed-out cathedral. The moon when it rises is almost full and scuds of cloud race across its surface.

We lie down on reed matting and Dhauba squats on his haunches some way off, silently and expectantly watching. He is a Mandean, which means that he believes that the world is divided between two forces, the world of light and the world of darkness. To Mandeans, man is a product of the forces of darkness and death is the day of deliverance when the soul leaves the body and starts on a dangerous journey into the realm of light. I cannot help but think of Monteith, my controller, and his words on the eve of the first Gulf war, his conviction that God and the Devil are engaged in a wager and the Devil has an even chance to defeat the Lord.

Dhauba means 'Hyena', which as I understand it, is intended to offer a measure of protection against the evil eye. But it is difficult not to look for further meaning in a name: there is something hyena-like in the prehensile curve of his back, his stiff hair and his watchfulness. I do not know whether to trust him. His long fingers never stray far from the knife in the sheath at his belt.

When I am sure that Miranda is asleep, I gently slide my arm out from under her head and ease myself off the matting. I go over and squat beside him, wincing at the pain in my bruised thighs and calves. Something shifts in the marsh and a sound like a groan travels across the water. I shiver.

'Do you know where the Yezidi is going?' I ask him, my voice barely rising above a whisper.

'Towards the ruins at the city of the moon,' he replies with grim certainty.

I do not ask him how he knows this and he shows no inclination to provide an answer. Instead I ask, 'Why do you hate him?'

He will not meet my eye. He looks down at the ground in what I take to be embarrassment. 'He lay with my sister; now she cannot marry.'

'The Yezidi has something, a silver-foil package. We have to recover it.'

'I know nothing of any package,' he says, with his fingers sliding up and down the sheath of his blade.

'Nevertheless,' I tell him. 'He cannot die until the package is recovered.'

'I know nothing of any package,' he repeats, dully.

I decide not to press him any further. I retreat back to the mat and ease myself in beside Miranda and we lie like spoons. I listen to the soft fall of her breath. I feel uneasy and despite my exhaustion I know that there will be no sleep this night.

An hour before dawn, Dhauba comes and squats beside me. The mudhif is surrounded by mist and dark shapes are moving in the marsh around us.

'What is it?' I whisper.

'We must go at first light,' he tells me, 'if we mean to reach the ruins by nightfall.'

We drink tea and dry bread and a few dates and watch the red disc of the sun break the surface of the water. The mist burns off, revealing a herd of water buffalo. When they have passed we slide the canoe back into the water and scramble aboard.

We move across the water, making barely a sound.

The heron stands motionless in the dusk light, surrounded by reeds as high as a man, its beak pointing like a dagger at the water.

I exist in a state of exhausted wakefulness and the further we travel into the marsh, the more I am burdened with a sense of ominous foreboding. I feel the familiar hollow pit in my stomach that precedes battle. With it, the lines come unbidden: *'For the thing which I greatly feared is come upon me, and that which I was afraid of is come unto me. I was not in safety, neither had I rest, neither was I quiet; yet trouble came.'*

She stares out across the expanse of reeds. By dusk light the landscape has a kind of sinister magic.

'Do you even have a daughter?'

I feel my face suddenly tighten.

'Yes,' I say. Not looking at her but aware of her eyes on me.

'What's your real name?'

'Jonah.'

She looks away again. We sit and stare in silence at the passing marshlands. I have no idea where we are or how to get back. I want to leap out of the boat onto dry land, to stretch my cramped legs and stride and stride through the night and find some kind of respite in motion, but there is nothing but the boat and the darkened mass of the marsh around.

'I haven't lied to you,' I tell her.

Her body is racked by a sob. 'I thought I was going to get my son back.'

'I know,' I tell her.

Tears are flowing down her face. I put my arms around her.

'I'm tired,' she says.

The sun sinks and the water and the sky run unimaginable colours.

'There is a storm coming,' Dhauba informs us.

Ground Zero

From the river an irregular stairway rises between broken bulwarks of ancient masonry. Dhauba poles between the reeds and we moor alongside an ancient stone jetty. At the bottom of the stairway, Dhauba lays his bamboo pole along the length of the canoe. He slips his knife out of its sheath and, without looking back, sprints up the stairway and within seconds he is lost in the darkness.

'Shit.'

There is a long slow roll of thunder. It appears that my concerns about Dhauba are well founded. He has abandoned us.

We look uneasily at each other. There is no choice but to follow. I stick the revolver into my waistband and we slowly climb the steps, feeling our way on the cracked steps with our hands. When we reach the top the moon, yellow as an old tooth, appears in a rent in the gathering clouds and the landscape is illuminated. Before us is a huge block of weathered basalt with blunted features that must once have been a lion and beyond it a waste of blanched soil, hunchbacked palm trees and formless piles of rocks. It is an ancient Sumerian city, dating back to the very start of recorded history, its canals filled with sand, its terraces obstructed with fallen bricks and all but one of its towers flattened. Occasional brick walls rise from heaps of debris and grey slag. And in the distance, thrusting up into the moonlight, there is a single, solitary tower.

The ground ahead is scattered with shards of pottery and enamelled brick and it crunches and crackles beneath our feet like thin ice as we run to the cover of the basalt statue.

We flop down in the shadow, breathing heavily. I am in lousy shape. My whole body aches. My bruised wrists throb.

'He's in the tower,' she says.

'Of course,' I groan, doubled up, with my arms wrapped around my chest.

'Are you OK?' she asks.

'Just great,' I say.

'Where's the Mandean?' she asks.

'It's a fucking trap,' I tell her. 'They're waiting for us.'

Painfully, I straighten up and pull the revolver out of my waistband. Opening the cylinder, I count the bullets again.

'What are we going to do?' she asks.

'I don't know,' I tell her and I truly don't. All I can think of – all I've ever really been able to come up with – is moving forward. Heedless motion. It's not exactly a sound basis for a world-saving intelligence operation. I'm such a lousy spy. I smile wryly and even that is painful. 'We'll make it up as we go along,' I tell her.

We abandon the shadow of the statue and scramble across the pitted surface and cracked, broken limestone flags of the processional way towards the tower.

My heart is beating like a hammer against my chest and I am gasping for breath.

There is a precarious path that leads up to a chamber at the top of the tower. Guttering light is visible through the open door. We stumble up the path towards the summit, grabbing at rocks for balance. Halfway up there is a flash of lightning that lights up the chaos of rocks and bricks and immediately after it a barrage of ear-splitting thunder.

In the silence that follows we hear another sound like keening issuing from the chamber above. We continue up the path. Miranda trips and dislodges an avalanche of stones. We both freeze.

The keening has stopped.

'Dhauba?' a voice calls. It is Malak's voice. A shadow falls across the lighted doorway and then he emerges and is lit up by the storm. He is naked and covered in a shroud of white dust – the smallpox. I raise the revolver.

There is movement from a rock off to one side and something dark whistles past me. It is Dhauba. There is the flash of a blade. The left side of my chest explodes in pain. I trip and, carried forward by my own momentum, I get to my feet again. I try to shake off the pain. Step by step I lurch towards the tower.

Malak is holding his arms like a crucifix, gouged palms outwards, fingers splayed and dripping blood, like an avenging spectre.

'I will show you death in a handful of dust,' he calls. Trails of blood snake across his ashen form, revealing the whorls and spirals of his tattoos beneath.

I stagger and then flail back down the slope in a cascade of stones. I land on my back and Miranda slides down beside me, her robes ragged as bat's wings.

I stare up into the storm and see the black sky whirling.

'Look at the moon,' Malak yells.

The moon slips from the whirling clouds and I feel its cruel and implacable stare.

Malak is triumphant, the germ on his body dazzling like salt in the moonlight. 'It's the end-time, Jonah.'

I am gasping for breath, my lungs heaving like bellows. The wind is roaring in my ears and my eye is opening and closing. Miranda's hands are in my shirt, tracking the passage of the knife across my ribs. The knife is still there, stuck in my clothing. She grips it by the hilt.

'Disarm him,' Malak shouts.

Dhauba pries the gun loose from my fingers. I cannot feel my legs.

'Have you come to try and kill me?' Malak asks. He looms above us. There is a bloody wound on his left side. He looks at me with cold curiosity. 'Have you?'

'I've come to stop you.'

'Then you have failed.'

'No,' Miranda says.

Beside her Dhauba is staring up at Malak with an expression of feverish adoration.

'The germ is the instrument of God, Jonah,' Malak says. 'It is His gift to us. And it is our sacrifice to Him. I am offering something sublime, something better than a life of humiliation. Soon the soldiers will come and they will find me. They will evacuate me and by the time they find out I am infected it will be too late.' I watch his gaze sweep past me and look out across the marsh. 'The germ will be free. It will spread like a vast and cleansing flood across the surface of the entire world.'

'You don't have to do this,' she pleads.

He looks down at her calmly. 'Of course I do.'

'You can be cured,' she says.

'Look at me. Look at what they did to me.' He rubs his bloody hands furiously across his chest, revealing the peacock tattoo, its fan of plumage and the cluster of iridescent eyes. 'It's just the surface; can you imagine what lies beneath? Can you even imagine the changes wrought? I was broken and remade.'

I reach out my hand to touch her. She shrinks against me. The lightning flashes again, lighting up the sky beneath.

'The world will be remade,' Malak cries.

A great thunderclap echoes across the ruins.

'It will be beautiful. Pristine! Free of barbarism and war. Free of tyranny and poverty. And risen from the ashes, from the weeds of the lesser races, a new breed of man.'

'No!'

Miranda plunges the knife deep into Dhauba. His pinched face slackens. His mouth falls open and blood spills out and he claws at the hilt of the blade. Then he topples over and the revolver falls back into my lap.

'No!' Malak screams.

I scoop up the gun and point it at him. A fork of lightning strikes the tower and we are showered in a cascade of sparks.

Malak howls in frustration.

I fire. And I miss. And I fire again. And miss. There is only one bullet left.

Malak stumbles backwards.

And I pull the trigger as if I am squeezing the life out of the gun. The shot crackles across my palm like an electric shock and the round goes in at the centre of his chest and shatters his sternum. He collapses backwards with his arms outstretched.

It begins to rain and within seconds we are deluged in a roaring downpour, a great unravelling that sounds like a stampeding herd; the rain hammering our exposed bodies and washing the germ off Malak's body and into the blasted earth.

Miranda is kneeling, looking up into the rain.

'It's over,' I tell her, placing my hand on her shoulder.

'Is it?' she asks. And I have no way to answer the despair in her voice.

'Come on.' I help her to her feet and together we limp up the crude path to the shelter of the tower.

We lie on the mud and straw of the brick chamber and I arrange her robe to cover us as thoroughly as possible. She leans into my shoulder and her tears run down my chest. I do not know how to console her. All I can do is hold her.

We sleep.

When I wake I am covered in a film of sweat and there is a barbed pain behind my eyes.

The sky is clear. I sit up and see the heaps of rubble and bricks glistening with moisture. On my knees I creep past Miranda and go outside. The storm has passed.

I examine myself. My arms, legs and torso are covered in bruises. There is a shallow gash in my ribs on the left side and there are electrical burns on my chest. My wrist and ankles are swollen and I am covered in somebody else's blood. Everything hurts. When I hear her stir I hobble back inside and help her stand. Her clothes are in rags and her hair is matted with blood.

She comes outside, shielding her eyes with her forearm.

'Look,' she says, pointing.

I turn to follow her gaze. There is a dark green hovercraft advancing across the marsh towards us. The soldiers on the deck are wearing chemical suits and gas masks.

'It's the Marines,' I tell her.

'They're too bloody late,' she says.

I grip her tightly. 'They'll isolate us,' I tell her, 'and probably separate us.'

'What are you going to do?' she asks, looking up at me.

I think about it for a minute. 'I'm going to give up cigarettes.'

And she smiles: a weary, heart-rending smile. 'And then?'

'I want to go home.'

'Home?'

'I want to see my daughter.'

She is silent for a moment.

'I'd like you to come with me,' I tell her.

DAR AL-HARB:
THE HOUSE OF WAR

The lands of the unbelievers

August 2003

'All that is needed is that a state of war should exist.'
George Orwell, *Nineteen Eighty-Four*

Barnhill

We stand on the deck of a passenger ferry moored on a remote island on the outer edge of Europe. There's no such thing as a clean slate, nor should there be.

The sky and sea are gunmetal. Light grey drizzle falls on the wharf, on the piles of creels and stacked wooden pallets and gantry-ways and on the piles of rusted chains. It falls on the still water of the sound and on the gently rising and falling mass of the ferry. Beneath us the cars roll off the ramp onto the Port Askaig slipway with a dull, repetitive thump. Holidaymakers mostly, but I know a few of the faces down on the car deck, the driver of the Duffies van and the island's butcher. We exchanged nods on the two-hour journey over. This is my ex-wife's ground: the isle of Islay.

I raise my head and watch Sarah's Land Rover sail down the incline to the port with its galvanized-steel roof rack visible above the foliage as it cuts back and forth on the switchbacks.

Miranda has her hands tucked nervously in the back pockets of her jeans and her elbows stick out awkwardly. I slide my hand in the gap and grip the belt loop at the back of her jeans. We are both skinny as rakes but eating wolfishly. She is back in the country to which she has paid a complex allegiance for the first time in eighteen years.

She leans her head into my shoulder and we snatch a final moment of comfort before the Land Rover swings around from behind the post office into the car park and we are in full view.

I straighten up and breathe in and out self-consciously. I want a cigarette but I will not give in. Same old reason; I have made a vow. Yes, again. A vow that sustained me through the long journey back, through long hours kicking my heels in holding cells and transit accommodation, in an isolation tent and on a military transport plane and finally in a familiar interview room in a windowless basement somewhere underneath the old War Office buildings in Whitehall. There were two chairs and a scratched metal table and a radiator that stank of burnt dust and sitting behind the table General Monteith: my controller, mentor, blackmailer and consistently disappointed father figure.

'Congratulations,' he said. 'You've been granted immunity from prosecution.'

'Does that mean I can quit now?' I asked.

Monteith sighed. 'Nobody ever really quits.'

'This is real enough,' I told him, sliding my resignation letter across the table towards him.

He glanced down at it and then at me. 'There's no particular hurry. No need to rush to a decision.'

'My mind's made up.'

'You know that we rate you very highly, Jonah.'

'I don't like being blackmailed.'

'Very well,' he said. He could tell that there was no point pushing it. He opened a drawer and produced a bulky envelope with Kuwaiti stamps on it and handwriting that I recognized.

'Your belongings,' he said.

I tore it open and emptied the contents on the table top, my wallet, my daughter's crayon drawing and the clipping of the polar bear.

'Where is she?' I demanded.

'Up the road and under a lion,' he replied. 'She's waiting for you.'

I unfolded the picture of the polar bear and pushed it across the table to him.

'You can keep that as a memento.'

He looked down at the picture and then up at me. 'Don't go doolally on us, Jonah.'

'Don't worry about me,' I told him, getting up from my chair and pocketing my wallet.

'You're covered by the Official Secrets Act,' Monteith reminded me, 'belt and braces. You breathe a word of just about anything that has occurred, including the fact that this discussion took place at all, and we'll throw away the key, comprende?'

'Yes.'

'You've been given an opportunity, Jonah. A measure of redemption. Don't mess it up.'

'I'll try not to.'

'And, Jonah . . .'

'Yes?'

'Well done.'

I didn't say a word. I wasn't sure that he wasn't just saying it. I wasn't sure that there wasn't a sneaky vein of disappointment in him that the germ hadn't got out.

'Keep in touch,' he said.

A plain-clothes policeman escorted me the length of an underground corridor and up a flight of concrete steps, through a series of internal doors with mesh-lined windows and eventually out into the empty lobby of the Telephone Exchange in Craig's Court. There I received a stern warning from the policeman, with his large, raw-knuckled hand on my shoulder, to stay out of trouble.

'Don't worry about me,' I told him, 'I want no more of your trouble.'

I went out of the door and up Whitehall to Trafalgar Square and found her waiting, as Monteith had promised, beneath one of Landseer's lions.

'Hey,' she said.

We stood a few feet apart, staring at each other. We hadn't seen each other for weeks, not since Iraq.

'You have a new eye,' she said.

I nodded. 'I'm a civilian now.'

'Good. You never really struck me as being a soldier.'

'I don't think I convinced anyone else either.'

There was a pause.

'You had a lot of people convinced of a lot of things,' she said.

I smiled ruefully. 'I guess I walked into that one.'

'I don't really know you, do I?'

'You know me well enough,' I told her.

Children and dogs stumble out of the Land Rover, his kids by his first marriage, mine, their joint child who is only a year old. We make our way down the stairs to the gantry and walk out onto the pier.

The handover has something of the Balkans about it. We should be at a checkpoint on the edge of an enclave in a bitterly divided city and not on this remote Scottish island. They are at one end of the pier and we are at the other.

But this too has been one of the wild places of the earth: the Vikings came here and the island is littered with their graves and the place names they left behind. It is not entirely inappropriate. Only the children and the steaming, wet lurchers are oblivious.

Esme is wearing a Brats backpack and a shaggy white fleece and red lights dance along the rim of her trainers as she hurries at tripping pace towards me, a conversation half-completed before she even reaches me. I don't know where she finds the time to breathe. I kneel midway down the pier and hug her. She smells warm and clean.

Then I straighten up again and watch as Sarah and Douglas approach. I find that I can watch them together and it no longer makes my brain boil. Something of the heat in the bruise has gone. I find that I have it in me to wish them luck with the future. I know that I cannot expect a similar response. I wish there was some way to say sorry.

Neither of them will meet my eye.

Douglas holds out Esme's bag by the straps and I reach out to grip it and for a moment our hands meet, knuckle to knuckle on the strap, and we are deeply aware of each other. What was done to him should not have been done. I should have stopped it. There is no excuse: when I squatted down beside him in that steading and waited for him to recognize me I did so for no reason other than the satisfaction of a vain and vengeful thirst. In doing so I lowered myself to the level of those I despise: the irregular militias and the fanatics, the soldiers of ethnic cleansing. I am the one who has brought the Balkans here. I have resolved to try and be better than that, to do all I am able to be a better man.

Sarah looks different and not for the first time I wonder who she is. The woman before me seems to bear no resemblance to the person I married and that I longed for through four desperate years. The person that I remember has been replaced. I hope she is happier.

'Fourteen days,' she says.

I nod in agreement. 'We'll be here.'

She nods and turns her back and strides back to the Land Rover with children, dogs and Douglas following and I do not, even for a moment, wish to call her back. I hope that I am cured.

We are not going to simply leave on the next ferry. I have remembered that I loved this magical place once and I want to rediscover it and show it to Miranda. We have our own Land Rover waiting for us. It's a rental with the keys in the ignition, parked in the queue for Jura, the island that is on the far side of the narrow sound.

Esme reaches up and takes my hand. She has her father's dark hair and her mother's blue eyes. She makes my heart soar.

'Dad,' she says, watching me carefully, 'what are you doing?'

'Thinking,' I tell her, 'just thinking.'

'You're funny,' she says, in the mock-adult way of children everywhere. 'What are we doing now?'

'We're going to Barnhill.'

'Right,' she nods, 'how long till we get there?'

'Not long.'

'Let's go then.'

Miranda holds out her hand and Esme grasps it without hesitation. We walk towards the Land Rover and at the count of three we sweep her off her feet and she lands running and we count again, louder this time and again like a fairground ride she sails up into the air.

Barnhill lies in a natural saddle on the northernmost tip of Jura. It is fifteen kilometres beyond the last tarmac of the county road, at the end of a rutted hardcore track that winds across open moor between outcrops of exposed rock that lie strewn across the heather.

It is a white-painted farmhouse with a grey-slate roof and a cluster of outbuildings that form a horseshoe around a grassy courtyard. The house looks out over the Sound of Jura, across hundreds of rocks scattered like specks of coal dust on the water, to the distant jagged peaks of the mainland.

There is an oil-fired Aga and a shed full of peat for the fireplaces and a diesel generator if you can bear the noise and a drawer full of candles if you can't. We opt for the candles. There is no television in the farmhouse and to be frank I am glad of the respite from its remorseless eye. I feel as if I have watched nothing else for the past few months: a catalogue of violent images and dire warnings; suicide bombings in Iraq, Morocco, Israel, Chechnya and Saudi; futures markets in atrocities and televised beheadings; Uday and Qusay's bullet-ridden bodies on a slab in July; the narco-lords back in power in Afghanistan; Bin Laden still in the basement. Things will inevitably get worse.

Barnhill feels like a world away from all that, but the feeling is deceptive: the house comes with its own significant history. George Orwell lived here in 1948, tended a vegetable patch that has long since gone and completed his final work, *Nineteen Eighty-Four*, before tuberculosis finally claimed him.

I sometimes wonder what Orwell would make of this frightening new world, with its doctrine of perpetual war between an intangible idea of freedom and an impersonal noun. I think he would recognize it.

Terror is a pitiless, amorphous enemy that follows no conventional rule book and affords no possibility of risk mitigation or zero danger, and the only response to it is the dehumanizing hope that the next inevitable atrocity is marked for someone else's city and someone else's children. Terror can never be exterminated. It feels like a charge of fear exploding beneath my heart. I do not know what to do in the face of such despair.

Except.

Except do jigsaws and paint pictures and make sandwiches and buses out of cardboard boxes and ziggurats with sticklebricks and fill baths with bubble bath and read books aloud at bedtime – Scarry, Sendak and Seuss – and brush teeth and snags out of hair and find some kind of sanity in the cocooned rhythms of meals, tasks and errands.

And her snug beneath the covers, with my hand on her forehead and her words, sleepily spoken. 'You're a puzzle. Love you, Dad.'

On the second day we look up as a shadow falls across the living-room window, to see a pony's unkempt white head pressed to the glass, looking in.

There are four of them, wild highland ponies, grazing on the neglected and hummocky grass lawn that slants down to the jumble of rocks at the shoreline. They are ghostly white, with thick, matted manes that reach to their flanks and black, mud-covered legs. They smell of sweat and horseshit.

I stand at the doorway with Esme on the bony jut of my hip and watch as Miranda goes barefoot out into the endless summer-evening light. Approaching them, she speaks soft and soothing words. She reaches out to the nearest and runs a hand down its neck. The pony snorts.

The ponies are the true heirs to this place. We are the impostors.

Miranda leans her head into the pony's flank. There will always be a part of her that she keeps hidden by force of will; that is only revealed in the dark hours, in moments of weakness or desire, the part of her that mourns a lost son and a lost decade.

I watch her, I do that a lot now, just quietly watching; the curve of her skinny hips, her irregular clavicle, the lock of hair that she tucks behind her ear.

'You'd better make it fiction,' she says, passing me a rinsed plate.

We do this now, picking up conversations started days before; it's surprisingly easy when you don't talk much to other grown-ups. I dry the plate and add it to the stack on the kitchen table.

Esme is drawing with crayons, lying half-across the table. The ponies are grazing in the field outside the kitchen window. We feel like a family, or my notion of one. We feel at ease.

'They wouldn't allow the truth,' I concede.

I have decided to write a book. Writers are perverse creatures. I think it might suit me. I'll write each page as it comes. It'll be like putting one foot in front of another and maybe someday I'll have a novel. And when I'm not writing I'll walk and no doubt I'll mutter and rub my face.

If I walk enough, maybe when night comes I'll sleep the uninterrupted sleep of someone at peace with himself.

'In your book, I want to be beautiful,' Miranda says.

'You will be,' I tell her. And she will be: beautiful and full of love and pain and yearning and rage.